The Scoop

The Scoop

Cat Walker

Red Door

Published by RedDoor
www.reddoorpress.co.uk

ISBN 978-1-913062-10-1

A CIP catalogue record for this book is available from the British Library

Cover design: Emily Courdelle

Typesetting: Jen Parker, Fuzzy Flamingo

Printed and bound in Denmark by Nørhaven

For my son, Albert, and my god-daughters, Emma and Polly, in the hope that they will find their rightful places in the world and, above all, be happy

*'We all travel the same journey…
…some people have better maps.'*
Printed on *Himalayan Map House* bag,
Kathmandu, Nepal

Brimful of Ashram

I've been sitting cross-legged on the floor of the Rezhen Ashram since 4 a.m. I'm numb from the cold and tiredness, let alone the fact that my legs haven't been forced into this position since primary school. Through the wall-to-wall window in front of me lies the highest valley on earth – the Tibetan Plateau – the roof of the world. The plateau is framed on all sides by beautiful icing-sugar-topped mountains whose names I can recite like an inner city school register: In the front row is the Nyenchen Tanglha Massif, flanked by Qungmoganze in the west, with Noijin Kangsang and Kalurong at the back beside the ragtag group of Himalayas, which run all the way round the back of the Ashram. In the middle of the front row, where the Nyenchen Tanglha gang meets the Namcha Barwa Himal stands the impressive class captain – Namchabarwa himself – over 7000 metres tall, with his little sister – Gyala Peri – a full 300 metres shorter but none the less impressive. I roll their names around on my tongue silently, enjoying the feel of their foreign exoticness.

The sun is just beginning to rise over Namchabarwa. Its yellow fingers take hold of the peak, then climb up and over and tumble down the pristine white slopes like an avalanche chasing a crew of show-off snowboarders. It plunges into the shadows at the bottom of the cliffs, then picks itself up and starts to creep over the foothills and stealthily across the plateau floor as if mounting an attack.

Inside, the room is filled with the reassuring low hum of chanting: 'Om, Mani, Padme, Hum', 'Om, Mani, Padme, Hum'. The prayer drifts over me; through me. It seems to travel to the four corners of the earth and back, permeating everything; holding me in its warm embrace. I'm barely even aware of the cloaked figures around me. It really is as if we are all one. One room full of humanity acknowledging the power and beauty of nature, breathing and chanting in unison. I've never felt this kind of belonging before.

Outside, the army of the sun is filling the plain like a flood and advances still, gaining speed as it draws closer. It hits the window suddenly with an almost audible ringing sound. Climbing inside, it begins to sweep across the rush-matted floor towards me, waking the very particles in the air, which glisten and sparkle in the blaze of morning glory. Like a precious gold cloth the sunlight climbs on to my lap and envelops my body in the richest of cloaks. As it rises to my face I can feel myself holding my breath, as if I might drown in the warm golden tide.

Suddenly the whole world is burnished gold and I have to close my eyes against the dazzling light. Its purity and radiance overwhelm me, and nothing else matters. I'm completely and utterly at one with the light in sublime serenity. I'm in the flow of the universe. I'm living inside this very moment. This is finally it: Enlightenment!

I open my eyes to let the sunlight in, and can't help sneaking a quick look around the room, smugly wondering whether anyone else has felt it too, or whether I'm the only one. I might be the only one. Perhaps I really could be the chosen one like I always hoped...

It takes me just a few glorious seconds of indulgent self-righteousness to realise that I've already blown it. I had it.

And I've lost it again. Somewhere between the sun rising over Namchabarwa and the moment it hit my eyes I'd achieved nirvana, but in the very *moment* of recognition, in that instant of being at one with the universe, I've bloody blown it! I've started overthinking again – about myself, as usual.

And once I start thinking I can't bloody stop. When I try to go back into a state of meditation, all I can think about is my failure. I try to concentrate on the beauty, on the glistening particles still flying in the air around me, but all I can think about is that it's really just dust; and what is dust anyway? Dirty, filthy, dead skin cells and bits of crap floating around and being inhaled and exhaled by everybody: second-hand, third-hand, old-hand dust. What did God create dust for? I mean, He (or She) may have clothed the sparrows of the air and the flowers of the field, but what spiritual purpose could dust possibly have? Remarkably unedifying stuff, even when it is sparkling like a thousand tiny stars in a Tibetan Ashram in the middle of a dawn meditation.

Watching the dust fly I have a sudden urge to sneeze.

Dammit. I can't sneeze now. It would shake the whole Ashram out of its meditative calm (I'm a loud sneezer). But, as in a library, this thought seems to be exactly what makes the sneeze seem so inevitable. The more I try not to, the more urgent the sneeze becomes. I go to put my hand up to my mouth to try to stifle it, but it's pinned down, not just by my oversized robes but by the weight of a sleeping twelve-year-old boy. Momentarily the urge to sneeze subsides as I look down at his tousled mess of hair and feel a pang of... something I can't quite name. I gaze down at the boy and think what a strange world this is, what a long journey we've all made to get this far, and how I didn't expect things to turn out this way.

Without warning the urge to sneeze returns with a vengeance and this time I can't stop it.

CHAPTER 1

The beginning and a surprise

'Midway upon the journey of our life
I found myself within a forest dark,
For the straightforward pathway had been lost.'

Dante Alighieri,
'The Divine Comedy: Inferno', 1867.

March 2006

When I was little I used to go on adventures all the time. I'd pack an apple, my penknife, a spare jumper and a compass into my brown school satchel, and Mum or Dad would find me tramping determinedly up into the woods behind our house. Thirty years on and the woods have been uprooted to make way for a new housing development, my adventuring days are long gone, and my compass is well and truly broken.

* * * * * * *

I'm staring at the apple perched on a corner of my office desk. Its wrinkled skin is pocked with little indentations and one side of it bears a burgeoning brown bruise from repeated falls to the floor. I wonder how long it could sit there before it

1

rots away completely. Probably longer than it would take for my resolve to eat healthily to kick in. Outside the thick glass window, London's skyline is struggling to make itself visible behind a misty veil of drizzle.

It's Tuesday, the most boring day of the week. It has no claim to fame. Wednesday is hump day – halfway to the end of the working week; Thursday is the downwards slope to Friday, gateway to the weekend and perennial excuse to skive off any real work. Even Monday has a caché – everyone's hungover and miserable and generally doesn't get anything productive done either.

I'm meant to be filing some really-not-very-important paperwork just in case of an unimaginable future need to look at it again. I stand up, briskly picking up the sheaf of papers to dispatch them to their retirement home. After all, this is my job, and if I don't do it... Well... Looking round the office at the nodding tops of people's heads behind their computer monitors I'm suddenly struck by a frightening existential thought. I sit back down at my desk with the papers still in my hand, blindsided by the sheer inconsequentiality of my own existence. God, I hate my job.

Once upon a time I genuinely thought I might achieve some sense of purpose and meaning through work. But in the brutally competitive job market of London I just ended up in a series of dead-end jobs I thought beneath me; until I sank to a point where I found it hard to imagine ever getting out from under them to anything better. The rest of the wannabe-somethings drifted through the office, usually only staying for a couple of years, three at the most, before drifting off again to what I imagined were better things. I felt alienated by their youthful enthusiasm and 'can do' attitude. I switched to 'can't, don't' long ago. So I remained, plagued by the thought that anyone with any get up and go would have already got up and gone.

I thought about quitting most of the time, but never did. I stuck at it, vainly hoping it might get better. But it didn't. I was trapped. If you've ever worked in an office yourself you'll be familiar with that law of modern science in which the space-time continuum does some sort of a double back-flip in the office, becoming stretched into a Mobius strip of 'office time', with us caught like rats in a wheel. A blink of an eye in the real world takes three weeks of office time and you can go in and sit down at your desk aged twenty-five and walk out of the door at the end of the day over a decade older.

One of the big ironies is that I work in a charity. I wanted to save the world, but the truth is I couldn't even save myself. My parents, of course, never tired of telling people how worthy my job was, as if I was single-handedly ending poverty in Africa: '*Yes, she's working in the City! In a* Charity, *yes! Oh I don't know all the details but it's something very technical and high up.*' The fact that 'technical' meant I got to plug in computers and do the office photocopying, and 'high up' meant on the twenty-second floor, didn't get mentioned. I only got to plug in computers because no one else wanted to, not because I was talented at it. I was an *IT Crowd* of one.

I wasn't even looking for any thanks for this tireless devotion. Well, maybe I was. But I didn't get it. As the years went by, I gradually realised that, although my job was, to my parents at least, one of huge importance, which was making society a better place to live in, on the inside it was just the same as any other office job – vague, tedious and even more underpaid. No starving children in Africa ever called me up to express their undying gratitude, nor did our celebrity patron ever *once* pop in for a cup of tea and a Hobnob and to shine my halo.

Almost without my noticing, the papers slip out of my hand into the wastepaper bin by my feet. I stare at them for

3

a moment and then calmly take the big wad of files from my intray and post them into the bin too. It feels very satisfying, as if I've finally understood the filing system. I open my desk drawer, pulling it out beyond its wooden runners until it's free, and empty its contents in one fell swoop. I feel almost delirious. Next I position the bin at one end of my desk and with one long sweep of my arm send my whole collection of pens, pencils, notebooks, business cards, gonks, stress toys, floppy disks, motivational flashcards and amusing vegetable-shaped pencil-sharpeners into its waiting jaws. The browning apple plops in last.

I stand up, suddenly light-headed, surveying my empty desk. Now what? I contemplate standing on it and yelling: 'Who's coming with me?' Like Jerry Maguire in the film, but I suspect I'd get the same response – just the fish. I don't even have a fish! I pluck the apple out of the bin and stuff it in my pocket.

Head held high I stride through the room, with a look that dares anyone to stop me. They don't. Heads nod sleepily behind monitors. Just one more corner to go to reach freedom, and...

'Casey?' My boss looks up from her computer quizzically.

Rumbled. She must have seen my scorched earth of a desk, and the paperwork, *her* paperwork, in the bin. I stop in my tracks, oscillating wildly between flight and fright.

'Get us a coffee while you're up, will you?' she orders casually and goes back to her keyboard tapping before I can tell her how I'm never getting her coffee again. How I've been fetching coffee for her and the rest of the team for the last twelve years without a murmur of thanks. How being a glorified coffee-fetching, photocopying, filing, computer problem-solving, turning-it-off-and-on-again dogsbody wasn't really the glittering career I'd envisaged for myself.

So I just walk brazenly past her, past the rest of the 'team' who never notice me, past the group of life-size cardboard cutouts of our charity patron, a scruffy but very rich musician from a defunct eighties band. Pausing at the door I take one last look around the office. Nobody has even noticed I'm going. I take a couple of steps back and punch the nearest cutout smack in the face.

'Shove your no-good goody-two-shoes bloody charity bloody job!' I yell, inwardly; adding out loud for our patron's benefit: 'You'll need your own bloody Band-Aid when I'm done with you!'

The cutout makes a muffled '*pth*' sound and sways gently on its weighted stand, grinning silently. Smug git.

I flounce out of the office, slamming the door, which closes slowly and quietly behind me on its mechanism. What do I care? Freedom starts now, I think to myself, as I reach the street. Life starts right now.

* * * * * * *

A month later and I'm sitting in the dilapidated café at Trowell motorway service station in the rainy North of England on a wet and windy Saturday afternoon in the middle of April. The café spans the motorway and I'm sitting right over the Southbound carriageway as if illustrating the long-ago betrayal of my Northern roots. The dirty beige Formica tables are circa 1975 and ingrained with God-knows-what grimy leftovers of travellers gone before me. All of us waiting for something to happen. Anything. It seems a pretty inauspicious place to start an adventure.

* * * * * * *

5

I've just dropped off my cat, Dixon, with my parents, and I've arranged to meet Danny here. Danny, who says he has a surprise for me.

* * * * * * *

Danny probably thinks I'm having a mid-life crisis, ringing him up pretty much out of the blue and asking him to meet me here. To be fair, I most probably am having a mid-life crisis. Let's face it – I'm in my mid-thirties; I have an unused History and Classics degree; no career prospects; I don't own my own home; I haven't had a relationship since she-who-must-not-be-named several years ago; and I have a cat instead of children. But most of all, I have a nagging little voice in my head (well, more like a loud shouty thing with cymbals and a megaphone) telling me that there must be more to life than this. Surely?

The last four weeks since I walked out of the office have been less than underwhelming. It should have been the glorious start of the rest of my life – an epic adventure, and indeed it was for a couple of days. Pure freedom. I felt like I could do anything I wanted, and ended up doing absolutely nothing but sitting around in my pyjamas watching daytime TV and eating Pot Noodles, planning my future in between episodes of *Midsomer Murders*. Then, on the third day, HR rang from the office and asked why I hadn't been in. When I explained, they told me in no uncertain terms that if I didn't come back and work out my notice then they'd sue me for breach of contract. So I had to slink back in, past that sly grinning cardboard git, back to my denuded desk. I filed and photocopied and fetched coffee for another three long, miserable and mortifying weeks.

As if that wasn't humiliation enough, I then had to endure a stilted leaving 'do' where nobody really talked to me except an enthusiastic new intern who seemed to think that the free sandwiches and plastic cups of cheap, warm white wine might presage a visit from our celebrity patron himself. As if! Before anyone could boozily suggest a speech of some sort I slunk out of the office as soon as I politely could, this time with my tail firmly between my legs. As I walked unsteadily down the street, I barely registered the black limo pulling up behind me, with a trendily scruffy guy in the back who bore a strong resemblance to a cardboard cutout I once knew.

* * * * * * *

Where's Danny got to? He was supposed to be here twenty minutes ago. I've given up on my cardboard sandwich, so start playing with a piece of loose Formica on the table top, prising it off the MDF underneath. I feel like I'm waiting for Godot. I'm certainly waiting for something, or someone, preferably in shining armour, to whisk me away to a sunnier and more meaningful life. Outside, the sky has darkened and rain is sheeting down on to the motorway below, creating small wakes at the sides of the cars, making them look like strange motorboats sailing away into an oily sunset. I catch my reflection in the dirty rain-streaked window – nothing to write home about. All geek and no chic, that's me. Geeky and awkward: *Gawkward*. A shapeless hoodie and a worn beanie pulled down low, masking most indications of gender. The small pointed nose and angular features nothing like my parents' big open faces. Open-faced but closed-minded. I give a wry smile to my reflection in the glass but it just looks like a lopsided grimace, so I quit trying. Hurry the hell up, will you Danny?

* * * * * * *

Back home, once daytime TV lost its appeal, which was pretty soon after I realised that I was the *Weakest Link* whether I got a *Deal Or No Deal*, I started properly planning for my future. Trouble was, I was having difficulty figuring out what I wanted to do. I'd become institutionalised in the office world, trained not to think beyond the next weekend. I realised with a shock how very small my world had become. And that's when it hit me. My big plan was forming.

* * * * * * *

So, here I am, halfway up the M1 at Trowell Services in the pouring rain. In a café that smells like a greasy hospital; eating a sandwich that cost me a day's wages and tastes like week-old breakfast cereal. Waiting for Danny, who's late again. Danny, who's spent his whole life being late. Late for class, late home, late for work, late to settle down. Late, late, late. In fact, the only thing Danny was ever early for was puberty, which arrived like Concorde when he was twelve years old, giving him wings and pumping him so full of hormones he practically exploded, and he's been like that ever since. Which is why I'm worried his surprise will be yet another unsuitable blonde bombshell with legs up to her ears who might ruin everything. Not that I'm jealous as such. Well, not in a conventional way.

* * * * * * *

I stare out at the rain wondering, not for the first time, whether I'm doing the right thing. Maybe I should change... Ah, there he is. I see Danny getting out of his battered old MG, unfolding all six feet two of his muscular frame like a boxer climbing into the ring, fighting with an umbrella against the driving wind and rain. He goes round to the other side of the

8

car and opens the door. I can't really see the passenger shielded by the umbrella. Danny pulls his collar up and guides the mystery woman through the parked cars and into the doors of the service station. Through the rain-streaked windows I can only judge that Danny's 'surprise' is petite, and surprisingly dressed in jeans and trainers instead of the expected mini-skirt balanced on high heels. Could it be that Danny has finally picked someone sensible and wants my blessing? It better bloody not be. That'd ruin everything. After all my grand planning...

My thoughts trail away as Danny appears at the top of the escalator, water dripping down his handsome face as he folds his collar down. If we weren't such good friends (and the other thing) I'd probably make a play for him, although you'd think a lifetime hearing about his philandering would put me off. I console myself with the thought that he's incapable of loving anyone as purely as he loves me. This train of thought is broken quite suddenly when Danny shouts across the café to me as I'm half-rising to greet him: 'Hey gay girl, how's life on the other side of the sheets?'

He's never been one to hold back, our Danny, and neither has he ever been in the slightest bit embarrassed or put out that his former sweetheart is gay (OK, so it was many, many years ago but I still like to think of us in those terms). Me, I'm not embarrassed by being gay at all – I got over that a long time ago, even before being gay became trendy. But when it's shouted across a Northern service station and all eyes in the room stop their conversations to stare at you over their steaming mugs of coffee and overpriced fry-ups, I go a little pink around the edges, if you'll pardon the pun.

Danny strides up to me and gives me one of his huge bear hugs, which I hide in, hoping that by the time I emerge everyone will have gone back to their own lives, satisfied at the semblance of normality restored by the big macho man hug, even if the funny-looking woman does looks a bit like a boy. His leather jacket smells reassuringly familiar, even if his aftershave is a bit overpoweringly masculine. And it's while hugging Danny, and feeling no particular desire for him to let go, that I begin to wonder where his passenger has got to. Straining to see over his shoulder I can see no lost-looking blonde waiting for the big man to notice her again. In fact, I can't see anyone standing nearby except a lost boy. A slightly bedraggled elfin-looking child of indeterminate age in a scruffy black hoodie is standing there staring at me with a kind of inner fury directed against all adults. I ignore him, still scanning the area for the blonde.

'So, where's your surprise?' I manage to gasp as Danny finally lets go with one last squeeze.

'Huh? Oh, right.' Danny looks around and seizes the scruffy little hoodie by the shoulder and drags its contents into an uncomfortable side embrace. 'Casey, meet Ari.'

The boy turns and sneers at me with all the grace of Vinnie Jones on a bad day.

'Wh...what?' I'm too stupefied to say anything more intelligent. 'What...? Who...? Why...?' I manage to pop out some elementary questions, at the same time as my brain is wandering through all the possible explanations – nephew, kid-next-door on his way to football practice, friend's son being looked after for the day by caring father-figure? What – Danny? Yeah, right, think again. Meanwhile, the mini street version of Legolas is looking distinctly unimpressed by my stammering, so I address him directly.

'Hi, Harry.'

'It's Ari.'

'Well, I think you'll find that we pronounce the "H" in Harry,' I correct him, and in return receive a long hard stare which Paddington Bear would be extremely proud of.

'Actually it's Ari. With an "A". Short for Aristotle,' Danny interjects helpfully with a grin.

Are you kidding me? I turn Danny slightly away from the child: '*Aristotle?* What kind of a person names their kid Aristotle?' I blurt out to him, oblivious as I am that all children have super-sensitive hearing when it comes to adult conversations they're not meant to hear.

'The *intelligent* kind,' Ari spits out, and walks off, leaving hanging in the air the unspoken (and momentarily accurate) implication that I am *not* the intelligent kind.

I shrug at Danny in disbelief.

'Aristotle – you know, the Greek philosopher. Casey, you did Classics for Chrissakes.'

'Oh, *that* Aristotle.' I manage a weakly ironic smile at Danny's improbable declaration. 'Well, of course, but tell me, Danny, who is he and what's he doing here?'

'Well,' Danny shrugs a trademark shrug, 'that's kind of a long story.'

CHAPTER 2

The philosophy of travel

'*Rather than love, than money, than fame, give me truth.*'

Henry David Thoreau,
Walden, or Life in the Woods, 1854.

The rainspray from the road blurs my vision as I drive back down the M1, homeward bound. It feels like my life – just one long grey blur. And just when I thought I'd found some sort of focus. I'm still trying to take in what Danny's just told me. The one person I thought I could count on.

Danny and I were best friends when we were kids, growing up in Scarborough – 'England's first seaside resort', as the billboards now proudly proclaim. We both lived in Valley Road on a wide green street that ran down under the Suicide Bridge to the sea. Everyone called it the Suicide Bridge, although our parents spoke in hushed tones about it and once, when someone they knew jumped off, they bundled us away and I got smacked for asking who the jumper was. I think the body was still there, under a blanket on the road. Danny and I went down later to look for spatters of blood but they must have cleaned it all up. Danny found a brooch that he said was from the jumper but I didn't think it was. He gave it to me that

Valentine's Day when we were seven, but I never liked to wear it. I think I still have it, in a box under my bed somewhere, along with all the other, more sanitised, curios of childhood. I'm a bit of a hoarder of happy memories.

* * * * * * *

A John Peel rerun plays mournfully on the car radio. I switch it off. No time to be listening to the dead, however cool. It feels like I'm driving through a giant carwash. The old-fashioned kind from when I was a kid, cowering in the back seat; with huge whirring brushes enveloping the car completely. This used to frighten and exhilarate in equal measure – like watching *Doctor Who* from behind the sofa. It makes me feel out-of-time, out-of-place with where I am now in my life. I slow to a steady cruising speed: the right kind of speed for deep thinking. And this is my thing, my curse: that I think too much.

* * * * * * *

I think of what Danny said when I first told him about my plan: 'Everyone's on a journey. True that, but it's just, well, it would be a whole helluva lot easier if it came with a map, or instructions – any hint or clue as to why we're here and what we're meant to be doing.' My mum and dad have a wall-hanging at home in the vicarage that says: 'Jesus is coming, look busy!' They naively think it's vaguely amusing and don't really get the irony. *I* think it hides a bigger truth – that nobody really knows what they're doing, or what they're meant to be doing. It's all guesswork.

How much easier this game of life would be if it did come with instructions. For instance:

Casey Jones: your mission, should you choose to accept

it, is to become CEO of a major international charity and save lots of lives, find a suitable female partner and two cats, and live in a nice quiet southern suburb (Brighton is quite nice). You should study Buddhism and yoga and be nice to your neighbours. (Optional: join the local golf club when you turn thirty and you will be club captain by thirty-seven.) Follow these instructions and you will lead a full and happy life.

With instructions we could at least have real goals and some concrete sense of success or failure, instead of this constant pervasive possibility, and fear, of both. But without such direction we're all floundering around in the dark. I mean, our parents do the best they can, I suppose, but generally still manage to fuck you up somehow. School, if you're very lucky, gives you glimpses and hints but generally just prepares you for modern life as they understand it (which is getting a 'good job' in order to pay the mortgage, and saving for your pension so that you can travel in retirement). The media hypes and rehashes instances and half-truths and in the end just serves to dull the mind rather than educate or inspire. Our peers are as clueless as we are, and then we turn into adults ourselves and become teachers or journalists or parents and start the mindless cycle over again, churning out the same old wives' tales we were handed down generation to generation. It becomes a nightmare guessing game of 'Chinese whispers'. I mean, the answer to the meaning of life, the universe and everything might just as well be forty-two. I exhale a deep, calming breath, which mists in front of my face in a tauntingly allegorical fashion.

I think about Danny, back in Trowell Services, so cocksure of himself in that way that most men seem to be. He was my kindred spirit when we were kids. We figured out early on that the best way to get to spend more time together was to pretend

14

that we were childhood sweethearts. Funny how even back then I knew it was pretending. So we asked each other very formally to be boyfriend and girlfriend when we were nine years old and our parents thought it was so cute. We were never apart. Both only children we were more like brother and sister. The boyfriend-girlfriend thing lasted about three years until Danny hit puberty, or rather puberty hit Danny, and after that he was only interested in one thing – other girls. I wasn't strictly speaking heartbroken, although I often remind him that technically he was my first broken heart, which sometimes earns me a free coffee. Really, I was too young to even know what love was, and I remember just being angry with Danny for not spending so much time with me after that, when he was off chasing girls and I discovered a new love – books – and was having different adventures of my own. But we always remained friends, tied together with that invisible thread which connects best friendships.

* * * * * * *

I drive past Donington Park where all the big rock festivals in the north were held in the seventies. I always wanted to go but Dad said it was the music of the devil, and I was too young to go on my own. Once, when I was fifteen, I persuaded him to come with me to an all-day concert in Leeds to see Motörhead, Def Leppard and Girlschool. I wanted him to see that rock music isn't evil. I'm not sure I succeeded. I mean, I know they say the devil has the best tunes, I just don't think my dad expected him to dress in so much skin-tight lycra and tassels. Dad stayed for a couple of hours then made some excuse about the whole experience having inspired him to write a sermon on the perils of youth culture. He left me with Danny and some of his mates, with an imperative to 'look after his little girl, or else'. I wasn't exactly sure what that 'or else' might have meant, coming from the vicar – perhaps death by tea party?

But after we left school Danny and I just kind of lost touch, like people did in the days before social networks; before even mobile phones. I used to get sporadic news updates from my parents – chiefly my mum who loved to gossip, though swears she doesn't as that's some sort of sin, I gather (most everything is, it seems). So I heard he'd got married and then I heard he got divorced over an affair with a blonde secretary at the company he was working at. The marriage surprised me, the affair and divorce didn't. Ever since then he's been doing contract work as a structural engineer on oil rigs in the USA and Middle East, earning a shedload of money and then blowing it on wine, women and whatever. Never anything permanent, never settling down, always on the run. A woman in every port, that's our Danny.

I guess a part of me was always a bit jealous of him. Of his carefree lifestyle, the freedom of it – never getting tied down, always moving on, a rolling stone and all that. Not that I'm excusing his behaviour as some sort of 'loveable rogue', just that I can see how this could have happened. Commitment and Danny have never been good friends, but I never imagined this. Now here he is, finally having to face up to his past, and ruining my present into the bargain. Of all the stupid, ridiculous, crazy things to surprise me with. Ta-daah! A scrawny rabbit leaps unbidden from a well-worn hat. Danny has become a father. How did all this happen?

* * * * * * *

I just passed the turning for the UK's National Space Centre – no, seriously – on the A6 near Leicester. Hardly Cape Canaveral. Especially in the enveloping gloom. It's still lashing down with rain, and getting properly dark now as the weak grey spring daylight fades, but I've no more lights to put on – I already have my fogs and full beam on, which barely illuminate my path. *Come in Houston, we have a problem.* It reminds me that when I was a kid I dreamed of being an astronaut. Whatever happened to *that* dream? It may have vanished in the mist but I still want to *be* something. I still feel the need to find my place in history.

I was born in the year that Dorothy died and man first walked on the moon; in the year of the Woodstock festival and the Stonewall riots: free love and unfree love; John and Yoko's bed-in protest against the Vietnam War; the year of *Easy Rider*, *Monty Python* and colour TV; when the first incarnation of the internet took to the cyber-airwaves; in the year that a new kind of self-realisation was in the air.

My parents were Baby Boomers, which is ironic since *they* couldn't have kids. I'm not even totally sure they really wanted one, just wanting to conform to the expected stereotype. No, that's probably too harsh. It's just that I think my mum had this very fixed idea of what she wanted – a mini version of herself – and I wasn't exactly that. By the time they realised this, of course, it was too late to give me back. Of course they love me in their own way, and in the freedom of their benign neglect I had a pretty happy childhood growing up in the 1970s, in my flares and fluorescent socks, and my denim jacket covered in sewn-on badges. We had Wagon Wheels as big as your face back then, and Walkman portable cassette players, ghetto blasters and Rubik's Cubes; and all we lived for was *Top of the Pops*. I remember the Queen's Silver Jubilee on a rare sunny day in the cold wet June of 1977, and my first stolen taste of warm champagne under the trestle table set up for the parish congregation in the vicarage grounds. My mum finding me laid out on the damp grass slightly tipsy with

Danny, singing the national anthem over and over again at the top of our voices.

But now here I am. A typical Generation Xer: underemployed, overeducated and unpredictable as Douglas Coupland tells it. Adrift in the world. Glued to *Big Brother* every season because we're afraid to lose touch with a world which is receding beyond our screens. Suspicious of a fame and fortune we crave. We are the newfound lost generation, the kings of the wild frontier, we are anarchy in the UK, the rave generation, the new wave generation, the glasnost and perestroika kids. We are the middle-aged rebels without a cause. We've escaped from the shackles of our agricultural and industrial past only to find ourselves shackled to a new monster of modernity. George Orwell was right: freedom is slavery.

And then there was that day when the planes flew into the towers. Of all days in my life, I thought that day changed the world, that life would never be the same again. And for a few weeks life wasn't the same, but as each day went by, the old familiar habits and routines overwrote that experience until it gained the same status as any event happening far away to people you don't know. And it became just a series of images stored in the mind's eye. A faint warning light flashing with a constancy that eventually makes it meaningless.

I have this terrible weighty feeling of not belonging in a world that has outpaced us, outsmarted us, outgrown us. Progress has never moved so quickly, so exponentially, as during the last century. In these days of hi-tech strip-lit darkness, in this modern crazy world, where can we find enlightenment? Or have I left that too late already? Is it down to the next generation now?

* * * * * * *

A vision of Danny's little 'nextgen' issue playing in the arcade section of Trowell Services comes into my head. I still can't quite believe he's Danny's son. It's true Ari has the same dark brown hair as Danny, although hanging on his head like a greasy mop, but he has a pointed impish face without Danny's square jaw, and the most startling green eyes, like a cat. They must come from his mother – a half-Greek woman called Niobe (named after a Greek goddess, which explains 'Aristotle', I guess). I suppose, as I watched him blast apart the living dead with a large plastic gun, that he has the same hint of a swagger about him as Danny, only ganglier. Or maybe all boys have that? Danny and Ari, champions of the world.

* * * * * * *

My dad tells me that when I was a child I asked him how I could *not* have children. Being a lesbian seemed, until recently, to have solved that one little issue. I don't really *get* them, and they certainly don't get me. No, I'm just not cut out to be around children. Danny may have to face up to his responsibilities now that his ex-wife needs to have an operation, but why the hell should I have to shoulder half the burden? The Boy Wonder is definitely NOT part of the master plan.

See, here's the thing, as I tried to explain to Danny: I've spent the last month formulating my Big Plan. Thirty-seven years in the making. I had it all sorted. OK, not in meticulous detail, but that's all actually part of the plan. Part of escaping the humdrum everyday existence I've been programmed into. I want to, just for once, fly by the seat of my pants.

The Grand Escape Plan, in all its glory, as scribbled on the back of a Trowell Services Café napkin while I was waiting for Danny:

1. Buy a campervan;
2. Travel the world;
3. Find ultimate happiness and the meaning of life.

OK, so number 3 is *my* ambition and not something I've really discussed that much with Danny, but hey, it seems we all have our little secrets. We'll go where the spirit takes us. Be free. Be a bit hippy. Shed the shackles of this overcomplicated modern life (which Blur and I concur is rubbish) and get back to the simple life, the good life.

And I'd planned to do all this with my best friend, Danny. Friend, confidant, drinking buddy and co-driver. Danny, the son-in-law my parents never had (so little do they know).

When we got back in touch a few years ago, Mum was full of new hats and ludicrous ideas despite the obvious *and* Danny's 'colourful' past, which she'd heard all about on the gossip train that is the Women's Institute. Well, clearly not everything. But if it gets me an easier life, I can put up with all the comments like 'well, you never know what could happen when you spend so much time together in the van', and 'if you can't be good, be careful' said with a wink from my uncle. Oh please! The only thing likely to happen between Danny and myself in that confined space is a few good bust-ups. And this is the first one. That devilish detail is NOT coming along for the ride.

'You won't even notice he's there,' Danny casually tries to assure me. 'I'll be looking after him. All you have to do is make a little room in your heart...' He grins at me endearingly as if presenting me with a cute puppy and not a wannabe borstal boy, and pinches my leg. I slap him away, but I can hear the note of desperation in his voice. Desperation no doubt planted by the sudden parental responsibility he's inherited. Reading quickly between the lines of Danny's garbled explanation, I gather that he hasn't really spent time with the boy in years, having walked out on Niobe and Aristotle when the boy was only two months old.

Funny, he never mentioned any of this when we got back in touch three years ago on Friends Reunited, and oddly enough his profile page doesn't mention the ex-wife, or the son.

'How come you never told me about this before, Danny?'

'Oh, I don't know, it never came up.'

'It never came up?'

'Well, obviously it did, actually...' He winked at me and we burst out laughing like kids again.

Men! In fact men and children, definitely not for me.

But then what happens to my big plan? I'm not about to give it up at the first little hurdle. Big hurdle. Boy-shaped hurdle.

* * * * * * *

As I cruise along the motorway I mentally readdress why I'm so desperate to do this trip. Why do I want to travel? Why do I feel this seemingly primeval urge deep down in my bones to *get away* and, contrarily, to *find myself*? It feels at once totally instinctive, intrinsic even, to this whole life experience thing, like a rite of passage. But also totally alien, frightening and even a bit self-indulgent. A couple of hundred years ago I might have been sent on a Grand Tour of Europe (if I was a boy), and most kids these days get it out of their system by taking a gap-year, I guess, but I never had that luxury. My dad's vicar stipend wouldn't stretch to supporting a feckless daughter gallivanting around the world; nor could his moral compass quite get the bearings for the concept.

When I was a student, so many years ago, we used to sit around in one of our rooms or the local pub on a Sunday afternoon drinking copious amounts of cheap plonk and talking about how to fill the vacuum of modern life. I always thought I'd have the answers by now. It feels like I've been waiting for my life proper to start all this time. And now, at that place somewhere near the midpoint of my life, I've realised that maybe I need to go find some answers for myself.

* * * * * * *

Sitting in Trowell Services, poring over the map unfolded between us on the coffee-stained, grease-smeared table top, the world looked a pretty big place for two thirty-somethings from the north of that little island there called, postmodern-unironically, 'Great Britain'... But it doesn't seem to faze Danny. I've only ever got as far as London and a couple of French exchanges with school, oh and of course that one ill-fated holiday in Greece with she-who-must-not-be-named. That certainly put me off foreign travel for a while. Danny's worked in the Middle East and the States, and has certainly had his fair share of air stewardesses from what I can gather. But neither of us are what you'd call real world travellers.

I wonder what Danny's real reasons for this trip are, and whether, deep down, they're anything like mine. I had suspected his reasons for coming along were less about the meaning of life and more about whether he can still pull women on all continents of this globe... although, in the end, does that amount to the same thing? Why should that be any less valid than some romantic notion I have of meditation and finding my inner higher self and absolute happiness? On the other hand, maybe he's just shallow and I should get used to that if I'm going to be in close quarters with him for the next couple of months.

It makes me wonder what kind of relationship he has

with his ex-wife, the Greek goddess Niobe. I imagine some demanding WAG type who spoils her son rotten. No wonder he 'has a few problems at school'. Doubtless a spoilt brat. But why ask feckless Danny to act in loco parentis? Loco, yes. Parentis, no. Doesn't she have *anyone* else to ask?

* * * * * * *

Suddenly, out of the gloom of the rainy night I see a looming orange glow on the horizon, reminiscent of a nuclear explosion in a permanent state of detonation. The Big Smoke beckons menacingly as I pass the sign for Watford Gap at last. Threshold of the Southern smoglands, and abandon hope all ye who enter here. At least I'm on the home stretch now.

* * * * * * *

I relive the final fateful moments of my conversation with Danny in my mind.

'But Danny...' I'd whinged. 'It'll cost more. It'll be too much, Danny. No, look, I've dropped my cat off with my parents – can't you do the same with your kid?'

Danny had frowned at me and leaned back in his seat, checking over to where Ari was still splatting zombies. 'Well, then, that's it for me I'm afraid. I have to look after Ari this summer and if you won't let him come with us then... I'm out.'

He had me over a barrel and he knew it. OK, so the cat comment was a bit below the belt, but... the thing is I really didn't want to be on my own. Oh God. Not God, just... bloody... pants!

I'd looked over at the little imp who's the cause of all this hassle, to see if I could picture what it would be like to spend more time with him. I'd tried to imagine Ari with a halo round

23

smiling cherubic features, but only caught him grimacing at the video screen as a large red splat mark appeared, signifying the end of him in that particular game. He'd sworn and thrown down the gun, marching over to where we were with a scowl the size of the Suez Canal adorning his far-from-angelic little face.

'Ari. Come and meet Casey properly.' Danny had held out his arms to the child who deftly avoided them, reminiscent of Diana avoiding Charles' kiss on their wedding day. Ari scowled more deeply, and thrust his hands deep into his pockets, from whence clearly no handshake was ever going to materialise.

'KC?' he'd said, mocking my earlier attempts at his name. 'Like KFC?' He let it hang in the air like a practised stand-up comedian putting down a heckler. He couldn't be more than ten years old, could he?

'Well...' Danny began, but I cut him off at the pass.

'No. It's Casey. Like "The Ballad of Casey Jones".'

'Or the Teenage Mutant Ninja Turtles,' Danny added, which actually made the boy grin, much to my chagrin.

'Or suitCase-y,' Ari joined in, triumphantly, at which even I tried hard to suppress a grin.

'So...' I began, trying to win back some control of the situation. 'How old are you?' asked in my best responsible adult voice (which I haven't quite honed yet).

'Twelve and three-quarters. Nearly thirteen,' Ari replied, folding his arms defiantly across his chest like a young warrior king.

'He'll be thirteen in three months,' Danny added, for all the world like the proud father, although I somehow suspect that he hasn't kept up with the birthday presents all of these years.

'Lucky number thirteen, huh?' I said, a bit sarcastically. The truth is I felt a bit unnerved by him. When did kids stop having any shred of respect for their elders? 'Well, you better

24

learn some better manners if you're going to come with us,' I'd finished in what I hoped was an authoritative voice.

'So… are you saying that he can come?' Danny leaned in, with raised eyebrows and his best little-boy-lost look. I quickly saw the trap I'd fallen into, but then I couldn't really see any way out – I either put up with this wannabe Damien and hope Danny takes on full parenting duties, or I have to give up on the whole plan. Which would mean, what? Finding another dead-end job and coming out ten years older and no wiser? No no no no no!

There was a long, pregnant pause, while I'd fought my better judgement which, it turns out, isn't so good after all…

'OK then, yes.'

* * * * * * *

Back at home, exhausted, I try to switch off, but my thoughts keep coming back to Danny and the super-surprising Aristotle. I pop a ready meal into the microwave and crack open a lovely cold can of beer. Ah, the freedom and joy of single life. Just as the oven pings to signal my meal's readiness, the phone rings. It's Danny.

'Look, Danny, can I call you back? My dinner's ready.' Making it sound like I've just created a gourmet delight that'll spoil if left a second longer.

'Oh, right, OK, it's… well… Happy birthday Casey! Sorry, I forgot.' He sounds genuinely bashful.

'That's OK – can't expect you to remember everything, eh? Not with your *surprise* and all.' I giggle forgivingly, although I had thought I might at least get a card.

There's a long pause on the line.

'Is there something else, Danny?'

'Oh, it's nothing. I'll call you another time.' I can hear a note of anxiety in Danny's voice, which is unusual. He's normally laidback to the point of horizontality about everything.

'Hang on, look, I can reheat my dinner. What's up?'

There's a pause, and then: 'No, it's OK, you eat your dinner. I'll talk to you another time. I've got to go now anyway, Niobe's waiting for me. It's nothing. Talk to you soon.' And he's gone.

I wonder what that was all about? How life has changed. Danny's all grown up with an ex-wife and a kid, and I'm... well, I'm older than I used to be. I coax my macaroni cheese out of its plastic case on to my plate and contemplate the nutritional value of adding the only sauce I can find in the back of my cupboard – a tube of ready-made wasabi – well, it's *green*.

The phone rings again. Hoping it'll be Danny calling to explain his mysterious silence I answer, and immediately regret it. It's Mum and Dad calling to wish me a happy birthday, hoping I got back safely, that I gave their love to Danny, and asking me if I've got everything I need for the trip. Even though we're not going for another six weeks. *Have* I got enough clean underwear? *Do* I have a first aid kit? *Do* I think they should invite Danny over for lunch before he comes down to London so that they can have a word with him and make sure everything's going to be OK on the journey, and that he'll look after me? And, for about the hundredth time: w*hy* do I want to go so far away on this big 'holiday' anyway? I take a large swig from my can for Dutch courage, and explode in one long outpouring: 'For Chrissakes Mum, I'm an adult now and I think I know how to pack for myself and organise enough clean underwear, and no way am I allowing you to have Danny over for lunch just so that you can ritually humiliate him and me. I've told you a thousand times why I want to do this trip, and, while we're on the subject of Danny: wake up and smell the pheromones – for the last time, I'M GAY and that's not going to change – get over it!'

There's a pause on the line, and I realise that I just said all that in my head and not out loud. I sigh, and tell her that I'll check on the underwear and first aid situation and that unfortunately Danny's far too busy with work to come over before the trip, and I miss out the bit about him looking after his estranged (and strange) son for his ex-wife because I'm still not sure what *I* think about it all and I sure as hell don't need to know what God thinks.

* * * * * * *

My macaroni cheese looks like a plastic prop left over from a sixties sitcom when I finally manage to get off the phone after forty minutes. I chuck it in the bin and crack open another beer instead. I grudgingly realise that Mum's right on one thing, though – I haven't told them the real reason why I want, no, *need* to do this trip. Just mumbled some vagaries about seeing the world and exploring new cultures. In my head I've blamed this vagueness on not wanting to talk to my parents about *finding myself* (and risk bringing up the whole adoption thing, or the religion thing), but I realise now that perhaps I'm not entirely sure of my own reasons. So I grab the pad and pen by the phone, have another big gulp of my beer, and sit down to make a list of my reasons for travelling. I jot down:

~~'Escape'~~

Escape from what? Wherever I go, there I am (as some ancient philosopher might say). I cross this out and have another think...

'Find myself'

Swiftly followed by:

'Find something'

More crossing out, and then:

'To find a better life'

If modern life is rubbish, can we go back to a way of life which was simpler, and more rewarding? Swap the laptop for the garden hoe, type of thing? But can we live without money? This trip is costing a small fortune already. Even the simple life would be so much easier if we were all rich. So is money actually the answer to happiness in life? Should I just give in and join the millions of people hanging on to the frankly ludicrous limbo state of hoping to win the Lottery and believing that this will make everything OK? Maybe this state of perpetual hope is easier than actually doing anything about this meaningless life?

I take another piece of paper and write a quick 'to do' list for tomorrow:

'Buy a Lottery ticket'

I look at it for a moment, then screw it up and throw it at the wastepaper bin. It misses and sits there on the floor taunting me like an enigmatic sign. I pick it up, straighten it out and go back to my original list and write:

'To explore the world and find answers'

The world has become so much smaller these days, now that Thailand has become the new Costa del Fish'n'Chips, and the exotic is more like the everyday. We seem to have lost a sense of the world as a place to explore. Paradise has become mundane. But there must still be something out there worth experiencing. There must be answers out there. I think somehow that the *quest* is about leaving behind what you know in order to find what it is you're looking for. Does that make sense? But answers to what? Maybe I need to define the questions.

I pause for another beer.

- *'What am I here for?'*
- *'What do I need in order for life to be meaningful?'*
- *'What is happiness and how do I attain it?'*
- *'What is love and how do I attain it?'*
- *'What is good and right and true?'*

I stare at these for a while, then finally write:

'To explore the world and find meaning and purpose in my life – to find, in short, the meaning of life'.

That seems right, somehow, even if it is still a little vague.

I sit back in my chair, drain the last of my beer and contemplate my list. What would someone else reading this make of it I wonder? I pick up my pen again, hesitate, then put it down again. I just don't know how to express the other unspoken questions in my head and heart – the stuff about being adopted, about not fitting in, about feeling that I'm the wrong shape – a square peg in a round hole, like I'm a missing jigsaw piece looking for my other 4999 pieces – about being gay and about God (or whatever). I guess I just hope that they'll get answered along the way.

I crawl into bed with the list still grasped in my hand. I'm so tired of all this thinking, but when I close my eyes it doesn't stop. Questions and thoughts whirl round and round inside my head like a sandstorm. Happy birthday to me. At 4 a.m. I finally drift off into a fitful and dream-laden sleep. I dream that I'm on the beach again. The dark water clinging to my ankles and the sand sucking me downwards. I think that I see her body floating just out of reach but I can't get to her. Every step is like wading through setting concrete as the sands clasp on to me. I cry out but no sound comes out of my mouth. Her body is sinking, sinking into the dark waters...

I wake with a start, tangled in the sheets and covered in sweat. It's only a couple of hours since I went to bed but I'm scared to go back to sleep again.

CHAPTER 3

The ice cream van at the end of the universe

'Taking a new step, uttering a new word, is what [people] fear most.'

Fyodor Dostoevsky,
Crime and Punishment, 1886.

Six weeks later, Mum and Dad are still reeling from the shock of me telling them about Ari. I try not to make him sound like the devil incarnate, although it's hard, to be honest, given the first impression he made. Danny has gone from golden boy to tarnished brass monkey and back again as I told them how he's looking after Ari for the summer. Now Mum thinks it's a thoroughly good idea and I can see her beginning to put us all together in some kind of *Little House on the Prairie* set-up.

Since I volunteered to look for our chosen mode of transport, I've been spending lots of time on eBay looking at campervans. That's been fun. Oh and, of course, now we need something big enough for the three of us – me, Danny and Ari – Aristotle, Aristo, the Aristotlater – 'the boy'. I have a budget of two and a half grand. One thousand from my savings and fifteen hundred from Danny's last contract (before he fritters it away on booze and birds – in fact I'm surprised Danny can come up with enough money to make the trip at all given he's never had so much as a piggy bank. I suspect he has 'borrowed' some from Niobe as a bribe for taking Ari off her hands for the summer).

I've spent three solid days and nights sitting at my computer on eBay in bidding wars. I've *almost* bought every single van of my dreams only to be pipped at the post in the very last second by people called things like WhiteVanMan, TheVanInFrontOfYou or VanDammit. Having finally figured out how to play the game I bide my time, waiting up until 2.17 a.m., 3.21 a.m., 4.40 a.m. and 5.15 a.m. in order to put in the last bid just as each item is closing, but still someone with a faster broadband connection than me, or just plain psychic abilities, seems to know what I am about to bid and bids a fraction more. I've bid up to my last penny and sometimes even been tempted to go that one extra fiver over budget, but seventy-two hours later I'm severely sleep-deprived, caffeine-hyped, no more psychic than a lettuce leaf and still van-less.

I have, however, managed to 'win' two really cute miniature VW campers which turned out to be salt and pepper shakers (and which will forever remind me of the perils of perspective when sleep-deprived); and a long piece of rubber tubing which is allegedly 'an essential spare piece of kit for any serious campervan journey'. (I've absolutely no idea what it's for and it came with no instructions, but I won it, so I'll pack it with pride.)

* * * * * * *

Danny calls. He's found a van. What? I didn't even ask him to look – that was my job.

'OK,' I say warily. 'When can we go and see it? Oh, and what are they asking?'

'No need,' Danny says breezily, 'we've already bought it.'

'*We?* Have *bought* it? *What? Danny?*' My mind is racing, wondering whether to scream in frustration or relief. I try to reassure myself that this is a good thing, that Danny knows what he's talking about when it comes to cars and vans and things. Right? He's just made an executive decision. I mean, God knows, my eBay skills haven't really done it for us. I try to remain calm. But what does he mean 'we'? He and Ari – the new Batman and Robin?

'Don't worry babes, it's a great van and it was a real bargain. I used your credit card, I hope you don't mind, only Gary said someone else was interested so I thought we ought to get in quick. She's a real cracker and...'

'How the hell did you get my credit card details, Danny?' I ask incredulously, trying not to get too angry until this mad story has unfolded to a place where I can understand it properly.

'You gave them to me.' Calm as anything.

'What? No, I didn't. Why on earth would I give you my...'

'You gave them to me to book the cinema tickets last week, when we took Ari to see Harry Potter and I didn't have any money in my account.'

'Oh right, I see!' I explode, not seeing anything but red. 'So because I very generously took you and your young Dementor to see the boy wizard, which, by the way, he didn't even say thanks for, you thought that it would be OK to use my card details to spend... how much? How much was it, Danny?'

'It was a real bargain, really. Look, calm down, Casey. It's all in a good cause. It's the perfect van for our trip. You'll love it when you see it, my most gorgeous, generous friend.' Danny tries to charm me.

'How much?' I reiterate, with as much patience as a sleep-deprived serial eBay loser can manage.

'A real bargain,' Danny repeats, although sounding slightly less positive than before.

'*HOW MUCH?*' I enunciate both words with venom.

'OK… Three grand.'

'Danny!'

The bank of Mum and Dad just opened another position.

* * * * * * *

It turns out that Gary is a mate of a mate of Danny's who deals in decidedly dodgy gear. Most of which probably fell off the back of one of the lorries currently lying around his yard in various states of disrepair. Danny and I pick our way carefully through the broken bits of engine, twisted plastic, and discarded packaging bearing fragments of foreign writing. This treasure trove of detritus looks like it's come a long way to end up, mysteriously, on the Walworth Road in South London. But there's no sign of the magical campervan, which Danny was in such a hurry to buy, and which was in such huge demand from the equally absent hordes of other buyers.

Gary looks like an extra from *The Bill*, but then so does half of London, and a quarter of them are (*Criminal Number 3*). He moves with the exaggerated swagger of a seasoned wheeler-dealer. We follow him over to an old shed at the end of the yard in which I can make out nothing but a large mass of brownish stained sheets piled up in a huge mountain, like the leftovers of an Iraqi hospital after a bomb attack. Gary pulls back the edge of one of the sheets, which I wouldn't have touched with gloves, to reveal a dust-covered wheel arch painted a sickly strawberry pink colour. I realise I'm actually shaking, but not with anticipation, more the potent mixture

34

of fear and anger (and the caffeine high of the past sleepless week, which hasn't totally worn off yet).

Gary, whose pasty complexion looks like a slab of wet cod, with gingery seaweed hair, pulls off the remaining part of the dust cover with a flourish and announces, in his 'Sarf Lundun' dialect complete with the obligatory Jamaican undertones, which seem very cool these days: 'She's a bitchin' pimped up ride, my man, is it. You're talkin' real vintage stuff here, real *Antiques Roadshow* gold-dust, yeah? She's well bling.'

Danny and Gary are both looking at me expectantly and I realise that I had zoned out again. I've evidently missed an important question. It was probably 'what do I think?' Well, now that the covers are off and the van is revealed in all its 'glory' I can see that the strawberry colour is quite apt.

'It's an ice cream van!' I exclaim.

'Yeah, bitchin' ain't she bitc— er, dude?' Gary catches the glint in my eye that's been there for days and is now ratcheting up to volcanic levels.

'She's fully conver'ed tho, innit, Casey, Gary's done a well-cool job on 'er.' Danny's accent has slipped into the practised Mockney he usually employs for charming London lasses, with a touch of added gangsta for Gary's sake, I presume. I look at him incredulously.

'And just what do you think we're gonna do, Danny – sell Mister Whippy to the Mongolian herdsmen? Ciderpops to the Siberians? 99s to the Nigerians?'

'We're not even goin' to Nigeria, Casey,' Danny says calmly with the same irritating tone he probably employs for Ari, while Gary bursts in eagerly: 'Nah, mate, you got it all wrong, see, the ice cream bit ain't there no more, it ain't a freezer on wheels, is it. Come an' 'ave a look inside.' He beckons me towards the rear door and Danny quickly grabs my raised fist and pulls me over.

35

Inside its pink shell, the ice cream van is like a Tardis – unfeasibly bigger than the outside belies – and I'm momentarily distracted from my anger. Gary shows me how the bunk beds cleverly fold down from the sides, the spacious under-seat storage units where the ice cream tubs and cones would formerly have been, the tiny fridge, gas-bottle cooker on top, electric hook-up, and sink with your actual running water. And there, in the corner opposite the fridge, is even a small child-size chemical toilet in its own lockable cupboard, with absolutely no knee room whatsoever, but still, privacy. I have to admit I'm fairly impressed. And if I couldn't still glimpse the strawberry pink out of the serving hatch window, clashing violently with all the fake oak veneer inside, then I might be able to forget about the fact that she is, or was, actually an ice cream van.

* * * * * * *

'Why don't you call it Winston?' Gary suggests as Danny signs the ownership papers in the office before I can change my mind (or fall into a sleep-deprived coma). 'You know, 'cos you'll be Brits abroad, innit. I could paint a Union Jack on it,' Gary adds helpfully. I briefly contemplate whether the Blitz spirit is really something we want to conjure up on our journey, but it's a moot point; the van's clearly female.

Danny mutters something under his breath about a van with a Union Jack on being a bit of a target in the current post-9/11 climate, while I contemplate whether a strawberry pink ice cream van isn't already such a target.

'How about Kylie?' I offer.

'Ow about 'er?' Gary and Danny chorus. Danny pauses in his form-filling to give me a perplexed grin that's clearly meant to convey something about my sexuality and implied penchant for the tiny singer with the celebrated rear-end.

'For the van, I mean. Let's call her Kylie,' I persist, ignoring his look.

'You can't call a van a girl's name!' Gary explodes, as if personally insulted. Danny grunts noncommittally and I decide then and there that the van will have to be called Alice, like in *The L Word*, because she'll clearly have to be bisexual to please both parties here. I don't bother trying to explain this to the boys right now. And if I need a backup reason (if my parents ever ask, for example) I could say it's after Alice B. Toklas, the famous salonista and legendary forerunner of Jamie Oliver (though he has never dared to try to repeat her infamous fudge recipe, so far as I know).

Happy with my unilateral decision, I join Danny in signing off the joint ownership papers and climb into the passenger seat while he drives us off into the smoggy Sarf Lundun sunset in our new home-from-home, playing a melodic blast of 'Greensleeves' every time he hits the horn. This makes me giggle with pleasure despite the jeers and funny looks we get. I bet Henry VIII (or whoever really composed it) never thought his tune would be the clarion call for hot sticky kids up and down the land to buy their strawberry Mivvis 500 years later. Even less, that it would become the theme tune to our little adventure, starting right now on the five-mile journey from Walworth to Tulse Hill. My delight lasts nearly through the first mile.

I have to admit that I am warming to Alice, our ex-ice cream van, and I'm almost prepared to forgive Danny for buying her so impulsively, although we might really need to change the blinking horn.

* * * * * * *

In the evening, Danny and I are sitting in my bijou kitchen with takeaway pizza, looking at the map. It's cold and dark outside the security-grilled window. Another dreary spring day and I can't wait for summer and a complete change of scenery. I feel like I've climbed over the wall of eBay-induced tiredness and landed on my feet the other side, fuzzy but wide-eyed and ready for adventure. So, we crack open a few beers and go over the route plan, such as it is:

Harwich – Holland – Germany – Poland – then a whole load of exotic and forbidding-sounding places in the former Soviet Union – a quick detour into Kazakhstan – then back into Russia – Omsk – Tomsk – Irkutsk (and other Wombles) – down into Mongolia – through the Gobi Desert and on into Made In China. After China, the backpacker heaven of South-East Asia beckons, and then who knows? I'm not totally sure how an ex-ice cream van will cope with the Himalayas, but I'm willing to give it a shot right now, from the safety of 8000 miles away in my South London kitchen.

Sometimes I wonder if I'm not, if *we're* not, going into this whole adventure a trifle underprepared.

I look at big, strong Danny for some reassurance. He's making Irish coffees for us, which, after all the beers we've drunk, is just about going to finish me off.

'So, why do you *really* want to go travelling, Casey?' he asks me without warning while he pours a large measure of whisky into the coffee.

'We've been through this, Dan,' I reply, catching even myself off-guard with my defensive tone, as if I'm scared that my reasons for going aren't good enough. Not *justifiable*. As if I'm scared that what my parents think is true – that I'm just skiving off for a year with no real purpose.

'The whole mid-life crisis thing?' Danny shoots at me over his shoulder as he pours cream expertly over the back of a spoon, making the coffee look like a perfect half of Guinness in the glass mugs.

I look up at him, and around my rundown rental flat. Dido is warbling on the radio in the background, about how her life is for rent, that she's never found somewhere she can call home. It's not really my thing this kind of music, but suddenly I'm fighting back tears. What the...? It must be the alcohol. And all the late nights on eBay. I quickly brush my cheek with my sleeve hoping that Danny hasn't noticed.

'Yeah, maybe. Maybe it is that.' I try to laugh but the effort just makes me feel like crying again.

Dido carries on obliviously about her dreams to travel more and live the simple life, as if addressing me directly.

I gesture towards the radio and say weakly: 'You know, it's just time, Danny, it's just... I need to find... *something*.' The exasperated emphasis I put on the word makes Danny look round and, frowning slightly, he brings over the Irish coffees and places one gently in front of me like a peace offering.

'So tell me about it, Casey.' He looks me directly in the eyes.

Danny's a man, right, but he can sometimes be sensitive; and I think he knows there's more to this than a song on the radio and what I've just said. So while Dido serenades us mournfully from the windowsill I try to gather my thoughts. After all, as my travelling companion, which is kind of a zen concept when you think about it, Danny should probably know what I'm trying to do, trying to find, trying to be... whatever that is.

As he drinks his coffee I tell him about the fact that I'm struggling with finding meaning in life, and how I'm not sure where I'm going and that I need to find *something* to make sense of everything. And all the time I'm worried he's going to think I'm either soft, stupid, or just plain crazy. But when I've ground to a halt and asked him to pass the Kleenex, Danny

39

leans over and gives me a big hug and says that he knows exactly what I mean.

'Do you, though, Danny? I mean, *you* don't ever think about any of that stuff, do you.' It's meant as a self-indictment rather than an accusation, although I can see how it could...

Danny gives me a strange look as if actually hurt by the insinuation and suddenly stands up, taking me completely by surprise. Grabbing his jacket from the back of the chair, he makes for the door, but hesitates for a second, and turns back to face me.

'You know what, Casey? You don't take me seriously. You never have. Nobody does. I'm just "good old Danny", "fun Danny". No one ever thinks there's anything more to me.' He hesitates for a second, and I notice the skin around his eyes redden and tighten.

'I'm a complete failure in most people's eyes,' he continues angrily. 'I've run away from everything in my life – my marriage, my kid, a steady job, any responsibility... Don't you think *I'm* looking for something too? That's why I called you the other night. I wanted to talk about things. I thought you of all people might understand. But you're too wrapped up in your own little world, Casey. You always were.'

He turns his back on me. I feel hurt, but more than that, I feel that I've let him down. I'm an idiot. I've underestimated him. I can't believe I don't even know my best friend any more. I stand up too, before he gets the chance to leave like this, and pull him into a hug, to show him... what? That I care? That I'm the same as him? That I understand?

He resists for a fraction of a second, then gives in and hugs me back. I suddenly feel tears pricking the back of my eyes.

'I'm sorry,' I murmur in his ear. My old friend. My childhood sweetheart. The runaway bridegroom.

'Oh my spiky little lesbian lunatic,' Danny says mock-soothingly. 'You know, for someone so clever you don't half act daft sometimes!' His anger momentarily forgotten, he rubs me affectionately on the head, and I have to laugh, even through my tears.

* * * * * *

I watch him walk down the road towards the train station, his square shoulders hunched against the spring night air and the black leather jacket catching the glint of streetlights as he passes. Back inside I stick on my new Arctic Monkeys CD to take away the bitter taste of Dido, and sit listening to Alex Turner's thick West Yorkshire accent rocking out about a bloke from Rotherham who's trying to impress the girls by pretending he's from New York. Makes me smile every time. And now I realise it also makes me think of Danny. Danny with his tall stories and northern charm. Danny, the best travelling companion a girl could want.

I think how lucky I am to have someone like Danny in my life. We're so different, but somehow also the same. I feel ashamed that I've been so wrapped up in my own reasons for travelling that I've not even thought that Danny might have *his* own reasons. Even worse, I seem to be guilty of labelling Danny as a simple *bloke* without the capacity to feel as I do. And after all the lecturing I give him about not labelling me. I guess I just thought he was up for a jaunt, a boy's own adventure. It certainly didn't take much persuasion to get him to agree to come with me, even though I hadn't seen him for a while. A long while. I never guessed that he could be on his own journey of discovery... just like I never saw the 'son' thing coming.

It must be fifteen years since Danny went AWOL from my life, nearly twenty since we both left Scarborough. When he finally got back in touch with me we exchanged a few emails, which led to a few late night phone calls and eventually settled into an irregular pattern of Friday night drinks (when he didn't have a hot date or a boys' night out). That closeness we had when we were kids just seemed to still be there. Like we'd never been apart. But I guess we didn't talk about stuff like this. I didn't think he'd be interested. The truth is I didn't stop to think what he'd be interested in. I really need to pay more attention to the people in my life – there aren't *that* many after all. Oh Danny boy! Bust-ups were one thing that Danny and I had all the time when we were kids, and it never meant anything then. I just hope that we still have that kind of bond after all these years.

I make a mental note to call Danny first thing in the morning and apologise, again. I eventually fall asleep to dream of winged monkeys screeching and swooping through the air, carrying off a helplessly warbling Dido in their clutches while the wicked witch swings from the back of a tram running helter-skelter down a San Francisco street towards the waters of the bay below.

CHAPTER 4

To Utopia and beyond

'It is not down in any map; true places never are.'
Herman Melville,
Moby-Dick; or, the Whale, 1851.

'Anyone for a 99?' I quip, swinging the last bag into Alice and suddenly feeling high on life. It's 7.30 a.m. on a Friday morning at the beginning of June. The sun is shining and I feel alive with the possibilities ahead, the sense of adventure, the freedom of the open road.

The van is packed to the gills with our *stuff.* 'Travel light' all the guidebooks told us, but between my inalienable right as a woman (yes, even a gay woman) to bring twice as many clothes as the menfolk, and Danny and my joint love of gadgets and camping gear, we've managed to fill up all the under-seat lockers, the cupboards, the over-cab space and jam up the toilet cubicle as well. A few (or *possibly* more) of the gadgets fall into the 'just in case' category; particularly my zombie apocalypse survival kit. But in this day and age, after 9/11, nothing seems too far-fetched. You never know when we might need flares, compasses, a fire striker, waterproof matches, water purification tablets, enough bandages to wrap a mummy, and a large hunting knife that's almost certainly illegal (sourced from pasty-faced Gary). OK, so I'm a bit of a geek, but I want to be prepared to survive this trip, even if a twelve-year-old child is the scariest thing I come across.

Ari is sitting in the back, squashed between duvets, pillows, a sack of potatoes and several bags of oranges (a present from Mum and Dad concerned that we might get scurvy, even though the first bit of our trip is in Europe).

'Mum always lets me ride in the front,' Ari pipes up petulantly, pushing the oranges and potatoes to the floor with a loud thud.

'Well, you can't right now, Casey needs to navigate for me.'

Danny locks the back door, leaving only me to overhear Ari muttering under his breath: 'Stupid ice cream van, wouldn't be seen dead in the front anyway. And *she's* not even your girlfriend.'

It's been a long week having Danny and Ari to stay while we made last-minute preparations. Ari's barely said two words to me, and Danny hasn't fared much better. I realise it must be strange and awkward for the kid but I wasn't prepared for the angry silent treatment. I've been treading on eggshells for days wondering how to *be* with him. I think Danny's much the same.

'What if I get car sick?' Ari moans, banging his bag against my headrest as he unpacks it.

'You won't,' Danny says, and the tone sounds more like a threat than reassurance.

Oh boy, the little fella certainly does have a knack for bursting bubbles. My optimistic mood is sagging at the thought of weeks of this warring. Still, onwards and upwards. Next stop Harwich Ferry Port.

* * * * * * *

Harwich is a two hour drive from South London, according to the AA. The AA, however, were presumably counting on you having a car of average weight, speed and age, *not* an overloaded twenty-year-old ice cream van. Two hours after leaving Tulse Hill we still haven't reached Colchester and I guesstimate we've about another hour to go. It's half past nine and our ferry is leaving at 10.40. This is not a good start, and to cap it all Ari hasn't quit moaning since we started.

'I'm hungry, Dan.'

I've realised the serendipity of Danny's name for a boy who hasn't used the term 'Dad' since he arrived at my flat. Said in his dropped-consonant adolescent way it sounds almost identical. Danny looks quickly over his shoulder and shoots Ari a glance. It glances off him. I guess *Dad*'s not been around enough to hold much sway. I can see this is going to be a *long* journey.

'Have an orange,' I yell at Ari over the engine noise, and ignore his screwed-up 'yeuch' face. Don't children eat fruit any more?

'Do you think we'll make it?' I ask Danny anxiously. He pouts, rather like Ari, and jams his foot to the floor. The engine gives a little start, roars a bit louder and the cab begins to shake like a fairground ride. I cast a worried look at Danny who eases off the pedal slightly to lessen the juddering. Alice still stubbornly refuses to go over sixty-five miles per hour. He shakes his head.

I'm trying to be philosophical about the whole trip, so I suppose I'd better start here. It's meant to be very laissez faire this journey, not overplanned, going where the wind blows, etc. So why worry about missing our first little ferry trip?

'They won't give us a refund you know, if we miss it. It said on the website.' Danny neatly cuts across my philosophy with the razor wire of fact, and we all sit in rather sullen silence for the next hour, watching the minutes until our hugely expensive ferry crossing tick by one by one.

* * * * * * *

At 10.30 Danny rounds the last corner into the Ferry Port. We swing through the gates almost on two wheels, sending Ari bashing violently against the window in the back with a worrying crack. We whizz past lines of waiting cars with me frantically trying to get all the paperwork out of the plastic folder and in order, which is tricky with Danny playing Formula One in an ice cream van. Screeching round the last corner we're just in time to see them hauling up the back end of Stena *Searider* in a very final-looking fashion. A man wearing a dayglo vest and waving a clipboard runs towards us.

'Check-in closed half an hour ago,' he informs us helpfully, waving aside my proffered handful of paperwork. 'You'll have to go to the office and see if they'll put you on another one, but it's busy this time of year; you might not get one till tomorrow.'

I'm heartened by the fact that we may not have to buy new tickets, but Danny seems to think we'll have to pay a penalty and is swearing under his breath, cursing at Alice. Clearly we're going to have to factor Alice's slowness into our journey plans. Progress could be slightly more leisurely than we anticipated.

* * * * * * *

Inside the terminal I'm having little luck in switching our tickets with the woman in the ticket office.

'It's discretion'ry,' she tells me, with the flat finality of a practised jobsworth.

Apparently we'll have to pay a penalty fee of £100 and book on to another ferry, only they're all full. She's just looking at ferries for two days' time when Danny strolls up with Ari. Her face instantly brightens.

'Any problems, Casey?' he enquires casually, giving the woman behind the desk a big, lazy smile. He turns to the kid and lifts him on to the desk top like a little child. 'Now, Ari, I'm sure the nice lady... er? Bronwen,' he reads her name badge, 'can get us on to the next ferry so that we can get to Disneyland in time for your birthday.'

'But it's not...' Ari begins.

'Yes it *is*... important,' Danny cuts across him firmly.

'Oh, what a sweet boy!' Bronwen purrs. 'Oh now, let me see what we can do.' She picks up her phone, all the time ogling Danny so obviously that I wonder if she's forgotten that I'm standing here, or the conversation we've just had. I've seen this kind of reaction to Danny before, of course, but usually just before he disappears off leaving me with two drinks to finish. This time I might let it pass, and not say anything just now about the lying in front of Ari or the bad example he's setting as a father.

'Right, OK. Thanks Sue.' Bronwen's smiling and winking at Danny conspiratorially as she's clearly pulled in some favour to get us on to the next ferry. If I was Danny's wife or girlfriend I'd be livid at the level of flirtation, but I'm not, so I'll take those tickets, thanks.

'Thank you, Bronwen,' Danny is saying into those simpering eyes. 'You've made a young boy very happy.'

Two young boys in my opinion.

Danny lifts Ari off the desk again and, giving Bronwen one last smile, he leaves me to do the paperwork, swaggering off with that 'job done' look on his face.

'You're so lucky.' Bronwen beams stupidly as she hands over our new tickets.

'Yes, aren't I?' I say, grinning sardonically at her over my shoulder as I go to find 'my boys'. I wonder why Danny needs to search for meaning in life. I mean, when you can twist people round your little finger like he can then isn't life just a breeze?

* * * * * * *

Ten thirty p.m. and all safely aboard the Stena *Britannica*, halfway through our crossing on the first leg of our epic adventure: so far, a day trip to Harwich. Ari is curled up asleep on the leatherette bench beside Danny. The onboard 'curry special' and the rolling motion are not making me feel too good and all I want to do is read my book, *Spinsters Abroad*, tales of Victorian lady explorers, which Danny belatedly bought me for my birthday. But Danny's in the mood for talking.

'So, first stop Holland, Casey,' he begins. 'What's on the itinerary? Tulip fields? Van Gogh Museum?'

What am I – a glorified tour guide and children's rep?

'Actually I've heard that there's this amazing place...' I falter, suddenly hesitant about saying it out loud.

'Oh yeah? What's that then?'

'Well, it's called YouTopia. It's in Amsterdam.'

'Utopia? What is it, a nightclub?' Danny sounds a bit taken aback.

'No, it's a... a commune. I read about it online.'

'What, on dubya dubya dubya hippydippy dotcom?' Danny scowls.

'Well listen,' I start, feeling a bit miffed that *my* plan for discovering the world and new ways of *doing life* are now having to pass through the Parental Guidance filter. 'It *is* a hippy commune, as it happens, and if you don't want to come with me because you've got to look after Ari then that's fine with me.'

'Oh come on, Casey, don't tell me that you actually believe in utopia?' Danny asks with what sounds a lot like sarcasm in his voice.

'Well, I'm just curious,' I say, a little defensively. I mean, the word utopia really means a good place that doesn't exist (my History and Classics degree finally pays dividends), and I just want to see if it could, in reality.

'Haven't you seen *The Matrix*?' Danny asks me.

'What? Well yes, of course, but...'

'The whole point about *The Matrix* is that utopias don't work,' Dannys says, as if this is self-evident to anyone with half a brain. And because I must look puzzled, he continues: 'That's why the first *Matrix* went wrong, because people are never satisfied with what they've got. They always want more. They want the nice garden *and* the forbidden fruit.'

I'm temporarily stunned into silence, because I'm seeing a side to Danny I never knew existed. I mean I enjoyed *The Matrix,* and I loved the special effects and 'bullet time' (and I had a crush on Trinity like everyone else), but I'm not convinced that I really got it. At least not as clearly as Danny.

'Well,' I hesitate momentarily. I dig deep into my historical memory banks for something to come back at him with. 'I grant you that More's Utopia was fictional, but maybe that was because socialism hadn't developed sufficiently at that point for it to be a reality? Maybe, like Plato's Republic, Utopia could never work because humans are, well, human?' I trail off, aware that my argument is not very well thought through.

'Humans are a species that define their reality through the misery and suffering they endure. There's no such thing as the perfect world – that's just a dream that their primitive brains keep trying to wake up from,' Danny says, paraphrasing *The Matrix* again.

A line, or the ghost of it, suddenly comes back to me from nowhere, so I try it out: 'Er, having a choice is just an illusion conjured up by those with power and tacitly accepted by those without.' I smile triumphantly, warming to this little celluloid duel over our next destination.

It's all getting a bit surreal, so when Ari stirs, disturbed by our random conversation, it seems like he might just save me from my own private Matrix. He sits up, rubbing his eyes and scowling – his usual expression, only it's a slightly greener shade than normal. I'm guessing he's finally got the travel sickness he was banging on about earlier. Danny looks at him, and then at me.

'Casey, would you take Ari for some fresh air?' Danny asks casually. The cheek. Still, if it means I can escape from the Matrix for a break... Ari looks less than happy, but too green to argue.

'Come on then,' I say, in my best attempt at motherliness, and Ari gets up from the seat and follows me, keeping just far enough away for us never to actually touch clothing or anything.

I haven't realised until I stand up just how much the boat is rolling, and as Ari and I weave our way across the floor we're thrown left and right by turns, looking for all the world like a couple of drunks trying to find their way home. I lean with all my might on the outside door and hold it open against the wind for Ari as we step out into the dark cold and get hit by a face full of seaspray. The deck is wet and slippery and I pull my jacket closer around me, following Ari to the rail.

'Do you think you're going to be sick?' I ask him. I have to shout to be heard above the roar of the engines and the sea.

'What do you care?' Ari shouts over his shoulder and I'm stung simultaneously by another whip of wind and salt.

His response stops me in my tracks. What *do* I care? After

50

all, he's not my child, but as an adult I feel strangely obliged to at least *act* like I do.

'Of course I care,' I shout, but the lie sounds hollow, even to me, as the wind howls in my face.

'In... van, when I hit... on the window... you looked like you... cared whether the glass... cracked... didn't care if... was hurt.' Ari's words spindrift angrily over his shoulder.

'What?' I shout into the wind, but I've caught the gist of it, and he doesn't bother to repeat it.

'Oh,' I yell, pointlessly. '*Were* you hurt?'

Ari stands with his back to me for a few long seconds before turning briefly to say: 'No.'

I stand on the wet, cold deck, with the wind and seaspray battering my face, gripping on to the rusty salt-encrusted rail, and I don't know what to say. There is nothing to say. I feel exasperated and exhausted after a week of these hostilities; and way, way out of my depth. I just don't think I've got the gene to cope with children. I wait in the icy wet darkness for Ari to feel better, and then we stagger back in silence.

* * * * * * *

When we disembark at around 1.45 a.m. it's raining lightly, and I've volunteered to drive – more to give my mind something concrete to focus on than from actual desire. I've never driven on the right before, and it's dark and windy and rainy and I'm tired, and all I really want to do is pull up for the night and get some sleep.

I pull into a petrol station on Dirk Van Den Burgweg street to ask if there's a campsite nearby. The guy says there's one near Oranjesluisweg. Despite my tiredness I'm already loving this country. I feel that somewhere between Dick Van DykeBurg and Orange Juice Street I could be happy. However, navigating a foreign country on the wrong side of the road in the now driving rain and pitch dark is another matter; and after driving around in circles for ten minutes I admit defeat and head for the highway, hoping we'll just come across something soon.

Ari is asleep in the back, slung across the mountain of duvets and pillows, and my co-pilot Danny is lolling in the passenger seat with his chin on his chest, so I figure no one's going to argue with me. I grab the AA printout of the route from Danny's sleeping hands and try to read it in the puddles of orange motorway lights as they flash past. We're only about an hour from Amsterdam but I'm betting not many campsites are going to be open at this time in the morning, so I think our best bet is to head for a service area. At least there'll be clean toilets and coffee shops and things. According to the directions there are two – at Leiburg and Den Ruygen Hoek, if I can just get myself on to the A4. What did that sign say?

Thirty minutes later I miss the turnoff for Leiburg Services. Bugger! I slew to a stop on the hard shoulder and momentarily consider the motorway madness of reversing to the exit. As visibility out of my side mirrors to the rear is virtually nil and I haven't had much (OK, any) practice at reversing the van, I decide against it. It's only another thirteen kilometres to Den Ruygen Hoek, near the airport. Danny rouses at this point to mumblingly ask why we've stopped, and are we there yet?

'Nearly,' I say reassuringly. 'Nearly there.' Thinking to myself that I've been 'nearly there' all my life, but never in an ice cream van with one and a half men.

At Den Ruygen Hoek, finally, I pull into a corner of the practically empty car park and park up. Waking Danny I grab my jacket and run round to the back of the van trying not to get too soaked in the downpour. Ari needs a few good shakes to wake up enough to get the bunks sorted, which we all do in a semi-stupor. I can't decide which I would prefer – to sleep in one of the dodgy-looking hang-down bunks which are attached to the roof struts with chains or to sleep below one of them on one of the benches. Luckily the choice is made for me when Ari climbs into one of the top bunks and Danny hoists the potatoes and oranges on to the other one, settling below. I hope those chains hold tight.

I try to settle down to sleep but am assailed by the sound of planes taking off and landing at nearby Schipol airport, the rain battering on the roof, the grating and straining of the chains as Ari turns over, and snoring from Danny's bench. What a great first night performance.

As I lie, totally exhausted but irritatingly awake, in my morgue-shelf bunk, I turn over in my mind the events of the day, including Matrixgate. I begin to wonder how 'normal people' deal with life's big questions. Most people, I'm sure, don't feel the need to go off to the far ends of the earth in an ice cream van looking for answers. In fact it seems to me that most people, when confronted with the whole meaning of life thing, tend to either ignore it and just get on with things, or look first for a higher being – something that created us and therefore *knows* what we are here for. Problem is, they haven't exactly told us, these higher beings, unless you count the ten commandments, Koranic principles, Buddhist mantras and various instructions to convert all peoples to *this* or *that* religion: the *one* true religion; one ring to bind them all.

I suppose that some people are provided with their raison d'être by family. Some people's entire goal in life is to find the right man or woman, settle down and have children. Their sum purpose is to procreate – the most basic biological reason for existing. Only, there must surely be more to it than that? If that was all there was, why would we have evolved as we have? We could just be cavemen and women, hunting and gathering and mothering and fathering and that's that. What's the modern human for? Why do we need brains, society, culture? There *is* more to life. There *has* to be. Humans have evolved into these amazing creatures who've built cities and the internet and spacecraft and... What's that all for? What are we seeking to do with all of our knowledge?

The whole family thing's not for me, I think, reminiscing on tonight's little shipside drama. Not just because I'm gay. I just don't seem to have that biological urge. Although, as I get older, I can see the attraction of this – the continuation of the gene line, the unconditional and constant love and feeling of being needed generated by offspring; the fact that there'll be someone pretty much guaranteed to be around to look after you when you're older. Perhaps I am, after all, approaching the menopause? I glance up at Ari in his bunk, scowling even in his sleep, and instantly change my mind. It's much more responsible of me to do my bit for our overpopulated globe and stay childless, otherwise you never know what you might end up with.

I suppose, in a way, I've deliberately shied away from the usual 'crutches' people use to get through life –marriage, children, career, religion – because I felt pushed into them. And just as rudely pushed out of them. My mind flickers briefly on painful memories of my relationship with she-who-must-not-be-named, and the abrupt ending to my church-going, before I drag it quickly back into the present. All those things are traps, tricks, Mogadons. They somehow stop us from finding the true meaning in life. But, having shied away from all of these, having 'purified' my life, somehow I can't help feeling it's a little bit empty... But perhaps that's just because I haven't found the true meaning of life yet?

My mind is slowly grinding to a halt somewhere between the known unknowns and the unknown unknowns. Oh God, life's too short for this. I stuff the duvet over my head trying to shut out the thoughts, and hope that sleep will finally overtake me (or I'll suffocate). Either way, it'll release me from this endless thinking.

CHAPTER 5

Red light Green light

*'You start a question, and it's like starting a stone. You
sit quietly on the top of a hill; and away the stone goes,
starting others.'*

Robert Louis Stevenson,
The Strange Case of Dr. Jekyll And Mr. Hyde, 1886.

I'm woken by a bursting desire for the toilet, which I've been
suppressing since we arrived last night in the dark and pouring
rain. I can't get to the chemical toilet for all the stuff in the
way, so instead pick my way to the back door through the
debris of discarded clothes and shoes. Luckily I was too tired
to get changed last night, so I'm still fully dressed. I stagger
across the car park in the dawn light, gradually aware that
cars are pulling in and out and that I must look a complete
state: crumpled, scarecrow-haired with wild, barely slept-in-
days starey eyes. I'm reminded of my eBay trauma.

I furtively creep into the toilets, hoping I've chosen the
right ones as the little picture seems to have clogs on and is
wearing a funny hat and sort of a skirt (I assume the little boys'
room will be a picture of a little fella with his finger in the...
well, you know). It's all very modern and clean. They have
those taps that are like an IQ test – no visible means of turning

them on and off. I'm glad there are so few people around as I swipe my hands over, under and around the taps. I move from sink to sink repeating these hand movements like Harry Potter trying out a new magic spell or enticing out Moaning Myrtle. Eventually I accidentally move through some invisible beam or other and a torrent of piping hot water spills into the bowl and splashes out on to my jeans. Brilliant. I can't see anything to operate the plug device so I stand to one side and wave and splash my face with scalding water until I feel I'm sufficiently parboiled for the day.

When I open the back door of the van again I'm hit by a wave of what I can only describe as 'eau de l'homme' – that faintly urinal, musty man-encrusted sheet smell that I remember from Danny's bedroom when he was a boy. There's one thing for sure, there's way too much testosterone in this van for my preference. So I go get a big strong coffee and lean on the fence looking out towards the airport. It's 7 a.m. and last night's rain is drying away in patches across the car park's surface in the growing sunlight. Given the shaky start we've had I suddenly find myself questioning the sanity of the whole trip.

Why am I so obsessed with finding the answers? The elusive 'truth' that I keep talking about. Why can't I just be content with my lot, with vague promises and hopes, which seem to keep other people happy? Maybe I would've been happier if the church hadn't thrown me out and shattered my belief system? Oh I'm sure they wouldn't see it like that, but that's basically what happened when I told them I was gay. My parents and the rest of our church told me I was 'wrong' in the sight of the Lord. Would've signed me up for conversion therapy if they'd had that back then in Yorkshire. That's why I left home the summer before university and got a job until I could move out permanently. It's also why my relationship with my parents is still somewhat strained all these years later. We've never spoken about it, just left it as the holy elephant in the room that we all feed and water and pet without acknowledging it's there.

I have a huge problem with the church saying that God hates gays, because as I see it God is love, and a loving God doesn't hate. Somewhere in the Bible it says: 'Test all things and hold fast to that which is good.' But therein lies the dilemma – who says what is good and right and true?

Now I've got this feeling of crazy emptiness you get when you realise that something you believed isn't actually true. And then things feel even more weird when you realise that actually the thing you believed *might* be true and *might not*. And you'll never really know. The Greeks called it 'aporia', from the word for 'impasse'. I call it incredibly annoying. You can't take your thinking forwards or backwards. You can't KNOW for sure what's real and true. That's how I felt throughout my History and Classics degree, and ever since then, if I'm honest. Like Schrödinger's blasted cat – I never knew if I was in the box or outside it, or both. Is God out there or, like Elvis, has s/he left the building?

There's this little part of me which hankers after the old certainties, which misses the blithe spirit and security of a childlike faith. Can you have a certain faith? Or is faith always a blind leap? I think about last night's *Matrix* conversation. Neo was born into a prison he couldn't smell or see or touch: a prison for the mind. Like in Orwell's *Nineteen Eighty-Four*: 'War is Peace; Freedom is Slavery; Ignorance is Strength'. And the more I think about modern society and life with all its supposed 'freedoms' the more I think it's slavery.

So does utopia exist? Maybe YouTopia is it? Perhaps my journey was just leading here, to Amsterdam, to a new community of freedom and living the dream?

* * * * * * *

'Anyone for a bacon butty?' Danny jumps into the cab half an hour later and hands round a big bag from the service station McDutchlands accompanied by a cardboard tray with three steaming styrofoam cups wedged in it.

I munch through my butty still thinking about YouTopia and what it'll be like. Wondering when I should mention to Danny that I've unilaterally decided to go there whether he likes it or not.

Danny drives us to an incredibly neat and clean campsite we've been directed to by a kindly stranger at the service station, just on the outskirts of the city. We're greeted by an enthusiastic gaggle of kids thronging round the van all shouting for ice cream, which makes us all laugh. From here, Danny, Ari and I have decided to mosey into town to do some sightseeing. Ari has been remarkably quiet since his little outburst on deck, but none the less surly. Ah, roll on YouTopia where I can be free of this pseudo-parental responsibility.

* * * * * * *

Through the windows of the taxi we see the city centre metamorphose from chic industrial urban to olde worlde twee as we near the canal which bisects it. Tall, thin, richly gabled facades jostle for position; white, red and brown; eyeing us as we go by with their excessively numerous windows. All the better to see you with, and to see at all, given their deep recesses. I read that Vermeer lived in a similar canal house in Delft, taking advantage of the particular light it afforded. I'm still feeling no oil painting myself after last night, and in desperate need of coffee. I'm also quietly keen to try to find

YouTopia, so I split from the boys as soon as we reach the centre, agreeing to report back later.

* * * * * * *

I'm halfway through my second cup of coffee when an annoying young man sits down opposite me. I say *annoying* because I just want to sit quietly and drink my coffee, but he turns out not to disappoint my cynicism.

'Hi theer,' he says cheerily. 'Ha'ye goat a light?' He's holding an enormous joint in one hand and a cake in the other.

I consider pretending to be deaf, or Dutch. I really just want to drink my coffee and figure out how to get to YouTopia.

'I don't smoke,' I answer curtly without looking up.

'Are ye English?' he asks, and waits until I finally look up. He has a heavy Scottish accent and is, I suppose, in his mid-twenties, with a bush of crazy curls on his head, which bob around his face when he speaks.

'Er, yes,' I have to concede. He smiles, but I've committed the cardinal sin now and shown interest in the other. Now I'll never get back to my coffee. Now I'll have to sit here and be nice to this complete lunatic happy stranger and nod and smile and pretend to be having a wonderful 'connection' until he goes. Or perhaps I could go to the toilet and climb out of the window. I'm not very good at talking to people I don't know.

'Well, cannae be helped, ye being a Sassenach. Ahm Sincleer bah the wae.'

'I'm Casey, Casey Jones. Nice to meet you Sinclair.' I offer him my hand.

'Casey Joans? Like th'railwae man?' Sinclair asks, with slight amusement.

'Yes, yes,' I say with a sigh. 'Like the railway man.' Except

60

that in this life I'm the runaway train not the one who stops it.

After an awkward pause I blurt out: 'I'm looking for YouTopia. Do you know where it is?'

Sinclair's face lights up like a dozen reefers tied together.

'This is yoor lucky dae Casey Joans,' he exclaims.

* * * * * * *

Now, you may believe in things like fate and destiny, or you may not. But right now, with Sinclair sitting in front of me telling me that he lives in the YouTopia Commune, I'm prepared to believe.

'It's, like, a real U-topia, hen. Pure stoat.' Sinclair's heavy Glaswegian accent seems slightly at odds with his hippy leanings.

He tells me that YouTopia was founded by someone who'd been living in the Christiana hippy commune in Copenhagen before they had to stop trading in weed to make a living. This guy set up his own version of utopia in the backstreets of Amsterdam and, like *The Beach*, word of this quasi-mythical place passes amongst backpackers as the last true hippy commune where drugs can be bought and used freely and where all is sweetness and light. According to Sinclair, that is, who says he'll take me there 'later', when he's finished doing whatever it is he's doing here, besides smoking.

After a few tokes on his reefer, Sinclair tells me how he used to believe that devolved government would save Scotland from the misery of the twenty-first century and bring newfound peace and happiness, but it didn't. And now he seems to see himself as a quiet revolutionary looking for a brave new world and willing to help build it. A commune seems a bit of a conundrum to me, 'cause how can you build a brave new world by sectioning yourself off from the rest of society and shunning its rules? But, Sinclair asks, how else can you change the system?

'From within?' I wonder.

'Bin tryin' tae fer centuries, aye, ye ken? Yer got yer wee people, wee cogs i' the greet machinery o' the system, thee try tae change things but after a while thee realise tha' one wee cog cannae change the whole greet lumbering beastie. We're no livin' i' the taems o' Braveheart anymoor,' he explains.

'But what if that one cog influences the next slightly bigger cog and so on until there's enough force to move the whole thing in a different direction?'

'Cannae be done,' Sinclair says emphatically. 'Sooner oor la'er the system realises the wee cog is tryin' tae change things an' takes it oot the system – replaces it, an' any other cog who's seen tae ha' been influenced. Issa witch hunt,' he concludes with the air of one who has tried to be that rebellious wee cog, and been removed, silenced.

'That's a bit *Big Brother*, don't you think?'

'No, hen. Tha's the reality o' politics. If ye wanna be free ye ha' to break oot, be an ootsider, live wi' like-minded people an' create yer own worrld. YouTopia is wha'ah've been looking fer all mah life. It's the on'y thing tha' feels like haem to me. Naebody tellin' yer wha' tae dee. Naebody tellin' yer wha's reet an' wrang. Ye jus' dee wha' seems true for ye, ye ken? Pure freedom. An' that's as rare as rockin' horse shite,' he concludes.

I'm finding it a bit hard to follow everything Sinclair is saying – partly because of his accent, and partly because I'm distracted by wondering whether this YouTopia place really could be the answer. But what about Ari and Danny? I can see 'free love' appealing to Danny but what on earth would the Boy Wonder make of it all? And would it really be the kind of environment his mother intended for him on this trip? I mean I'm no prude but I was brought up in a vicarage, and hippy culture seems a bit, well, out there – all that nudism and chanting and experimenting.

'And the drugs help I suppose?' I ask, perhaps a bit cynically, but Sinclair isn't affronted.

'Aye, the drugs help, ye ken.' He smiles and waves his cartoon-sized big joint around.

'Dee ye wan' some?' he asks proffering it towards me.

'No! No, I didn't mean... I'm er, I'm fine thanks...' Oh God I'm going to sound so uncool. 'Isn't it illegal and all?'

Sinclair looks mildly amused or perhaps bemused by my comment.

'Did ye no know it's legal i' coffee houses heer?' Sinclair grins.

I didn't. But I'm not about to admit that, so I just repeat the line that I don't smoke, even though I realise it makes me sound really square. Believe me, I wanted to be a smoker. It had always appealed to me as a look: cool, like. I tried really hard during my teenage years with 'borrowed' fags I nicked from my granddad's pack when he was out pottering in his shed, but they always made me gag.

Sinclair just sits there grinning at me, and I wonder if joints taste different from normal cigarettes. Perhaps they don't taste as bad? I'm on the verge of giving in when my eye is caught by a brown muffin sitting on the counter. Hash cakes! It's chocolate, and it's got a mild high in it – utterly irresistible. Ah what the hell. I'm on my own personal voyage of discovery here, and Danny's not around to give me a lecture (and I'm sure he's no stranger to the odd spliff or even something stronger himself). So I buy one and tuck in, realising that I'm actually quite hungry, it's been hours since I last ate. I wolf it down, despite Sinclair's plea for me to 'take it easy'. But surely they can't be that strong? Anyway I'm feeling nothing from it.

* * * * * * *

Some hours later – I'm not sure how many – the table has filled with empty coffee cups in a corresponding and equal manner to which my brain has emptied of any sensible thought. There are muffin crumbs everywhere and a half-eaten hash cake. Was that my second, or third? I can't remember. In fact I've pretty much forgotten why we're here or where we were meant to be going.

Too late I find out that hash cakes take longer to work than joints, but boy are they just as strong. With an unpleasant sudden rush my mind appears to have grown urgent wanderlust and is trying to leave me. I feel like if I lose concentration for just one second it might just float off into the atmosphere and never come back to my body again. And far from being a pleasant release it's a panicky feeling of losing control. I try to relax and keep hold of why we're here. Why are we here?

'Godot. God dot. Geddit. Gottit,' I keep repeating, every few minutes or so, as much to myself as to Saint Clair over there, as if it's a mantra which will somehow bring me enlightenment. It seems to keep me here, just, inside my own body and mind. Here. Wherever here is.

The sky outside has darkened and the café has filled with an early evening crowd of pre-dinner tokers. Every now and then Sinclair's approached by some stranger, disappears for a few minutes and then comes back again. I feel a little bit sick and think I ought to go outside and get some fresh air, but I'm scared that if I do I'll lose track of where I am and who I'm with. So I decide it's safest to just keep sitting here and wait. For what? I don't know. But I'll just sit here for a while longer.

Sinclair breaks through the waiting. I'd forgotten he was

there. Maybe he knows why we're here. He starts telling me a story about the fact that he's actually related to Jesus, and as he talks I feel like he's already told me this before. Then he tells me again. He says that the St Clair family, about which, after whom, he's named, is one of the oldest and most famous... clever... something... families in Europe. And somehow... somewho? This is connected with Jesus, who married Mary Magdalene, and had kids and then went to France... for some reason. I feel like I know this story. That I've heard it before. Is it the Bible? I try to place it.

'*The Da Vinci Code*!' I say.

'Da wha'?' replies Sinclair, and I get the feeling that conversation finished a long time ago.

I feel like something is finally making sense and the fog is lifting a little bit. It all falls into place. Like history repeating. What really happened to the Holy Grail and Da Vinci and everything and... all connected somehow. Saint Clair here is your actual Jesus' great great great great great great, etc., etc., grandson.

I think there's a bit more to that story that I'm forgetting, but that's the gist. Jesus – Sinclair, one family, and who'd've thought Jesus would be French, eh? Well, the French probably always thought it. Oh, my, thing... mobile thing, is vibrating...

'WRU? We bn 2c an frnk hse n cnl bt trp. Mt u bck @ Alice? D'

What? I understand the word 'Alice'.

'Muss... get back... to Alice...' I mumble.

'Alice? Who da feck is Alice?' Sinclair asks me, sending me into a fit of giggles.

I stare at the phone like it's a cryptex. What is it with txt language? It's *not* a language, it's a... cryptic code... intended to befuddle... people, and only for... teenagers and the criminally insane. It's a Da Vinci code of its own. And I haven't cracked it.

Jesus Saint Clair grabs my phone. 'They wanna meet yer back at Alice,' he says, confused.

'Why?' I ask him.

Jesus' long-lost relation shrugs at me through a cloud of yellowish smoke.

'Tell 'im no. Tell 'im to come and get me. Tell 'im where we are,' I say, looking around, wondering.

'We're in Wallen,' JC Sinc says.

'Walden! That's right. That's right Sinc! We're in Walden... Pond. Tell Dannyboy to come on over for a dip... in the pond. Tell 'im in that... texlanguage.' I thrust the phone back into his hands and stumble off in search of the toilets, hoping that my wandering mind will be able to navigate its way back again.

* * * * * * *

I'm awakened by a loud banging noise. I open my eyes, which hurt, as sunlight streams directly into them from all around, and try to focus on where I am. I'm lying down, in a bunk (so I can't be in a toilet cubicle, which is the last place I remember), in a place that smells faintly of strawberry ice cream.

'Casey? Are you awake?' Danny's less-than-dulcet tones reverberate around my brain.

'Oh,' I whisper. Unable to raise my voice any louder and unable to think of anything more sensible to say until I figure out what's happening and where I am. Images of Dutch coffee shops, clouds of mystical smoke, empty beer bottles, the smell of Indonesian food, a Christ figure, a pond and a quest crowd my mind. Am I in YouTopia? Am I? Is that it? Have we finally reached YouTopia? If it is then it doesn't feel very good. I drag myself upright enough to reach the door handle and open the door. Danny is standing outside looking harried.

'And where am I, Danny? Is this YouTopia?' I'm still dazed and confused.

'Well,' Danny cracks a weary smile, 'you might say that, but I doubt it. You're in the van...'

'So... er, what happened? How did I get back here?' I ask him cautiously.

'Well, Ari and I spent a lovely father and son day together going round the sights and then I had to leave him in the van while I spent half the evening searching for you.'

I leave aside the 'father and son' comment for another time, when I'm feeling better able to do sarcasm and Danny's in a better mood to take it. 'But, didn't Sinclair text you? I asked him to text you where we were. At least I think I did, in between him telling me he's the new Messiah or something.'

'What? Oh, never mind, I don't want to know. I did get a text. Hang on. Here it is: "Hi u2 C gd no prb got smks no pln bt Jesus my grndpa so no prblmo cu son Saint Clair".'

'Oh.' I think I might have a bit of grovelling to do with Danny.

* * * * * * *

I spend the day at the campsite guiltily tidying the van and nursing my hangover while Danny and Ari do more sightseeing. I wonder whether I should text Sinclair and ask if I can come over to YouTopia but he texts me first and says he's coming over to us instead.

Danny's not best pleased to learn this when he gets back. I think after last night's shenanigans he was hoping that we might just forget about YouTopia and move on. He's been barely civil since Sinclair turned up, offering to man the barbecue and heading off to the camp shop intermittently to buy beers. Sometimes I can't tell if Danny's chilled or annoyed.

Ari seems to have made friends with some of the other kids staying at the campsite and is playing football with them, occasionally showing up to wolf down a sausage.

So here we are, in the post-barbecue glow of the campfire, under the clear sky, which is now darkening and lighting up with bright stars. Danny's finally sat down with us, although he seems more interested in his beer than the discussion. My head seems to be finally clearing, although Sinclair is still puffing away like a trooper. It's like a religious ritual. The heat from the wood crackling in the fire-pit warms our faces while Sinclair talks intently about YouTopia.

He's telling us that in YouTopia everything is right and everything is permitted – drugs, sex, whatever. They don't impose concepts like *right and wrong* and *good and evil*, and besides there's no leadership to impose any rule of law anyway.

'But if you have no rules and no concept of right and wrong then what about things like cheating, lying, crime, murder?' Danny asks, somewhat morosely, out of the darkness where he's been fetching more beer.

'Tha' doesnae happen. It's on'y 'coz o' roolz tha' ye get rool breakers ye ken. Wi'out roolz theer's nae need tae break 'em,' Sinclair explains. 'An' anyway, ever'uns so spaced oot most o' th'time it jus' wouldnae happen.'

Opium is the opium of the masses, I think to myself.

'Listen mate,' Danny interjects sombrely. 'I've been around a few drug addicts and they are *not* pleasant people to be around.'

'Well, ah think ye'd think diff'rently if ye both partook,' Sinclair concludes.

He goes on to describe the mind-expanding qualities of drugs and how the experimentation with LSD and magic mushrooms in the sixties was the first step in the modern search for an alternate way of seeing things. He describes how taking more and more drugs is like a path to enlightenment, a brave new world, a new paradise...

Danny snorts audibly and walks off towards where Ari and the other boys are playing football. I get the distinct feeling he's not really into this whole YouTopia thing. I'm sure he's done his fair share of party drugs, but I'm beginning to suspect there may be more to it than that. Sinclair offers me his joint but after last night I'd much rather have a clear head to discuss this.

'Ye see, Casey,' Sinclair says. 'Ye pass on this joint, bu' this joint could take ye to wheer ye could understan' wha' ahm sayin'.'

Somehow I sincerely doubt that. And this catch-22 argument just confuses me further – if I take drugs I'll understand how drugs are the answer. Just have faith. It sounds like a cult. Like religion, you have to either buy into the idea wholesale or steer well clear. There's no middle ground. But I want something which makes sense in the clear-headed light of day, to anyone, not just those in an altered state of consciousness. I want something that makes sense on a Monday morning, not just at 3 a.m. on a Saturday.

It's hard for me to imagine that drugs are the answer. I can see that they might dull the pain of modern living, but is that really the answer? I somehow can't see myself fitting into Sinclair's YouTopia, and I begin to wonder where Danny and Ari are and when they're going to come back and rescue me. Maybe I'm too middle-class for this kind of utopia? Perhaps I would have been better off in Skinner's *Walden Two* with its choirs and string quartets and am-dram productions? On second thoughts no, that sounds a bit like hell to me as well.

I sneak off to find Danny when Sinclair goes to the loo. I find him leaning against a fence whittling a stick with the hunting knife, watching Ari trying to play football still, in the near dark.

'He's enjoying himself,' I say, with some surprise. Ari hasn't really smiled since I met him a couple of weeks ago, and I've never seen him evince any social skills. All he does all day usually is sit and listen to loud bassy, tinny music or play games (usually 'Street Fighter') on his PSP thingy.

'Yeah. He is. Good to see that *someone* is,' he says sarcastically. 'The two of you seem to have found your utopias already.'

'Look, Danny,' I begin, but he cuts me off.

'I just don't think that what you've got in mind for this "trip" is really...' He searches for the right word in his slightly beery brain. One with enough impact to convey his mood. 'Good.' He couldn't have settled on a worse word for someone brought up in a vicarage where being good was all that counted. All the wind is instantly knocked out of my sails.

'You want to stay? You want to expand your mind in YouTubia?' Danny half shouts at me. 'Go ahead! Be my guest! Don't worry about me and Ari. We'll be fine.' He shrugs off my tentative hand from his shoulder, turning away from me.

'I... Look, Danny, I...' I begin, but tail off, not knowing what to say. I realise that I haven't exactly been thinking of anyone but myself since we started this whole trip. And it's true to say that I was a bit taken in by the utopian thing. I really thought that... Well, I'm surprised at my own gullibility.

'Look, I already lost one good friend to drugs. I don't want to lose another.' Danny suddenly looks vulnerable in the darkness and I desperately want to hug him.

'It was a long time ago now, but... And I just don't know what I'd do with Ari on my own if you went off. I'm barely coping as it is, and I promised Niobe...'

I feel like a total heel.

'I'm sorry Danny, I didn't know... Of course I'm not going to leave you. I really don't want to fry my brains in Ectopia. I was wrong about the whole thing, it's a crazy idea.' I give him my best smile, and his hand touches mine for a brief instant. 'Do you want to help me get rid of Sinclair then? He looks like he's settling in for the night.'

Danny sighs. 'You invited him along, Casey. This is *your* problem, *you* deal with it. I never signed up to a utopian dream when I came on this trip with you. I'll go and fetch Ari in.'

I watch Danny stride over to Ari and join in with the football for a minute. I realise that this trip is only going to work if I accommodate Danny and Ari. Whatever their motivations are, they have to be taken into account too. We're all in it together. I decide to go back and tell Sinclair to return to YouTopia without me. We're heading on out in the morning.

CHAPTER 6

Ich bin ein Berliner!

*'From this hour I ordain myself loos'd of limits and
imaginary lines,
Going where I list, my own master total and absolute,
Listening to others, considering well what they say,
Pausing, searching, receiving, contemplating,
Gently, but with undeniable will divesting myself of
the holds that would hold me.'*

Walt Whitman,
'Song of the Open Road', 1855.

As soon as we're on the road again I feel a palpable sense of relief. It's not just that there was something deeply disturbing about Sinclair's druggy YouTopia, but also that being on the road, the motion, the journey itself, brings some sense of liberation. It's not even the feeling of getting somewhere, but the endless possibilities that lie between A and B. The sense that the journey itself holds its own secrets and life, that it could lead us anywhere. Like Emily Dickinson, I have this profound sense of the happiness of dwelling in possibility that I've never felt before (or not since I was a kid anyway). The morning sun lights up the road ahead like a beacon and life feels good.

I wind the window down and the cool June morning air

rushes in and seems to pat me on the head, as if to say: 'Well done for choosing life!' I'm on top of the world, and start to bip the horn rhythmically in time with some inner disco of happiness, letting out syncopated bursts of the old ice cream music.

'Roll up! Roll up! The ice creams are on us! Just one Cornetto!' I shout into the wind, the words shooting straight back past me and out into the wide world almost before they're out of my mouth.

We're on the autobahn to Berlin, baby, and everything is tickety-boo. The sun is shining and the smog of a million Amsterdam joints is fading in the rearview mirror, along with my naïve thoughts of utopia. The fresh air is clearing out the staleness and awkwardnesses of yesterday. Danny's sitting in the back of the van playing cards with Ari on the fold-down table, for all the world like the picture of familial bliss. Ari has even put aside his PSP for once, and is actually smiling and even laughing at some of Danny's crappy jokes, and I can see a kind of nascent bond there that looks like it could develop into something good.

We're travelling eastward across the top of Germany to Berlin, and then beyond that to Eastern Europe – Poland and Russia. The mighty Russian Federation; formerly the Soviet Union. And in many ways that breakup all started in Berlin with the fall of the infamous wall in 1989. It was a bit like dominoes after that: many of the Baltic states overthrew their former Communist mantles and grasped their independence with both hands, some with velvet gloves and others with iron fists.

This is *my* Europe, *my* continent, *my* history, I'm driving through, but I feel like I hardly know anything about it. Even a History degree can't cover everything, and since Alice only comfortably does around sixty-five miles an hour with a following wind, I figure we'll take a leisurely stroll through some of it now. It's a funny thing, but when you think about it, nationality is a total whim of parentage and birthplace, but the history gets attached to us nonetheless. And history gives us some sense of place in the world, even when we don't know what to believe and who to trust, and even when we know that history is just someone's version of what happened. What's that saying? History is always written by the winners; or, more extremely, it's a tool of the powerful to keep the rest of us in our places (or so said one of my history lecturers). Still, it anchors us and gives us some sense at least of how others see us, complete with the perks and quirks of our ancestors.

So I feel a bit apprehensive about arriving in the lands of our most feared enemies of the last century: the Germans and Russians. Old wounds on such a scale are hard to comprehend, let alone heal. I wonder if it's gloating or fear that makes the Germans an object of ridicule for us old-fashioned Brits even today. We say they have no sense of humour, and joke about them bagsying the sun loungers with their towels in an act of invasion on foreign holidays. We stereotype and categorise them, and not just the Germans. We pigeonhole everyone we meet with the least possible effort, in order to avoid dealing with each person as an individual, pretty much like us. We prefer to see difference. No, we seem *wired* to see difference before similarity. I resolve to at least try not to mention the bloody war (and avoid any *Fawlty Towers* scenarios where possible).

* * * * * * *

I've also decided to make a concerted effort to be nice to *everyone* I meet on this journey because you never know what you'll learn from them, despite the false start with Sinclair. So when I see a young guy hitchhiking by the side of the motorway outside Hanover I feel it's the right thing to do to offer him a lift. Danny appears less keen on the idea, but I've already stopped by the time I tell him why and the guy's opening the passenger door before Danny has a chance to say 'prestidigitation' (which he wouldn't have said, I'm sure it was going to be much ruder than that).

'Hi,' I say.

'Hi, thanks for stopping,' he replies with a home counties undertone. My similarity recognition system jumps for joy. An English accent, at least I'll understand him better than Braveheart St Clair.

'Where are you headed?' I ask.

'Berlin.'

Bingo! I gesture to the empty front seat and brush away the crumbs of my elevenses.

'Hop in... Oh, wait, you're not a hippy, are you?'

He looks a bit put out but shakes his head nevertheless and, receiving due approval, hops on to the faded leatherette front seat with a nod to Bonnie and Clyde in the back. I realise, as he closes the door and I catch a whiff of something in the air, that if anything, we're the ones who resemble hippies. The van is picking up a distinct odour of camping-without-proper-bathroom-facilities, and our clothes haven't been washed since we left. I have a bit of a hang-up about hanging-up my underwear around the boys so I'm eking out my supplies. I make a mental note to get to a laundrette next time we see one.

I give the new boy a once over as I pull out into the motorway traffic again. He looks about twelve years old on his way home from Scoutcamp with his neat little backpack, but I imagine he must be seventeen or eighteen; nineteen at a push. His strawberry blond Tintin hair and bright blue eyes come from his Anglo-German parentage, it turns out, and he's on his way to Berlin to catch up with his estranged grandfather. And as we bowl along the Germanically-well-kept autobahn as fast as Alice's little wheels will take us, Peter unfolds his strange story.

Peter's grandparents became trapped in East Berlin during the last days before the Berlin Wall was completed in 1961. His grandmother managed to escape across the border with her infant daughter, but Peter's grandfather (who was behind them) was stopped trying to bring a small cartload of their belongings over with him. Border guards seized their belongings and because he argued briefly with them, he was arrested and subsequently forbidden permission to cross the border. Forced to remain in East Berlin during the twenty-eight years of the 'Wall of Shame', when in 1989 it finally came crashing down it was too late – he didn't have the strength left to leave.

Peter's grandmother, 'free' but stranded and alone on the other side of the Wall, eventually moved to Britain with her daughter, Emma, where she settled and where Emma, years later, married an Englishman, Peter's father. But his grandfather was never spoken about in the family, and Emma having been so young when it all happened didn't even really remember him very well. Peter's grandmother recently told him this story on her deathbed, Peter confides to me, and I suspect he hasn't had the chance to discuss all this with anyone outside the family before.

'It was never spoken about at home,' he says, his big puppy eyes shining, and I can relate to that (the vicarage being a place of hushed whispers and unspoken emotions). 'I guess Grandma just wanted to forget all about it. But to think I was born in the year the Wall was demolished, and she never even mentioned it after that...'

'Did she remarry, your grandma?' I ask him.

'No, she never did. In fact I don't think she ever had another

76

male friend, not like that. But she adored my dad. Treated him like a proper son.'

'Wow, so all that time she remained faithful to your granddad while not even knowing if he was dead or alive or whether she would ever see him again?'

'Yeah, I guess.' Peter doesn't seem the romantic type.

'But,' a voice in the back of the van pipes up from nowhere, making us both jump, 'why didn't she go back to see him when the Wall came down?' It's Ari, and I realise that he must have been listening to the whole story as both Danny and he have put away their cards.

'I... I don't know why she didn't. I asked her when she told me the story, but she was very frail and she started crying and I... I felt terrible. I didn't know why she was telling me all this anyway. I wasn't even sure she knew who I was – she was a bit doddery in the end... dementia.' Peter is visibly fighting back tears now and seems to dissolve into a child of around Ari's age.

'It's OK Peter.' I put a gentle hand on his arm, keeping the other one on the steering wheel. I want to stop the van and give him a hug and mother him (why doesn't Ari engender this kind of maternal feeling in me? I can see him in the rearview mirror looking disgustedly at Peter, as if to say 'Come on, pull yourself together; boys don't cry').

'But it doesn't make any sense!' Ari shouts from the back, oblivious to Peter's feelings. 'Why wouldn't she go back and find him? Couldn't she afford to? She could have flown on Ryanair or EasyJet, they're really cheap.'

I glare backwards at him in the rearview mirror, which is hard to do when you're sending all your sympathy to someone on your left and keeping one eye on the road. I glare at Danny for good measure too, as if to say 'He's your son, you keep him in line', but Danny just smiles at me as if 'his son' has just asked a really good question.

'Look,' I cut in, 'Peter doesn't know why his grandma didn't go back to see him. She must have had her reasons.'

'No, it's OK,' Peter turns round in his seat to face Ari, 'to be honest with you I've thought a lot about that and I think she was scared to go back.'

'Why?' Ari asks, slightly more gently now – he's curious if not tactful.

'Because... she didn't know what she might find? Twenty-eight years is a long time. He might have changed. I don't think East Germany was a very great place to live. The people had nothing and lots died young. I did a bit of research before I came. So I think maybe she didn't want to go there to find that he'd suffered, or died, or...' Peter trailed off.

'But what if he'd actually been waiting for her all those years and she didn't go back to him? And why didn't he go to find her?' Ari is relentless, and I'm beginning to sense that actually his interest is genuine, and that maybe, for him, it's also a replaying of what his own mother and he might've gone through with Danny? I glance at Danny but he's apparently busy fiddling with Ari's PSP.

My mind flickers to *Captain Corelli's Mandolin* and the moment when Corelli goes back to the island and sees Pelagia, but is too scared to go and speak to her. He was afraid – afraid that things might have changed, that something might have been lost, that the passionate love they had once shared might have gone. And that would have been the cruellest blow of all, and suddenly I can see why both Corelli and Peter's grandparents might have been too afraid to go back to their past. Fear and love – the two most potent of human emotions.

Peter has fallen silent and the whole van with him, each of us lost in our own private reveries on the subject as we roll remorselessly along the faceless four-lane autobahn towards Berlin.

* * * * * * *

'So, why have you come to Berlin? How do you know where your grandfather is? Why didn't your mother come with you?' Ari is throwing questions like howitzer shells and Peter, who climbed into the back when Danny switched drivers with me a while back, is doing his best to keep up. I want to tell him that he doesn't have to humour the kid, but something tells me that he would rather talk it out than keep it in. It seems almost as much a mystery to him why he's here as it is to us. I'd like to join in but I can't hear the whole conversation from up front where the monotonous roar of Alice's engine tends to drown out the interesting bits, so I leave them to it and settle down for a bit of a kip while Danny steers us ever eastwards.

The engine noise has a strangely soporific effect, almost as if this is what the world first sounded like through the walls of the womb (if your mother lived near a building site). I'm soon dozing into the strangest dream about Annie Lennox running through a maze like a rat in a Skinner box and then coming up against a huge wall and she can't see a way round the wall and it's far too high to climb over and Dave Stewart (the other half of Eurythmics) is trying to give her a leg up, only she keeps slipping through his grasp and then all three members of Bananarama turn up and try to help by forming a human pyramid and Annie, who is also somehow me, is climbing up and singing 'No more I love you's' and then these German stormtroopers appear in the maze and start shooting, and I'm seeing the shots in *Matrix*-style slowmo-bullet-time and this one bullet's heading straight for Annie Lennox/me and the stormtrooper who fired it suddenly comes into focus and it's she-who-must-not-be-named and then there's this huge bang and a pain in my head and I wake up with a jolt.

'You OK?' Danny is looking at me concerned and I'm still

half in dreamworld and wonder for an instant if I actually got shot, and then, suddenly realising where I am, I wonder if I shouted out loud.

'You nodded off and banged your head on the window.' Danny looks amused.

'Oh. What a doughnut.' I blush and hope that the boys in the back didn't notice, but out of the corner of my peripheral vision I register that the all-seeing Ari has noted it. It's just a split-second but it looks like he's grinning like an evil gargoyle. Must be the bang on the head.

* * * * * * *

We're driving into the ragged industrialised outskirts of Berlin now and the buildings are starting to take on that overbearing Teutonic, Third-Reichian, *Deutschland Deutschland über alles* kind of feel; like Big Brother in building format. We run the gauntlet of colossal statues bearing eagles and armoured men on horseback, parading in front of massive arched colonnades. From our van vantage point it feels like we're Kafkaesque beetles scurrying in a land of giants, with the mid-afternoon sun striking echoing shadows at all angles across the streets, and making me feel a bit uneasy. The plan is to drop Peter off at his final destination and go find a campsite to make our base for the night, then spend a day looking round Berlin i'the morrow morn. But Peter has suddenly got the jitters about seeing his grandfather, and the fact that he has never been abroad on his own before and doesn't speak the language, and begs us to let him stay with us.

I feel sorry for the lad but Alice simply wasn't built to sleep four with all our kit and all, and it's already testosterone-heavy. Danny, however, seems to think that Peter and Ari are getting on well and, I suspect, happy to delegate responsibility,

80

he asks me to reconsider. I've decided (since the whole Sinclair / YouTopia debacle) that compromise is the best way forward, so I offer to go with Peter to the youth hostel and get him settled in (me, with my German language ability culled straight from *Auf Wiedersehn Pet*) and to meet up with him again tomorrow morning to help him try to find his granddad. I also take the opportunity to take some dirty laundry to the city laundrette so we don't have to air it all in public.

Ari scowls at me when I get back into the van.

'You don't care about anyone but yourself! You could have let Pete stay with us in the van but you don't want to share.' He turns his back on me with an unspoken 'I hate you', and goes into an almighty sulk. I'm stunned into silence by his outburst. Danny suddenly leaps out, goes round to the back of the van and pulls the door open violently.

'How dare you talk to Casey like that!' he shouts at Ari. 'This is *her* trip and pretty much *her* van, and *you* are a guest, and *you* will start to behave like a young man and not a spoilt *brat* if you want to carry on with this trip.'

'I don't *want* to be on this *stupid* trip. I don't want to be with *you* or *her* or this *stupid* ice cream van. *I want to go home!*' Ari yells back.

'Well...' Danny softens slightly. 'You know you can't go home, Ari. Your mum's in hospital and you've got to stay with me this summer. After all, I am your father.'

Ari turns round, for all the world like Luke Skywalker discovering the identity of his pater, and fixes Danny with the most evil look I imagine a nearly-thirteen-year old can muster.

'You're *not... my... dad,*' he enunciates slowly. 'You never have been and you never will be.' And Ari turns away and folds his arms, and that's that. I'm suddenly not sure whose outburst I'm more taken aback by and who I'm meant to feel sorry for. I shrink into the front passenger seat wishing myself anywhere but here in this loaded silence. I'm barely breathing so as not to attract any of the ill will and invective which is circling menacingly around the fetid air of the van just waiting for a hapless victim to latch on to.

Danny stands shaking at the back of the van and I know he hasn't the faintest idea of how to deal with this. One minute they're getting on fine, the next this. The delicate and tentative strings that bind him to Ari aren't strong enough to withstand much testing, and I realise that he hasn't spent enough time with Ari to know whether he should leave him be or take him on. Ari, meanwhile, is stuck between turning his back on me in the front, and Danny in the back, and so is at an awkward sideways angle facing the van wall with his arms folded so tightly around his chest I think he'll suffocate himself. Locked in this mental battle Danny gives Ari one last desperate look before slamming shut the van door and jumping back in the driver's seat. He guns Alice violently out into the noisy rush-hour traffic and tries to steer us out of this messy stalemate.

* * * * * * *

Tentstation Berlin is an immaculately-tended grassy field full of happy families grilling sausages and playing volleyball together around an empty outdoor swimming pool in the heart of the city. The contrast between the atmosphere inside and outside our van seems almost enough to cause a spontaneous implosion. I can see Danny still fuming away as he angrily cranks up the stabilisers at the back to level Alice up, connects the gas stove then the water pump. He brusquely shoos away the first kids coming to queue for the ice creams we don't have, even though the atmosphere is frosty enough for them. Ari hasn't moved a muscle since the altercation, locked in a self-imposed straitjacket of spindly arms. I suspect that since he can't feasibly run away he may intend never to move again if given the choice. I have no intention of intervening in this one and so I suffer the mood in silence and grab the chance to go to the campsite shop to buy food and drink for the evening meal. Since it's likely to be a very sullen affair, I buy an eight-pack of extra-strong German beer, and might even consider sharing it with Ari if it helps.

When I get back, Ari is still in the van, although it must be pretty hot in there with the sun still shining brightly in the afternoon June sky. Danny is sitting in a folding camp chair scowling at the happy families. He brightens momentarily when he sees the beer and reaches out automatically for one before I'm even within passing distance.

'Er, yeah, sure, Danny, have a beer. In fact have two.' (I'm a firm believer in the healing power of alcohol, or at least its emotional numbing properties.) I hand him a cold bottle, which he deftly opens on the folding bit of the camp chair – neat trick – and gulps in that first cold draught, which I'm gasping for, and doesn't stop until the bottle's three-quarters empty. He gasps at the air like a fish out of water. Almost without thinking, he finishes off the rest and reaches for his second. I haven't even got the cap off mine yet.

'I don't know how to do this,' he says in a low voice so that Ari can't hear, even with his evil superpowers, and reaches over to open my bottle for me.

'Thanks. Neither do I,' I respond, in case he's thinking of asking for my help on this.

Danny looks up at me quizzically as if to say 'but you must, you're a woman', and I neatly deflect by unfolding the other camp chair and plonking it down beside him so that it's not so much a psychiatrist's couch as a drinking buddy's La-Z-Boy. I'm happy to talk to him about it, but I'm just as much in the dark as he is; more so. Plus, it's not really my problem – *he's* the errant father in this scenario and me, I'm just the innocent bystander caught in the crossfire.

* * * * * * *

The warmth of the day has given way to the chilly onset of evening by the time the last bottle is drunk (Danny wins 6–2 after much needed fortification became well-deserved fiftification, and then it was just too late to go back). It's still light out though, and the happy families are all washing their dishes together and laughing and getting their littlest, cutest kids ready for bed. I glance over to the campervan where Ari is still huddled in the darkness of the interior, hugging his knees. Brat or not, you've got to feel sorry for the kid. I mean, after all, his mother has just gone into hospital for a serious operation (although come to think of it, what has she gone in for? I've never been told – well, I mean, I've never asked – I've been so busy trying to get the trip organised and accommodating Danny and Ari that it hasn't occurred to me). And here's his long-lost non-father-figure showing up out of the blue like the Lone Ranger and whisking him off into the sunset and expecting him to be OK about it. And me? I'm just Tonto – not exactly a mother-substitute (we in heap big trouble Kemo Sabe).

After the strong beer and no dinner I'm beginning to soften up a bit. So maybe his manners *are* a little bit lacking today (and everyday), and yes he did laugh at me when I banged my head, but I guess I ought to cut the kid a little slack. He's having a rough time, and Danny doesn't look like he's ready to make peace just yet, or know how to; in fact, he's just gone to get some more beer at the shop, so here I am, Tonto sans the Lone Ranger, out on the range without a clue what to do. For once I kinda wish that I had had a more normal childhood set-up so that I'd know what it is to be able to understand a child.

'Hey Ari.' I climb into the van all cheery-like, but I'm not getting too close in case he bites. 'How're you doing?'

He doesn't even look at me this time. No withering stares, no instant cut-downs, no clever one-liners. He must be in bad shape.

'So, er...' I haven't actually thought through what I'm going to say to him, which I now realise is a big mistake. Should've at least prepared an opening gambit. I decide to jump straight in (I'm kinda impulsive like that when I'm cornered, and tipsy): 'Look, Ari, I know this is tough for you, with your mother having her, um, operation and all, but it's only for a few weeks, and besides, it'll give you a chance to get to know your... er, Dan, Danny. And he really wants to spend this time with you, you know...' I falter and trail off.

Ari doesn't move a muscle, giving no sign of whether he's even listening. I peer round his head to see if he has his PSP headphones in. He doesn't. I hesitate, unsure how to proceed from here, and not wanting to provoke another outburst. So I soldier on, more of the same, and no, I don't have the faintest idea what I'm trying to achieve.

'Look, your mum'll be out of hospital soon enough and then things will get back to normal and... hey, are you crying?'

Ari's bony shoulders are starting to heave. He tries to suppress it, but in vain. Oh God, I've made him cry. Now what do I do? I look over my shoulder guiltily to see if Danny is on his way back. I'm not sure if I want to run away quickly or try to get him to stop before Danny sees what I've done. I kind of wish I hadn't started this now... but I did. Dammit. What now?

I approach Ari like I would a wounded wild animal and sit down beside him. My hand hovers indecisively in mid-air, caught apprehensively between a rock and a hard place. I put it down agan.

'Hey,' I say, in as comforting and peaceful manner as I can. I don't know what else to say. I wait for inspiration but none is forthcoming. I wish I had another drink in my hand right now.

'Hey, don't cry.' I put out my hand again and, this time, make contact. He flinches, which makes *me* jump, but he doesn't pull away; he doesn't run, he doesn't scream, he doesn't shout. Just this agonising near-silent sobbing.

We stay like that for a minute or so. Probably neither of us knowing what to do next, but I'm the adult (apparently), I should be the one to make the move here, and I'm contemplating what that next move will be when Ari splutters through his tears: 'What if she's *not*?'

'Eh?' I say it as softly as I can but I don't know what he means.

'What if she's not OK?' he repeats, with more emphasis.

'I'm sure she will be, Ari, the doctors will take very good care of her, and they know what they're doing. They'll have her up and about before you know it.' Dammit, I wish I knew what operation she was having. That would kind of help in this situation. How come I never asked? I should have asked.

'What if they don't? What if it comes back, again?' Oh cripes, it's cancer? Ari is still looking away from me but now turns his shoulder towards me as if waiting for my answer. I have to be very careful here. I have no idea if it is cancer, and if it is, what stage it's at and how aggressive it is. I know nothing about it. I wish Danny would hurry up and get back here. I'm so out of my depth my feet haven't touched the ground for twenty minutes. I decide to take a leap of faith (if such I still have in me).

'Look, Ari, you er, you have to believe that the doctors will get it' (whatever *it* is) 'and that she'll be OK – your mum, she'll be OK,' I say with all the optimism I can muster.

'But you don't know that,' he retorts, not aggressively,

just hoping against hope that perhaps I do know that and can promise him categorically. I take a deep breath, toss a metaphysical coin and…

'No, I don't know that.' Ari's shoulders drop palpably and I can almost feel the fear rising. 'But I believe that she'll be all right because I know that medicine is very advanced these days and that the doctors will do all they can. And, if she's a strong lady, which I believe she is,' (she must be to have put up with Danny through all this and raise Ari) 'then she'll fight. And besides, she has you, so she'll want to make herself better for you, won't she.'

That's the best I can do. And I hope it's good enough, I really do, not just because I want out of this situation, but because I genuinely want Ari's mum to be OK, for his sake. He's just a kid. A tough kid, granted, but just a kid. And I know that cancer doesn't care, doesn't respect any boundaries, doesn't choose its victims by any rational system, and it takes and takes and keeps on taking. Dammit, all I want is for this one lady to be OK, for Ari and Danny's sake. I squeeze Ari's shoulder and look heavenwards.

Is that a prayer? If it is, who am I praying to? Or is it just a wish? And can God, in whatever form I choose to believe in her or him, know the difference? I'm not holding my breath after all the prayers I sent up when I was a kid, lost and alone, and living with a family who I couldn't understand and who couldn't understand me. Why would I think praying would help now?

Ari turns to me – his eyes are red and tear tracks stain his cheeks. He gives me a half-smile half-frown, and then he suddenly pushes past me and runs out of the van towards the empty swimming pool where couples are starting to gather for a drink after putting their kids to bed. And he runs right through them all and I'm afraid for one moment that he's going to throw himself into the emptied pool but he just keeps on running, and he's actually out of sight, darting in and out of the shadowy figures poolside, before I can shout after him. And I'm left in the dark van alone and wondering what the hell just happened.

CHAPTER 7

Crying on the Cold War shoulder

'Nothing gives small minds a better handle for hatred than superiority.'

Marie Corelli,
The Life Everlasting, 1911.

Danny rounds the corner at a running jog, his beer bottle still clutched tightly in his left hand.

'Nope. No sign of him. Are you sure he didn't say where he was going? What the hell did you say to him anyway, to make him take off like that?'

I can see that this isn't going to go in my favour, or show off my UN negotiation and peacemaking skills in a good light, even though I was only trying my best to make things better – and it's not even my mess to fix. I try another bout of reassurance (although it didn't seem to work the first time round I'm all out of alternatives right now).

'Danny, just calm down, I'm sure he's not gone far.'

Danny gives me a look that's almost identical to Ari's quizzical 'but how can you be sure' expression, and I'm left wondering desperately to myself how to interpret Ari's last enigmatic glance before he ran, but it's like trying to translate hieroglyphs without a dictionary. I don't understand children, sometimes I think I don't understand people or emotions at all.

It's half past eight and getting pretty dark. The chill air of the June evening is spreading across the campsite sending the worn-out parents back under canvas to squish the mosquitoes on their tent walls and retire to their squeaky camp-beds. I'm tired and cold and hungry, and if I am, then Ari must be doubly so.

'He'll come back when he's hungry,' I say from nowhere, and suddenly hear an echo of my mother saying the same thing about me when I was hiding out from some minor misdemeanour in our back garden, or had run off into the woods again. I guess we all do come crawling back sooner or later when the necessities of life hit us and we figure out that a hot supper, a cold drink and a warm bed count for a lot more than wounded pride and a short telling off. I wonder what Danny has in store for Ari when he shows up, or will he just be glad to see him? Another test of his fathering skills.

When it becomes clear to Danny that looking for Ari is hopeless (especially in his half-inebriated state) he sinks down in his camp chair in a kind of resigned stupor and opens another beer. Ah what wonderful coping mechanisms we've evolved in our couple of hundred thousand years on this planet. I can't see what else I can usefully do so I start to cook the sausages and onions on the campfire, and open another beer for myself.

* * * * * * *

Right on cue (ah, mothers are always right), the sausages are just browning and the onions achieving optimum stickiness when two shadowy figures approach us across the twilit field with a torch-beam swinging wildly between them. The larger

90

of the two figures points the torch-beam in my direction blinding me and almost stumbles over Danny slumped in his camp chair at the same time.

'*Entschuldigung, bitte, ist dieser Ihr Sohn?*'

'What?' both Danny and I chorus, but the material fact is plainly before us in the form of the errant twelve-year-old accompanying the German. Ari appears to have a black eye. Danny eyes the German man warily but it doesn't seem likely that he was the one who gave Ari the shiner as he's got a paternal hand on the boy's arm and Ari isn't struggling. Danny grabs Ari roughly and pulls him towards him, and for a split-second I'm not sure if he's going to hit or hug him, and maybe he's not sure himself as he throws his arms out and around the boy, pulling him into an embrace neither finds comfortable but which expresses a bond deeper than any words right now.

'Um, look, thank you, thank you for...' Danny tries to offer the German man a beer but he has already turned, apparently satisfied in merely returning the lost article to its owner, and walked away.

'Thank you. *Danke*,' I shout after him in my best schoolbook German.

'What the hell happened to you?' Danny is saying to Ari while still hugging him.

Ari shrugs and tries to get out of the embrace but Danny has him locked in tight.

I tuck the sausages and onions into their rolls while Danny talks to Ari in the gathering darkness. I can't hear what he says but they seem to make some sort of peace and I'm sure I'll find out later what the hell happened. As for me, I've realised I need to know what's happening with Ari's mum, and I need to start paying some proper attention to his feelings. He may be a kid, and therefore not top of my 'likes' list, but he's clearly been dealt one of life's great blows at an early age, and he's feeling it, and that makes him an equal sufferer of the slings and arrows of outrageous fortune in my eyes. Plus, I don't want him to run off like that again. What would I say to his mum?

* * * * * * *

In the morning, we all set off to fetch Peter from the youth hostel and our lovely clean laundry from the laundrette. A fresh start for everyone. Ari has calmed down, although he tossed and turned all night and did his fair share of crying into his pillow – you don't get much privacy in an ice cream van, I'm afraid. His shiner doesn't look so bad in the cold light of day, although I'm not sure he's told Danny what really happened there. Niobe told Danny that he gets into a lot of fights at school and she doesn't know if he's being bullied or if he's the bully. He seems to have a lot of pent-up anger. Danny had a pretty restless night too, which inevitably kept me awake, so we're a sorry-looking bunch who turn up outside Peter's hostel at 10 a.m., and I'm not sure any of us really wants to be there, but a promise is a promise.

Peter, in stark contrast, is looking very chipper. He seems excited about finding his long-lost grandfather and is keen to understand more about his family's past. Perhaps there's also an element of wanting to delay the moment of ultimate truth with his granddad, as he suggests that we all go to visit the Mauer Museum at Checkpoint Charlie – one of the infamous crossing points between the old East and West Germany.

* * * * * * *

Checkpoint Charlie is infamous from many Cold War films, with its famous sign: 'You are leaving the American Sector' spelled out in English, Russian, French and German. A replica of this sign marks the entrance to the museum, our passport to learning about the significance of the Wall and what it must have meant for Peter's grandparents.

To understand the Wall and Berlin's past split, you have to go back to what happened after the Second World War in 1945. In 1945, when Hitler's Germany was defeated by the Allied Forces (US, UK, the Soviet Union and the French), what remained of Nazi Germany and Berlin – Hitler's Third Reich seat of power – was divided into four zones, each controlled by one of the Allies. The original intention was for the four Allies to govern Germany together as a single unified country; however, the two major superpowers (the US and the Soviet Union) had major ideological disagreements about how this should be done – the Soviets preferring Communist methods while the US, well, did not – firmly and categorically (did I hear someone whisper McCarthy witch-hunt?).

So the Allies paired up and the zones became separate 'states'. The US, UK and French zones becoming the Federal Republic of Germany (FRG), while the Soviet-controlled zone became the German Democratic Republic (GDR). Berlin, the capital city, was also split into two sections, even though it was deep inside the Soviet zone; with West Berlin under the control of the US, UK and France, and East Berlin under Communist rule from Moscow. Divide and rule – almost like an experiment in how different ideologies and political and economic systems could work in the same city. And the result was crystal clear. At least, to us Westerners, it was clear that under the post-war recovery programme of the Capitalist Allies the FDR boomed from the 1950s onwards, while in the GDR, the Soviet-controlled (and I mean controlled in every sense of the word) economy made some progress but couldn't rival its Western counterpart.

'Now I can understand why people began to flee from

East to West Berlin,' Peter says. 'Because if you could get into West Berlin you could also get into West Germany and then anywhere in Western Europe. That's why they put up the Wall.' He points to a board on the Wall which proclaims that in order to stem this outpouring of people from East to West, the mayor of East Berlin proposed a border barrier be erected. This was duly sanctioned by then Soviet leader Nikita Krushchev in 1961. The wall was constructed almost overnight, in just a few days and comprised 165 kilometres of barriers, which cut Berlin in two and completely surrounded West Berlin (the Allied zone in the Eastern Bloc).

As Peter talks, I see Danny and Ari deep in conversation at the rear of our little troupe. I wonder if they're talking about last night. Peter carries on reading the next information board.

During the twenty-eight years that the wall stood, between 125 and 1,245 people were killed attempting to escape from the Communist East into the Capitalist West (numbers vary according to which side of the political divide you're on). The last was twenty-year-old Chris Gueffroy, who was shot on 6th February 1989, just nine months before the toppling of the wall.

I'm left thinking about how history is littered with 'he said', 'she said', 'he started it', 'no, she started it', like a child's playground. In the East, the Capitalists were seen as the enemy, with the Wall being hailed as an 'anti-fascist protection barrier'; Communism and Socialism were hailed as the great saving ideologies of the war-destroyed nations and the way forward for mankind, and Marx and Lenin were folk heroes. To us Westerners, our picture of the Eastern Bloc was of a stern, cold, grey world, overseen in *Big Brother* fashion by Moscow, with no personal freedom and everybody totally accountable to the state. It was the world described for us in George Orwell's *Nineteen Eighty-Four*. A world where everyone was spied upon, either informant or informed upon. Suspicion and mistrust were the everyday grist to the Communist mill. All in all you're just another brick in the Wall.

I catch up with Peter, Danny and Ari at the last exhibit before the exit. They're staring at a picture which looks familiar. An iconic image of nineteen-year-old East German border guard, Conrad Schumann, leaping to freedom and West Berlin and thus escaping his duties to shoot any defectors. Ironically, Schumann himself never managed to quite come in from the cold shadow of the Wall. He committed suicide in 1998, nine years after the fall of the Wall, declaring that only then had he 'felt truly free'. He hanged himself in his orchard in Bavaria.

Finally dragging ourselves away from this heartbreaking image of freedom won and lost, we tumble out of the museum and back into the bright light and jarring hubbub of modern-day Berlin. I realise how stuffy the museum had been, or perhaps it was the things I'd read which had made it seem more claustrophobic. I feel like gulping down the fresh air as if it's freedom itself. Peter is standing by himself blinking in the sunshine and looking very serious, while Danny and Ari are talking in low voices nearby.

'Did you find out anything interesting, about what might have happened to your granddad I mean?' I ask him.

'Only that he must have suffered hugely in the East, away from my grandma and my mother. Did you read all that stuff about the Stasi and how they were suspicious of all intellectuals and what they did to them?' he replies, all the bravado of this morning knocked out of him.

The East German secret state police had the most extensive network of informants in the world according to the museum. Peter seems lost in thought and I want to give him a big hug, but I'm too British. He catches me looking at him.

'By the way,' he asks shyly, 'what happened to Ari?' He motions to his eye.

'Oh that. He, er... he just tripped... over a tent peg last night. He's fine.' It feels like I'm trying to cover up for something even more sinister, and I suddenly realise why Peter has been eyeing Danny warily all morning. 'Really, it's nothing. He's fine.' I try to smile cheerily.

'So, what's the plan, Pete?' Danny asks as he and Ari surface from the museum. Ari is still looking pale, but I don't know how much of that is from last night and how much from the museum – I heard him asking Danny questions all the way round – he was clearly fascinated by all this war and spy stuff and he's old enough and intelligent enough to ask the right questions, believe me: 'Why did people tell on their friends and neighbours? Didn't they care if they were hurt?', 'Why didn't people just tell them it was wrong and they wouldn't help them?'

'Um. I have... well, I just have an address for my granddad...' Peter begins hesitantly.

'Do you have a phone number? We could ring him and check if he's in and where he is.' Me being reasonable and rational again.

'Um... no, I... er. He doesn't actually...'

'His granddad doesn't know he's coming. It's a big surprise,' blurts out Ari and immediately realises he's made a big mistake as both Danny and I round on Peter.

'You're kidding me, son.' Danny's barely recovered from last night's shenanigans and is still in fledgling father mode.

'You've got to be joking, Peter,' I add. 'You came all this way not even knowing if he's alive or dead?'

'No, I...' Peter looks entirely crestfallen. 'I just know he's alive though. I just know it.'

'So where did you get the address?' Dan asks.

'I looked it up on the internet. The old files. The old Stasi files and old East German records – they've computerised some of them in the records office. I searched for hours and I found only one Peter Gustav Eichardt, and this is his address.' Peter produces a piece of paper on which he's scrawled the name and an address in East Berlin.

'But you don't even know if he still lives there or, or... anything.' Danny isn't showing too much enthusiasm for the poor boy's quest, and it does seem a bit of a wild goose chase, but realising how important this is for Peter, and not entirely sure whether his mother even knows he's here, I make an executive decision (another one – I'm getting good at this).

'OK. Well, what's the address? Let's go find out.'

Danny looks incredulously at me, but before he has a chance to say anything, Peter has leapt forward and grabbed me in a big bear hug, saying: 'Thank you! Thank you!' into my crying-shoulder and I feel like a hero again.

Back to the van one and all: we've got a missing granddad to track down.

* * * * * * *

The address is a huge, grey apartment block sitting in a chequerboard of huge, grey apartment blocks – each one as drab and nondescript as the next – the very epitome of East Berlin and the Communist era (except that they also remind me strangely and semi-nostalgically of South London – funny how things at a distance can seem much more romantic than they are up close). The entrance area to Block B is grubby but neat, with a scrubby little bit of grassland (patchy but still neatly trimmed) on which a couple of dogs are exercising their elderly owners. Everything has a sad air of preservation about it, as if a slice of history has been hermetically sealed and everything within it – inhabitants, dogs, cats, buildings – has remained stuck at that point in time. I can imagine this place looking exactly the same during the war and during its enforced cutting-off from the rest of Germany and the West. Inside, the stairwell has the same air of historic tiredness. Not the piss-stinking, graffiti-overlaid, crime-riddled feel of South London sink estates; but a dark, mirthless, stale and lifeless feeling that creeps over us all like the shadow of the angel of death or a dementor's kiss.

I have to almost push Peter forward to make him go up the stairs, which he does tentatively, holding out the scrap of paper bearing his only connection to his granddad in front of him like a map. He's practically shaking, the poor kid, and I almost want to hold his hand. Danny must sense this too because, to my surprise, he steps up and puts a guiding hand on Peter's shoulder as we all file up the dank concrete stairwell. The walls are cold to the touch, despite the sun outside, as if it's always sunless in here. Two floors up we stop, unsure of whether the Germans count the ground floor as zero or as the first floor. We inspect the door numbers which are faded and chipped. This is it. Second floor. Peter locates the right number and falters. He suddenly looks a lot younger and I wonder if he can actually be any older than sixteen or seventeen. He's lost all colour from his face. Right now he's probably thinking through all the possibilities that might lie beyond that door – granddad or no granddad, alive or dead, intelligent or senile, welcoming or hostile.

Danny steps forward and knocks on the door, still with his hand on Peter's shoulder. He's clearly taking to this paternal role a bit more seriously since the uneasy truce broke out between him and Ari. A heavy pause. Silence. Nothing. Ari points up to a small button on the side of the doorframe and Peter reaches up and presses it diffidently. Inside, a crackling buzzer sounds intermittently far off down a corridor. Another long pause as we all crane forward to listen, and finally hear the shuffling sound of someone making their painstaking way to the door. A figure appears behind the frosted glass panel, accompanied by a rattling of chains and clacking of locks. A small white head looms close to the glass as the door opens a fraction and an elderly voice says: '*Wer ist dort?*'

We all look at each other, each of us hoping that someone else will take charge on our odd little Mission Improbable. Emboldened perhaps by the presence of the three mouseketeers, Peter takes a step closer: 'Excuse me. I'm looking for Mr Pay-ter Guz-tav Eye-chart,' he enunciates his best German accent as loudly as his fluttering nerves will let him.

A metallic scraping announces the chain being taken off and the door opens a fraction wider; wide enough for us to make out a little old man with a shock of white hair and a passing resemblance to Einstein peering out at us suspiciously. He must be a bit taken aback to see four Westerners standing outside his door, and maybe mistakes us for a sightseeing family lost in East Berlin. He blinks at us slowly, looking from one to the next, clearly sizing us up for potential damage-control.

'*Sind sie Engländer?*' he asks us. '*Warum suchen Sie nach Peter Eichardt?*'

Between us we recognise the words 'English' and Peter's grandfather's name. Peter puts up a hand to attract the old man's attention. He turns to look at the boy.

'Are *you* Pay-ter Eye-ch…Eye-kart?' Peter adjusts his pronunciation to the old man's rendering of the name and points to his chest, signalling in international semaphore 'you'.

'Why… you… vant to… know?' the old man says suddenly in haltering English.

Peter takes a leap of faith.

'Because I'm Peter, your grandson… *en-kel*.' Peter produces his pièce de resistance – the German word he has probably been saying over and over to himself for months in preparation for this moment. 'Emma, your daughter, is my mother, *meine mutter.*'

Peter draws out a battered old black-and-white picture of a smiling young couple with their little daughter forming a bridge between them, holding both their hands and staring half-shyly, half-cheekily into the camera lens. The man is wearing smart pleated trousers with braces and an army-style shirt, with horn-rimmed glasses and slick jet-black hair; the woman has a pretty white blouse with embroidered edges and a prim-looking skirt. Their daughter is wearing a little frock coat buttoned up to her neck, her little chubby legs in socks and sandals beneath. The picture is pretty faded and worn around the edges, as if someone has lovingly fingered it many times over the intervening years.

The elder Peter takes the photo carefully in his hands and stares at it for a long time in silence. Then, as if he were in a private reverie, his eyes moisten and become blurry. He pulls out a large white handkerchief from his cardigan pocket and blows his nose loudly.

'This is my Lisbeth, and my little Emma.' He looks at the picture and then more carefully at Peter, as if to see if there is any resemblance, or whether this young pretender has just happened across this photograph in an attic somewhere and tracked him down, hoping perhaps for a reward, or a story, or both. He casts an eye around mistrustfully, but young Peter seems ready for this and is already digging inside the plastic folder to bring out more proof. I imagine he wanted as much reassurance about the identity of his grandfather as old Peter seems now to need about him – the grandson he never even knew he had.

Peter brings out some more photographs, this time of

Lisbeth and Emma in England, Emma looking a bit older now. Then Emma as a teenager in school uniform, Emma and Peter's father on their wedding day and finally a family photo of Emma, Peter's dad and a young Peter. Peter the elder stares at the photographs as if they are of a Martian landscape. His little girl, grown up, married, with a son, this Peter! Slowly he seems to accept the truth of the situation and, smiling, he opens his arms to Peter and pulls him into a huge hug, and now the crying begins in earnest, on both sides (and I'm not immune to a prickling sensation behind my eyelids either, which I try to hide by looking away). Danny and Ari are both grinning stupidly, but I can't help hoping that this touching spectacle of familial lost-and-found is having an effect on them too.

Now personally I would love to hear more of the old man's stories, and I'm sure Ari would too, but I sense that this is Peter's private history we're intruding on now, and anyhow, it's time that we moved on. Our work here is done. We have our own journeys to travel and these two need some time to get acquainted properly. So we leave the two Peters with promises to stay in touch and grateful hugs all round.

'Good luck!' I wish them as they stand arm-in-arm at the doorway, but somehow I think they don't need it now.

CHAPTER 8

Any old iron curtains? Revolution in the new Europe

'"All hope abandon, ye who enter in!"
These words in sombre colour I beheld
Written upon the summit of a gate.'

Dante Alighieri –
'The Divine Comedy: Inferno', 1867.

The visit to Peter's grandfather seems to have lifted all our spirits, and Danny, Ari and I hang out chatting round our campsite barbecue pit well into the dark of the evening, just like the other happy families. The smell of the burning wood and the homely crackle of the fire fill the air. It's a coolish June evening and we huddle in close to the pit until our faces are glowing red, although our backs are still cold. We're full of smiles and stories.

Ari wants to know all about East Berlin and the Stasi and what might have happened to Peter's grandfather during those dark years behind the Wall. I have my own questions about the Wall and how it was allowed to stand for so long in the 'modern' world. I wish that we could have stayed longer with Peter and his granddad, and talked about some of this with them, but I think the shock of finding a new grandson on his doorstep was quite enough for the old man for one day. So I promise Ari we'll keep in touch with Peter and find out more one day.

After Ari goes to bed, Danny and I chuck some more wood on the fire and get to discussing the more mundane issue of our route. From Berlin the plan had been to go straight over to Warsaw and from there through Belarus and up to Moscow and across the huge Russian Federation. But now that I'm here in Europe I'm starting to get a real sense of its history ('continental Europe' I should say – we islander Brits sometimes forget that we are actually a part of Europe). I have a new yearning to go south into some of the new Baltic republics formed in our lifetime after the fall of the Berlin Wall, which broke up the old Soviet Union and the grip of the Cold War. It'd be quite something to explore the burgeoning republics of the brave new world: Czech Republic, Slovakia, Croatia, Serbia and Montenegro, Bosnia and Herzegovina (names I've only really heard of through the *Eurovision Song Contest*). The map of Europe has changed hugely in the last twenty years.

Danny's not so taken with the idea, however: 'I'm just not sure how safe some of these places are, and we don't have visas or anything.' Killjoy, I think to myself, wondering at the same time how much more he's known about some of his women.

'That would be the *adventure* of discovering the new Europe.' I try to appeal to his sense of wild frontierism.

'It's the same old Europe,' Danny replies a bit grumpily, poking at the fire with a stick, 'just with different names.' I restrain my urge to push the old curmudgeon in the fire-pit.

He must still be feeling the effects of the shenanigans with Ari last night. He'll be back to his old fun-loving adventurous self in the morning I reason with myself, hoofing a large log right into the centre of the fire and sending sparks high into the air.

We agree to go to the internet café the next day and look up the Foreign and Commonwealth Office information on travelling in the new Europe. If it looks safe (and I'm curious about carefree Danny being so hung up on safety) I might be able to persuade him to go the long way round (perhaps it's his newfound paternalistic instincts?). The world's a funny old place sometimes – things are never exactly what they appear to be. Constant evolution, that's the way of everything.

I settle down in my bunk and thank my lucky stars that we have trusty Alice, our little home away from home, to keep us feeling safe. I really am beginning to enjoy life inside an ice cream van. It even smells like home now – an indescribable mixture of testosterone, chemical toilet and strawberry Mivvi. I go to sleep dreaming of being Davy Crockett, King of the Wild Frontier, all fur hats and gunslinging. The Disney lyrics come back to me like it was yesterday (where the hell were *they* lodged?). You know, about him being born on a mountain in Tennessee, raised in the woods knowing every tree. That Davy Crockett, King of the Wild Frontier.

* * * * * * *

In the morning, full of pioneering spirit (and sausages), we trek into town to an internet café – guru of our age. We split up and grab a terminal each, as if the battered old computers are really our familial gods. I ask the online oracle that is the Foreign and Commonwealth Office's website how fares our first proposed destination – the Czech Republic (part of Czechoslovakia back when it was a spelling test under Communist rule). The oracle spake most surprisingly thusly: 'There is an underlying threat from terrorism. Attacks could be indiscriminate, including in places frequented by expatriates and foreign travellers.' (FCO website, 2006)

Erm. Right then. So that's not sounding all that safe. I look up in turn Slovakia, Croatia, Serbia and Montenegro, Bosnia and Herzegovina, and all say the same thing (with added threat from landmines and other unexploded ordnance in parts of Croatia and Kosovo). I'm seeing a theme emerge, so out of curiosity I look up Germany and back comes the same response. So I'm thinking fine, I've been living in London for the past fifteen years, and I guess the threat of terrorism is just a fact of life in the twenty-first century anywhere on this planet; and if I can survive in Brixton then I can survive in Bosnia.

I decide not to tell Danny and Ari about the overcautious advice – after all, what good's an adventure without a bit of risk? But I will tell them the other exciting news I found, that Europe's newest country has been formed in the week since we left home. Montenegro declared independence from Serbia on 3rd June 2006. A new country this week! Back in my school days there was just Czechoslovakia and Yugoslavia in this area of Europe, and now look at it – blossoming into independent states like rampant wildflowers.

I grab a quick coffee from the friendly bearded man in charge of this online heaven and check my emails. There's one waiting for me from Mum (alongside three offers to enlarge my manhood and the usual updates from Amazon and iTunes):

Dear Casey,
Your father and I have been a bit worried as we haven't heard from you since you departed.

[What? All of six days ago? Funny, it seems like a lifetime and the blink of an eye.]

I'm sure everything is fine but you did promise to keep in touch. Please call or email as soon as you get this to let us know that you are all okey-dokey.

In other news, the vicarage garden is coming along nicely and my flower arrangement won second prize at Scalby Village Fête on Saturday. We have lunch with the Smiths on Friday.

Please give our regards to Daniel. I do hope you two are getting along well.

Best regards,

Mum x

Righty ho. Okey dokey. I don't even know who the Smiths are, but clearly they're important in my mother's social calendar. I guess I'd better email them back, remembering to be careful what I say about Danny.

Danny and Ari are crowded round the next-door computer screen looking at emails from Ari's mum. I glance over to see that she's included a pic of herself in her hospital gown pulling a funny face. I stop breathing for a second. I can't quite compute the tragedy and hope wrapped up in this one picture. And there's something else. It's so wrong, but I can't stop my brain from telling me this information... she's really... there's no other way of saying it but... drop dead gorgeous. That's probably the worst metaphor I could have thought of in the circumstances, but that's what my stupid brain comes up with. Granted, she looks a bit drawn, but determined and smiling (presumably for Ari's benefit). She has the same elfin features as Ari, and mesmerising cat-green eyes. Her hair looks slightly too short and I wonder if she's had chemo or radiotherapy. I realise again how little I know about Ari's mum. She certainly doesn't look like the air-headed WAG I'd conjured up in my own head. I can't believe Danny's never shown me any pictures of her. I can't believe I never asked to see any. Now I can totally see why Danny fell for her. He catches me looking over and I blush furiously.

'She's going in for her operation today.' He thankfully misinterprets my blushing as caught out being nosy. His voice sounds like he's trying to be cheerful for Ari's sake but I can see a worried look in his eyes. I think back to last night's whispered conversation round the campfire, after Ari had gone to bed. Danny telling me that this is the second operation Niobe has had for breast cancer. That she doesn't talk much to him about it. She didn't even tell him the first time she went in, three years ago, until after they'd removed the first malignant lump and given her the all clear, but she did track him down then, and it occurs to me that maybe she got back in touch with him in case... well, in case anything serious happened, or it reoccurred, or...

Come to think of it, three years ago was about the same time that Danny settled back in the UK and got back in touch with me. Maybe he realised then that he needed to stop running and start to take his responsibilities seriously. But I'm sure none of them really expected the cancer to come back. Oh God, what if this is more serious than I thought? What if something does happen to Niobe; maybe she wants Danny to... God, that's a huge thing. But Danny? With Ari? Suddenly this trip falls into a sharper focus. Danny also confided in me last night that Ari won't say how he got the black eye, but he suspects he took out his frustration on some kid at the camp and paid the price for it. He doesn't think Ari is coping very well with his mum's illness. Well, blow me down with a feather Dr Obvious.

Danny leaves Ari typing out an email in reply to his mum

and comes round to have a look at the FCO stuff. I guide him through some carefully chosen pages, and repeat my thing about Bosnia and Brixton. This seems to cheer him up somewhat. I think he'd rather take on an unexploded bomb and Bin Laden's boys than face thinking too much about Niobe, the operation and Ari's future.

* * * * * * *

So here we are on the road again. This time en route for the Czech Republic – formed in 1993, following the 1989 'Velvet Revolution', after the Berlin Wall fell. Imagine what it must have been like for those Czech students overthrowing the Communist regime, which had ruled for the previous forty years, by holding flowers out to soldiers in riot gear.

Forty minutes past Dresden we're at the border crossing from old Europe into new. We don't need a visa but we're stopped at some sort of customs checkpoint where the officious little bureaucrat makes us all get out of the van while he searches it, none-too-delicately, for whatever it is he's looking for. He opens all the bags and looks bemused to find large quantities of potatoes and oranges on board a converted ice cream van. I half think he's going to confiscate them, but instead he produces a piece of paper and hands it to us, saying in a heavy accent: 'Must have!'

The list, written in what I take to be Czech and broken English, states that all car-drivers in the Czech Republic must carry the following items or they will not be permitted entry:

1 First Ade Kit [sic]
1 Warning Triangal
1 Spare pare designated glasses
1 Set spare bulb for light

1 Fluo essent green jacket
1 tax permit motorway

The first aid kit and warning triangle we can lay our hands on almost immediately and I smugly produce these. The spare bulbs Danny digs out of the tool kit in the bottom of the toilet cubicle after some strenuous shifting of bags and gathering of scattered potatoes and oranges. Neither of us wear glasses (which Mr Border Bureaucrat is at first reluctant to accept, asking us both to read various number plates at different distances until he's satisfied, and he almost tests Ari too). We're a bit stuck on the last two items, however. I'm sure we haven't got a green, or any other colour, hi-vis jacket (I mean, why would we?) and we haven't had a chance to purchase a tax permit (which I knew we needed – the FCO site said as much, but I thought we could buy it inside the country). We show him the defunct emergency satellite kit from Gary's dodgy lockup, but he remains unimpressed – it's not on the list, you're not coming in.

I ask Mr BB if we can buy the permit from him – which isn't meant to sound like a bribe, although as I'm saying it I realise it sounds a bit like that; and I really hope that it isn't a crime to try to bribe an official because he's carrying a very large gun. He waves us towards a desk where, to our relief, they seem to be able to sell us the requisite pass.

I'm hoping Mr BB will forget about the hi-vis jacket once we have the permit, but I hope in vain because every item on that old boy's list has to be ticked off before we can set one tiny little foot into the Czech Republic, and I'm beginning to have some doubts about our route change. If the Czech Republic is like this then maybe the newer states will be even worse?

I'm racking my brains for a solution to hi-vis-gate, and wondering whether a bright green Gap jumper I've got in my bag will do the trick when Ari suddenly appears from inside the van with a look of triumph all over his little face. He thrusts a handful of, yes, green hi-vis material into the hands of the border guard who shakes it out and recoils at the same time. The jacket must once have been part of the ice cream selling gear (did the former owner moonlight as a lollipop man? – no pun intended) and Ari found it screwed up somewhere in the depths of one of the storage units (it's been behind the water tank for a while is my guess from the brown stinky stuff dripping off the thing). Mr BB swears at us in Czech (at least I assume he does – I would in his shoes) and hands the jacket back to Ari who shoves it back into the locker, grinning. Mr BB hovers his pen over the last remaining item on the list and, with a wipe of his gloves on the side of the van, he ticks it off and stamps the list – we're in!

* * * * * * *

On the road through the Czech Republic en route to Prague the country looks distinctly more Eastern European compared to the pomp of Germany. The countryside and houses and people look a bit poorer here. Even the weather has changed – a skyful of clouds has blocked out the sun, making new Europe look even more grey in comparison. A couple of hours in we stop in the small town of Terezin to refuel. As I'm stretching my legs I see signs for Terezin (Theresienstadt) Concentration Camp and Jewish Ghetto Museum. It's been a tiring day so we have a vote on whether or not to go in. Danny has reservations about it being a bit too much for Ari who retorts that he learned about Hitler in year seven. After Danny explains to me that means the first year of secondary school, I think it's the boy's choice, and it's a part of history that everyone needs to learn about.

'Lest we forget, and all that,' I say to Danny.

'Yeah, right,' he retorts, 'because people really learned a lesson from that, didn't they? Because there hasn't been anything like that since we all learned our lesson from the Nazi holocaust?'

Mmmm, I think, listing inwardly: Rwanda, Burundi, Darfur, China, Cambodia, Korea, Afghanistan, Kurdistan... My brain runs on now unbidden: Yugoslavia, Kosovo, Bosnia... Endless TV reels of Kate Adie reporting from yet another war zone against a backdrop of blue-helmeted UN peacekeepers standing helplessly by. Did I really think that this 'shiny new Europe' came into being completely peacefully?

Sobered, suddenly, I feel drawn to exploring sweet Terezin's dirty little secrets. We follow the signs past garrison after garrison of yellow walls with red tile roofs. A pretty church stands incongruously on one side of the tree-lined central square. The museum is framed by two signs – the first, the concentration camp motto 'ARBEIT MACHT FREI' (work makes you free), and the second a Hebrew inscription saying, simply, 'REMEMBER'. Along one of the walls a simple wooden gallows is still standing. Better that than the fate which awaited inside?

I take a deep breath and walk inside the museum with Danny and Ari right behind me. We seem to be the only people here, which makes it even more eerie. The sign tells us that the prison here first accommodated the assassins of the Archduke Ferdinand, the incident that sparked the First World War. Who could have foreseen then how a Second World War would turn this place into a Jewish ghetto and transit camp to places like Auschwitz, Sobibor and Treblinka? We're informed that 150,000 people passed through here, and 35,000 died within these walls. It makes me shiver despite being inside and out of the cold wind, which has started blowing outside.

Terezin was a work camp providing Jewish slave labour

111

to the German war effort. It housed men, women, children, the elderly and disabled, all living in appalling conditions and spending their days breaking rocks or sorting through possessions confiscated from other Jews. This was still preferable to the gas chambers of the death camps where millions of Europe's Jewish population were disposed of by the Nazis. 'Disposed of.' To dispose of something is to put it in its place, to toss on the rubbish heap. We won't ever know exactly how many died. Some figures put it at twelve million. Twelve million people suddenly and brutally taken from their homes and incarcerated in camps like this. Forced to work in terrible, inhuman, degrading conditions; experimented on like animals and then 'disposed of'. Gassed, shot, decaying of hunger and mistreatment, their corpses thrown into the crematoriums and 'put in their place'. Assigned to history's rubbish bin. Imagine how different the world might have been if all of those people had survived.

And alongside the Jews, not many of the history books will tell you how many gay people also died in concentration camps. Tens of thousands, possibly more, appeared on police 'pink lists', were arrested and convicted of homosexuality. In the camps they were made to wear pink triangles and undoubtedly faced harsher treatment by guards and other inmates alike. To add insult to injury, come the liberation, the gays remained imprisoned because homosexuality remained a crime in Germany until 1969. It was never talked about, and they were never compensated. In the year 2000 the German government finally issued an apology to these forgotten victims. The Terezin museum is a horrific reminder of terrifyingly recent history.

I look round to see where Danny and Ari are, to check that they're safely with me. Ari is looking even paler than usual and I suddenly think that maybe this wasn't such a good idea. I'm pretty sure they won't have covered this kind of detail in

Year Seven. Ari's sticking very close to Danny and I find myself moving closer too, instinctively seeking and offering protection at the same time. In the next section we're confronted with life-size pictures of some of the children who lived and died here: Ari's age and younger; much younger. I'm struck by how even stick-thin Ari looks like a fattened calf next to them.

In the final bit of the museum, there's a film produced by the International Red Cross, which made official visits to the camp early on in the war. They'd been fooled into thinking that they were visiting a city built for Jews to 'protect them' during the war, or so the propaganda went. It was even called 'Paradeisghetto' by the Nazis. The film shows prisoners with forced smiles playing football and putting on concerts, with clean clothes and shops full of goods, which promptly disappeared after the visit. Over the film a narrator tells us how healthy-looking Jewish children were bussed in for the occasion, and how both they, and their hidden emaciated counterparts, were shipped out to be gassed afterwards. I feel sick to my stomach.

When the lights go up Ari turns to Danny and me, looking bewildered.

'Why didn't they help them?' he asks.

Ignorance is bliss? Who knows who did know and who didn't? How many pretended not to know? Turned a blind eye. But even if they had acknowledged it, what would they have done? I think back to when I went on the anti-Iraq war demonstrations in London in 2003. After we'd been hoodwinked by the sexed-up dodgy dossier alleging that Iraq's weapons of mass destruction could be deployed within forty-five minutes. The dossier that the weapons inspector himself, Dr David Kelly, ultimately committed suicide over, knowing it had been tampered with by the powers that be. They were the largest anti-war demonstrations in living history; bigger even than the anti-Vietnam protests in the sixties; but did they stop the war? No. Faced with the atrocities that man does unto man, what can most of us hope to do? We recoil in horror, we denounce it privately, write a few letters, send on a few email petitions, wear a coloured shirt to work one day to show our solidarity, or go on a march with our mates. But in the end we feel pretty powerless. And that powerlessness feels almost overwhelming.

* * * * * * *

Too exhausted to continue on to Prague we drive in silence to a local campsite in the grey drizzle that's now falling and eat a quick cold supper in the van before bed. Danny and I try to make normal conversation but Ari won't be drawn and I wonder if we're totally overdoing it with all the holocaust stuff on top of him worrying about his mum in hospital.

The drumming of rain on the roof is soporific, but nevertheless I slip into a fitful sleep studded with nightmares. I dream that I'm in a holiday camp in Scarborough but each chalet door has a dark handprint on it, and the people inside are dragged out and thrown into cages. Suddenly I see that Niobe is one of the people in a cage, looking gaunt and vulnerable, and behind her, is that Ari? And I want to set them free but there's no one to help me, and all the redcoats are telling me that the people are happy to be in the cages and I find myself wanting to believe them so that I can just go home and not have to look at them any more.

CHAPTER 9

The spectre haunting new Europe

'Through clever and constant application of propaganda people can be made to see paradise as hell, and also the other way around, to consider the most wretched sort of life as paradise.'

Adolf Hitler,
Mein Kampf, 1925.

I wake in a cold sweat tangled in my sleeping bag with an urge to put distance between us and Terezin. After a not-very-satisfying breakfast of fried potatoes and an orange each we hurry on our way to Prague. The rain has stopped and the clouds have parted to reveal a new sun. Prague is chocolate-box chic once you clear the more industrial suburbs and the five-lane highway. Its sunny demeanour and crowds of snap-happy tourists are a stark contrast to Terezin's gloom. We grab lunch by Wenceslas Square where the big demonstrations of the Velvet Revolution took place. Named after good king Wenceslas of the Christmas carol, Czechs believe that in times of trouble, Wenceslas will arise from the grave, summon a great army of dead knights and come to the aid of the people. Perhaps that's what happened in 1989, in the same spot where twenty years earlier twenty-year-old Jan Palach set fire to himself in protest at the Soviet invasion of Czechoslovakia.

As we drive out of Prague, the suburbs become increasingly grey and grim, and the sunlight seems to exacerbate the effect. Lifeless underpasses lead to paltry out-of-town shopping centres which look like they've only just updated from the Soviet-style queuing system. I guess Capitalism doesn't cure all ills. I think I read that some of the older generation actually mourn the loss of Communism with its zero unemployment and 'security'. Go figure. Freedom is slavery?

The rest of the day is a long drive into the southern part of the Czech Republic, Moravia, and on towards the Slovakian border. The countryside is pleasant but unremarkably flat and it's a pretty undistinguished drive down the D1 motorway to Brno, Czech's second city (also dubbed the Manchester of Moravia), and then on to the border and beyond that Bratislava, Slovakia's capital.

Pretty Prague appears to have cheered us all up a bit, though. It's a pleasantly warm day and Danny takes the wheel and tears up the dotted line of the open road. I absent-mindedly gaze into the rearview mirror while Danny drives, watching Ari in the back reading some pamphlets... until I realise with a jolt that he's got our passports in his hands and is smirking.

'Hey, Ari.' I turn to face him. 'Gimme those!'

Ari looks up with a grin and I see that he's got my passport open in his grimy little paws.

'Nice photo!' he says mockingly.

'Give me that now!' I lunge towards him through the tight space between the front seats and the rear of the van, knocking into Danny's arm and making him fight not to swerve the van.

116

'Hey, watch it Casey!' Danny shouts. 'What's the big deal?'

I manage to grab the passports out of Ari's surprised grasp and wriggle back into my seat awkwardly. Danny is looking at me like I've completely lost it.

'What's the problem?' he asks.

'Nothing,' I say, blushing. 'I just don't want him playing with the passports. He might lose them.'

Danny raises his eyebrows, gives me a look and shakes his head as if to say that he can't fathom women.

'Your photo can't be *that* bad, surely,' he adds, smirking, and I feel a bit embarrassed that I may have overdone it a little bit. But these things are important, and privacy should be respected. I settle back into my seat holding tight to the passports and resolving to hide them somewhere safe when we next stop. I get out my guidebook to deflect any further comment and start to read up about New Europe, avoiding looking at either Danny or Ari who doubtless think that I'm totally barmy. But I have my reasons.

* * * * * * *

New Europe is a place of huge contrasts – East versus West, history versus progress, Communism versus Capitalism, rich capital cities versus the poor countryside, McDonald's Big Mac wrappers littering the roads of former Soviet satellite states. You can even see it on the motorway, where the old Eastern European doyennes of the car world, Trabants, bimble alongside new Mercedes and Jags driven by men in suits and women in furs. *Arbeit macht Frei*? I feel like I'm on the verge of discovering something, some universal truth, but haven't quite got all the pieces yet.

When we switch drivers Ari takes a turn in the passenger seat up front as Danny goes for a nap in the back. I expect him to be a bit subdued after all the dark museums we've seen, plus the email from Niobe and everything, but Ari surprises me by being the epitome of lively conversation.

'Casey?'

'Yes, Ari?'

'Why did the Nazis kill all those Jews?'

Oh boy.

'Well, it's pretty complex Ari. Basically the Nazis believed in racial purity. They believed that blonde-haired, blue-eyed 'Aryan' Germans were a master race destined to rule the world. Even though Hitler and the rest of them were dark-haired, right. So they wanted to rid Germany of its migrant populations, especially Jews who they believed were an inferior race. They also thought that there was a worldwide Jewish conspiracy to take over the world.'

I can see Ari looking at me with wide-eyed disbelief, trying to figure out if I'm pulling his leg. I mean, who'd believe that bunch of guff?

For all he was a bad house painter, Hitler was extremely clever at exploiting people's intrinsic weaknesses, based on petty prejudices, greed and a basic desire to be on the winning side. Nazism was really a cobbling together of a load of different philosophical ideas out of which Hitler and his party grabbed just the bits that suited them.

'Take the Swastika – that square cross with wing-tips that was painted everywhere in the museums in Terezin and Berlin. It was originally an ancient Hindu symbol,' I tell Ari; '*Svasti* is the Sanskrit word for "good" or "lucky". But in the convoluted thinking of the Nazi ideology it became the Aryan symbol of the new German master race. And at the head of the master race: the ultimate dictator – Adolf Hitler – German Chancellor and Führer of a totalitarian national socialist republic.'

Ari is furrowing his brow as I finish my little rant.

'What's a totalitarian national socialist republic?' he asks.

I can't help but smile at him, thinking how weird it is to be sitting here trying to explain the finer nuances of the world's historico-political systems to a twelve-year-old who's the estranged son of my estranged childhood sweetheart in a bright pink travelling ice cream van in the middle of new Europe.

After what I hope he will remember as a coherent and persuasive analysis of Nazism and the reasons behind two world wars, Ari falls into a long silence. Probably digesting it all...

'Mum's never been with anyone since Dan,' Ari pipes up suddenly, causing me to swerve the van ever-so-slightly.

Caught off-guard I find myself blushing involuntarily and hope that he doesn't notice.

'Well, not if you don't count that weird one from the college where she teaches. What a tool.'

I think about pulling him up on his description, but decide against it, not wanting to draw attention to the fact that I'm still blushing. Bloody hell, this is Ari's mum we're talking about here, and Danny's ex – get a grip! After she-who-must-not-be-named I hadn't found anyone remotely attractive until I saw Niobe's photo. I wonder why Ari's offering this information, and whether he's reading my mind – consciously or unconsciously. I tune back in to catch the end of his sentence.

'...didn't like me, but I don't *care*. I don't *want* to be liked.'

I glance at him, wondering again at what damage Danny might have inflicted by running away from being a father and husband. Ari doesn't seem to require any kind of answer to this, however, so we settle back into a slightly uneasy silence that sends my brain into overdrive.

* * * * * * *

I was brought up to believe in a world where God takes care of everything. 'Let go and let God', as Dad is fond of saying. But at the same time, there's that pesky issue of free will; because I was also taught that everything that is wrong in the world is our own fault; that when people asked the dumb question: 'Why does a loving God allow wars and famine and disease?' that the standard dumb answer is because God gave humans free will and with that free will, combined with 'human nature', came all kinds of wrongdoing and evil.

But if humans are inevitably weak – and I believe that in some ways we are – then won't those weaknesses always get in the way in society, in any political system – whether Socialist, Communist or Capitalist? I fear that the proof of that is all around us here in the collapsed Union of Soviet Socialist Republics. The parallels between utopias, dystopias, Socialism/Communism and Capitalism are all about humankind trying to (re)create paradise on earth and it all going badly wrong. Why is it that we're not capable of creating a world where everybody is happy and nice to everybody else? Humankind's inability to overcome our fundamental human selfishness and greed sabotages us every time. This is what we need to figure out. But that begs the question: Why didn't God make humans a better creature in the first place? Why is human nature so flawed?

* * * * * * *

'You never asked me why I ran off the other night,' Ari abruptly proclaims out of nowhere.

The tone of his voice seems like a challenge, and I'm not sure how to meet it. I've not asked him because I didn't want him to think I was prying into his private affairs; and, if I'm honest, I didn't really know what to ask – I'm not his surrogate parent here. But clearly he thinks my not asking betrays a total lack of interest. I realise that I'm also afraid of going there, of getting closer to Ari like this, of knowing why he does things, of what he thinks about his mum, Danny, his life, anything. I'm afraid of a twelve-year-old boy! I am. I can't lie to myself about this. But what exactly is it that scares me about this? Does it actually show up an underlying fear or inability to get involved with anybody? Or have I been reading too many *Marie Claire*s? I'm getting all confused and going places in my head where I really don't want to go right now, and all because Ari has asked a very simple and straightforward question. Now I wish he'd ask me about Hitler again.

I realise he's looking at me as if to say 'well?' I wish I was better at thinking on my feet. I wish I was somewhere else altogether... He's still staring at me. I decide to jump in with both feet again and try to wing it (at least he can't run off this time). I smirk involuntarily at this twist in my thinking and immediately regret it. Ari fixes me with a harder stare than even Paddington could manage on his really, really bad horrid days. I feel like he wants to shout at me but instead he turns away and looks out of the window.

'No, Ari, look, I didn't... oh cripes!' The van swerves across the bumper strip as I reach over to him and he twists away from me. I straighten it up pronto. Ari looks at me as if to say 'Get a grip, crazy lady.'

'Ari, look, I didn't mean to smile. I was just smiling at myself, at how badly I handled things with you the other night, when you ran off. Not because it was funny, but because I was worried I would do the same again, or you might. That's why I didn't say anything to you.' My confession catches us both a bit off-guard. Ari is the first to recover.

'It's OK,' he smiles. 'I know you're not used to being around young people. Dan told me you're not married.' He says it conspiratorially, like it's a delicate subject which one shouldn't mention in polite company – a little secret that he's letting me know he knows.

I use the pretext of concentrating on the road to not say anything for a minute. I'm not sure whether Danny has actually told him that I'm gay (it hasn't occurred to me before to wonder whether he has or hasn't. Now I've no idea what else Danny has told him). But I can't think about that now.

'So, why *did* you run off then?' I ask him gingerly.

'Because I wanted to be alone. Because I was sad about my mum and I didn't want to talk about it. Because I thought I might cry.'

I wasn't expecting this to turn into a confessional. I want to ask about the black eye but don't want to push him too far on this first opening up.

'You know, Ari, it's OK to cry. In fact it's a good thing, it just means that we care about something or someone.'

'But Mum told me to be a big boy and not to cry. And I don't. Not... normally.'

'Well, I know your mum wants you to be brave and not to be sad, but really, crying is natural and boys are allowed to cry as well as girls...'

Ari pulls a face but I go on regardless.

'...It's not a sign of weakness to show your emotions, Ari. You should never be afraid of that.'

Ari looks up at me as if quizzing my features for signs of the truth to this statement. I don't know, I just feel like his mother would tell him the same thing if she was here. She didn't look the type to bottle things up, she looks more Mediterranean. It's us Brits with our stiff upper lips who bottle things up, and it's so unhealthy and then it comes out in other ways, like violence towards self or others – QED black-eyed pea.

'OK,' Ari says hesitantly, and that's that, another of

life's strange little lessons to be mulled over, chewed and contemplated during the journey. Ari goes back to playing on his PSP and we drive on in a more relaxed silence under the sun, punctuated by electronic beeps and (good) vibrations.

* * * * * * *

We finally reach the border with Slovakia at a place called Kúty-Břeclav. It's late afternoon and I'm exhausted from the long drive and Ari's chattering. He's now mercifully slumped against the door in a slumber, so I'm hoping to get through the border without waking him. Things here seem much more relaxed than at the Czech crossing, and we're just about to sail through when I spot a little fracas taking place at the booth next door. A middle-aged woman... No, I take that back – a woman of broadly my age but who actually looks middle-aged – is having an animated conversation with the man in the booth and two other border guards who are crowding round her. There's lots of arm waving and proffering and refusing of her passport. I wind down the window to see if I can hear what's going on. I catch something in a plummy English accent that sounds like: 'Refusenik!'

And then a heavy Eastern European voice saying: 'No feet entry!' in the very officious sort of way these uniformed pen-pushers have of trying to make themselves sound like they are very important people. The problem is that these ones do have a certain power – they can refuse entry, or delay you, or make you fill out a hundred forms or make you pay some fictitious fine, as long as they think they can get away with it. And they also have guns. The woman's wearing some sort of Jesus sandals with kitten heels, so I can see their point about 'no feet entry', but I hate to see these jobsworths picking on a woman.

So, perhaps against someone else's better judgement, I yell over: 'Can we help you? Are you having trouble?'

As if wakened by a Bat-Signal Danny pops his head up from the back and sees the damsel in distress. He has that built-in knight in shining armour thing that's initially very attractive but is hard for men to maintain when they fall off their horse drunk after the second date and leave spur marks in the rosebeds. The woman looks up and, seeing first a strawberry-coloured ice cream van, frowns in despair. Then she sees Danny, all sunny smiles as he jumps out of the back door. She goes all gooey-eyed, smiling in evident relief (and something more), and walks over.

'Oh I'm so glad you've stopped. Do you know I've been here for fifteen minutes trying to argue with these morons and they simply won't let me in. I don't know what's wrong with them. I have my passport and my itinerary for the conference in Bratislava this weekend, and I simply must get there. Do you think you could talk to them for me?'

She sounds almost aristocratic. Danny immediately grabs her documents and goes to talk to the border guards who are eyeing us suspiciously, as if we might be about to kidnap their hostage and zoom her over the border without the proper paperwork. Seeing the size of their guns I'm not contemplating Alice getting shot up while doing a Steve McQueen-style Great Escape so I raise my hands off the steering wheel as if to say 'I'm not going anywhere, please don't shoot.'

'Um, why are you...?' I gesture vaguely around, thinking why is she here on her own sans horse and carriage and ladies-in-waiting.

'Oh, I'm hitching.' She answers my query absent-mindedly while she watches Danny dealing with the guards. I can see that look of admiration women get when he's doing his thing.

Right, yeah, makes perfect sense – plummy English conference-goer, clearly not short of a bob or two, hitching across Eastern Europe on her own. Apparently also a mind-reader.

'It's the only way I can get a real *feel* for places.' She emphasises the word 'feel' like she's stroking a pedigree cat. 'I'm a sociologist,' she adds sibilantly, as if that explains everything.

Danny comes back over with one of the border guards – an affable uncle Joe sort with a moustache.

'The thing is, ladies, you can't cross this border on foot,' Danny says with a friendly pat on the border guard's arm, as if they are explaining something very technical to some silly schoolgirls. 'But if we're willing to take..."

'Oh, Arabella.' She does a little nodding movement with her body which is almost a tiny curtsey of greeting.

'Right.' Danny grins momentarily. 'If we're willing to take Arabella across the border in our van and make sure that she gets to Bratislava, then it's fine. He says it's not safe for a lady to hitch-hike alone in this country.'

The fat little guard is leering rather comically at Arabella, which makes me want to burst out laughing, but these things can get you shot, so I just agree to take on board yet another hitch-hiker, this time with a Prada bag and designer shoes. At this rate we should charge for tickets.

* * * * * * *

Arabella, it emerges, during several long diatribes en route for Bratislava, is not only a sociology lecturer at some home counties redbrick but also a Socialist. Yes, a Socialist – you know, those people who don't agree with individuals having riches. Her Farah Fawcett wavy hair moves like a peculiar brown seascape as she talks animatedly, and her designer glasses have a tendency to slip down her nose, forcing her to constantly push them back up like a fishing boat bobbing up and down in the harbour. To complete the look she's wearing a Louis Vuitton scarf wrapped round her neck in the way that revolutionaries or German youth do. Never has a Socialist looked more bourgeois. I don't know what to make of her, and neither, I can tell, does Danny, who's opted to stay in the back of the van and allow the 'lady' to sit up front. She's not unpretty (although a bit horsey) but her commanding manner and the way she holds forth as if she's constantly addressing a full auditorium make him unsure whether to chat her up or go and brush down her horse.

Ari, however, seems oddly captivated with her, and hangs over the back of her seat asking questions as she holds forth on Socialism, Communism, Capitalism and every other 'ism under the sun. I feel a pang of something. Jealousy? Because *I* don't captivate Ari in the same way? I mean, what on earth does Miss Rebel with Everything have that I don't have (apart from money)? Slowly a penny winds its way round the charity collection-box of my mind and drops: I wonder if this woman actually reminds him just a little bit of his mum? Not physically, but by all accounts Niobe's a bit of an intellectual and lectures at her local college, so maybe Ari senses similar vibes? I vaguely wonder what Niobe lectures in and whether she's a socialist too? Then I remember that she's just had her cancer op. I don't think we've had a solid mobile signal since leaving Harwich so we really need to get to a payphone and place a call later today.

Danny eventually takes over at the wheel and Arabella, perhaps sensing his slight unease with her, takes the opportunity to switch into the back of the van so that she can lecture Ari properly. I'm torn between wanting to escape from her grating plummy accent and wanting to hear more. My mental coin is tossed in the air once more and lands on the side of the free lecture. She accepts another student into her class with a condescending nod of the head and ploughs on, while Ari and I furrow our brows ready for the seeds to be scattered.

'So, you see Communism is a *political* system, Aristotle, whereas *Socialism* is really an *economic* system that can exist in a wide range of political systems. In its ideal form, Aristotle, Socialism would eventually lead to a state of perfect equality, freedom and self-fulfilment for everyone everywhere.'

'That's what they all say,' I chime in, thinking back to the definition Ari read about Capitalism earlier.

Arabella gives me a withering stare, one which she has clearly honed to perfection in years of lecturing and speech-making, and carries on.

'The aim of Communism is a workers' revolution to overthrow the bourgeoisie, and the creation of a state in which the government runs factories and businesses for the good of the workers, rather than the workers being exploited for someone else's private profit.'

'Power to the People, eh?' I raise a clenched fist imitating Wolfie Smith, Citizen Smith, of the Tooting Popular Front. This time both Arabella and Ari look at me like I'm the class clown disrupting their lesson.

'Whereas in a Socialist system, things are run like a cooperative,' Arabella says scathingly.

'Like John Lewis,' I add helpfully.

This time Arabella doesn't even look up, but continues without a second's hesitation.

'In both a Communist and Socialist state there is no private ownership of property...'

Yeah, and I'm sure that her Prada bag and her Louis Vuitton scarf and her daft kitten heels are part of some huge collective wardrobe that she shares on a weekly basis with the Surrey Golf Club Popular Liberation Front. But I say nothing.

'...so no one individual gets rich over another and everything is based on equality, justice and cooperation.'

It's like she's describing a pleasant middle-class nursery school where the kids all play nicely together and everyone has the same toys. It doesn't really sound like the same Stalin's Russia I was taught about at Uni, where millions died because of his policies of collectivism and his autocratic and brutal dictatorship. She surely can't be so naïve as to think that Communism actually works, can she? I think about the poverty we've witnessed in the new Europe and how it's driving so many to seek a 'better life' in the Capitalist West now that the Wall's down.

I mean, don't get me wrong, I would *love* Communism to work, beacuse on paper it's brilliant, but like I said, once you add in human nature – greed and selfishness and addiction to power – then you're on to a loser whatever you do. That's why Capitalism flourishes – because it allows, supports, encourages private greed. Jeez, I sound cynical. What happened to the young idealist who almost got sucked into YouTopia? That was *days* ago. I've grown up since then. I pick at a loose woollen thread in the seat and try to bite my tongue.

'The Soviets were the first to have their revolution and install a Communist government,' Arabella instructs the rapt Ari. 'And do you know why the Americans were so scared of them during the Cold War? Why they invaded countries like Korea and Vietnam to stop them from becoming communist countries?'

'No. Why?' Ari leans forward intently as if he's Luke Skywalker and Arabella is Yoda.

'The Soviets were so powerful *because* of Communism, because the people had taken power from the tzars and kings who once ruled them. The Soviets put the first man into space; the Soviets established universal literacy and education while the Americans are *still* illiterate; the Soviets had good healthcare, zero unemployment, low rent and affordable food.'

'Even if you had to queue for hours to get a loaf of bread?' I can't help interjecting again. I feel as if Ari is being brainwashed and I want to protect him. Or I just plain disagree with Arabella and feel like she's stealing my thunder. One or the other.

'That was only so that prices didn't have to go up. Everybody could afford the bread, and they only had to queue when supply was short.'

'But supply shouldn't have been short if the economy really did work, and what about the millions who died of starvation in the fields?' I splutter.

'Sometimes people died because they didn't work hard enough to fill their quota. You can't be lazy or everyone suffers. From each according to his ability, to each according to his contribution, as we Socialists say.'

'Are you kidding me? You'll be telling me next that Stalin was a nice man.' I can't help myself being sarcastic, Arabella's apparent naivety astounds me.

'Well, the people *loved* Uncle Joe. They worshipped him. Because he actually brought them true freedom.'

'True freedom meaning real slavery?' I add, to Ari's bemusement.

'The problem with Communism,' Danny unexpectedly interjects from the front, 'is that there's no incentive for people to work. Everyone, no matter what job you do – whether you're a doctor or a dustman – you get paid the same crummy wage. And if you're working in the fields then everything you produce is pooled and given out to everyone else. There's just no reason to work hard. Once people begin to realise that they'll only do the bare minimum to get by. *That*'s why the Communist economy never thrived properly.'

Arabella and I look at the back of Danny's head in open-mouthed wonder.

'And the other thing is,' he adds, 'wherever you have someone in charge you'll get abuse of power. Just like with communes and utopias.'

'Power corrupts and absolute power corrupts absolutely,' I chip in, wondering where Danny got his knowledge from – nights in with Niobe discussing world politics and history over a glass of wine? Hard to imagine.

'And do you really think that Capitalist governments are any better?' Arabella bursts out angrily. 'Do you really believe it when they say that in Capitalist states the government doesn't still control everything? Do you think there is ever such a thing as a truly "free" market?'

She spits out accusing questions as if *we're* the naïve ones spouting platitudes at her.

'Western politicians are just as bad as some dictators,' she continues. 'Do you think that the atrocities committed during the Vietnam War, in Cuba or Nicaragua, were really justified in the fight against Communism? Do you really think that George W Bush is any better than Stalin?'

It's an interesting question. I momentarily thaw my attitude towards Arabella, but it seems that we've poked the hornets' nest too hard to stop her now.

'Who really killed JFK? Who's really running things in the West? Is the CIA or FBI any better than the KGB or Stasi? It's all just espionage and counter-espionage. Do you think that Bush's *New World Order* is any less threatening to the world than dictatorship? Do you think that the UK ever really does anything on the world stage these days without America's say so? Do you really think that you are more *free* because you happen to live in the West? Western governments are spying on us all the time. Capitalism is the "they" in the "them and us". "They" are *Big Brother* – watching us, monitoring us, censoring us, trying to control us. Every privacy law in the land, every secrecy act, every CCTV camera – who is it designed to serve? Them, not us. They're monitoring our phone conversations, our mobiles, our emails, everything. Somewhere there is a file on you and me and every one of us – even Ari! Political agendas control funding for research and that then dictates which "truths" are pursued. And if you go it alone and do the research you think is important but is against their agenda then they'll make sure that your findings never reach the light of day. The media is totally state-controlled. Watch the news! See what drivel they feed to us and expect us to swallow as truth.'

Arabella has gone red in the face and there's a shocked silence in the van as we all try to absorb her speech. I think of the biased reporting we see on the news every day: which wars are reported and who is shown as the good guy and who the bad guy. I think of how different social groups are vilified or justified according to the line being taken by those in power at the time. How huge injustices by our 'allies' are excused for and how tiny misdemeanours by our 'enemies' are made into world-shattering events. Politics and policy determined what 'truths' we were told, and to find the actual truth about anything you pretty much have to be there. It's all about 'history' – 'his (or her, but usually his) story' – the gospel according to Tom, Dick or Harry and whoever is paying them and pulling their strings.

Ari is looking thoroughly confused now.

'But isn't it better that the people have the power? And if they're working for each other then wouldn't that make them work harder?' he asks.

Arabella cuts in, recovering her composure now that she

has an apparent supporter amongst the gloomy naysayers of the good ship Alice.

'Yes, that's right, Aristotle. And during the 1930s when the rest of the world was in the Great Depression, Russia's economy was flourishing.' She says this triumphantly, as if it proves her entire thesis. 'And it was this wealth and power that helped them to defeat Hitler's Nazis and to bring Poland, East Germany, Hungary, Romania, Bulgaria and Czechoslovakia into the Soviet Bloc under Communist rule. And following that, Yugoslavia, Albania and North Korea established Communist governments because they saw how successful the Soviets were. And then China – now one of the world's most powerful economies – became Communist too. Did you know, Aristotle, that at one time around one-third of the world's population were under Communist rule?'

I half expect her to burst into a hearty rendition of the 'Red Flag'.

'But… why did the Soviet Union lose the war when the Berlin Wall fell down?' Ari asks. Clever boy, he *is* taking this all in.

Arabella looks momentarily flustered. I wonder how many of her students she's converted to her version of Communism? And here she is brought up short by a twelve-year-old.

'Gorbachev! Glasnost! Perestroika!' She spits out the words, enunciating each one with a precise Russian intonation making everyone jump a little.

Gorbachev. The eighties Russian leader with the Harry Potter scar. The strange words which were emblazoned in newspaper headlines, although none of us knew at the time what they really meant. Gorbachev's response to our letter to Brezhnev. An opening up and a restructuring of the Communist system, the end of the Cold War, and eventually, an unforeseen consequence – the total collapse of the Soviet

Union's Communist reign in Eastern Europe. The fall of the Berlin Wall and its domino effect. The end of pogroms and gulags and the beginnings of perestroika and glasnost. The heavy machinery of politics. From the Greek word *politikos*, meaning: 'of, or for citizens'. But somehow always seeming to end up being about how to control them.

'They should put kids in charge,' Ari concludes after a short silence. 'We'd do a much better job.'

CHAPTER 10

Creme Puff Gay Whisper

'There are certain queer times and occasions in this strange mixed affair we call life when a man takes this whole universe for a vast practical joke, though the wit thereof he but dimly discerns, and more than suspects that the joke is at nobody's expense but his own.'

Herman Melville,
Moby-Dick; or, the Whale, 1851.

We bowl into Bratislava in the late afternoon still debating the relative merits of different economic and political systems. The one ineluctable truth being that power and money are inextricably linked, and dangerous for the mortal soul. Talking of harmful to the soul, Arabella's ceaseless lecturing, while informative and thought-provoking, is beginning to remind me of those irritating wind-up monkeys that clang their cymbals together ceaselessly. I can't help wishing her batteries to be the cheap kind that run out sooner rather than later. On the upside, however, she's been educational, and Ari's never been so attentive, or spent so long away from his PSP. Besides, we'll be rid of her soon enough – I can't see her wanting to go to a gay bar as I've persuaded Danny we will tonight. Not that I've offered. She has, however, asked to be dropped off at the nearest backpacker place, although I can't help feeling that as soon as we're out of sight she'll hotfoot it to the nearest Hilton.

Bratislava turns out to be much like Prague, only smaller. It doesn't seem to have benefitted from as much Capitalist investment since the Wall Fall, although some modern developments along the Danube riverfront complement its historical architecture. The skyline is dominated by the new capital's massive castle, rebuilt in the 1950s with white stone walls and the ubiquitous red tiled roof.

Alexander Dubček, once leader of Czechoslovakia, was exiled to Bratislava, the guidebook tells us, after he was expelled from the Communist party. It was his attempted reforms that led to the 'Prague Spring' anti-Communist movement in 1968. The Soviet Union quelled Springtime by invading Czechoslovakia and deposing Dubček, who was taken to Moscow and allegedly poisoned with radioactive strontium. It was against this invasion that the young Jan Palach set himself on fire – a famous image literally burned into history. It reminds me of the Italian writer who later set himself on fire in St Peter's Square in Rome to protest against the Catholic Church's discrimination against homosexuality. Such an unthinkable act, self-immolation, making a sacrificial offering of one's own body.

The last time this was the Slovak Republic, in 1939, the government was complicit in rounding up Jews and other dissidents (including gays) and sending them to Terezin and other camps. So all in all I think it only fitting under the circumstances to go out there and be relentlessly and unapologetically gay! The *New York Times* named Bratislava amongst its Five Great Gay Destinations in 2005 and tonight I'm determined to go to the Apollon and check out twenty-first century new gay Europe.

*   *   *   *   *   *   *

Campsites and campervans don't make for the best dressing rooms for a night out at the old discotheque. My other problem is that most of the clothes I brought would definitely be categorised under the 'practical' label and not 'nightclub attire'. Still, sensible shoes mean I won't have sore feet in the morning. I head off to the camp loos and leave Danny to change in the van, as I'm already treated to his prancing around in tighty-whiteys twice a day and they're not getting any whiter. Do boys have no shame in the underwear department? Mind you, it's not so long ago that men's Y-fronts and boxers were the staple of every trendy young lesbian's knicker drawer. Thank God these days we have girl boxers and boy-leg briefs so at least we're not uncomfortably lumpy in the nether regions any more.

I settle for a black vest-top with the words 'trailor trash' emblazoned over a curvaceous blonde in dungarees, juxtaposing with my rather flat chest beneath, and my best jeans – the ones with fewest holes. I do my make-up. Well, when I say I do my make-up, that might conjure up images of a woman who knows what she's doing with the stuff, whereas all I own is one eyeliner which I squintily and inexpertly smear along my eyelids; some old and clumpy mascara which I only brought along to get rid of and which leaves dots and splots all around my eyes; and Max Factor's Creme Puff Gay Whisper powder (clearly bought only for the name, and in a shade of orangey-brown which makes me look pretty Eastern European, to my eyes, so I'll blend right in). I can't fathom how some women do this whole make-up routine every day – 'putting on their face'. My face is just there, every day, not getting any younger.

I attempt to sweep up my hair into a semblance of a Hoxton fin but it's kind of outgrown that style and is a bit too

Mr Whippy-looking, so instead I put my trusty beanie back on and skew it to what I consider a rather jaunty angle. When I climb back into the van Danny wolf-whistles.

'You're wearing make-up!' he smirks.

I shrug, a bit self-consciously. Never heard of a lipstick lesbian? Ari is less appreciative.

'You look like a boy,' he challenges. 'And you smell like one too.'

'Oh, yeah, Danny, I hope you don't mind but I borrowed your aftershave,' I admit.

'The Drakkar?' Danny gives me a playful cuff on the ear. 'We'll smell like twins.'

'Yeah, we can see who pulls more,' I challenge wickedly, pinning Danny down on the seat and drawing a thick line of eyeliner under his lashes (which, I note, are longer than mine).

Danny pushes me off but doesn't entirely manage to wipe off the kohl with his ham fists.

'Listen, Ari, are you going to be OK?' he asks, with what I can tell is meant to be fatherly concern, and I suddenly realise that I hadn't even considered the fact that we're leaving a not-yet-thirteen-year-old boy alone in a campervan while we go off partying. I have a moment of panic. Pictures of kidnapped children flash before my eyes. But looking at Ari is enough to persuade me that he is more the Home Alone type – resourceful and resilient with more than a touch of this-is-my-house-I-have-to-defend-it. He doesn't answer straight away – the silence presumably meant to convey his disdain of the patronising question.

'Yes,' He answers tersely when Danny continues to stare at him. 'I can look after myself. I'm on my own all the time at home.'

'No you're not,' Danny cuts in, rushing to the defence of his ex, or perhaps exculpating himself.

'Yeah I am, when Mum's at work or in hospital.'

'Only for a couple of hours maybe, and your neighbour looks after you when your mum's in hospital... usually. Anyway, we'll only be a couple of hours, won't we Casey?' Danny looks to me for some sort of backup. 'Listen, maybe I should stay with him?' he whispers to me when Ari's back is turned.

'Well, maybe we shouldn't go at all,' I whisper back, hoping Danny won't agree. 'Or maybe we should take him with us?'

'I *can* hear you,' Ari pipes up from the corner (I guess an ice cream van isn't a big enough space to hold secret conversations). 'You can go. I'll be fine. I'm old enough to look after myself. And anyway,' he pauses for effect, 'you both look like drag queens, I wouldn't be seen dead with you!'

* * * * * * *

The *Apollon* is dark and cavernous. It's Thursday night so it's not so busy at first, and come eleven o'clock Danny and I are feeling tired and ready to go back to check on Ari (even though we've asked the campsite's owner to keep an eye on the van). But eleven seems to be the magic hour for clubbing in Bratislava, and the Apollon is now beginning to fill up with asymmetric haircuts and nineties-clad youth. So we decide to stick around for a little while longer. We've been playing 'round Europe by beer', tasting every brand on offer – Czech Staropramen, Bavarian Schoferhoffer and Ukrainian Obolon (pronounced Avalon or thereabouts). It's taken the edge off the cheesy eighties pop the DJ's been playing all night. Danny is *not* impressed – devotee that he is of China White, Ministry of Sound and Fabric.

I was also amused when Danny went to the loo and I watched about ten guys follow him with their eyes, and two of them with their feet. Must be the eyeliner. Actually, it's not just the eyeliner. I've noticed that Danny gets just as much attention from the boys as the girls – lucky beggar. Thank God he's quite an enlightened twenty-first century guy, otherwise I'd never bring him to a place like this.

He emerges with a wry smile on his face, so I assume that he noticed his followers.

'You didn't tell me I still have eye make-up on.'

'Oh, that. Well, it suits you.'

'I look like Tim Curry in *Rocky Horror*.'

'Then you fit in perfectly, my dear.' I pat him proprietorially on the arm and order him another Obolon.

'So, tell me, Casey,' he swivels his bar stool to face me, our knees knocking together, 'how's the trip working out for you so far?'

I realise this is the first time since setting off that Danny and I have been away from Ari and able to talk properly. Our last little heart-to-heart was back in my kitchen in Tulse Hill when he made me cry. Well, all right, *he* didn't make me cry as such, but nevertheless. Anyway, how to sum up my experiences so far? Getting high in Amsterdam searching for utopia; reuniting young Peter with his East German grandfather in Berlin; Ari losing it after my inept questioning at the campsite and running off and getting a black eye; visiting a Czech concentration camp; picking up a garrulous bourgeois Socialist who never shuts up; oh, and discovering that I kind of fancy Danny's ex who has cancer…

'Yeah, good,' I say, my Britishness taking over. 'How's it going for you, Danny?'

He shifts on his bar stool and gives me a look as if sizing up how to approach his 'yeah, good' in return. But Danny's time abroad, it seems, has cured him of some of his British reticence, as he now looks me in the eyes and says: 'I just haven't got the first idea about how to handle Ari, Casey. He wants nothing to do with me. And I can't really blame him after all these years.'

'Wow. Yeah, that's a tough one,' I blurt out. My counselling skills are second to none, I feel, especially after all those Obolons. I wasn't prepared for Danny opening up like this. I wish *I* was as open and easy.

'I should have stayed.' He's already continuing, ignoring my uselessness. 'I should have been there for him. I could've tried to be a proper father instead of running away.'

'...with your secretary?'

Danny gives me a sharp look. But if I've overstepped a line, it's a well-trampled one – his nickname as far back as I can remember has been Romeo.

'I didn't run off with Sadie.'

'You *didn't*? That's what everyone said. Mum heard it from the verger at the church whose cousin used to do the hair of someone who worked at Niobe's college in Derby, and she said it was the talk of the town: you leaving Niobe and "running off to America with that floosie" – quote.' I make those irritating little bunny ears signs for quote marks before I can stop myself. No one had mentioned a baby – that was obviously an embarrassing family secret too far.

Danny looks deep into his beer bottle for a good answer, but it appears to have evaporated, so he orders up another one for us both.

'It wasn't quite like that,' Dan says slowly.

'Er, wasn't quite like what? Did you or did you not run off to America with a leggy blonde secretary deserting your wife and child?'

'Things aren't always as black and white as you want them to be,' he says a bit snappily. 'I did run off, and Sadie was there, but she was nothing...'

I roll my eyes.

140

'Well, anyway, it was actually much worse than what you've heard,' he finishes in a quiet voice that has a slight tremor in it, and even I can sense the emotion.

Danny takes a big swig from his beer bottle.

'So, what happened, really?' I ask gently. He hesitates for a moment, then leans in closer until I can feel his breath on my ear.

'Niobe was the first, the *only* woman I ever loved. I mean *really loved*. And it was a bit of a shock to me at twenty-five. I was a confirmed batchelor, a bit of a...'

'A dirty cheating lowdown lothario?' I offer. Danny sits back and grins ruefully.

'A Romeo is what I was going to say, but er, yeah, I suppose I might have been seen that way by some people.' He quickly continues to stop me from commenting further: 'So I tried to fight my feelings for Nib. I tried to stay away, but I always came back eventually, and then... then she got pregnant and I felt trapped. I mean how stupid is that? There I was a grown man in my mid-twenties, who's found the woman he loves and she's having his baby. It should have been perfect, but I was an idiot. I told her to have an abortion, that I was too young to be a dad. She said no, that she was having this baby whether I stuck around or not. And I couldn't stay away, and I couldn't bear the thought of any other man having her. So I married her.'

'You married her just to make sure that no one else could have her?'

'Yeah, I know, I was so stupid.' Danny hangs his head unable to look me in the eye now. He's turning back into the little boy I used to know. 'As soon as the baby was born I started feeling even more trapped. I felt I had to find a way out. There was nothing Niobe could do. This perfect woman, whose only fault had been to return my love and give me a son.

This woman who I loved so much it tore me apart. She was *so* beautiful, *so* kind and gentle and funny and clever...'

He takes another big swig of beer.

'... So I started staying away. Just short trips at first, contract jobs. But they got longer and longer; and then I got offered a big contract in the States and I jumped at it. Never even stopped to think twice about Niobe and Aristotle. I barely knew him even then; I just hadn't been around enough. And just the sight of him made me furious with rage and guilt for not being a good father to him, and a good husband to her. So I went. I took that job and I went.'

'With Sadie?'

'Well, yeah, I mean, I needed an assistant, and she was a good one, and, well, you know how it is.'

I didn't, but Danny obviously did.

'So what about Niobe? Didn't she try to stop you?'

'I never told her I was going,' Danny says with a grimace. 'I just packed up one day while she was round at her friend's house with Ari, and I left. I didn't contact her, or anyone, for about two years. By then it was all just too late. I'd ruined the only really good thing that ever happened to me.'

Danny falls into a silence, and I join him, not knowing what to say to him. Am I shocked? Yes, a bit, despite having known him all my childhood years and knowing his tendencies. But he's still my best friend. I summon the barman and ask him to bring us something strong and medicinal. Alcohol – fuel of champion world-putter-righters. The barman takes one look at Danny's downcast face, which somehow lends him an air of Caravaggio-like tragedy, and brings out a small bottle from under the counter, and assures us it is: 'Very good thing.'

And three small glasses. Clearly medicinal drinking is not to be entered into alone. He pours us each a very generous tot of a clear viscous-looking liquid.

'*Na zdravie!*' the barman salutes us before downing his in one.

'Cheers,' Danny and I say with little enthusiasm and upend our glasses too.

The deceptively innocent-looking liquid takes my breath (and mouth lining) away.

'Tastes like meths,' I splutter.

The barman grins.

'Slivovitza,' he says triumphantly, pointing at little blue berries on the bottle which turn out to be plums.

Plums mixed with rocket fuel. The legal version is 40 per cent proof, he tells us, but the homebrew we have just imbibed is his own personal stash of 70 per cent. After taking another shot while we're still recovering, he leaves us the rest of this bottle of 'very good thing', presumably in the kind hope that if we can't drown our sorrows we can just burn them out of our heads.

'So, this trip is your attempt to make good?' I ask Danny when I've recovered enough to speak, and find my tongue looser than before.

He shrugs, knocks back another slug of meths and tries to smile weakly.

'Yeah, I guess,' He says, and I find myself wishing fervently that it works out for him, Ari and Niobe. There must be some happy endings left in the world, surely? And I put all unwholesome thoughts of my own about Niobe to the back of my mind. Or as far back as I can – out of reach of the Slivovitza mind-stripper anyway.

* * * * * * *

Another hour and all the Slivovitza is drunk. And so are we. Completely. Danny and I make our tipsy way to the door and flag down a taxi. In the back, Danny leans his head against

143

my shoulder and is promptly asleep, like a toddler after an emotional day at playgroup.

Somehow we get back to the campsite in one piece and stagger into the van, tripping over bags and waking Ari in the process.

'You two stink of booze,' he says grumpily.

'And you, young man, stink of… uncouth youth,' I retaliate, pleased with my rhyme. He turns over and ignores us both while we shrug out of our dancing clothes and into PJs, in my case, or just pants, in Danny's.

I fall into bed, only to find my Slivovitaza'd brain defenceless against the old dreams of she-who-must-not-be-named. Waves of clear liquid wash over my head, over her head, and I'm trying to swallow it down but there's too much and I can't breathe. I can't breathe.

* * * * * * *

At some ungodly hour of the morning I'm rudely awakened by someone shouting and throwing stuff around inside the van. My head is pounding and when I try to open my eyes the glare of sunlight through the window is excruciating. I try to turn over to go back to sleep but the motion is not good. I retch involuntarily and suddenly the taste of bile is in my mouth making a bid for freedom. Nowhere to go buddy. I launch myself towards the toilet cubicle only to be met in mid-air by an all-in wrestler who turns me around and bundles me out of the back door of the van, in my PJs.

* * * * * * *

The sudden rush of fresh air and the manner of my ejection from the van on to the daisies seem to have shocked the vomit

144

into retreat. Danny, the wrestler, is standing in the door of the van looking at me like I've just beamed down from another planet.

'Feeling better now, are we?' he asks gaily, smiling.

I hate him. I try to say this to him but opening my mouth right now is not a good option. How come he's not suffering?

'Casey, we're going to have to get going,' he says.

'Go without me,' I mumble into the grass, still not properly awake.

'Don't be stupid. Come on. You'll be fine once you've had something to eat. I brought you a bacon butty.'

My stomach turns at the thought of food but then Ari appears with a bottle of water, grinning like a Cheshire cat. He offers it to me.

'Thanks Ari.' I remember my promise to myself to be nice and I ignore his grin, although truth be told he actually looks quite concerned as well.

'You should get a shower. You need it,' Danny suggests. He's no Florence Nightingale, that's for sure, but I guess he means well.

I look down at myself, sitting here in my men's pyjamas like a teenager on a back garden camp out. I have one sock on and a smear of eyeliner on the back of my hand. Danny catches the look of horror.

'You should see your face,' he says, grinning.

* * * * * * *

By the time I regain some semblance of normal service it's late afternoon and we're crossing the Hungarian border into Croatia. I briefly poke my head up to see out of the window. Croatia looks pretty, but I'm in no fit state to really enjoy it. So I just sit in the back of the van and look wanly out of the window at the countryside. I feel rather like a Victorian lady in the *Spinsters Abroad* book Danny bought me, only I'm sure they wouldn't have overdone it on the Slivovitza like I did. Danny and Ari sit up front, and I hope that a bit of father-son bonding might take place in my absence. Although all I can hear is loud, angry-sounding hip-hop coming from the van stereo, Ari's choice presumably. I'm glad I'm safe here in the back with my ladies, sipping tea.

* * * * * * *

Next day we cross into the former Yugoslavia, which, since the Wall Fall and much brutal in-fighting, split into Croatia, Bosnia and Herzegovina, Serbia and Montenegro, Macedonia and arguably (most arguably) Kosovo. In fact the changes are ongoing and history is still very much in the making: Last Saturday, a week ago today, Europe's newest country was born – Montenegro. Having kind of missed out on Croatia I'm determined to see this little parcel of land which has just gained independence from Serbia.

Talking of newfound independent states, I've been thinking about how I feel, now that we're truly underway on our little adventure. I mean, how I feel apart from the hangover. I guess Danny's questioning in the club set me off. In some ways my soul feels like it's expanding into these new horizons, but at the same time I realise that, just like my Victorian counterparts in their carriages, I'm only sightseeing from a safe distance.

Yesterday I crossed Hungary without even knowing it. Today I'm speeding through Croatia and into Bosnia and Herzegovina – places which have been torn apart by bitter feuding and fighting in the last fifteen years – and all I'm seeing is the pretty countryside. In my protected van life I'm not sampling anything of the real flavour of the places I'm passing through. Not even their food. We're living on noodles and Western basics, which we buy at campsite shops. We may as well be at home watching the TV, or on a cruise ship passing through (although without the luxury cabin or Captain's table, onboard cinema, wave pool, and sea-sickness, although...)

I'm beginning to wonder if I'm really getting the experience I was looking for. This comfortable Western shell we're hiding in is like a thick screen between 'us' and 'them'. Apart from the odd traveller that we've met, we've not really had any contact with the real world. I don't know, this little adventure story seems just that – a kid's jaunt, not a real experience of what's out there – just a sightseeing trip.

Watching the Bosnian countryside whizzing past outside I can only imagine the war that raged here and the thousands who were viciously killed in the genocide, and I find that my imagination is not enough. My guidebook says that crossing the border between Croatia and Bosnia and Herzegovina means that we're traversing an ancient and invisible religious faultline. First the Great Schism of 1054 when the Croats opted for Roman Catholicism while the Serbs chose Eastern Orthodox Christianity. Then in the sixteenth century it became a militarised border between the Habsburg Hungarians and the Ottoman Turks (the Christian and Islamic worlds). These seemingly simple decisions about what one believes created the conditions for centuries of bloody conflict. Oh fateful, fatal, fissured, fractured faith. That, I can relate to.

CHAPTER 11

The Balkan ethnic cleansing service

'I must confess that I lost faith in the sanity of the world when I saw it suffering the painful disorder of this island.'

H.G.Wells,
The Island of Dr Moreau, 1896.

We roll into Banja Luka in the middle of Bosnia and Herzegovina around lunchtime and, full of new resolve to be a more hands-on traveller, I insist that we stop to have a look round, even although I'm still feeling a tiny bit green around the gills. It's another pretty town on a river (the Vrbas) and is full of tree-lined avenues and green parks. We find a nice-looking street café and, despite the stiff breeze blowing up the valley, we sit outside and order some Bosnian lunch. Luckily for us the menu has pictures, so we all point at items that resemble something familiarly edible. Then I get out my trusty guidebook to read a bit of the history of this place to the others.

Banja Luka is a place with a troubled and troubling history.

It was a centre for the deportation and extermination of tens of thousands of Jews and Serbs in the Second World War by the Catholic and pro-Nazi Croatian majority. During the 1990s, following independence for Bosnia and Herzegovina, the majority Orthodox Christian Serb population carried out an ethnic cleansing of the Croats, some of whom were put into more concentration camps. Tit for tat genocide. An eye for a bloody eye: a blind man's paradise.

It's hard to believe that this pretty town in the foothills, with its hotels, restaurants and parks, surrounded by lush green countryside, could have been the site for so much bloodshed. I realise that here we've crossed another invisible boundary between those largely peaceful revolutions after the breakup of the former Soviet Union – the Velvet (Czechoslovakia), Rose (Georgia), Orange (Ukraine) and Tulip (Kyrgyzstan) – into something entirely different.

Today there is an independent Croatia, an independent Bosnia and Herzegovina and within that a separate Serbian Republic (Republika Srpska) of which Banja Luka is the capital, and everyone now accepts this situation as the best way to all live together peacefully. Bosnian Muslims, Catholic Croats and Orthodox Christian Serbs all live here, although many are still refugees of sorts.

Underneath the Communist veil (and kept in check by it) some ancient racial, nationalist, ethnic and religious tensions were just waiting to surface when 'freedom' came to town. The ethnic Serbs, ethnic Croats, Bosnian Muslims, ethnic Muslim Albanians and others all took sides in the fighting on religious and territorial grounds. The same battles in 1941–45 had led to the formation of the Socialist Federal Republic of Yugoslavia in a bid to bring these tensions to an end. So, far from being new countries: Croatia, Serbia, Slovenia, Bosnia and Herzegovina, Macedonia and Montenegro, are all the original constituent countries of Yugoslavia – it's all just a little bit of bloody history repeating.

'So, who was fighting who?' Ari asks, looking a bit confused, and I can't blame him.

I try to clarify: 'The conflict started when the Serbian president, Slobodan Milošević, decided to try to extend Serbia's borders into Croatia and Bosnia. Milošević claimed that he was protecting the Serbian minority from the fascist tendencies of the new governments in the years before the Wall Fall. This involved terrorising, raping and killing non-Serbs, in what became known around the world as ethnic cleansing.'

'What does that mean?' asks Ari.

Danny intervenes: 'It's when one group of people from a certain ethnic group try to kill all the members of another ethnic group.'

'But I thought ethnic was something to do with hippies.' Ari screws his eyes up against the sun and wind.

'Yeah, well, it's sometimes used to mean hippy-type clothing and beads and stuff, but really it means a group of people who feel like they belong together because of all the things they have in common: like religion, culture, where they come from, that sort of thing.' Danny comes up with the goods, and good on him – I'm not sure I could have defined it as well.

'Like tribes?'

'Yeah, that's a very good analogy. Like tribes.' Danny smiles approvingly at Ari.

I carry on. 'Serbia invaded Croatia and Bosnia, including Sarajevo – the old Yugoslav capital. Then the Croatians and Bosnians started to fight amongst themselves for territory. In 1994 the UN stepped in and tried to patch up things between the Bosnians and Croats, which was partially successful in that it united these two forces against the Serbs, which resulted in more ethnic cleansing. Around 200,000 people died in the whole conflict.'

'It makes it sound like cleaning up,' Ari says curiously. 'Like they're just doing the spring cleaning like Mum does every year to make the house smell nicer. But what they're really doing is killing each other just because they have different religions and stuff. It stinks.'

Danny looks at Ari with what I think is a touch of pride. 'Yeah. It does stink, son.'

Ari looks up sharply at the word 'son' but doesn't comment. In the nick of time our food arrives, looking nothing like the pictures on the menu, and distinctly, well, 'ethnic'. So I stop the history lesson to allow us to attempt to identify and dissect our various dishes. Danny's 'stew' looks like a cross between goulash and curry with an unidentifiable meat and equally pernicious greens in a bright orange sauce. What I thought was a bland-looking spaghetti carbonara turns out to contain fish, which turns my fragile stomach instantly, and even Ari's sensible option of a toasted sandwich contains chillies and a tomato pasty substance rather like a lime pickle. It's not the best lunch we've had but it's more authentic than pot noodle.

After a few tentative bites, which are slowly and carefully chewed, with the occasional bit spat out, Ari puts down his toastie and asks: 'Why didn't anyone stop the fighting? Didn't anyone know it was happening?'

Ah, this old chestnut again. 'Well,' I begin, 'people did know about it. It was on the news all the time, and...'

'You saw it on the news? You actually saw what was happening?' Ari is incredulous.

'Yes, it was on the news. Far away in another country, more people were killing each other,' I say, more world-wearily than I

151

really feel, as if to excuse my own and everyone else's inaction.

'But, but... why didn't anyone *do* anything?'

'Well, they did,' I begin hesitantly. 'The United Nations...' Ari looks quizzical. 'It's an organisation that tries to keep the global peace. They sent in peacekeeping forces, but, well, they weren't very effective.'

'Did they stop them killing each other?'

'Not exactly,' I sigh. 'Wait, here. Read this bit.' I offer Ari the guidebook, which has a special section on what the UN did or did not do in the conflict; allowing me to dissect my lunch and slightly disassociate myself from this whole sorry affair at the same time.

He reads it quickly, ignoring his half-eaten sandwich. 'It says here that the UN peacekeeping troops were only allowed to make sure that food and medicine got through to the refugees but they weren't allowed to actually stop people from getting killed. They were forbidden from using their weapons. What's the use in that?' he asks angrily.

'Well, the UN is a neutral body...' I begin, but Ari cuts me off.

'It says that the UN soldiers were meant to be guarding "safe havens" for the refugees, but once the Serbs realised that they wouldn't take sides they just carried on and killed thousands of Croats in front of the troops in Sere..bren.. ika.'

'It's pronounced *Srebrenitsa* I think.' I recognise the name from countless news reports of the 1990s.

'Then what was the point?' Ari is agitated. 'They just stood there and let them kill each other?'

He's outraged and I can't say I blame him. I used to believe that the UN was this fantastic organisation for world peace and I even thought about joining them once, before I got my great charity job in London; but that was before Rwanda, the

Balkans, Darfur, the Israeli–Palestine conflict and every other huge killing field they've failed to stop. Now, like Ari, I find it hard to see the point in something that seems just about as useful as a tooth fairy in a war zone.

'The guidebook says that Sere…brin…itza was the worst mass murder in Europe since the Second World War. It says that all the men and boys aged twelve upwards were killed – that's my age. And the women were raped.' Ari's voice has been steadily rising during this dialogue and now I'm suddenly aware that people at other tables are looking over.

'Give me the book back, Ari, I don't think you should be reading all that. It's… well, it's a bit upsetting.'

'Upsetting?' He looks at me incredulously. 'All those thousands of people were killed and nobody did anything to stop it.' He's almost shouting now with the full indignity and shock of a boy who's just found out some of nature's hardest truths about being human.

'Lower your voice, Ari.' Danny leans across and places a big calming hand over Ari's. 'These people lived through all that.'

I'm not sure if any of them understood what we were saying but Ari looks around and, seeing several people looking at him, blushes and puts his head down.

'Sorry,' he mumbles. 'It just makes me so angry.'

'It's OK.' Danny's arm is around his shoulder now, as he turns to me and hands over the guidebook with a look that says 'I don't think you should be giving this sort of thing to my young and impressionable son'.

I raise my eyebrows at him but I don't protest. What do I know about age-suitable reading?

Ari looks up after a moment's thought and whispers: 'So, were the people here the killers or the killed?'

Danny and I exchange another glance and I shrug to tell

153

him that I'm not going to venture any more opinions on what we should be telling his son. Danny pauses for an instant and then whispers back truthfully: 'Probably both.'

* * * * * * *

After lunch we go for a walk. On all sides there's new building and restoration work. Where other cities we've passed through have boasted beautiful cathedrals and mosques, here they're in the process of being rebuilt. But we can see no bombsites or mortar shell holes, no sign of sniper fire or blood on the streets. And it's surprisingly quiet. We walk past an internet shop and Ari says he wants to go in to email his mum, so he and Danny stop there while I walk on in search of more history. But all I get is sore feet and more of the same – no real signs of the conflict except perhaps a certain heavy sadness in the chill air coming down from the mountains. History is so intangible sometimes.

* * * * * * *

I find a park bench in the sun, out of the wind, and sit to reflect on this place, our journey, and on what Danny told me in the nightclub. Love seems a frivolous thing to get worked up about when you're surrounded by war atrocities, but love and hate are two ends of the same circle I think. And love is one of the abiding hang-ups of our species.

I'd never considered that Danny might ever have been properly in love. That might seem harsh but I grew up with him, and our nine-year-olds' love was about as deep as I thought he ever got. I figured the long trail of heartbroken females inured him to real feelings. I'd no more think of Danny in love than Danny on the moon. But it seems I was wrong, again.

He'd probably say the same about me, mind. Not the sowing-of-wild-oats bit, but the not-being-one-for-love bit. I've never told Danny about she-who-must-not-be-named. It happened when we weren't in touch and I guess it's never come up since.

Poor Niobe. I can't imagine what she must have gone through. Ari too. Jeez. To meet someone like Danny and fall in love with them, get pregnant and have their baby even though you already know that they don't love you the same way you love them; or rather, and worse, you know that they do but they can't seem to admit it. I guess she never got over it if she hasn't properly been with anyone since, according to Ari. Does she still pine after Danny, I wonder? Damn. What a mess.

I'd never fallen in love until she-who-must-not-be-named, and boy did I fall hard. I knew the moment she walked into the room that she was the one. Of all the gin joints in the world she pulled up a bar stool in mine... I thought she felt the same. Until...what happened happened.

No wonder Ari was so anti-Danny to start with. He wasn't just the absent father but the emotional screw-up too. I can't quite believe Niobe is even speaking to Danny, let alone allowing him to look after Ari, but then I guess he is the kid's dad. Nib must be a *really* forgiving person. And as for Danny himself... Bloody hell. I can't pretend to understand that whole 'I love you but I can't be with you' crap, but it must have been killing him too. I wonder if he thinks that by doing this trip with Ari he can really make amends, and even get back with Niobe? I resolve to ask him later, if we get any time on our own again. Danny is really trying with Ari, even I can see that, and I think Ari's beginning to respond, maybe; a little bit, anyway.

* * * * * * *

I meet Danny and Ari coming round the corner en route for Alice. They're both looking a bit grim.

'What's up?'

Danny shoots me a 'not now I'll tell you later' look, but Ari isn't so cautious.

'Something went wrong with Mum's operation. They took her to a London hospital for special treatment,' he says agitatedly.

'There were... complications,' Danny adds, clearly trying to downplay whatever the reality is. 'They took her to the Royal Marsden. It's a specialist care hospital for...' Danny trails off and I realise he doesn't want to say the 'C' word in front of Ari.

'Oh, OK.' I'm not sure how serious this is, but taking Danny's cue not to overdramatise the situation, I add: 'So, er, is she OK now?'

'We won't know until we can get through to them, but she's in the best hands,' Danny says, shooting me another look that says, as if to a terrier: 'Leave it'.

Ari shrugs heavily and turns away, not wanting us to see how upset he is. Poor little fella. Here he is stuck with his estranged dad and some random un-motherly-alien type. I have a brief urge to give him a hug but Danny gets in first, reaching out and trying to put his arms round Ari's shoulders. Ari accepts it for a moment then gently, almost gingerly, twists away. Danny looks faintly hurt.

'I've been looking at our intended route, Casey.' Danny turns to me with a frown. 'And it's not looking all that promising. The FCO website says that you can't cross into Kosovo from Serbia unless you started off there. Plus, Kosovan local authorities might ask for "documentary evidence" of the reason for our stay.'

'Oh, right,' I say, distractedly. I'm not sure what official-sounding reason we might give for our stay in Kosovo: 'A

156

prurient desire to see this former war-torn country'? 'Searching for the meaning of life'? 'No good reason except for it's en route to our destination, so please could you let us through, Officer, we won't be no trouble'? We might have to have a bit of a rethink. 'Well, let's get to Sarajevo and see how the land lies. Maybe we could find a phone there and try to call Niobe?'

* * * * * * *

The road to Sarajevo is what you might call 'a bit hairy'. On the one hand we have the Vrbas river winding its merry way through the mountains below a sheer drop, and on the other hand a cliff-face. The road is narrow and the locals tend to drive like maniacs – overtaking on blind corners and dodging round the trucks and convoys of military vehicles on the roads like they're all in *Wacky Races*. There are also several tunnels, which are all unlit, so you go from blinding sunlight to pitch dark in an instant. The whole experience is like a fiendish arcade game, and as the designated driver this afternoon I'm very happy to at last spy, round a corner as the afternoon fades, Sarajevo, site of the 1984 Winter Olympics.

Danny has been quiet all afternoon but now starts humming a tune I vaguely recognise as that U2 song with Pavarotti singing in the middle, about a beauty queen competition in the middle of the war, Miss Sarajevo.

'La la la la la,' he sings pretty tunelessly, having forgotten everything but some words of the chorus.

'There's never a time for East 17,' I tell him firmly. What the hell did Bono mean by that anyway?

'Oh, that reminds me,' Danny says, 'there was an email from your mum asking me to get you to call home.'

'What on earth is the connection between East 17 and my mum?'

'Just postcodes. Made me think of back home, that's all. Oh, and there was one from Peter to all of us…'

'It was sent to me,' Ari pipes up from the back where he's been listening to tinny pop music on his PSP, shunning my choice of Kylie on the stereo.

'Yeah, well, it said hello to all of us,' Danny clarifies.

Ari pops his head through the opening between the two front seats: 'He said he's spending a couple of weeks with his granddad and he's having a great time, and that his granddad's agreed to come and visit his mum in England this summer.'

'That's great,' I say.

'Yeah, he says his granddad has started telling him about what happened to him. He was made to fight for Hitler in Greece and that saved him from being sent to the Soviet Union, and then he was actually there when the Wall came down, and Pete says that he might help him to write a book about it all if his granddad agrees. And Pete says he hasn't stopped talking about his wife, Pete's grandma, and that they must have been so in love…' He looks from Danny to me with an odd look in his eyes.

I'm thinking: yeah, like your dad was so in love with your mum that he ran away to another continent. But I say nothing. Ari goes back to his PSP.

'So, are you going to call your parents?' Danny asks, ignoring all this.

'What? Oh, yeah, I guess.'

'Your mum said I was to make sure to look after you at all times and that we should enjoy our time together,' Danny teases. 'So I emailed her back telling her about your newfound love of Slivovitza and that club you took me to.'

'You didn't?' I squeal, digging him in the ribs.

Danny smiles for the first time today and maintains an annoying silence on the matter.

* * * * * * *

In the morning we're treated to the magnificent sight of the sun coming up over the Dinaric Alps surrounding Sarajevo. We dress quickly, bolt our cornflakes and hurry out to explore this city that endured a four-year siege in the 1990s. The town is split between 1960s-looking Communist-grey tower blocks, rebuilt mosques and churches harking back to a more ancient civilisation, and cute Swiss chalet-style houses dotting their way up the mountainside either side of the picturesque Miljacka river. It's a confused, schizophrenic-feeling place.

Wandering the streets we see Sarajevo Roses everywhere, the mortar shell scars on buildings and pavements that have been filled with a red resin, a bitter reminder of the thorny conflict. An average of 329 mortar shells hit Sarajevo every day during the siege, and almost every single building in the city was hit at least once. These scars feel very real somehow, in a surreal kind of way.

Ari is intent on finding another internet shop or somewhere we can call his mum from. I suppose I ought to call home as well. We find a backpacker place with phone booths. It's not very private but it's cheap.

'Hello, Mum.'

'Who is this, please?'

'Mum, it's me, Casey – your only daughter, remember?'

'Oh Casey, well, you know we've been waiting to hear from you. Wherever are you? Are you all right? Is Danny looking after you?'

'Yes,' I sigh, too battle-weary to fight the patriarchy today. 'We're fine. We're in Sarajevo. In Bosnia.' As soon as the words are out I know I've made a mistake.

'Bosnia?' she shrieks into the handset. 'Casey, isn't that a war zone? Oh my goodness. Ted? Ted! Come here and talk to Casey. She's in a war zone! She's in Bosnia!'

The handset goes quiet while I hear my mother's muffled voice in the background telling my father to tell me to get out of there as soon as possible.

'Casey?' My dad comes on the line. 'What are you doing in Bosnia? Your mother's worried.'

I guess I'd better not tell them I'm headed for Kosovo then.

'Yeah, Dad, it's perfectly safe. The war's been over a long time. I'm fine.'

Backpackers young enough to be my own offspring look up with amusement from their computers and I just hope they couldn't hear my mum shrieking just now.

'Look, Dad, everything's fine. Tell Mum I'll email again soon. Everything's under control… Er, Danny's looking after me.' I roll my eyes at giving in to this ridiculous charade, but if it'll keep my parents happy…

'All right then, Casey. Do take care. Love to Danny and, er…'

'Ari.'

'Yes, Harry, that's right, well… um…'

'Well, goodbye then, Dad.' I'm not about to get into another conversation about Danny and Ari on the phone. I had enough of that when I was still in Britain. I feel, like I always do, both relieved and guilty when I get off the phone. Guilty that I should have had a longer conversation, but relieved that I didn't have to open up to them. I've just never felt able to communicate properly with them.

Beside me, Ari and Danny have been trying to get through to the Royal Marsden Hospital but it seems they've not been able to get connected to Niobe.

'She's due in for surgery later. That's all they'll tell me,' Danny says, looking pale, and placing a protective arm on Ari's shoulder.

'Oh, right. Well, I'm sure she'll be OK.' My reassurance feels as effective as it was with my parents. I mentally cross counselling off my list of future career possibilities.

Ari shrugs Danny's arm off and walks intently out of the internet shop, heading for Alice. I suspect he's fighting back tears that he doesn't want Danny or me to see, so we let him go off ahead of us. I exchange looks with Danny, who shakes his head at me as if to say 'don't ask' and I can see that he's quite emotional too. I feel totally unprepared for this. This isn't what the trip was meant to be about. But this *is* real life. I vow to myself to try to be more understanding of both of them.

* * * * * * *

There aren't that many roads into and out of Montenegro. In fact, on our atlas I can see only one real option – Route 18 that goes straight through the middle to the capital Podgorica. That'll take us right down south, meaning we'll have to go through Albania to get to Kosovo and then down into the Former Yugoslav Republic Of Macedonia and southern Bulgaria to eventually get to Turkey. There are so many countries to visit, it feels like we'll be lucky to get there in time for Christmas dinner.

We're just rolling out of Sarajevo to try to find Route 18 when Ari, who's sitting up front with Danny, lets out an excited shriek.

'Look! It's Arabella!'

You've got to be kidding me. Not *again?* But sure enough, when I look out of Alice's side window there is Arabella Rockefeller hitching by the side of the road with her Prada bag slung over one arm, and a sign in the other saying in rather pretty scroll handwriting 'Montenegro or bust!' Her Louis Vuitton scarf is flapping in the breeze as she picks her way daintily along the side of the road.

Danny pulls over before I can stop him. Arabella sees us and is now trotting towards the back of the van. I open the door at the last second.

'Hello again,' she beams. 'Fancy meeting you three here. What luck!'

Yes, what luck. Like losing a pound and finding a bad penny.

Arabella climbs in and arranges herself on the seat opposite me. She smiles ingratiatingly.

'Well, you've rescued me once again. What knights in shining armour you are.'

She pats me on the arm condescendingly.

'So, what happened to your conference in Bratislava?'

'Oh that was only a one-day thing. My paper on "Emerging Democracies in the So-called *Post*-Communist Europe" went down very well, and I've been invited to do some research in Montenegro – Black Mountain. Europe's newest country. How exciting! I'm researching what it's like to create one's own country after conflict. Well, strictly speaking it's *re*creating one's old country since Montenegro first existed in the fifteenth century, which is even more interesting, of course.'

She makes a small, almost imperceptible, grimace, which says to me that she would have found it much more interesting, and academically saleable, if Montenegro was a completely new country and that it's a little bit inconsiderate of it to have already had a previous incarnation. What a load of old Balkans.

'Well, hold on tight!' Danny yells from the front as he careers round another hairpin bend on these largely unmarked roads. Arabella's presence seems, unaccountably, to have lifted the mood, or perhaps it's just the opportunity to do some rally driving. 'Next stop: the world's newest border crossing.'

I grab hold of the chain holding up the top bunk and try not to think about that fact that it was in Sarajevo that a driver took a wrong turn and accidentally facilitated the murder of Franz Ferdinand, triggering the First World War.

CHAPTER 12

Broke in Black Mountain: the world's newest country

'If the doors of perception were cleansed everything would appear to man as it is, Infinite. For man has closed himself up, till he sees all things thro' narrow chinks of his cavern.'

William Blake,
The Marriage of Heaven and Hell, 1906.

'So what do you think of the Balkans then, Ari?' Arabella asks when we stop for a cuppa at a roadside café, which is really no more than a collection of dusty plastic chairs arranged round wooden trestle tables.

Ari shrugs. He's been pretty withdrawn all day, just sitting listening to loud music through his earphones, or playing some violent game on his PSP (I guess this isn't so surprising with his mother in hospital and all).

'The Balkan war zone, what a testament to religious intolerance! Under Communist rule there was none of this.' Arabella ploughs on regardless of the indifference of her best audience member.

Ari looks up briefly, and this is all the encouragement Arabella needs.

'Yugoslavia used to be Communist after the Second World War, you know, under the great Marshal Tito. It was stable, well run and there weren't any religious tensions as there are nowadays.'

'There was no religion, Arabella, it was outlawed under Communist rule,' I cut in, eager, for some reason, to defend the church and give a more balanced view to Ari. It must have been the phone call to my parents back at the vicarage this morning.

'Exactly!' she counters triumphantly. 'There was no religion and therefore no tension and no bloodshed. Tito was a great man who rescued Yugoslavia from the Nazis and reformed the country under Communist rule to prevent ethnic bloodshed. The Allies even helped him to do it because they recognised that he was a strong leader. Tito was one of the greatest Communists who ever lived.' Arabella's eyes light up with what I assume to be genuine admiration. 'His profit sharing system in Yugoslavia should have become the blueprint for all Communist states after the Soviet Union started to lose its grip. If he hadn't died in 1980 I don't doubt that Yugoslavia would never have broken up, and would still be a model of living Socialism today,' she continues, well in her stride now, and hardly noticing that she is losing Ari's attention.

'But he was still a dictator,' Danny adds his two penn'orth worth.

Arabella pulls a face, obviously hurt on Tito's behalf.

'If he was a dictator then he was a benevolent one,' she says, almost petulantly.

'No such thing.' Danny laughs.

Arabella continues obliviously. 'He maintained a peaceful Yugoslavia for thirty-five years. That's more than many would have managed. Under Tito, Yugoslavia was the most religiously tolerant Communist country on the Bloc. He feared religious uprisings more than anything, but he understood that oppressing religious groups only led to their beliefs becoming stronger, so he allowed a degree of freedom of speech unheard of in the Soviet Union.'

'But it's all still *degrees* of freedom isn't it,' Danny argues.

'Total freedom is just chaos by another term,' Arabella counters. 'People *need* systems of government. People *need* to be told what to do in order to have true freedom.'

'Now you're sounding very *Nineteen Eighty-Four*,' I chip in.

'And you two are sounding like wishy-washy Western liberals who advocate *"freedom"* without seeing that freedom always comes at a cost. Freedom is just a construct dreamed up by people who can't find their niche in society – poets, dreamers, anarchists, outsiders, loners, tramps, dilettantes...' (I wonder which category we fit into just now) '...to explain and justify their doing nothing. Society can't function without government, without rules and regulations to tell people what they should and shouldn't do. These rules are what you vote for in a democratic system.' She's on a real roll now, down a steep hill with no runaway stop strip.

'What I'm saying is that the current Western democracy doesn't work precisely because people are too ignorant to know what's good for them. They've grown up with a Western media that tells people that they can have it all, that anyone can be famous even without any talent, and that you don't have to work for anything or wait for anything but just have it all right now, on credit. In a Socialist system the government does what's in the best interests of the people and just gets on with it. Westerners look at such systems and say that they're dictatorships or that they're exploiting the people but actually it's the West that's exploiting people, giving them ideas above their means, filling their heads with Hollywood fantasies of what life is like. Is that any better than the so-called deceptions of Socialist politicians? If you asked the people here, they'd say that they *miss* the old Yugoslavia, the peace and prosperity and the multi-ethnic multi-dimensional Socialist culture.'

Arabella is red in the face from waving her arms about so vigorously and I surreptitiously move her super-strength coffee out of reach. She pauses momentarily, just long enough to give one hope that she might have finished, but no such luck. She takes a deep breath and begins to go on:

'Tito really should be hailed as a hero...'

'Stop it!' Ari suddenly bursts out, unable to contain himself any longer. 'I don't care about Tito or Communism or religion or anything else. Just, please, *stop talking!*'

He gets up from the table hurriedly and runs back to the van, slamming the back door behind him emphatically. There's a stunned moment of silence in which Arabella's mouth flops open like a fish.

'Sorry, Arabella, I should explain...' Danny begins but falters, looking over at the van.

'Ari's mum's in hospital having an operation today for, er, cancer,' I finish Danny's sentence for him.

'Oh lawks! I'm so sorry. I didn't know. I wouldn't have...'

'No, it's OK. I thought it might distract him to listen to you,' Danny says, before getting up and walking over to the van. 'Just give us a minute, would you?'

'Of course.' Arabella's eyes follow Danny for a few seconds then turn back to me. 'Is it breast cancer?' she asks, quite matter-of-factly.

I nod, still looking at the closed doors of the van.

'I had a lump a couple of years ago,' Arabella says, as if this is just another chance to talk about her. 'I thought it was the big C. But it turned out to be just a benign cyst. I had it aspirated.'

She motions towards her left breast and for one awful moment I think she's going to show me her scar or something, but she touches it briefly, almost without thinking, and places her hand back in her lap.

'That… must have been terrible for you,' I say falteringly at this admission; although, in truth, I don't know how it must have been because I haven't had a scare, yet. Touch wood. This is the closest I've been to cancer since seeing Kylie on her *Showgirl* tour last year, just before she had to cancel.

'It was the not knowing that was the worst bit. Waiting for the test results, not knowing if one should prepare oneself for the worst or keep a stiff upper lip about it all.' She smiles wanly, and I find it hard to picture Arabella, the confident hitch-hiking bourgeois Socialist academic, frightened by anything. But I suppose the threat of death is hard to prepare oneself for. I think about Niobe back in England, missing Ari and putting a brave face on. She deserves a medal at the very least.

Well, I guess that's Tito-time well and truly over for now. We drain our cups of bitter coffee in silence and head back to the van. I motion to Arabella to ride in the front with me and leave Danny with Ari in the back. When we get in I can just hear the sound of heavy sobbing, so I don't look in the rearview mirror but just drive.

* * * * * * *

The border between Bosnia and Herzegovina and Montenegro is virtually non-existent – just a big makeshift sign by the side of the road. After all, it's only been a week or so since Montenegro's independence. According to reports I read on the BBC website this morning, *'true independence'* won't be confirmed until 13th July, when approved by the EU, US and UN. Makes you wonder about who's really in charge around here.

* * * * * * *

I'd hoped I'd heard the last of Tito, given Ari's little outburst, but Arabella just can't seem to help herself.

'Did you know that the capital used to be called Titograd before they renamed it Podgorica?' she enlightens me as we emerge from yet another tunnel round yet another blind bend in the mountain road. We can finally see, far below us on the plain, a collection of white houses and minarets. It looks like a pretty Greek village nestling in the valley as it catches the last of the sun and I can see why Tito wanted it for an eponym.

'I thought they liked Tito?' I grin at her.

'They did,' she pouts. 'It just wasn't the done thing to keep Communist-era names after the revolution.'

A car horn blares at us. It's been a very long drive through a pretty mountainous region and poor slow Alice has caused quite a few tailbacks on the inclines today. Drivers are pretty hyper round here. Must be the Mediterranean climate. Lots of gesticulating and shouting and horn-blowing. Luckily we can't understand a word, so Arabella and I have been doing the Royal wave out of the window as they huff and puff past us at 40mph on the 1-in-2s.

'So, what happened after Tito died?' I can't help myself being interested now that we've got this far in the story.

'Milošević. He was a former Communist, but also a Serbian (Tito was half-Croatian), and when he took over in the late 1980s he envisaged ruling the whole Yugoslavian bloc on largely Serbian terms. The place was in chaos, economically and politically, and Milošević's ultra-nationalistic tendencies did nothing to help the situation. After everything that was happening in the rest of the old Soviet Bloc, and the Velvet Revolution in Czechoslovakia, the United State of Yugoslavia just couldn't hold itself together any more. The old nationalisms resurfaced. In 1991 Slovenia and Croatia unilaterally declared independence, then Macedonia, and Bosnia and Herzegovina in early 1992. This outraged Milošević whose response was that if he couldn't have the whole of Yugoslavia he would use the mainly Serb-national Yugoslav military forces to grab more land for an independent Serbia, and thus the Balkan War ensued.'

'So freedom brought conflict?'

'That would be a very simplistic way of looking at things, yes,' Arabella says patronisingly, but with a smile, as of a weary teacher acknowledging the naïve grasp of her cheeky pupil. Milošević carried on as Serbian president until he was ousted in the Bulldozer Revolution of 2000. A bulldozer operator, called Joe Đokić, stormed the state television building with his machine after Milošević tried to rig the elections. I've met him several times now. He's something of a popular hero.'

'The Wolfie Smith of Belgrade,' I offer.

'Yes, well, something like that. In fact Joe and his bulldozer inspired other Balkan nations to follow this example of largely peaceful demonstration. In the end even Russia had to take note of changing public mood and abandoned Milošević. After that, the colour revolutions began: the Rose Revolution in Georgia in 2003, Ukraine's Orange Revolution in 2004, the Tulip Revolution in Kyrgyzstan in 2005.'

'So, are you pro- or anti- the revolution if it's not a Communist one?'

'Communism is much more than a system, dahling. It's a way of thinking. It's power for the mass populace. Freedom for the working classes. Of course I wouldn't dream of backing a monster like Milošević just because he said he was Communist at one time. However, I fear that the new resistance movement was just a shoehorn for Capitalism. The truth is that it wasn't Communism that did for Yugoslavia, but religion and greed.'

* * * * * *

It's getting dark out as we roll into Podgorica, the capital of the world's newest old country, but we can still see signs on the streets of the recent election victory. There are banners and placards propped against important-looking buildings and drifts of coloured bits of paper confetti, the remains of political pamphlets and ticker tape, blowing in the wind. It's Sunday evening, but there are lots of people on the streets seemingly still celebrating.

'Where do you need to be?' I ask Arabella.

'Oh anywhere, dahling. Anywhere will do. I'll find something.'

She motions down a side alley, which is full of drunken youths singing and shouting outside what look like brothels.

Against my better judgement, and perhaps influenced by her earlier confession, I find myself saying: 'Look, Arabella, why don't you stay with us tonight and we'll find you somewhere in the morning?' I suggest.

She looks at me as if I've just propositioned her, a mixture of surprise and amusement on her face.

'No, look. Um, it's just that it might not be safe in the centre, what with the celebrations still going on, and there might be trouble.'

It's not like I *want* her to stay with us in our increasingly crowded quarters with all our oranges and potatoes and zombie-fighting gear.

171

'Oh tush, I'll be fine. I'm old enough to look after myself, and young enough to find myself someone to look after me.' She twinkles mischievously and goes to open her door although I haven't quite stopped the van, just slowed down enough to argue with her.

'You're staying with us,' Danny suddenly says imperiously from the back reaching an arm round to grab Arabella by the shoulder.

'Oh,' she half-simpers, doubtless thinking that perhaps Danny could be her to-knight in shining armour after all, shuts her door and settles back into her seat and starts making small talk with Danny.

I roll my eyes and drive on in search of a castle keep for the night. When will I be somebody's Guinevere? Actually, I always fancied myself as Lancelot. There was a large stained-glass picture of him in the vicarage when we moved in and I was always drawn to it. I used to sympathise with the poor guy – on the one hand a pious knight and best friend of King Arthur, but he just couldn't help himself fancying Arthur's wife Guinevere.

I think that in many ways Plato was right when he said that sexuality, in any form, was dangerous because it resulted in 'mental frenzy', making rational thought impossible. I tried it, but only once. In my experience love hurts. And it messes you up. It encourages recklessness. If love is blind then it shouldn't put on roller skates and charge round the china shops which are our lives, in my humble opinion.

Luckily for me there hasn't been anyone since she-who-must-not-be-named. After what she did I couldn't be blamed for never trusting anyone ever again. Inexorably my thoughts are drawn back to that fateful holiday in Greece, to 'the incident'. And then further back to the time when I got washed off the seawall in Scarborough and nearly drowned, leaving me with a lifelong fear of the sea. How could she do what she did and leave me feeling so helpless, like I'd lost everything? I can never forgive her for that. Almost without noticing, a tear has formed and run down my face. I wipe it away quickly before anyone can notice. All of that's in the past now. And the past is buried. Only the present matters. I shake my head sharply as if to dislodge the unpleasant memories, and drive on.

* * * * * * *

As it happens, it's lucky that Arabella does stay with us because both Danny and I have run out of ready cash and, being Sunday in the middle of independence celebrations, we've no way of getting any more until the morning. So Arabella pays for the campsite, and also for dinner, waving away any offers of repayment.

'All for one and one for all,' she smiles, flashing her Fendi purse. So we dine in style on the campsite's best Montenegrin fare of cabbage and pork stew.

'The biggest crime is that Milošević killed one more person before he could be indicted for war crimes at The Hague,' Arabella engages her captive audience as we chow down. She really is like a Duracell bunny, in many senses.

'Who?' Ari asks, seemingly much recovered from earlier. 'How could one death be worse than all the others?'

'Himself,' Arabella says gravely. 'He died in his cell in March this year as he awaited trial for all his crimes. He was the first head of state ever to be indicted for crimes against humanity. Do you know what that means? How significant that is for all world leaders? The precedent it sets for history? It means that in some future Socialist world even George W Bush or Tony Blair might be brought to book for their war crimes...'

173

'How did he kill himself?' Ari seems gruesomely drawn to death right now.

'Well, there are many conspiracy theories about that one,' Arabella confides. 'It happened only days after one of his key accusers apparently hanged himself in his cell. Some people say Milošević poisoned himself. Others say he was poisoned. The official view is that he had a heart attack... but that's not the point. The point is that he evaded justice by dying, however it happened.'

'But now everyone's better off, right, now that he's dead?' Ari surmises.

'Well, not exactly, Aristotle, no. You see when Communism was defeated, the Capitalist vultures moved in and decimated what was left of the economy. The same happened in every Eastern European country since "opening up" to the West. The Iron Curtain falls only to reveal the Capitalist clowns are in town. Capitalism brings nothing but economic, social and cultural disaster. Look at Russia – the West calls it a success story, but all that has happened is that a few opportunistic Russian Capitalists have made obscene amounts of money out of privatisation while the rest of the country has slipped back into the Middle Ages in terms of social welfare.'

'But what about religion? I thought you said religion was the real factor in the Balkan wars,' I throw in testily.

'Ah yes. Religion. The West is very afraid of religion, especially in countries where people still believe, like in the East. But Capitalism is the West's religion and Capitalism is what they believe will override everything. On this one point Communism and Capitalism agree.'

'But England and America are Christian countries and pretty tolerant with it,' I say, perhaps a little naïvely, even for me.

'Tolerant only because they know that most people don't

really believe any more. They know that Christians won't go to war *explicitly* over religion. They can't be called Crusades any more.'

'But what about terrorism and Islamic extremists?' Danny wades in, having finished both his and Ari's helpings of campsite cuisine.

'Make no mistake. It's Capitalism that terrorists are targeting, not Christianity. Religion is just a mask for them to wear, their propaganda smokescreen. People will fight for money, but die only for their gods.'

'But I read somewhere that while most people believe that religion is the world's biggest killer it's actually Communism. Stalin and Mao killed more people in their pogroms and programmes than all the crusades and religious wars put together.' Ha! I think. Got you there. (Never thought I'd be quoting my old man in public though.)

But Arabella is surprisingly calm about this revelation of mine.

'People give many excuses for the atrocities they commit. Whatever, in fact, they think they can get away with. The fact remains that as systems of thought and government, Communism and Socialism would make the world a better place.'

'As long as the world wasn't filled with power-hungry monsters like Stalin and Milošević?'

'Well, you can't control human nature, of course,' Arabella says calmly. 'The revolution will still come. Just look at Russia now – rebuilding its national pride and starting to push off the American way of life. I believe another Cold War will come soon enough, and this one may be a bit hotter. Nuclear,' she adds, just in case we didn't follow her drift.

This silences us all for a minute. It sounds to me like she's waiting for some sort of Socialist Messiah – one who won't misuse the power and who will bring a truly Communist way of life to all people who will live happily ever after. Now wouldn't that be nice. Although personally I find it hard to accept that Putin could be the anointed one. But she's right that it's not ideological systems or actual religions themselves that cause all the world's problems, it's the people behind them. Power corrupts, and human nature is foul and weak.

We take our plates up to the counter and head back to the van where, although it's been interesting, I'm hoping the lectures won't continue and we'll be able to get a good night's sleep – I'm rather tired from the day's driving and practically having to pedal Alice up those hills.

But Ari, it seems, has other ideas. He wants to go into town to call his mum. In fact, he's pretty frantic. I think all the talk of killing and suicide has played on his mind. Danny is trying to dissuade him, but Ari is adamant. In the end, Arabella steps up and offers to taxi us all into town so that she can take a sociological evening stroll. Exhausted, I offer to stay and get Alice cleaned up a bit.

Arabella's long speeches have drained me today and I'm practically falling asleep as I toss stray oranges, potatoes and pot noodles into their respective cubby holes and get the bunks down. Not that it's not interesting stuff. Countries in this area have formed and reformed and borders have moved, melted and been militarised so many times it's like a patchwork quilt. But when I start thinking about the genocide it makes me shiver. What drives one 'tribe' to try to exterminate another just because of some religious, ethnic or cultural difference. How are people capable of such atrocities? Are we all, deep down, capable of murder? Not just at a distance – like a sniper – but up close and personal, cutting a throat, hacking off limbs, turning the dial on the gas chamber and watching people die in front of us. How are we able to view other humans as nothing more than animals, or waste, and just decide that we are better than them and that they deserve to die? It's chilling. Way, way more than chilling but I have no words to describe it. Are all humans born with this capacity to be so utterly evil? What bewildering creatures we really are.

I think again about the persecution of gays – people who love differently. Not in a different way, gay people feel love in exactly the same way as straight people, just with different partners. In ancient Greece and Rome, two of the greatest civilisations this planet has ever known, homosexuality was completely acceptable (as it was in a great many ancient societies around the world). Male homosexuality was considered aligned with athletic skill and military courage, while women also took female lovers as the poet Sappho famously wrote about. Many Roman emperors (including Hadrian of the wall fame) had male lovers, and same-sex relationships were often considered more pure than 'straight' relationships. In fact it was Christianity, the religion of those who apparently believed in a loving Christ but who couldn't let go of the good old-fashioned fire and brimstone God, that crushed the acceptance of homosexuality in its steamrolling of minorities to create a uniform and subjected kingdom. Not that that stopped many monks and religious celibates taking male lovers (secretly in the cloisters, of course).

* * * * * * *

I've dozed off into a fitful sleep when loud banging on the back door of the van brings me heart-thuddingly awake. I stare at the darkness trying to recall where I am and who or what might be making the noise. Only Danny's voice calling out my name brings me back to reality. In fact, Danny and Ari's raised voices. I open the door.

'Look, you can't go and that's final,' Danny is saying to

a tearfully enraged Ari who resolutely refuses to get into the van.

'I can and I will! I'll go alone if I have to,' Ari is shouting at him.

'Look, just get in the van and let's talk about this.'

'No! I want to go right now. Let me go!' Ari is screaming and crying as Danny grabs him and lifts him bodily into the van. Ari kicks at him and yells but Danny is way stronger than him and he's inside before he knows anything more about it.

In between bouts of sobbing and shouting, I learn that Niobe's in surgery right now and the hospital's not giving away anything except that it's a bit more complex than anyone thought after what the surgeons in Derby Hospital found. They think the cancer may have spread to the lymph nodes so they might have to remove these too now. So she'll probably have to have a complete mastectomy. Understandably, Ari's very upset and wants to go home to be with her. Danny's trying to talk him down but he's way out there right now and I can't blame the poor kid. He doesn't want to be thousands of miles away in a campervan jaunting across Europe while his mum undergoes major surgery. But, on the other hand, this is what Niobe wanted – for him to be well away and distracted and *not* seeing her like this. Except, of course, she couldn't have foreseen the complications. Danny is clearly torn.

'Look, Ari, in any case, we aren't near any international airports until we get to Sofia, in Bulgaria. That's two days away. Let's just hang on until then and we'll call your mum every day and we'll see how she's doing, OK? Then if you still want to go back when we get to Sofia, I'll go with you. OK?'

Ari has stopped crying now and is looking defiantly at both of us as if we're conspiring against him (which, I suppose, we are, but only in his best interests).

'OK.' He finally sniffs, fixing us with an animal look that says: 'If you dare to go against your word I'll hunt down you and every member of your family and everyone else you ever cared about and kill them.' I'm beginning to understand a little more about what human emotions, especially fear, can drive us to.

Danny tucks him into his bunk and motions for me to join him outside the van. Arabella, it turns out, has decided to stay in a hotel in Podgorica rather than slum it in the van. Fond farewells were conveyed rather hastily due to the current predicament. Danny takes my arm and leads me a bit farther away from the van.

'Casey, I…'

'I know, you might have to go back with Ari.'

'Do you mind?'

'No. No. I'll be fine. I'll just… I'll be fine. Don't worry. You do what you need to do.'

'I might be able to fly back and join you later…?'

'Yeah. Whatever. Look, Danny, seriously. Just do whatever needs to be done for Ari and Niobe.'

Danny looks relieved.

'Can I just ask you one thing, Danny?'

'What?'

'Do you really think that doing this, this whole looking-after-Ari thing, and flying him back to be with Niobe, is going to bring you two back together?'

'What, me and Niobe?' Danny smiles for the first time all day and playfully cuffs me round the ear. 'Don't be daft, Casey. Didn't I tell you? She bats for your team now.'

CHAPTER 13

The long way round – five countries in one day

'I sometimes think if we knew all, we should be more glad to get away.'

Robert Louis Stevenson,
The Strange Case Of Dr. Jekyll And Mr. Hyde, 1886.

In the morning we rise bright and early, each of us embroiled in our own thoughts which, for once, all revolve around the same thing – Niobe. Besides the worry about the operation, a lot of things have now fallen into place for me, although even more still needs explaining – like why has Danny never told me this before? Now I visualise her face in my mind, as seen on the emailed hospital picture in Berlin, I think it's obvious – she has that *look* about her. You know, that inexplicable, indescribable *look*. A certain *gayness*. But there are so many more questions: did she always know that she was gay? Is that why she and Danny never got together properly? Did she in fact just use him to get 'with child'? Or did Danny make her realise that she was gay? When did Danny find out? Does Ari know? What does he think? Is it true that she's not had a proper relationship since Danny, or just no one that Ari knows about? Does she know about me? Is she really single?

I try to banish that last thought from my head as I look over at the boys washing up the breakfast things. Ari's face is still a bit red and creased from crying into his pillow, and a scowl the size of the Grand Canyon adorns his little brow. Danny is deep in thought. I realise with a jolt of rare self-awareness that their preoccupations with Niobe's health are a bit more pressing than my own musings, and that our collective priorities have changed. We now just need to get to Sofia as quickly as possible. After that, who knows?

Unfortunately there aren't that many roads in Montenegro, and we don't know exactly where the borders are, so for the next step en route to Sofia we have to go round the big black mountains in the east, south into Albania and come up through Kosovo, back down into Macedonia and on to Bulgaria. It's a bit circuitous but there are no straight roads in the mountains. From Sofia we (or I) can pick up the A1 and O3 motorways all the way to Istanbul.

We still risk getting turned back at the Kosovan border if we get asked for documentary proof of our 'intentions' in the region, but I'm hoping that one look at our happy little 'family' in our happy little ice cream van will be enough to persuade them that we're not terrorists. Or, perhaps, this is exactly the disguise that canny terrorists might adopt if they were trying to sneak across a border? We'll see... We wave goodbye to Podgorica, the world's newest and perhaps, at least temporarily, happiest capital (and to Arabella, wherever she may be and whoever she may currently be lecturing).

* * * * * * *

The first leg of our journey takes us down past the picturesque Lake Scutari where we cross the first border of the day into

Albania. The border cuts the lake in two, which must be interesting for boats. When we reach Shkodër at the far end of the lake we are rewarded with a beautiful view of the sunny Adriatic glinting azur blue in the distance between the shaded folds of the mountains. According to the guidebook this is where all the wealthy Balkans this side of the Black Sea come to holiday – hard to imagine given the poverty we've seen so far, but maybe we're not looking in the right places (campsites and internet shops)?

My guidebook tells us that Albania is also the world's first atheist state, since 1967 when its then leader (Enver Hoxha) sided with Mao instead of Stalin on Communist manifestos and destroyed all churches and mosques. What we notice most about Albania, though, is the poor state of its roads – not only are they preposterously vertiginous but also full of potholes, which we have to swerve around to avoid grounding Alice. The countryside views almost make up for that, if you're able to take your eyes off the treacherous road for a second, with beautiful olive groves and citrus fruit trees sheltering in the gullies.

At Shkodër we take the aptly-named Pukë road lurching through the precariously mountainous Balkan Peninsula to the Albanian-Kosovan border, which we reach around midday. After the FCO warnings about landmines, we don't leave the van to go for a pee in the woods for fear of losing a vital bit of anatomy. We do not so much as stick an arm out of the window as we drive up to the border crossing, and barely breathe as we are approached by UN officials who give a cursory look into the back of the van – revealing the mouldering sacks of potatoes and oranges, sleeping bags in various states of disarray and a twelve-year-old boy in a similar state of dishevelment nodding his head vigorously to whatever music he's got on his iPod.

After everything we've read and heard, we don't intend to stay in Kosovo longer than we have to, just making a dash across its lower reaches before ducking back down into Macedonia. Call me old-fashioned, but I'm not ready to risk life and limb in a violent area (even though I've lived next-door to Brixton for the last fifteen years).

Ari pokes his head through from the back of the van and asks me why there were UN guards at the border. I try to explain that it's because the area is under UN control, to keep the peace. NATO moved in in 1999 to try to quell the bloodshed and in the process contributed to a large part of the bombing of Kosovo and surrounding areas. When fighting subsided, and Milošević was finally removed, Kosovo was left intestate. Kosovans want to be fully independent. Serbians want it to go back to being an autonomous region within Serbia. Since 1999 Kosovo has been governed by a set of impressively acronymous entities: UNMIK, the PISG and KFOR (the United Nations Interim Administration Mission in Kosovo, the Provisional Institutions of Self-Government, and security provided by the NATO-led Kosovo (K) FORce). Things are still far from settled: in 2004 there were large-scale riots between Serbs and ethnic Albanians; last summer there were bombings and shootings in the capital Pristina; and in January this year the Kosovans' much-loved President Rugova died, followed by the resignation, in March, of the prime minister (the one before him having been removed for questioning over war crimes). We definitely won't be hanging around to find out what happens next. Perhaps, for once, my parents were right to be worried.

We stop at the Kosovan capital, Prizren, for a quick lunch and to try to get further information on Niobe as we've had no signal in the mountains despite Danny's attempts: At every summit he's pulled over, jumped up on Alice's roof, and run through a series of yoga-like poses attempting to get some bars, but enlightenment is not forthcoming. When we stop at a roadside café, Danny tries to get Ari to eat, but he barely picks at his food, only scoffing down the last two baklava so that we will finish earlier and go find an internet shop. So we soon find ourselves in 'Charlotte's Web' down a small side street, which is full of the usual complement of backpackers huddled over out-of-date computers. Danny tries to get through on the phone while Ari logs into his email.

'Nothing!' he cries out despairingly, looking to Danny for news.

Danny appears to have got through to someone who is willing to discuss his gay ex-wife's condition with him and is nodding gravely on the phone. Ari waits impatiently for him to finish.

'It's good news, I think,' he explains to us when he gets off the phone a few minutes later. 'She didn't have to have her lymph nodes removed after all. The cancer hasn't spread. But she had to have a more "inclusive" lumpectomy,' Danny puts the word in bunny ears with his fingers, 'and she'll need to have radiotherapy, but... It's all gone well. "*Really well*" they said, Ari...' Danny is overwrought and clearly just so relieved at the good news that he's garbling his words.

Ari and I look at him rather blankly.

'So the lump-ecto-mony thing is a good thing?' Ari tries to clarify.

'Lumpectomy. Yes, Ari, it's a good thing! Not a mastectomy or anything,' Danny adds, more to himself than Ari, and looks at me in slightly embarrassed relief.

'So, what's the situation?' I ask him while Ari asks simultaneously: 'When can I go home?'

'Well...' Danny pauses, 'look, Ari, the nurse said that your mum's going to be recovering for the next few days and they'll monitor her to see how she does before they move her back up to Derby Hospital. And she'll have to have radiotherapy when the wounds heal, but all the indications are that she'll recover really quickly. So... we could go back, Ari, but really she won't be in any... she won't be feeling very well right now, and everything's gone well with the operation and, you know, she really wants you to be here with me until she's a bit better.'

'But what if she doesn't get better?' Ari is still frantic, having wound himself up like a spring from the moment we heard that things might not be going according to plan.

Danny puts his arms round him and gives him a big hug.

'They said there's no more risk of it recurring than before. She's going to be OK, Ari, I promise.' Danny's relief at the news is palpable, although 'no more risk than before' in this case doesn't sound all that reassuring to me.

Ari looks up at him as if promises from a big loser like Danny are worth less than a burnt Lottery ticket.

'Listen, Ari,' I wade in to give Danny moral support, 'we'll go on to Sofia and contact the hospital again and see how well she's recovering. You might even be able to speak to her tomorrow...'

Ari doesn't answer but picks up his stuff and heads for the door. He's already on his way to Sofia airport.

* * * * * * *

We take the low road from pretty Prizren, with its cobbled streets and octagonal domed mosques, round the end of the Sar Mountains and down into FYRO Macedonia in beautiful sunshine. Apparently the FYRO bit (Former Yugoslav Republic Of) was something Greece insisted on when (FYRO) Macedonia claimed independence, because the name 'Macedonia' was already taken by the ancient Greek kingdom of Macedon while the FYROM is a Slavic Ottoman concoction.

FYROM is Europe's third poorest economy behind

Albania and Kosovo. It's hard to really gauge this when you're in an ice cream van surrounded by Western comforts, and visiting international campsites and tourist places. Driving through some of the tumbledown mountain villages with their ragamuffin grimy-faced but grinning children shows us a glimpse of another story – but one which we don't really get to read properly on our whistle-stop tour of middle-Europe.

We comfortably make Skopje, the capital, in a couple of hours. From here it looks like a pretty straight route up between the mountain ranges to Sofia. Danny reckons that if we gun it we could make it this evening, even in a vintage ice cream van. Looking at Ari's anxious face we both think this is the best option. Sofia was on our original route anyway, or not very far from it. The only problem is that by the time we get there it'll be too late to phone the hospital, so we'll have to wait until morning. Still, we'll be on the spot if Niobe does want Ari to come home. Although I think that's far from certain, what with her having gone to all the trouble of arranging this trip with Danny, right? But the boy's convinced himself now. Danny urges Alice through the brief motorway section outside Skopje and on to Bulgaria.

As we descend the mountain roads and I watch the scenery change from slopes of Macedonian pines to fields of early-blooming sunflowers and scattered olive trees, I'm beginning to seriously consider what will happen if Danny and Ari do go back. How will it change things for me? Will I really be able to go on, all the way, alone? Would I still make the same choices and gaily sail into places like Kosovo without a second thought? Will I be OK alone in Alice with those night noises mere inches away? Even more scary: what would I tell my parents?

* * * * * * *

'Camping Sofia' is a busy little field tucked away from the road near the airport. Despite the number of tourists, it turns out to have only a small café and no internet connection. Ari is all for us driving to the airport straight away, or looking for another internet shop, but Danny assures him that we can't do anything at this time of night and that we'll go to the airport first thing in the morning and get in touch with the hospital to see what's what. I think if he weren't so tired Ari would object more, but he eventually acquiesces. When I look in on him half an hour later to hand him a sandwich, I find that he's packed all his stuff neatly into his bag, which is sitting ready by the foot of his bed. He's also roughly piled all Danny's gear on his bunk as a hint to his temporary guardian that he means business.

Danny and I sit up round a small campfire drinking warm Bulgarian Pils. The mood is oddly sombre despite the good news about Niobe.

'So, what's the story then?' I ask him. It's been hard for us to properly talk in the van with Ari's cat-like ears radaring in.

Danny glances towards the closed doors and lowers his voice.

'I really don't know. Niobe's always seemed so blasé about it, I never know what to think.'

'But it hasn't spread, so that's good, isn't it? I mean, doesn't that indicate that it's all under control? And with the lump gone, won't she just… get better?' I wince a bit at my own naivety.

'I dunno, Casey.' Danny looks pale and haggard tonight. 'I wish I knew more about it but I was, well, I was too scared to look it up. I just wanted it all to go away, I suppose. It's a bit stupid, isn't it?'

'No it isn't,' I try to reassure him. 'It's a natural reaction. If you don't know what could go wrong I guess you can still be positive about it.'

'You mean I could continue to stick my head in the sand

187

and hope that it'll go away again, like last time,' Danny says morbidly. 'She was lucky the first time round. It was... I don't know, the non-spreading kind, and it was so small she didn't even need radiotherapy. This time she does...'

There's a pause. The fire crackles loudly.

I blurt out: 'I know what you said to Ari, but doesn't the fact that it recurred once make it more likely to come back again?' I'm not sure I should be asking this, but I am.

Danny looks at me sharply.

'Don't ever let Ari hear you saying anything like that,' he hisses.

There's a heavy pause between us for a few moments before Danny sighs in resignation.

'I don't know. I thought that when Niobe got in touch with me three years ago, after the first operation, that it had all gone away and that everything was going to be all right. That I could start trying to build up some sort of relationship with them, with him.' He motions to the van where we can hear Ari tossing and turning in his bunk. 'When she told me it had come back... I panicked. I nearly ran again, Casey.' Danny hangs his head and rubs at his eyes with the back of his fists as if smoke has got in them.

'So, what stopped you?' I ask gently.

'Niobe asked if I would have joint custody of Ari with her parents if anything... *happened*. It brought it all home to me how serious the situation was, and that this was *my* son.' Danny looks at the van distractedly. 'I think up until that point he'd just been this kid that I knew about, somewhere in the background of my life. Something I'd tried to ignore.'

Danny is shaking his head slowly now as if in disbelief at himself and I reach out and take his hand in mine and squeeze it, and I realise that the relief in him at Niobe's successful operation is only part of the story – there's a whole future

188

to worry about now. Danny goes on: 'If anything happens, Niobe wants me to have regular contact with him until Ari's old enough to choose what he wants to do.'

Only if anything *happens?* 'And if it did, where would he live?' I ask.

'With his grandparents at first, in Greece, but Niobe wants him to be in England. So if I got a place near Matlock he could come and live with me, if he wants to. If his grandparents let him... They're not too keen on me.' Well that's understandable, I think, but don't say it.

What I do say is: 'Hmmm. And is that what you want to do – live in Matlock permanently? Where would you work?'

'Look, Casey, this is worst case scenario stuff. Let's not go down that road just yet, eh?' An edge of emotion sounds a warning in his voice.

We sit in silence for a minute and stare into the flames. The soft crackling of the wood as it expands and splits is hypnotic, and the bright dancing tongues of light emphasise the quiet darkness around us. It feels like everyone and everything else has melted away, like we're the only people alive right now. Danny eventually looks up at me.

'Can I ask you something, Case?'

'Yeah, sure.'

'What was it like when your mum and dad told you they'd adopted you?'

I give an involuntarily shiver and wrap my arms round myself. I don't think anyone's ever asked me that before, and I guess I'd kind of repressed the memory. I frown, trying to think what to say.

'After the initial shock and anger... I suppose it was like everything finally fell into place, and broke apart at the same time,' I say slowly. 'I felt rejected and accepted in equal measure. I... I can't explain it better than that.'

Danny nods. 'And how did you feel about your biological parents?'

'Well… I guess I felt pretty abandoned. Like an unread book that's just been left on a shelf.' The analogy comes to me unbidden, as if my unconscious mind has long ago assigned this image for my conscious brain to find one day. Perhaps the product of so many Sunday mornings collecting in hymn books in my dad's church.

'I'm sorry.' Danny frowns, and although I think he's apologising for a different abandonment, it's nice to hear. We both fall into silence, wrestling our own demons and glugging on our warm beers.

Later in my bunk an earlier memory comes back to me of my (adoptive) mother singing to me. What was that tune? Something about… My brain traces the melody back to its origin. 'It's a small world after all… it's a small, small world.'

*   *   *   *   *   *   *

Predictably, Ari is first up in the morning and makes as much noise as possible as he starts to stuff all of Danny's gear (which Dan had removed from his bunk last night but left unpacked) into a bag without paying too much attention to the niceties of folding.

'What time is it?' I groan, turning over in my bunk to see greyish light creeping through the van window where Ari has pulled back the curtains.

'It's 5.45 Ari, for Chrissakes go back to bed!' Danny yells and covers his head with his sleeping bag.

'No!' Ari yells back, leaning over to make sure his mouth is near Danny's ear as he does so. 'I want to get to the airport and get the first plane home.'

'Grnnnnnphh.' Danny turns to face him and bats Ari

190

lightly away as if swatting an annoying fly. This is his sign of capitulation. 'OK. OK. But we may not be going home, Ari, it depends what your mum says. You know that.'

'Yes, OK!' Ari has finished packing Danny's stuff and heaves the overflowing bag up, to dump it straight on to his full beer-filled bladder.

'Aaargh!' Danny shrieks. 'Let me through!' and makes a mad dash for the toilet cupboard, tripping over Ari's bag en route.

With all this commotion I can see it's futile to try to resist, so I raise my head and am rewarded by a big fat beery Danny-fart right in the face.

Ari's face creases with the effort of not laughing, until finally it explodes in a snort of near-hysterical laughter and he dives under his sleeping bag for cover, as I'm left in the fug to muse on toilet humour saving the mood of the day.

* * * * * * *

At the airport I can't drive Alice into any of the car parks as they all have low clearance bars and I don't want to get her stuck, so I offer to drop Dan and Ari at the terminal and rendezvous with them in half an hour. Ari is insisting on taking the bags with them in case there's an early flight but Danny's adamant that they wouldn't be able to get checked in that soon, and anyway I know that he's holding out for Niobe saying that everything's OK and they don't have to go. Ari reluctantly lets go of his bag and I wave them off, wondering if I'll be waving them off for real soon.

I drive round and round the airport perimeter trying to find somewhere to leave the van. Eventually I give up and pull up outside an ubiquitous McDonald's to wait for the appointed meeting time. I feel suddenly alone, seeing Danny and Ari's packed bags sitting on the back seats... I have a pang of longing to have Dixon, my cat, sitting here with me to keep me company. Dixon, who turned up on my doorstep one day in the pouring rain howling to be let in, as if he lived there. As if I'd ordered him from the supermarket and he'd been delivered and wasn't going away. A bedraggled pathetic-looking monster with big paws and a yeowl bigger than himself, which reminded me of a small police siren. Hence his name: Dixon, of Dock Green. 'Evening all, this is your friendly neighbourhood watchcat.' I think of him now, being pampered in the vicarage, with my father practising his sermons on him, although not being let up on the good furniture.

* * * * * * *

When I get back to the drop-off zone, Danny and Ari are waiting. Ari's arms are folded tightly and he's not looking at Danny. Not a good sign. Danny comes round to my window.

'They wouldn't let me speak to Niobe but basically she's going to be in hospital for the next couple of days before they move her back up north. Her parents are with her but Ari's still insisting he wants to fly back. I don't know what to do.'

'Well,' I say, 'the only thing that's going to stop Ari from getting on a plane is either you, in which case he'll hate you for ever, or Niobe, in which case you're going to have to try to get a message to her and get her to tell Ari not to fly back.'

Danny looks at me for an instant, clearly admiring my pragmatic summary.

'Right, OK. Wait here.' He grabs Ari and tells him to stay with me, then turns and runs back into the terminal.

Ari looks at me quizzically and stays where he is, challenging me to make him get in the van. I keep a watchful eye out for the police who are moving on overstayers, and stand my ground. In a few long minutes Danny comes running out of the terminal building again and comes to a standstill beside the motionless Ari.

'Why aren't you in the van?'

'I'm not going in the van. I'm waiting for you so we can go catch a plane.'

'Look, Ari.' Danny turns the boy to face him, which he does reluctantly, hearing that tone in Danny's voice that sounds like all planes are grounded. 'I just spoke to your mum...'

'*What?* Why didn't you take me? I want to talk to her!' Ari is instantly near-hysterical.

'Look, calm down, I didn't actually get to speak to her...'

'But you just said...'

'Well, I meant that the nurses went to speak to her and tell her what I said and then she sent a message back through the nurses...' Ari looks dubious, but Danny soldiers on: 'So she said that she's doing fine and that she doesn't want us to go back home right now. She'll be in hospital for a couple of days and Yaya and Pappou have come over to look after her [his grandparents, Danny says in an aside to me], and then she can go home, but she'll still be tired and... So basically she wants you to carry on with the trip.'

'I wanted to speak to her,' Ari repeats plaintively.

'I know you did, son, but you can't right now. She's not... they can't take the phone into her room because it interferes with the... the machine,' Danny finishes hesitantly.

Ari takes this in and mulls it all over, looking mutinous and pitiful at the same time.

'OK,' he says, finally, 'but I want to speak to her as soon as the machine is out of her room. And... I want you to promise that I can go back if Mum says it's OK.'

'OK, I promise.' Danny makes a criss-cross over his heart

193

with one hand and guides the forlorn little fella to the back of the van. As he helps Ari in I notice in my wing mirror that the fingers of Danny's other hand are gently crossed.

* * * * * * *

After a quick trip to McDonald's (well, if ever there was a time for it it was now) Ari and Danny settle into an uneasy truce in the back. Ari with his earphones in and Danny looking helplessly on, and occasionally, futilely, attempting to engage him in conversation. In the front, I steer Alice on to our first straight road in ages, the motorway to Turkey. I find driving quite calming when things in the van are a bit tense, plus the engine noise of an ice cream van trying to reach 65mph drowns out any arguments very effectively.

The A1 runs between Sofia and Plovdiv, Bulgaria's second city, nestled in the mountains. Its hotchpotch architecture reflects both old and new Europe and the increasing preponderance of minarets announces our approach to the East. Then we're back on A-roads again, skirting the Greek region of Macedonia until we reach the border control for Turkey where we purchase our visas and off we go. At Edirne, just inside the border, we pick up the O3 all the way to Istanbul. I wonder what O stands for: Ordinary road? Outstandingly beautiful? Oh I do like to be beside the seaside? Oh My God, don't you have any rules of the road here? It is all of these in turn. And for the last half-hour or so, where we border the sparkling Aegean-Black mixture of the Sea of Marmara, and draw within sight of the city that spans two continents, I'm filled with the feeling that at last I've arrived somewhere truly 'other', 'foreign'; somewhere quite unlike anywhere I've ever been before.

Istanbul shimmers by the water's edge, straddling both

sides of the Bosphorus Strait which marks the boundary between southern Europe and Asia. Studded with needle-like minarets pointing up to bright blue skies it seems full of Eastern promise. I can understand why Turkey's bid to join the EU has provoked so much debate – it doesn't seem very 'European' at first sight. The city is bursting at the seams, with buildings on every spare inch of land, even when that land is one of the near vertical slopes that enfold it. And it's bustling with Turks and tourists. I'm instantly captivated, and I can see Ari staring out of the back windows almost open-mouthed. I suppose we've been up in the spartan mountains for days, seemingly thousands of miles from 'civilisation'.

I'm really glad that it's distracting Ari from thoughts of home, and after being cooped up in the van for days I wonder if we should stay here for a couple of days and look around properly – not just seeing the world through the strawberry-rose-tinted windows of our ice cream van.

When we finally pull into 'Londra Kamping' I'm torn between wanting to sit down with my guidebook and read all about this fascinating place and actually getting out there and experiencing it. I realise with a start that I'm a little bit afraid of experiencing it. I don't know if it's the Islamic quality of the place or whether the Victorian attitudes of my 'Spinsters Abroad', and the four comfortable walls of Alice, have sheltered me too much. I'm suddenly world-shy, so I'm really glad that the boys are still with me and that I'm not forced to wander forth alone – or worse, not wander forth at all. But Danny and Ari are also keen to explore, so we park up, pay up, wash up and head off into the unknown for the evening.

* * * * * * *

When I wake up in the morning I'm excited, in a way that I realise I haven't been since the start of the trip. The muezzin calling people in for prayers rang out across the city at dawn and sounded so achingly beautiful. Outside Alice lies a world rich in mystery, in difference, in sheer exhilarating *foreign*ness. Our little foray last night was a sensory explosion of sights, sounds and smells. The heat from the long, hot, dry day hung around into the evening, intensifying the heady scents of cinnamon, nutmeg, cloves, dried fruit and coffee in the exotic spice bazaar mixed with the sweet, sugary stickiness of lokum and baklava. The dusty winding streets left us reeling from the architectural beauty and bizarreness of the tenements, tourist shops and ancient mosques jostling for pride of place. While our taste buds were finally sated by the darkening waterfront where row after row of seafood restaurants vied for our attentions, offering live fish in tanks to choose from (although being eye-balled by our future meal was slightly off-putting). Just so much life everywhere. The walk back in the dark, feeling drunk with all that we'd seen, and with the lights shimmering over the water, was magical.

The boys are already up and I can hear Danny outside in the sunshine trying to teach Ari the words to 'Istanbul (not Constantinople)' from *Puttin' on the Ritz*. He's prancing around in mock-music hall manner with a ridiculous grin on his face singing, and trying to put all thoughts of the C word out of both of their minds for a while. As he concludes his performance he grabs Ari and whirls him around while he serenades him about his date waiting in Constantinople for her rendezvous in Istanbul.

'Don't even think about it Danny,' I yell out of the window. 'You'll never get a date in Istanbul or Constantinople. Not unless you're a good Muslim boy anyway!'

'That's OK, I don't want one – the women here must be really ugly,' he flips back.

'Why do you say that?' I thought the women I saw were rather attractive.

'Otherwise why would they cover themselves from head to toe in black veils?' he replies, making Ari collapse in a fit of politically incorrect giggles.

Oh Danny boy. What would I do without these two to keep me amused?

* * * * * * *

A quick perusal of my guidebook tells me that in actual fact Istanbul has had three names. First it was Byzantium, the seat of the Roman and Byzantine Empires; then under the Emperor Constantine it became known as Constantinople and formed his base for the spread of Christianity in the region; then, after a brief spell of being ruled by the Sultanate of Women, the city fell to the Ottoman Muslim Empire in the 1400s and was renamed Istanbul (meaning simply 'the City', or 'the City of Islam'). In the process, it was officially made totally Islamic, although in reality Jews, Christians and Muslims lived here side-by-side in a truly cosmopolitan society.

During the First World War, the Ottoman Empire was defeated and the modern Turkish state was established by Mustafa Kemal Paşa, known as Atatürk, the father of the Turks. He abolished the sultanate, moved the government to Ankara, introduced the Roman alphabet and Westernised clothing and, even more revolutionary, gave women much greater political and social freedom. Ataboy Atatürk!

Danny, Ari and I spend a glorious morning visiting the magnificent Haghia Sophia, a huge Byzantine church built in the sixth century, which was converted into a mosque in the fifteenth century, with its massive domes and delicate minarets. The equally stunning Blue Mosque, next door, was built by some of the same stone masons who built the Taj Mahal, and gets its name from the stunning blue Iznik tiles that cover the interior, making it feel as if you're inside a fishbowl when the light catches them. Iznik, incidentally and rather ironically, is also known by its ancient name of Nicaea, from whence the Nicene Creed, the manmade agreement about what Christianity was and is all about, and the source of much conflict since, not least in my own head.

I'm relieved to find that women are allowed inside the mosques (although only if you cover your head with one of the scarves they give out at the entrance, and take your shoes off) although if I was praying I'd have to do that in the women's area at the back, or upstairs. I'm not sure how interested Ari is, but he seems impressed at least by the size of these places and the rich tapestry of colour everywhere. He is, however, keen to get to lunch and an internet café as soon as the one o'clock call to prayer sounds, ending our visit.

We sit at a streetside café and have kebabs with houmous and Greek salad. I even feel recovered enough to try a tot of Raki, the local liquor, which I regret almost instantly as it turns out to be a quite harsh version of Greek Ouzo and takes off the inside of my mouth. I'm looking forward to seeing more of Istanbul's palaces, bazaars, mosques and museums, and definitely looking forward to my evening meal, but first we need to find an internet place to see if we can get through to Niobe. When Ari disappears to the toilet, Danny leans over to me and whispers urgently: 'Listen, we can't let Ari talk to Niobe before I've spoken to her.'

'Why not?'

'Because I made it up.'

'What? Made what up?' Danny's not making any sense.

'About Nib telling him not to come home. I made it up because I couldn't get through to her... You gave me the idea,' he says defiantly when I look askance.

'What do you mean?'

'Well, you said that was the only thing Ari would listen to... Shush, he's coming.' Danny leans back, leaving me open-mouthed at his audacity, or is it his ingenuity?

CHAPTER 14

Playing chicken in Turkey

'I never married because there was no need. I have three pets at home which answer the same purpose as a husband. I have a dog which growls every morning, a parrot which swears all afternoon, and a cat that comes home late at night.'

Marie Corelli,
Fortnightly Review, 1926.

At the internet shop Danny persuades Ari to check his email first, promising he'll call him over to talk to his mum if he manages to get through, but he's interrupted before he can even dial the number.

'I've got a message!' Ari yells, startling other internet users.

Danny looks concerned.

'Who from?'

'From Mum. Look.' He reads it out: "Darling Ari, the nurses told me that you've been trying to get in touch with me. I'm sorry I haven't been able to get to the phone. The operation went well and now I'm recovering. Yaya and Pappou are here with me and I know that you are thinking of me too. I've been thinking about you the whole time my darling, hoping that you are being good for your father and Stacey...' Ari looks up at me and grins at this, quite unnecessarily I feel for what's obviously a slip of the finger. 'I'm sure you're all having a wonderful time in all those exotic places you're visiting. Hopefully we can talk soon, but you shouldn't worry about me. Everything's going fine and I'll be able to go home very soon. I love you very very much, Ari. Say hi to Danny for me. Lots of love, Mummy xxxxxxx."

Ari is silent as he reads it through again. Danny practically wipes his brow in relief. I'm relieved too, although somewhat peeved at being called 'Stacey'. Hasn't Danny mentioned me much at all? Or maybe it's just her medication.

'Look, I'll still try to get through. Why don't you come with me?' Danny obviously feels that the coast is clear enough now, and takes Ari off into the phone booth.

I take over Ari's session and log into my own email: The usual junk mail and offers to '!NCRE@SE YOUR M@NHOOD 7 INCH£S!!!!!!'; a couple of worried lines from Mum and Dad. Nothing from any of my exes wanting me back (not that I would, in a million years, but it's the principle of the thing). Nothing from any other future lovers on the horizon. I suddenly realise that I haven't even considered another relationship since she-who-must-not-be-named. That part of me kind of died. And now here I am having these odd thoughts and feelings about my best friend's ex-wife, mother to my pseudo-ward. A woman who's lying in a hospital bed recovering from a cancer operation. Life is weird. Or is it just me? I reply briefly to update Mum and Dad, not mentioning Kosovo, then start Googling information about our next bit of the journey to take my mind off other things.

I'm trying to book us on a car ferry across the Black Sea as a bit of a shortcut to arrive directly in the Russian Federation rather than having to drive round through Georgia. It looks like there's a ferry '2 or 3 times a week' from Trabzon to Sochi. It costs maybe 2000–3000 roubles which, my trusty internet currency exchange website tells me, is around £40–£60 (per passenger I assume, I can't find a price for cars or vans). I'm getting slightly concerned that we're increasingly flying by the seat of our pants as travel information becomes more sparse. But what the hell, this *is* meant to be an adventure.

Istanbul is like a breathing space. The first place we're going to stay for more than a day. There's a practical reason for this besides the beauty of the place (and the great food): we'll soon be entering serious visa territory. Both Kazakhstan and China require visas in advance of entry and Istanbul seems a good place to get them. We've travelled over 2000 miles so far, but this is nothing compared to what lies ahead – Kazakhstan (at least 1400 miles) and China (at least 1200 miles). So the ferry would save us some mileage, and give Alice a bit of a break. She's been doing valiantly so far, for an ice cream van that's more used to trundling round the block at 20mph.

Ari and Danny emerge about twenty minutes later looking much relieved, and Ari is even smiling.

'I got to talk to Mum!' he exclaims, like a little boy on Christmas morning after discovering a huge present. 'She's in re-habitation. The doctor says she can go home soon.' He's grinning from ear to ear. '…And she said that I can come home as soon as she's well enough.'

'Which won't be for another few weeks,' Danny hastily adds, to make sure Ari hasn't got the wrong idea.

'Oh, and I told her your name isn't Stacey it's Casey, and she said "Crasey?" She thinks your name's "Crazy Casey" now!' Ari is giggling madly. Oh great, so now she thinks I'm just some madwoman.

* * * * * * *

When we ask around about a visa service we're directed to the roadside desk of a swarthy man with a luxuriant red-tinged beard who looks the spit of Barbarossa, the infamous Turkish pirate. With much charm he gives us a totally ludicrous price for Kazakhstani and Chinese visas for the three of us. Now haggling doesn't come easy to us Brits. We like to be told a price and we pay it, then grumble about it afterwards in secret. But Danny's worked in the Middle East so he manages to get the price down to something more reasonable and we reluctantly hand over our passports to this perfect stranger and arrange to pick up our visas from his brother in Ankara in a few days' time. Not at all worrying.

* * * * * * *

In the afternoon we visit the Topkapi (Sultan's) Palace with its stunning Iznik-tiled Harem apartments, and get lost in the Grand Bazaar, which is like walking into Aladdin's cave. We end the day at the Orient Express Restaurant at the train station down by the ferryport – the old end of the line for European travellers – under portraits of Agatha Christie who frequently stopped here on her adventurous way to Asia. It feels incredibly exotic to be sitting where she sat, no doubt composing her next thriller.

We're accosted dozens of times by Turkish shopkeepers and stallholders, crying out 'beautiful lady, for you only', and I can feel my inner feminist's heckles rising. They rise again when I overhear a couple at dinner talking about a restaurant in nearby Edirne where women have to sit in a separate section from the men, and where single women would not be served. Ari thinks this is amusing, but I'm horrified, and it's so much at odds with the more relaxed attitude towards Islam and women visible in Istanbul. I guess life in the provinces is the same everywhere – decades if not centuries behind the big cities.

The next day we go looking for Turkish baths and a good

soak, and I'm equally horrified to find that the majority of them favour the men – having either separate (longer) times for the men, or separate sections for men and women – with entrances on different streets. What are Turkish women supposed to do while the men frolic in merry hairy nakedness, homoerotically soaping each other down? Do the shopping? Cook a meal? This is not the Turkish Delight I'd hoped for. So it surprises me slightly that Istanbul has a 'lively gay scene' according to the guidebook, although unsurprisingly it says it's 'mainly for men'. I decide to give it a miss this time.

Four days, five mosques, two palaces, some whirling dervishes and a boat trip up the Bosphorus later and I think we have well and truly 'done' Istanbul. We even got to see the tomb of a bloke called Eyüp, who was a standard bearer for the prophet Mohammed (may his name be praised, I add almost automatically now having heard it so many times from tour guides). The tomb is, however, disappointingly unreminiscent of God's own country: Yorkshire. On the Saturday morning we set off for Ankara to collect our passports, hopefully complete with visas, for our onward journey. After that we'll head north again to Trabzon, and the ferry, over 500 miles away.

Ankara's (formerly Angora's) white high-rises glisten in the hot dry sun like Mediterranean seaside apartments, although it's landlocked and practically in a desert. Like a small mirage of London with whom it's oddly twinned. It lacks the charm of Istanbul but has plenty of great places to eat. Good job as I'm really enjoying the Turkish cuisine, especially the kebabs (a million times better than your after-pub drunken doner experience back home). Ari's favourite is the 'balaclava' desserts, as he calls them, dripping with syrup. They also keep him quiet – so everybody's happy.

The one thing I can't get used to (besides the attitudes towards women) is the coffee. Turkish coffee is so thick and strong you can literally stand a spoon up in it. You order it according to how much sugar you want in it, no milk. But all the tooth decay in the world can't mask the bitter aftertaste. It really is rocket fuel, but on our mammouth drive it does the job, as we set off again for Trabzon across Turkey's arid countryside.

* * * * * *

It takes us two long hot days to cross the rest of Turkey up to Trabzon. The potholed dual carriageway cuts through the scrubby, sparsely-populated countryside, briefly alleviated by the domes and minarets of simple mosques flashing past.

Alice is starting to grumble with the heat and dust, and feels like she might cut out at times. I'm starting to feel the same way as my stomach's been a bit gripey. Danny says it's all the doner kebabs I've eaten, and the heat's not helping. It's a bit like being in a tin can in the desert. Even with the windows rolled down the moving air is just as hot, so it's like being blasted with a hairdryer; and when the wind gets the sand up you get a thorough exfoliation as well. Alice's cooling system isn't up to blowing cold air in this heat – rather surprising for an ice cream van – so we're slowly basting in our own sweat in Turkey. Shame it's not Christmas.

Added to this, the rules of the road in Turkey appear to be more a matter of playing chicken. Drivers seem to drive as fast as they can, regardless of the state of the road, corners or inclines, and use their horn to indicate everything: from 'I'm here, get out of my way' to 'It's Sunday and I'm happy' or 'It's Monday, I'm angry'. Alice's horn, unfortunately, having never been altered from her former days of Soft Scoop glory, can't really compete, with her melodious Casio organ rendition of 'Greensleeves'. It may be very British to respond to the onslaught all around us with: 'Alas, my love, you do me wrong, to cast me off discourteously' but really it doesn't cut the mustard, and after several sustained bars of this, Danny and I give up on using it and resort to waving or flashing the lights. Luckily Alice is a little too slow to really compete in the chicken games, and even more fortunately for us, her brakes are still good.

* * * * * * *

As we eventually board the Trabzon ferry on Monday I think what a long way we've come since Harwich. The ferry is packed with huge Turkish families spreading themselves out with epic picnics of magnificent-smelling food. We end up having to share a table with some young backpackers who look like they haven't eaten (or washed) in weeks. They tell us that they've been travelling the old Silk Route, sometimes hitching lifts by camel, which explains a lot. Henk and Maria are gap year students from Europe and Rob is doing the Australian thing, travelling for fun and working when the money runs out. I ask them what they think of Turkey and we somehow end up in a huge discussion about women's rights and Turkey's application to join the EU. I suddenly feel like a student again.

'The problem with Turkey joining the European Union,' says Henk, 'is that it's still essentially an Islamic country. It's not a question of geography but politics and culture. The EU is essentially a Christian club. They don't say it, but that's what it is. Then there's Turkey's human rights record and their attitudes towards women.' Henk is a politics student at the London School of Economics.

'An' the unemployment,' adds Rob, the burly Aussie, in his broad twang. 'Ah couldn' git a job inywhere.'

Plus, of course you have to take into account the fact that, as all mothers at Christmas know, the size of Turkey is crucial – it would be by far the biggest country in the EU, and just look who our neighbours would be then.

'The point of the EU originally,' Henk is continuing, 'was to stop future war between member nations and to reinforce democracy as the political system of choice. But really, it was all about control. After the two world wars, European countries needed a way to control each other and make sure no one country had too much unilateral power. Turkey's just too big to control. Too much of a threat.'

Maria, an attractive raven-haired olive-skinned Tunisian, who's studying Women and Democracy at Leeds, chips in: 'Turkey isn't the same as the Taliban you know, Henk. Just because women wear a hijab doesn't mean it's something repressive that's forced on them. In fact, in Istanbul at least, there are a lot of fashion-hijabs. Some women choose to wear the veil to avoid sexual harassment and because they're genuinely proud of their religion.'

'Yes but that's *Istanbul*,' Henk emphasises by slapping his hand on the table. 'Istanbul is another *country*. We shouldn't confuse *Istanbul* with *Turkey*.' More hand table slapping. 'Just like the Turkish government doesn't represent everyone, just the enlightened few. If you believe what the *government* says, or think that all of Turkey is like *Istanbul*, then you'd let them into the EU like that.' He clicks his fingers imperiously. 'But it's all smoke and mirrors.'

Rob, Maria, Danny, Ari and I listen on.

'Look, it's all about where you draw the battle-lines. Turkey only backed the Allies at the *end* of the Second World War. But in 1949 they became one of the first members of the Council of Europe and joined NATO a few years later. It was also a founding member of the Organisation for Economic Co-operation and Development and the Organization for Security and Co-operation in Europe. So why won't the EU let them be a full member of the European Union?'

We all lean in for the big reveal.

'Because Turkey's more *complex* than that. Just because the government says they sign up to human rights legislation doesn't add up to much in the east of the country where many people would rather be part of the Soviet Union or Middle East.'

Smoke and mirrors indeed. Or the dance of the seven veils. Lift one and there's always another one beneath it hiding more stuff. It's the old freedom and slavery argument again. Is wearing a veil an enslavement or a liberty? And does that depend on whose choice it is? And is their choice really free or are they fooling themselves? It reminds me of the black population taking back the 'n' word, or gays reappropriating the word 'queer'. But how much of a freedom is that in reality? Isn't it just reinforcing the old values while pretending they mean something different? Can it be an act of rebellion to do the very thing 'they' want you to do? How would anyone know if you were doing it for your own reasons or theirs? Is freedom truly to be found in the language that we use, or the things that we wear? Or is it in our hearts and souls?

I turn to Maria, who's looking put out by Henk's diatribe, for some further confirmation: 'Putting the veil aside, no pun intended, what about those restaurants and places where women are kept separate from the men?' I ask her. 'You can't tell me that isn't repressive?'

'Kind of. Sometimes. But you know, sometimes also it's nice for a single woman to be able to get away from the men who might harass her. So it's also a refuge for women. And anyway, is it any different from when the British women retire after dinner to a separate room leaving the men to discuss politics and suchlike?'

'Hmmm. Yeah. I see your point, but that doesn't really happen any more.' No, now the men just have separate clubs to go to instead, or do all their business on the golf course. Is it really so different? I think of my Victorian 'Spinsters Abroad' who had escaped from a society dominated by men and by social etiquette, but who, in their freedom from these structures, found that they needed an excuse still, to be a single woman traveller. Just travelling wasn't enough, for the world, or for them, to justify their escapades; so they ended up calling themselves botanists, ethnographers, artists. This also provided 'meaning' for them, something to do with themselves aside from just 'travelling'. Something providing depth and meaning in a world where a lady's pursuits were rarely granted such profundity. Men don't appear to have the same issues. Their place is already provided for at the top of the tree.

I turn to ask Danny what he thinks, but before I can get the words out, Danny, being Danny, winks at the guys and says mischievously: 'All right lads, maybe we should leave the womenfolk to it and go and find some more manly pursuits, such as the video arcade?'

Henk, clearly a 'new man' looks suitably disgusted, but Rob and Ari jump up like the fire alarm's just gone off and follow Danny in search of their own raison d'être. My feminist case somewhat proven by this, I settle in for a long evening of verbal and mental stretching with Henk and Maria to see if we can find some more profound answers; accompanied by some doner kebabs, Turkish wine and some sweet, sticky baklava to feed the old brain cells.

* * * * * * *

An hour or so later, Danny returns with a sleepy-looking Ari and we all decide to turn in for the night. Somewhere overhead a disco is thumping out a strange mixture of Turkish traditional tunes and cheesy eighties pop. I find the rhythmic bass quite comforting and dream of dancing with k.d. lang (bearing a striking resemblance to Niobe) who has been playing a concert on board a lesbian cruise ship, but stopped the instant she saw me walking into the room and is now declaring her undying love for me – the famous feminist activist – as we waltz effortlessly around the dance-floor with everyone looking on admiringly. I awake hugging my pillow and with a very stiff neck, still a travelling spinster without a cause, with a very loud klaxon declaring our landing in yet another country and the feeling that I'm no closer to cracking this meaning of life thing yet. Oh and now I have a decidedly dodgy stomachache as well.

CHAPTER 15

Ice cold in Alice

'What good is religion if it collapses under calamity?
Think of what earthquakes and foods, wars and
volcanoes, have done before to men! Did you think that
God had exempted [us]? He is not an insurance agent.'

H. G. Wells,
War of the Worlds, 1898.

By the time we land in the CIS – the Commonwealth of Independent States that replaced the Soviet Union in 1991 – I'm feeling really quite ill, so Danny takes the wheel. As he turns inland at Tuapse to head into the mountains en route for Stavropol I climb into the back clutching my stomach. Outside the sky is blue, and fluffy white clouds skid along as we climb further up. I open the back window for some air, until Ari shouts that he's being frozen 'like an ice lolly', but I'm burning hot and for the second time I'm feeling as if the contents of my stomach are about to go on a trip of their own.

It's nightfall by the time we reach Astrakhan on the Volga river delta; forty miles from the border with Kazakhstan and, quite frankly, in the middle of bloody nowhere. Ari keeps calling it Azkaban and since I feel as if my insides have been sucked out of me I'm inclined to agree. Danny has had to stop the van several times for me to be sick at the side of the road, and now I'm wrapped round a bucket shivering, alternately burning hot and freezing cold.

I just can't go on, so for the first time on our journey we camp wild, by the side of a tiny little road leading towards the river. It should be picturesque and exactly the sort of rugged setting I'd imagined when I first planned this trip. Instead, all I can think about is a nice warm bath with candles, Mum's homemade tomato soup and wrapping up in my snuggly duvet in my own comfy bed.

I wake to a banging noise so fearsome my first reaction is to try to call CSI CIS before a murder happens. Danny is halfway out of his bunk and wrapping a towel round his waist to go open the back door from whence emanates this noisy banging. He opens the door gingerly to find what looks like a Russian Cossack standing there hammering on the back window.

'*Sdrazweecha! Shto vee zdyes delaech?*' he says. Or something along those lines. He doesn't look very happy and I gingerly stick my head out of the window, risking throwing up in the process, to see that we are blocking him and his herd of what look like bison from getting to the river, presumably for their morning swim. I point this out to Danny who does his best to placate the Cossack and gestures that we will move the van. The man says something else which doesn't sound too complimentary, so Danny leaps out of the van in just his undies, runs round to the driver's door and manoeuvres Alice back up the track with Ari and me rattling around in our bunks.

'Hey, watch out!' Ari yells, hanging on to the side of his top bunk shelf as Alice lurches over ruts and what feels like bison toes. He grips on to the chain that attaches his bed to the roof of the van until his knuckles go white. Danny meanwhile has turned the van and is heading off down the road.

'Hey, where are we going?' I yell through the partition queasily. I have visions of us arriving in central Astrakhan with me and Ari still in bed and Danny in just his pants.

'I'm just getting us out of the way. I'll pull up in a second.' Danny rolls Alice on to a large verge at the side of the road and our swaying eventually comes to a halt. What a start to the day! Still, it could have been worse – one of us could have been very surprised by a bison in the bushes.

After this very false start I'm feeling no better but we decide to push on as there's no point just sitting here in the middle of nowhere. And I'm starting to feel like a prisoner of Astrakhan. Traversing the Volga delta with the aid of a rickety old wire-guided ferry barge we eventually cross the border into Kazakhstan. Though one of the largest countries in Eurasia, Kazakhstan has very few major roads, which means that once again it looks like we'll be taking a circuitous route. I ponder on the fact that there don't seem to be any shortcuts to finding the meaning of life.

The road is getting unbelievably bad. It alternates between asphalt and desert track and some of it looks like it's been bombed to pieces and never repaired. Apparently Genghis Khan's five million horses turned Kazakhstan's grassland into desert in the twefth century so now all that's left is arid scrubland – over a million square miles of it. The existence of so few roads doesn't seem to have had any bearing on the amount of care and maintenance given to them and far from becoming more careful, the drivers appear to have become correspondingly more reckless. In the back of the van every jolt and swerve is magnified through my intestines, so it's a small mercy every time we stop.

And we're stopping with increasing regularity, as Danny is getting worried about Alice overheating in the semi-desert and

I have to admit that she's been making some worrying sounds in recent days. Perhaps we're pushing her too hard. She's used to a few more stops on her '99' rounds. But taking things slightly more easily makes our progress seem interminably slow. Stuck in the back I sit through the oven-hot day and ice-cold night, waiting patiently for my stomach to start obeying the usual laws of nature again.

I'm pleased to overhear in the front of the van that Ari's entire demeanour has changed now that Niobe's successfully out of her operation. He smiles and laughs, and, within reason, chats happily with Danny. He's almost like the nice little boy that in a drunken moment I thought I might have one day. Weird to think of it like that. Niobe can't be much older than me, so Ari could have been my kid. I could have a twelve-year-old son like Ari. I must be feverish.

* * * * * * *

Finally we roll into Aral, an important fishing port by the Aral Sea. I sit up to take a look around and find, to my amazement, that both my head and my stomach feel quite normal. The doners have left the building. Hurrah! I practically leap out of the van, eager to see the sparkling sea and maybe even dip my toes in. But what greets me is a ghost landscape: Single-storey white buildings clustered at the edge of salty mudflats, which stretch as far as the eye can see. Even the main roads are dusty sand tracks lined with shacks, which wouldn't look too amiss in developing world villages. Aral, also called Aralsk, reminds me of a deserted set for a wild west film. I expect tumbleweed to blow down the main street at any moment.

Danny and Ari arrive at my side looking equally bewildered. I quickly unearth my guidebook. It turns out that Aralsk used to be a huge port on the fourth-largest landlocked body of water in the world. But massive dessication in the area has meant that the sea's receded some 100 kilometres away leaving a totally dry dock and a mass of slowly-rusting ghost ships in the middle of what is becoming desert.

The drying up was largely due to the Soviet Union diverting the rivers that used to flow into the Aral for irrigation of cotton and food crops in the 1960s. According to my book the Aral Sea (like the Caspian) is dying. The concentrated salination, plus run-off from fertilisers, and poisoning from nuclear and bio-weapons testing in the area, is killing everything. Apparently childhood mortality rates here are amongst the highest in the former Soviet Union. Nice to know. Maybe we'll avoid the seafood in Aralsk, and the vegetables, and the meat. And the water.

Danski and Ariski want to find an internet shop to contact Niobe, but I've been cooped up in my sick bed for days so opt to walk around for a bit of fresh air instead and maybe to find a café for a nice cup of tea. Just as I'm tucking into something faintly resembling a scone, or maybe a teacake, Ari and Danny walk into view chatting animatedly with a tall, willowy blonde girl. Alarm bells start to jingle inside. What kind of Juliet has Romeo found this time?

'There you are!' Danny cries heartily. 'We've been looking for you.' He pauses. 'Anyway, um, Casey, meet Epiphany. She's on her way to the other side of Kazakhstan to work with a Christian charity project so I said we'd give her a lift.'

You have got to be kidding me! I mean I'm in a much better mood now that I'm feeling back to normal, but I have my limits and I think Arabella's already pushed those too far. What is Danny playing at? And is that a Bible she's carrying?

'Epiphany.' I raise my eyebrows. 'So, er, what do your friends call you – Piff or "Phany"?'

'Neither,' she replies, perfectly straight-faced, with a mid-American drawl.

'Right,' I say, smiling broadly at her.

Danny shoots me a warning look and adds: 'I'm sure even you can manage four syllables can't you, Casey Jones?'

'Casey Jones?' Epiphany says with a warm smile. 'Like the...'

'Yes,' I say irritably, thinking Danny didn't need to say that. 'Like the railway man.'

It effectively shuts me up, but somewhere in a deep recess of my warped mind a parrot from a long-forgotten childhood storybook is squawking 'Pifflebunk! Pifflebunk!' and I have to stifle a snort of laughter with a pretend sneeze. Danny and Epifflebunk are both staring at me curiously. Actually it's more like glaring in Danny's case. But really, what is Danny thinking of? An American Bible-basher for crying out loud.

We walk to the van and climb in out of the sun, although it's a bit like climbing into an oven to get away from the grill. Danny's looked at some maps of Kazakhstan in the internet shop and thinks that since the drive to the next town is a pretty long one we should wait until the next day so we're going to treat ourselves, and see if we can find a hotel for the night. I see that the decision to take Epiphany with us has already been taken without my consent, so I guess we're stuck with her until we get across Kazakhstan. That's hundreds of miles.

* * * * * * *

'So where are you from, Epiphany?' I ask as Danny gets the drinks in the hotel bar. I say 'the' because it's the only one in Aral, and I say 'hotel' because that's what it's called, but it looks and feels more like an office block, such that I feel like we're at some weird work leaving do, and let's not even go there.

'Beverly Hills,' she drawls.

'Really?'

I'm momentarily impressed until she adds: 'Near Waco, Texas.'

Oh. This gets better and better. I secretly wonder if she's a Branch Davidian as well?

'So, George Dubya territory, eh?' Danny shoots me a warning look as he plonks the beers down, but I ignore him. I'm enjoying my newfound wellness and am in the mood for a bit of verbal sparring.

'Oh yeah, we're very proud of him,' she twangs.

'Are you? I thought even the Texans had disowned him now.' Epiphany looks at me like I've just stabbed her grandmother. I decide to try a change of topic: 'So, er, what are you doing here Piff... Epiphany?'

'Well, I've been travelling around some of the early Christian sites in Europe. I just left Mount Ararat...'

I wonder, impiously, whether she met Noah while she was up there, and if he thinks the recent flooding we've been having in the UK is really due to global warming or whether it's God's judgement on Gloucestershire? I reluctantly tune back in to Epiphany: '...now I'm on my way to join a Church Mission project in the Xinjiang Uyghur Autonomous Region in North East China. I took a bus from the port in Sochi, only when it stopped at Aral I got out to stretch my legs and it took off, leaving me stranded here. And that's when Danny turned up and offered me a lift.'

She smiles and twinkles at her apparently God-sent knight in shining armour (an epithet that's beginning to get a bit tarnished, with me at least), then gestures vaguely towards the roof of the van outside where perhaps God is sitting cross-legged looking after her.

'And what are you going to be doing in the *Xinjiang Wee...* place?'

'The Xinjiang Uyghur Autonomous Region, or Uyghurstan – only the Chinese don't like it to be called that. I'll be working with the Uyghur people.'

'The wee what?'

'The Uyghur people, they're an ancient tribe, well, actually a conglomeration of nine tribes, one of the most noble of the Turkic people. And my church back home in Texas adopted them.'

'Adopted them?' Ari interrupts, his face a mass of confusion and disbelief.

'Yes, they're our church's chosen cause,' Epiphany explains patiently, her large Bambi eyes smiling. 'They need our help. These poor people don't even have Bibles! So we send them translated gospels and other church booklets, and we occasionally send someone to visit, to make sure they're doing OK.'

'And, er, what religion do they normally practise. I mean what did they believe before you sent them the Bibles and converted them to Christianity?' I ask her.

'Oh, they were mainly Sunni Muslims,' she tells me, without a trace of shame and more than a hint of missionary zeal.

'And now Jesus wants them for a Sunni beam,' I say, smiling sweetly, and go on quickly before anyone can admonish me: 'And why did you decide to adopt the "wee grrrs"?'

'Well, Pastor Dave did a pilgrimage to some of the ancient rock churches in Turkey, where I've just been, and while he was there he met some Uyghur tribesmen who were trading there. It was as if God had led them all to meet right there at that specific time and place. He knew immediately that the church had to adopt them and create a religious bond with them, and encourage them to take Jesus Christ as their Lord and Master.'

'So they became your cause célèbre because Pastor Dave met them on holiday?'

'Sort of,' she replies, hesitating only fractionally. 'Before that we adopted the Bulsa tribe in Ghana because one of the Church Elders had a cousin whose family were originally from there.'

'Right,' I say, thinking it's sounding more like fostering now, or just flatout invasion. 'And the fact that they're Sunni Muslims and that's part of their cultural and ethnic heritage, that doesn't bother you at all?'

'Oh yes, it does. It bothers us a lot. That's why we're sending them Bibles and inspirational church tracts so that they'll...'

'...accept Jesus Christ as their Lord and Master, yes, OK. I didn't quite mean "bother" like that, but never mind. So you don't think that their religion is as worthy as yours?' Epiphany baulks at the word 'yours' as if she has assumed that every white Westerner is automatically a God-fearing Bible-bashing Christian like her. She looks around herself, fearing suddenly for her moral well-being (and sitting beside Danny I'm not surprised). She looks so genuinely frightened that I relent, slightly, and rephrase my question.

'What I mean, Epiphany, is do you believe that the Muslim God, Allah, is so different from the Christian God, and that only Christians are entitled to immortality and being *saved*, however that might be perceived.'

Epiphany's eyes widen and she looks at me as though I'm a witch casting spells around her. I admit to feeling a little heretical right now and try not to think of Dad, sitting in the vicarage, praying for my soul.

'But *of course* there is only *one true God*. That's the whole point. No other religion is...' She casts about for another word but fails... '*true*. All other religions are idolatry. "Thou shalt

219

have no other Gods before me, saith the Lord." And no one can come to God except through Jesus Christ His son and our saviour. And if we don't convert them then they'll die in sin and never get to heaven.'

She is a little pink in the face and slightly breathless from this little recital of this version of the Nicene Creed that's been spoon-fed to her. Not from embarrassment but from religious fervour. Even Danny is looking at her a bit askance now, instead of giving me the evils. I'm beginning to wonder whether the bus leaving her here was totally accidental. I'm also not sure about the however-many-more days of this between Aral and the Xinjiang Autonomous Region of United Wee Grrrs. I might have to have a word with Danny tomorrow. What was he thinking? Did he just see a pretty blonde and... yes, of course he did. We drink on in silence for a while, like a Billy Graham after-party, then decide on an early night since there's no other fishing to be done. Somewhere God or the devil is having the last laugh.

As Danny hasn't persuaded Epiphany to share with him, or maybe because he's now too scared by her, I end up sharing with Ms Waco 2006. Epiphany modestly goes to the bathroom to change and comes back wearing pink fluffy pyjama bottoms and a sweatshirt, saying 'Jesus Loves Me!', which covers her from neck to knees. I watch in fascination as she climbs into her bed and gets out her Bible to read herself some comforting stories to send her to sleep. Just like I used to do when I was a lonely kid in the vicarage. My heart destonifies somewhat at this thought.

'Epiphany,' I pipe up from my bed, 'where does your belief in God really come from? I mean, besides the fact that all your family and their family before them and all your town and state and most of the country believe in a God. Where does your own personal belief come from?'

220

You might think I'm just winding her up but I'm not. Not this time. I'm genuinely curious. Being the relapsed daughter of a vicar and all. And who knows, perhaps Epiphany was sent here to bring us all a… well, an epiphany. So I'm waiting with just that hint of reverent expectation for the answer…

'Gourds,' she says.

'What?' Wondering whether I'm misunderstanding her accent.

'Back in Beverly Hills, we grow a lot of gourds. And I was always fascinated that every single one of those gourds was unique. Not one was exactly the same as another one, and I just got to thinking that if there wasn't a God then all those gourds would be exactly the same. Only a creator God would make every single gourd, and every single human, completely unique.'

My brain racks itself for some rational evolutionary argument for me to use to cut down this plainly silly little girl, but it can't find one. Instead I find myself thinking about what she said. And some part of me is shocked to find itself somehow agreeing.

The fact is that Epiphany is happy. Naïve. But happy. In fact, she reminds me of me when I was younger – totally secure in my world view that God is in charge of everything so there's nothing to worry about (except sin). All you have to do to be happy is to follow God's laws, go to church and perhaps try to convert others along the way. But now I'm like someone who's been unplugged from the Matrix, floundering about in an alternate reality that's much more grim. I've been given the knowledge that this 'God view' is only one view of the world, and that when you actually test it out it's found wanting. There are other ways of living and seeing the world. There are other 'Gods'. There are other 'truths'. It's disconcerting and liberating at the same time. Freedom is slavery.

I dread to think what my dreams are going to be like tonight.

* * * * * * *

In the morning we have trouble starting Alice, which I immediately take to be an omen regarding our new passenger. This has never happened before. But eventually she sputters into life and seems good to go, even with Epiphany Jonah on board. Half an hour later, however, disaster strikes. Alice begins to jump and sputter like a fairground bucking bronco. We're all thrown about like ragdolls, and oranges and potatoes fly everywhere as Alice grinds noisily to a halt and refuses to go on. Dead as a dodo. We're kiboshed in Kazakhstan.

* * * * * * *

We decide to sit tight and let her cool down for a bit. Maybe she'll start when she's good and ready, and we can just get her to the next town and have her looked at properly. So we sit in the back and make tea and play cards for half an hour then try again. No good. Alice isn't going anywhere.

Plan B: We flag down a passing motorist. Easier said than done. Traffic is zooming by, hooting at us merrily, with drivers and their families waving back at us madly as if we are some sort of fairground attraction. I suppose we are – a foreign pink ice cream van stuck out in the middle of the Kazakhstani steppes. Finally someone stops who speaks a few words of English and agrees to drive Danny back to Aral to fetch a mechanic. I'm not so sure this is a good idea leaving us girls and Ari with the van in the middle of nowhere but the Kazakhstani man has a plan, he leaves his wife with us as extra security and we all wave as he drives off in an enormous cloud of dust with our knight.

More tea and cards. The best we can do is snap – you try explaining the rules of gin rummy to a non-English-speaking Kazakhstani woman who's been left a hostage to fortune in a broken-down ice cream van in the middle of nowhere. So we're all really excited and relieved to see Danny and the husband returning, trailed by a Fiat 126 out of which two burly guys in overalls squeeze out with some effort. They indicate that they are going to tow us, clearly oblivious to the relative size difference between Alice and their Fiat. Stoically they indicate that Epiphany, Ari and I should squish into the Fiat with them and Danny should steer the van. The Fiat roars into life and takes the strain as Ari, Piff and I all try desperately not to touch each other, which is not easy in the back of a boiling hot Fiat 126.

After a few false starts Alice starts to move at a snail's pace behind us in jerky little starts until the Fiat guys get up enough steam on the verge to wave madly out of the driver's window and pull into the traffic. The 126 sounds like it's going to blow up any second, and what with the traffic hurtling past us at full tilt, horns blaring, jammed in like sardines in forty degree heat, and a tow rope the length of a London backyard washing line between us and Alice, it's a stop-start scary rollercoaster of a ride into Aral. In fact it's possibly the longest hour and a half of my life.

We pull up outside a small garage and the burly mechanics get out, slap each other on the back (they're obviously amazed we made it too) and detach the tow rope. A man in a shiny office suit appears, and tells us in broken English that we should book into a hotel while he and the Super Mario brothers will get the van fixed.

'How long will it take?' Danny asks.

'Maybe one day, maybe two... Maybe ten,' he adds for good measure with a smile. 'Can get part not easy.' He gestures around us as if to say 'we are in the middle of nowhere you know'. And we do know.

* * * * * * *

Booked back into the office block hotel with nothing to do but wait, Epiphany takes the opportunity to regale us with tales of her travels in Israel, Syria and Turkey, visiting biblical sites.

'Did you know that Turkey was where the original Christian church met? The Cappadocia province is where the Cappadocian fathers first wrote about the Holy Trinity. It was awesome just seeing those places. And the ancient rock churches, carved out of the hills, where the Christians hid from persecution.'

Now I'm sure Epiphany's trip was lovely and even moving, but personally I feel that those Cappadocian fathers have a lot to answer for. They're the ones who created the liturgy of Christianity, the ceremonies and trappings that came to define how Christian worship takes place. They told us what we were to believe and not to believe; and I'm sorry, but however divinely inspired they felt themselves to be, at the end of the day it was just a bunch of old men sitting around and making stuff up. One religion. One true path. One saviour. One chance and all the others are dead ends. In my humble opinion it's this kind of fundamentalism that may hold the church together but it alienates all others. It's about fear of difference and otherness, not tolerance and love. And while we're at it, it's misogynistic and homophobic as well.

But for all Epiphany's naivety there's something about her that I grudgingly admire. Why? For sticking to her faith in the face of overwhelming opposition and 'proof' to the contrary. Now that's either pure stupidity or pure faith. As Epiphany herself chided me last night – you need to have the faith of a child to believe in God. But let's not go into that one right now, I have a splitting headache from the Fiat fiasco.

* * * * * * *

'Casey, you're clutching at straws. I think we need to face the fact that this could be the end of the road.' Danny is holding court in the hotel bar in the mid-afternoon. He's just come back from visiting the garage and it isn't looking good for Alice. Parts for last-century British ice cream vans don't come easy in this part of the world.

'Shall I pray?' offers Epiphany.

No. No. This can't be happening. It just can't be the end of the road. We're only halfway to where we planned to be. We're nowhere. We haven't got *there*. I haven't found any answers. This can't be the end of the road for me.

'I have to go on,' I say rather theatrically.

'How?' Danny asks, irritatingly pragmatic as always.

'I don't know, but look, Danny, this is the trip of a lifetime for me, I can't just turn back now. I just can't.'

'And what about us?' Danny asks. 'What if…' He leaves unspoken 'what if Niobe's recovery doesn't go as planned, or Ari can't cope any more?'

Danny regards me for a moment, and I suddenly feel very vulnerable contemplating carrying on without the boys or Alice.

'Well, let's sleep on it and see what's what in the morning, but I'm going to try to call Niobe again and see how the land lies with her. Whether she's ready to take Ari back yet if need be.'

At this announcement Ari simultaneously smiles and grimaces, caught between desperately wanting to see his mum and apparently wanting to continue the trip. There's a pregnant pause.

'I think I want to stay,' he says, finally, to both my and Danny's surprise.

* * * * * * *

After we all go to bed I lie awake for a long time thinking about the trip and my faith in things, anything, something, myself. Something my dad used to say comes back to me, about Pascal's bet on religion. Pascal said that if you're putting a wager on there being a God or not you have to consider the stakes: if you win, you win everything, but if you lose, you lose nothing. Dad uses it as an argument for 'why not believe', but while I understand the logic I think it's just lazy. It's like deathbed confessions of faith, hedging your bets. I want something more positive than that, but the two positive choices seem so stark: You either choose to go for the comfy, cosy religious life where you don't ask too many questions in return for the knowledge that there is an Almighty Power that loves you dearly and it'll be quite nice when you die; or you can go for the atheist route where you know that What You See Is What You Get and you're completely free to think what you want, but you're on your own.

I sleep fitfully, and dream that Alice washes up on a tropical beach, and suddenly there are hundreds of ice cream vans all washed up, left to rust, and in the very last one Jesus is at the serving hatch doling out free Cornettos to a long line of angelic little kids and raggedy old tramps. And I'm standing at the back of the line when this beggar in front of me turns and asks me what I'm doing there and aren't I in the wrong queue? He says that this queue is only for children and the meek who shall inherit the earth. And I think: 'He's right, I'm not the meek, I'm not worthy' and I turn away from the queue but I don't know where else to go and I can't find Alice anywhere, and I'm so hot and thirsty, and I so want one of those Cornettos…

* * * * * * *

I wake confused as to where I am. When I look over, Epiphany is already awake and reading her Bible.

'Ah, you're awake. Did you sleep OK? You were thrashing around a lot. Did you have a bad dream?' she asks. 'Danny and Ari are waiting for us downstairs.'

When I finally emerge, forty-five minutes later, dressed and in a semblance of readiness, Danny looks like a man with a plan, while Ari looks like a boy with no joy. And I'm with him for once. There's still no news on the van but Danny wants us all to go the internet café and figure out our next steps.

I'm just delving into the far reaches of cyberspace for any stray pearls of wisdom on this when Ari sticks his head round the wall of my cubicle.

'Mum wants to speak to you,' he announces.

'Er, what? Me? Why?'

'*I* don't know,' he says sulkily and disappears again. I get up and go to the phone booth where Danny is just finishing a sentence hurriedly:

'…sure, but he's twelve years old and I'm not sure he should make this sort of decision on his own… anyway, Casey's here. I'll talk to you in a minute.' He hands the phone to me, covering the mouthpiece and whispering: 'Try and make her see sense.'

Now, I'm not sure quite why I'm being summoned to the phone, nor what 'sense' it is exactly that I've been charged to make Niobe see, bearing in mind that I've never met her. So I'm already thinking it's going to be a weird conversation.

'Hello?' I begin.

'Hi Casey, it's Niobe. Well, of course you knew that,' she laughs gently, 'it's, well, it's hard to believe we haven't spoken before.' Her voice is silky and slightly posh with only a trace of a flattened Derbyshire accent. I try to conjure up a living picture from the photo I saw on Ari's email, and wonder if she's as good-looking in real life. This is a totally inappropriate thought but it's too late, it's in my head now.

'Hi, no, we haven't met,' I say in a fluster. 'Danny's obviously been keeping you hidden away!'

There's a slight pause, and I realise the ambiguity of what I've just said, but I'm not sure how I can neatly disambiguate it so I plough on, hoping to override that slip.

'How are you feeling after the operation?'

'Oh, you know, pretty ropey. But I'm back at home now. Just trying to rest up. Listen, Casey, can I ask you something?'

Oh God. Suddenly the snippets of casual daydreams and ridiculous notions I've secretly been having about this woman I've never met come crashing in around me, and I feel as if she can read my mind. I feel myself blushing ridiculously at the thought. I'm such an idiot.

'I wanted to ask you woman to woman...' she continues.

Help! Am I woman enough for this? I start panicking and hold my breath.

'...how do you think Ari has been getting on with Danny?' she asks. Oh, right. I breathe a sigh of relief. 'I mean, the thing is that Danny told me that the van's broken down and he's all for bringing Ari home, and that would be lovely, of course, although I'm a bit tired still, but, you see, the thing is that I really wanted Danny and Ari to spend some quality time together this summer. And it's only been three weeks now and when I spoke to Ari he seemed to want to carry on, and, well, actually he seemed quite attached to you, and I just wondered if he's been getting on OK with Danny, in your opinion?'

Wow.

'Well, I can't say that I'm an expert on these things, Niobe. I've not had any experience with children myself, and I'm not sure that I would say that Ari is quite "attached to me".' My mind boggles at what Ari might have said. 'But certainly him and Danny have been getting on fine.'

'Fine?' Ah, my powers of description are quite something.

'Well, "good" really, I suppose. I mean... OK, for example...' I tell her about the times when Danny and Ari have ganged up on me, when they've laughed together at daft things I've said or done, the times when they play cards together and joke around, the times when Ari has almost called him 'Dad'. I don't tell her about Ari running off at the German campsite or the screaming matches he's had with both of us. I mean, all in all, when you weigh it up and consider his age and the circumstances, I guess he's a pretty decent kid.

Niobe laughs.

'So, he's keeping Danny on his toes then? And you too by the sound of it.'

'Yeah, well, we all get on OK. It's been... fun.' And you know, as I say it I realise that it has been fun, actually. It's been a big shared adventure and we've learned lots of stuff, and I really don't want it to end here. So I say as much to Niobe.

'I thought it must be something like that. Ari sounds like he's really enjoying himself. Of course he doesn't say it in so many words.'

'No.' I laugh in agreement, thinking of Ari's penchant for monosyllabic conversations, but there have been times when he's really got excited about stuff too.

'So, do you think that Danny and Ari should carry on travelling with you for a while longer then?' Niobe asks.

I smile.

'Yes. I do.'

229

'Good. Then that's settled then. Thanks Casey, I really appreciate it. And I really appreciate you taking Ari with you on your trip. I know it wasn't planned, but I think it's doing him the world of good.'

'No worries,' I tell her. 'It's been good for me too.' Realising this truth only as I say it.

'Good. Listen, we must make time to meet up when you come back… Could you put Danny back on please, I need to have a word with him.'

'Yes, yes, well, you look after yourself, Niobe. Um, nice talking to you. Bye then,' I say hurriedly.

I hand the phone back to a scowling Danny who has appeared at my side like the shopkeeper in *Mr Ben*. Perhaps I didn't make Niobe see the 'sense' he was thinking of? Well, that's his lookout. She seems very… well, you know, in control, sensible, nice. I liked her. I look forward to meeting her. It's silly that talking to her made me feel nervous, but it's probably just the fact that I'm half in loco parentis for her only son, I tell myself. Me, the inveterate child-hater. How times change!

So, the journey's not over for us yet. But how can we continue when this is clearly the end of Alice's adventures in Wonderland?

CHAPTER 16

Go Big or Go Home

'Dimidium facti qui coepit habet: sapere aude
("He who has begun is half done: dare to know").'
  Quintus Horatius Flaccus (Horace), *Epistles*, 20 BC.

'So what did Niobe want to talk to you about?' Danny asks me in this strange kind of faux-casual way, hanging over the side of my internet booth.

'Oh, nothing in particular,' I reply in a similar tone. 'She just wanted to check me out: That I'm not a completely raving mad Southernised lesbian, and that I'm not being a bad influence on the poor, impressionable young boys I'm travelling with.'

Danny gives me a look that says, very clearly: 'Get lost!' But I'm not about to divulge the lovely intimacy of my first conversation with Niobe. I want to savour every word and hoard it for myself.

I turn back to the computer where I think I've found a way for us to continue our journey without Alice. We can hop aboard the Trans-Aral Train and connect with the Trans-Siberian or Trans-Mongolian railway which will take us all the way to China. The only drawback is that it isn't cheap and our budget never had much room in it for unexpected extras.

I gather the troops for a discussion about tickets and

routes, which is when Epiphany drops the bombshell that she is totally skint, having relied on the kindness of strangers and the bounty of the good Lord for most of her trip. Oh brother. The Trans-Trains have recently been upgraded, which has taken them beyond the affordability of most backpackers and ice cream touts such as ourselves. Basically, we can't afford it.

* * * * * * *

Epiphany only adds to my woes by insisting on giving me a pep talk on the way back to the hotel.

'You know, Casey, you should really make more of yourself,' she ventures, for all the world like she's my new BFF. 'I thought you were a boy, the first time I saw you. For a start, you need to take off that...' She grabs for my beanie but I deftly squirm away. 'You should be proud of how God made you. You have quite a pretty face really,' she concludes to my horror.

'How God made me, dear Epiphany, is GAY, GAY, GAY!' I want to scream in her doe-eyed Disney princess face. 'Stick that in your Bible and smoke it!' But I force myself not to. She's having a hard enough time dealing with our challenges to her beliefs as it is. I'm not trying to bring the world down on her head or tell her that her faith is bad, or her life is bad, or that the truth that she believes is in any way inferior to the truth that I believe (whatever that may be). But I do believe that everything we think we know can be challenged, that true knowledge is one of the keys to real freedom. In my own way I think *I* actually want to save *her*.

'Have you ever considered that not everything they tell you about at church might be the literal truth?' I venture at last, exasperated by her giving away yet more coinage I've lent her to the queue of Kazakhstani urchins that has miraculously appeared en route to the hotel. I'm rewarded with another one of those 'you're going to burn in hell' looks of complete incredulity at my incredulity.

'I believe in the Word of God as written in the Bible and in the divinely inspired words of the elders of the church,' she recites from some inner litany.

'So you believe that the world and everything in it was created in literally seven days?'

'No!'

Aha. At last, a chink in the armour.

'God created the earth in six days, and on the seventh day he rested,' she corrects me with characteristic guilelessness.

Oh for crying out loud. I want to put my head in my hands, or maybe her head in my hands. Not that I'm an all-out evolutionist. Far from it. I'm an intelligent designist of sorts, I guess. Which means that I believe that the theories of evolution and creation are not mutually exclusive. I also believe that the theory of evolution can no more be proven than God. Science begins to look an awful lot like magic when you look at it closely. Even the best of evolutionary accounts requires a Lemony Snicket-like concatenation of coincidences and serendipity in order to arrive at the humanoid. Even Einstein and Stephen Hawking ultimately accepted the idea of a creator God. This by way of saying that I'm not entirely hostile to Epiphany's view, but I graduated from Sunday School a long time ago, and I don't believe it was literally six days, more like millennia.

'But, Epiphany, what if the Bible wasn't divinely inspired? What if it was written by mere men who wished to manipulate others?' I know I've gone way too far too fast, but I genuinely want to understand the basis of her seemingly unshakable belief system.

She looks at me for a moment, then laughs uncertainly.

'Oh, right. I never get the British sense of humour,' she says, and I leave it at that for now, unable to gather the strength to carry on in this unstoppable force meets immoveable object contest.

* * * * * * *

Back at the hotel we call an emergency powwow in the boys' bedroom about our future plans. Perched uncomfortably on the lumpy mattresses, Epiphany and I carefully try to avoid sitting on the balled-up twists of thin cotton sheeting and threadbare brown blankets, which Danny and Ari have failed to fold up. I'm dreading this conversation. All my half-baked dreams of finding myself, finding paradise, finding the truth, now looking like primordial amoebas floundering in a dried-up sea. I just can't go home now. What will everyone think? What will Niobe think? Her words are still ringing in my head as I look at Ari's crestfallen face, and Danny's defeated scowl. I know what Mum and Dad will think: That we fell at the first hurdle, that we were only playing at travelling anyway with our silly ice cream van, that we don't have what it takes to be proper adventurers.

Suddenly, in the middle of the conversation, Danny jumps up and runs out of the room shouting that we should stay where we are, he'll be back shortly.

* * * * * * *

Ari has well and truly trounced Piff and myself at gin rummy and pontoon and is trying to teach us a charming game called, he assures us, 'shithead', when Danny comes flying into the room waving a rather large fistful of dollars.

'I sold her!' he yells excitedly, grabbing me by the shoulder.

234

'What? Alice? You sold our Alice?'

'Our dead-as-a-dodo 1970s ice cream maker? Yes.'

I'm torn between feelings of elation and ones of remorse. I'd really bonded with Alice. She was our shelter, our home from home. I felt that her seats and bunks had finally moulded to our forms. She was our safe haven, our shelter, our protectress... But on the other hand she's now no more than a useless pile of scrap metal, which I wouldn't have thought you could even sell for parts. Time to face facts.

So Danny, who bought her impulsively a month ago, has now just as impulsively sold her.

'So how much d'you get?'

'Well,' Danny starts, 'not as much as you might hope... but then, there's not much to sell now that she's not actually roadworthy.'

He's right, I shouldn't get my hopes up – all we need is enough to finish our trip, so even if he's only made back three-quarters or two-thirds of her overinflated original value it'd be good.

'So how much?' I press him, eager to calculate whether we'll have enough for some internal flights as well as our flights home.

'Well, look, here's half of it, he's got to go to the bank and get the rest this afternoon.' Danny thrusts the wodge of dollars into my hands and sits down with Ari and Epiphany to play cards still looking very pleased with himself.

The oily dirt-besmirched dollar total comes to $980, mainly in very used twenty dollar notes. I wonder who keeps this much money in their house, but perhaps the banks round here aren't so reliable. So, if this is half, then that means that we have sold Alice for the princely sum of $1,960 give or take, or around £1,000, just one-third of what we paid for her just four weeks ago. Now *that's* depreciation, I sigh.

On the positive side this'll allow us to carry on our trip for a while, but God knows how we're going to get home: strapped to the back of someone's motorbike or flapping our arms on some dodgy bucket airline. After some negotiation, Danny and I reluctantly agree to pay for Epiphany's ticket. I try to consider it our down-payment on good karma for the rest of the trip (if not thereafter), but I can't help begrudgingly feeling we've been ripped off right royally somewhere, or everywhere – from Gary on the Walworth Road, to the cheap-suited garage owner whose brother's first cousin's wife's sister's husband is apparently buying Alice as a tourist attraction for people coming to see the dry harbour. I guess they're going to convert her back into a real ice cream van. It seems fitting somehow. It's all she really wanted to be in the first place. But the best thing is that we've got some money and we can carry on with our journey.

'Well done, Danny.' I half-heartedly congratulate the man who didn't even seem to want to carry on a few hours ago. Men! I'll never understand them.

* * * * * * *

By five o'clock we've collected the second instalment of slightly less-soiled money from the bank account of Mr Cheap-suited garage owner's brother's cousin's first wife's sister's husband and bought tickets for all of us on the Trans-Aral express to Arys in the far south. From there we transfer on to the Turkestan-Siberian railway (the poor (affordable) cousin to the Trans-Sib) and travel up through Tashkent and the old capital Almaty to Aktogay (yes, really) from where we can pick up a train into China. We'll leave Epiphany at Urumqi which is the capital of Uyghurland, while we carry on right the way across the Chinese hinterland to Lanzhou where many railways meet and the whole of East Asia becomes our oyster.

No more bad roads and watching out for potholes, playing chicken with the traffic and the constant cacophony of horns. All we have to do is sit and look out of the window and see the world rushing by. Perfect. We'll also be real backpackers now, getting in amongst the people: 'the common people', as my Victorian spinsters (and Pulp) might say.

I clamber out of the van for the final time tooled up like GI Jane in a low-budget sequel. Sporting a black wife-beater over cargo shorts, with a heavy duty lanyard slung round my neck boasting the essential survival tools of a plastic compass, whistle, torch, tin opener and foldaway shopping bag; a red bandana on my head; and a large knife sticking out of my army surplus stores webbing belt. I feel pretty cool. Danny and Ari take one look at me and burst out laughing, while Epiphany looks horrified. I reluctantly decide to tuck the knife and lanyard into my rucksack instead, and swap the bandana for my trusty beanie again, despite the heat.

I'm sad to say goodbye to dear old Alice, our ice cream mystery machine. Especially in the state she's currently in, looking like a blown-apart *Transformers* toy. It's like saying goodbye to one of our little gang of adventurers. Now we're back to being just the lost lesbian, her philandering friend, his estranged son and the adoptive hitchhiking Bible-basher – what a team!

* * * * * * *

As the train moves out of Aral we're shown to our bunks by a uniformed guard who looks like a fully-paid-up member of the KGB. Certainly we aren't going to argue with him when he points brusquely towards four bunks in a compartment sleeping six. It isn't the Orient Express, that's for sure, more British Rail in the 1970s – all rattling windows and faded glory – but it's cleanish, and exciting to have a new home from home.

In due course, a number of young backpackers from other sections begin to crowd into our space, lured by the new passengers' stocks of crisps, nuts, oranges, chew bars and other durables from back home that we'd filled Alice's nether regions with.

Epiphany is studiously trying to ignore the rising commotion by sitting cross-legged on one of the top bunks and praying with her hands together, which is making her rather an unintended centre of attention – like the elephant in the room everyone's too polite to point out. Eventually, one of the four young female backpackers from Manchester who is squished into the seat beside me whispers: 'Is she OK? Or is she, like, you know, a bit mental or what?' Now a Mancunian whisper is more like a shout in any other part of the world but luckily the din of the train and the hubbub of the party prevents most people, especially Piff, from hearing it.

'She's a Christian missionary,' I say.

'Oh, right.' The girl looks a bit shocked, like I've just said that Piff's a terrorist or has the plague or something. Piff spends the rest of the evening sitting on her high horse while the rest of our carriage gets slowly pissed on cheap Ukrainian vodka, which even Ari has apparently managed to sample as he's sitting giggling away in the corner playing cards with some young lads who have procured a deck of 'Naked Ladies of Russia' for the occasion. Ah good times, as we roll on down the track through Kazakhstan, finally feeling the thrill of being unencumbered backpackers.

* * * * * * *

By the next morning we've reached Arys where we need to change trains for the Turkestan-Siberian railway, which will take us along the bottom of Kazakhstan, bordering Kyrgyzstan, and eventually all the way to the Chinese border.

Arys and neighbouring Samarkand have been very important stops on the ancient Silk Route connecting East and West since the first century BC. One of the oldest inhabited cities in the world, it was in Samarkand that the earliest paper mill in the Islamic world was created (the technology having originated in China and spread from here to the West). Up until then, everything had been oral. Now with the written word, knowledge and ideas could be spread much more widely and easily. Without this innovation, the guidebook in my hand wouldn't exist and we might never have made it here 2000 years later.

The primary purpose of the Silk Road, of course, was the import-export business (much like Gary, back on the Walworth Road). This trade route has been the conduit for things as diverse as maps, gunpowder, compasses, Buddhism and, of course, Chinese silk, which was lapped up first by the Romans. Apparently, they went so crazy for decadent silk togas that an edict was eventually proclaimed by the Senate to ban the wearing of silk on economic and moral grounds. The unfortunate consequence of this successful trading for the Easterners was that the Westerners could now find their way back along the same routes, sending missionaries to conquer the heathen hordes (which is the grand tradition Epiphany is now following). These were followed in the 1960s and 1970s by the hippies bent on 'finding themselves', 'seeking God' and 'communicating with other peoples'. So maybe I *am* a hippy, without the flares and flowers.

Back on board the new train, one of the young backpackers tells us about his destination in Goa, India. He's heard of a community there who have allegedly transcended normal human boundaries and are living like yogis. He starts to tell us the story of the founding of the community when one of its members ascended to a higher plain. The guy had been meditating on the beach, and experimenting with 'shrooms and some sort of liquid acid, and it also transpired later that he'd had a good few beers at the bar (presumably while he was having a break from meditating). Anyway, as the sun went down a beach party broke out as it often does in Goa and, around midnight when the tide was coming in, a young girl stumbled across the beach looking for her boyfriend. She found him dead drunk, lying face down on the beach, with the tide lapping at his feet. She dragged him up and out of the water and set about trying to revive him. As she did so, she noticed another guy lying face down in the sand at the water's edge – meditating guy.

She's torn between reviving her limp and almost lifeless boyfriend and trying to drag a complete stranger out of harm's way. Rather selflessly (and you have to remember this is her retelling of the story) she goes to try to drag out meditating guy but finds that he is quite a bit bigger than her boyfriend and she can't move him more than about a foot. Unwilling to leave her boyfriend any longer she shouts for help. The rest of the story is a bit confused. She claims not to have seen meditating man's body being washed out to sea, happy to adhere in the next days to the newly-formed cult's claim that he 'ascended' before the waters took him.

There's a moment's awed silence when the story finishes and I suddenly need some air. Excusing myself I walk hurriedly down the corridor to where an open window is blowing the hot desert wind into the corridor. Outside there's nothing but reassuringly flat sand in every direction. I immerse myself in it. A whole sea of sand, devoid of features except the occasional wild horse or marooned yurt. I stick my head out and watch the back of the train curl round the bend behind us like a snake coiling to attack. Closing my eyes, I let myself be blown about by the desert wind until I can barely breathe.

* * * * * * *

'Are you OK?' Ari is standing awkwardly in the corridor with his hands thrust deep into his jeans' pockets. I withdraw my head from the sandblasting oven of a window and look at him. Twelve years old, all social awkwardness and yet sensitive somehow. My heart thaws.

'Thanks for coming to find me. You didn't have to. I'm OK.'

'You didn't look OK. When Todd told that story you looked like you were gonna be sick or something.'

'Well... I *am* OK, Ari, thanks. It was very sweet of you to come after me.'

He looks at me and sighs at the word 'sweet'.

'I'm not a little kid, you know. I know when something's wrong.'

'I know you're not.' I can suddenly feel tears welling up and I fight them back. I can't cry in front of Ari. He's been through enough with his mum's illness.

'Look, really, I'm OK, I just need a bit of time on my own, that's all. I need to think about some stuff. Big stuff,' I add when he rolls his eyes.

Ari shrugs. 'OK,' he says, a bit hurt. Putting his earphones back in, he turns on his heels to go back to our carriage. Halfway down the corridor he hesitates and turns back in slow motion. I don't notice him until he's right behind me again.

'I do get it,' he begins, 'it's like Spiderman. He's always having to hide who he really is and he gets lonely as well.' He turns back again and is gone before I can react, leaving me in shock, and feeling suddenly terribly, terribly alone.

Eventually I turn to go back to the compartment but find that I'm rooted to the spot, unable to tear myself away. As if the window with its hot air is a release valve, an escape hatch, and I can't leave it for fear that the thoughts will overwhelm me if I move. I don't know how long I stand there, lost in my thoughts.

'Hey you! I've been looking everywhere for you. Ari sent me the wrong way, I've been right to the other end of the train. What's up?' Danny arrives by my side, giving me a big brotherly squeeze of concern.

'I'm fine, just feeling a bit queasy,' I lie. Some things are better not talked about, it just rakes up feelings that are better off left well buried. Luckily Danny seems to have other things on his mind and accepts my white lie quite easily.

'What's up with you?' I ask, turning the tables. Always a good one when in a tight spot.

'What do you mean?' He looks evasive.

'I mean, your behaviour in Aral. One minute you want to give up and go home, the next you turn up with a fistful of dollars for our train tickets. What's going on? Are you worried about Niobe? Or Ari? Or... me?'

Danny sighs.

'You always seem to know when something's up. Is that a woman thing?'

'You can't answer a question with another question,' I challenge, knowing I do it all the time.

Danny raises an eyebrow and gives a little laugh.

'OK, you got me. Look, it's not you or Niobe. It's not even Ari, although I have to admit it's been pretty touch and go at times...'

'So what is it?' It's like wringing blood out of the proverbial.

242

'Well, you're not going to like it…' Danny hesitates.

'Go on.'

Danny takes a deep breath.

'I've been offered a contract. A really *big* contract. The kind that I can't really afford to turn down. I got an email. In Aral. They want me to do the initial scoping trip.' Danny grimaces.

'And this field trip – it needs to be done *now?* And it has to be done by *you?* Where?' I try to fill in the blanks left by this bombshell.

'Saudi, and yes, it needs to be me if I want the contract. Just for a week, but it has to be in the next ten days. I was waiting for a chance to talk to you about it…'

'So what did you tell them?' I challenge him.

Danny blushes slightly and I gather he didn't say 'no'.

'I told them I'd get back to them. It's just such a big thing for me. It could *make* my career, Casey. It would mean that I could move up a step: be more permanent, be more secure, be able to provide for Ari and Niobe…'

'But not *be* with them? Not if you're in Saudi.'

'I'd be in Saudi for six months, and then I could oversee the project from the home office in Nottingham. I'd just do the odd field visit. The rest of the time I'd be around for them both. It would be like a new start.'

'But…' My head is filled with questions, not least about Niobe and her sexuality. Danny clearly reads my thoughts.

'A new start for my relationship with Ari. Being some sort of permanent figure in his life. And hopefully being a support, a *friend*, to Nib. I know the love bridges were burned from both ends a long time ago. I'm not stupid.'

I take a deep breath. This is a lot to take in. This certainly wasn't part of the plan, but somewhere inside of me a decision appears to have already been taken.

243

'It's a great opportunity, Danny. I think maybe you should go,' I hear myself saying.

'But Niobe wants Ari to carry on. I don't think she's up to coping with him right now.'

There's a long pause where Danny and I just look at each other. Then my mouth opens and these words come out: 'Look, Danny, I think you should go... but I think you should let Ari carry on. I'll look after him until you come back.'

'Are you kidding?' Danny looks incredulous. Maybe he's right. Maybe that's a stupid idea. I can't look after Ari by myself. But on the other hand, this is a huge break for Danny and he really should take it. Surely I can handle looking after a twelve-year-old for a few days on my own? I'm a grown woman, aren't I? Danny is looking at me still, but his expression has turned from incredulity to consideration: puzzling, sizing me and my capabilities up. It makes me feel distinctly uncomfortable.

'What are you thinking?' I ask, unable to bear his scrutiny any longer.

'That maybe you can manage to look after Ari for a week. But...'

'But what?'

'Well, it's not as if you're exactly *keen* on him, or him on you.'

Fair point, I think. But you know what? *I've* changed. At least, I think I have. I'm not the same cynical spiky child-hater I started out as. And Ari has grown *attached* to me. Niobe said so and I say as much to an incredulous Danny, who still doesn't look convinced. Now a deeper scowl crosses his face. I raise my eyebrows as if to say 'out with it'.

'Well, how's Ari going to take it? He'll think I don't care. That I'm abandoning him again. This time in the back of beyond with a total stranger.'

'I'm not a *total* stranger now, Danny,' I say indignantly.

'No, but you know what I mean.'

'Look, Danny, I think he'll understand if you explain it to him. He's not a child, you know. He'll get why you have to do it.' I'm aware of the irony as I repeat Ari's words back to Danny.

Danny shrugs with the weight of the world on his unaccustomed shoulders.

'Yeah, maybe. We'll see.'

We walk back to our compartment together, both lost in our individual thoughts. Just before we get there Danny turns to me and says: 'Look, let's not mention anything to Ari yet. Sleep on it tonight, Casey, and let's talk first thing tomorrow, just in case either of us changes our minds, yeah?'

Yeah. Good idea.

* * * * * * *

Danny and Ari spend the evening playing cards with some of the backpackers while Epiphany is trying to learn a few words of Wee Grrrr for her impending mission visit. I take to my bunk and try to read but find that I can't concentrate. I'm worried about how Ari will react, and how I'll cope with him on my own. Am I ready? Can I do this? Am I man enough to act as a mother? I realise that part of me wants to do it just to prove that I can; to myself, to Danny, to Niobe.

I think about the day's incidents and Ari's sensitivity towards me. Surely a good sign? Then I start to think about Todd's story about the beach and, as if an evil electrician has just powered up the slide projector in my brain, the images start to flash up in front of me: me and she-who-must-not-be-named at the bar in Greece; her getting so drunk; the vicious accusations; the hurled drink; her on the beach; walking out into the water; shouting at me in the darkness; getting smaller and smaller in the waves; me standing on the shore unable to move, my childish fear of the sea rooting me to the spot; and then that scene of her disappearing in the darkness playing over and over again, never getting to the credits. I open my eyes and force myself to focus on the twilit scenes flashing past the window – the arid ground of the Kazakhstani Steppe, the sandy dirt, the choking heat and the dust... and not a drop of water in sight.

CHAPTER 17

Mao, myself and I (and Ari)

'An oppressive government is more to be feared than a tiger.'

Confucius,
The Confucian Analects, 475BC-220AD.

'It's OK. I get it. You have to go for your work. I'll be OK. Mum wants me to carry on, she told me. It's OK, Dan. Anyway,' Ari spots that my eyes have opened, 'Crazy Casey can look after me.'

'I'm not sure which is worse, the nightmare I was having or what I've woken up to!' I joke, half-awake. It's still dark in the compartment but Danny and Ari are sitting on the bottom bunk discussing next steps. Clearly the boy has metamorphosed from ghoulish devil-imp to cheerful little adventurer at some point over the past four weeks.

'So, that's really OK with both of you?' Danny seems as nonplussed as me at this turn of events. And it seems the time for second thoughts may have already passed. Failed charity worker to full-time nanny in one easy leap. I think back to the behaviourally and emotionally-challenged 'yoof' I first met at Trowell Service Station months ago, and then to the kind, sensitive young man who came to find me last night to check I was OK. This is surreal. I realise Danny is waiting for final confirmation. No going back once I agree...

'Yes, of course we're both OK with it,' Ari says for me before I have a chance to think thrice. And that's that. In the next instant Danny's on his mobile to head office sorting out flights and I'm helping Ari pack Danny's bag for him. The nearest airport is at Almaty, the old Kazakhstani capital, and our next scheduled stop. This is also where we'll change for the train that will take us into China, so it's action stations for all of us. Danny, Ari, Epiphany and myself all jostling for elbow room, ramming clothes and belongings into bags and trying to look presentable after a night in a sardine can. Before we really know what's happening we're waving Danny off at Almaty station, and suddenly it's just the two mouseketeers, plus hangers on, heading off into the rising sun.

* * * * * * *

Half an hour later we're ensconced in our new Chinese train. Piff is reading her Bible and Ari is glued to his PSP playing 'Street Fighter'. I wonder whether I should be trying to talk to him instead. All that violence can't be good for him.

* * * * * * *

Forty-five minutes later again, Ari is still playing with his PSP. Surely that isn't good? He'll ruin his eyesight and how will it affect his social skills (what little he has)? I figure I should try to engage him in conversation but can't think how to start or what to talk about.

* * * * * * *

Almost two hours now since Danny left. Epiphany's praying and I'm 'looking after Ari'. He's still pretty unresponsive, although I haven't actually tried to talk to him yet, and…

'Casey?'

'Yes, Ari?'

'Stop staring at me. I'm OK you know.'

'Oh. I wasn't, well, good, you know, that you're OK. If you want to talk to me, at any time, just… Well, just if you want to. I'm here.'

'I know. I can see you. You're crazy!' Ari grins a very Danny-like grin and goes back to his PSP, which peeps and beeps reassuringly at him like an electronic pet.

Well, good. There we go then. He's fine. Everything's fine. I can go back to my book. Or maybe I *should* talk to him? Or I could talk to him later. If he wants to…

* * * * * * *

The train frequently stops for ten to fifteen minutes at stations where the platforms are lined with locals selling dense sesame bread, hard-boiled eggs, preserved fruit, turnips and souvenirs. From this we're able to supplement our diet in creative and relatively satisfying ways. I'm also able to stock up on a selection of 1950s postcards and Ari starts a collection of squished coins which the local kids put on the tracks for the passing trains to run over – an ingenious version of those ubiquitous machines you get at UK tourist attractions. We're also able to swap our chew bars and stuff salvaged from Alice with other passengers for sundry luxury items, including a crate of Tsingtao Chinese beer in exchange for a big bag of potatoes, one of our better deals. About 90 per cent of the passengers on this train are Chinese, mainly traders riding the iron horse home from the mid-West with almost every item imaginable, from beer and nuts to puppies and jewellery.

Just as I'm about to enjoy a Tsingtao beer after lunch Epiphany strikes again, out of the blue.

'You know, if you really want to be good role model for Ari you shouldn't drink in front of him. And you should stop being so sarcastic all the time,' she drawls.

'Wait. What?' Since when did this turn into a conversation about me and my values?

'It's not just about what we say, but what we do and what we feel that really counts…' Piff is on a roll now. '…I think the reason you feel lost in life is because you've rebelled against everything that is good and right and true – God and the church.' I think my jaw must drop open at this stage, as Piff goes on: 'You think I haven't been listening to your so-called *intellectual* conversations? You think I don't understand what you're saying? I do, and God does. God cares for you, Casey. I've been praying for you to open your eyes to God and see what His plan is for you and your life.'

'What?' I'm dumbstruck. And worse, Piff sounds just like my mum and dad. This is too much. Something inside me snaps. 'Who are you to tell me what to believe?'

'I'm not telling you what to believe, Casey,' Piff is relentless. 'I'm asking you to consider what you believe. God is forgiving and loving and…'

'Hey, just stop with the sermon, Epiphany! *I* don't preach to you and I'd ask you not to do it to me. You know *nothing* about my upbringing or my beliefs. You don't know what's brought me to where I am now, and you sure as hell don't know where I'm going.' And the fact that I don't either does *not* come into it. I'm livid. How dare she?

'I'm just saying,' Epiphany goes on a bit more plaintively, 'that you're part of a lost generation who think that they've found freedom by turning away from the church, but really they've lost their true sense of who they are in the world. Pastor Dave said it all started with women burning their bras. You see, women were the traditional keepers of the faith, and...' This is too much.

'Look, Piff,' I practically spit, 'I don't give a great big fig leaf what Pastor Dave and his misogynist and homophobic church says about bra-burning or anything else. And I certainly don't want to hear any more of *your* theories on *my* life. *OK?*' My anger is brief but incandescent. I fly out of the carriage, slamming the door loudly behind me, leaving Piff looking like a saint on the brink of her martyrdom (which might be nearer the truth than she realises).

Even as I walk out I'm aware of Ari staring at me with bemused concern. I've been in solo loco parentis for less than a day and I've already confirmed his view of me as crazy and unstable. Great. I'm such an idiot. Why did I let her get to me like that? It wasn't such a big deal. Why do I always let the whole religion thing wind me up so badly? Is it guilt? Or is it actually God giving me a sharp poke in the ribs? Bloody hell. Now I'll have to go in there and apologise, before Ari loses all faith in me.

* * * * * * *

By the time we reach the Chinese border, mid-afternoon, I think Epiphany has forgiven me (well, she kind of has to doesn't she – it's in the rules of the game for her). But I don't think I've forgiven her, or myself. I've apologised, more for Ari's benefit than hers, and we've left it at that. So it's an uneasy truce that reigns in our quiet carriage for now.

The train stops at the border for guards to come on board and check our passports and visas. I wouldn't want to try to argue with them in their terribly smart uniforms and terrifying array of hardware, and I become slightly concerned (or is it hopeful) that Epiphany might get turned back for carrying Bibles and religious tracts but (un)fortunately they don't search us, just inspect our visas and give us a hard look: a lost and lonely lesbian in loco-loco parentis, a British street urchin and a tanned blonde American in a Disney sweatshirt. Lord knows what they think. In Britain, a bearded olive-skinned man with a rucksack looks like a terrorist, while a young blonde American girl looks innocent; while round these parts it's probably the opposite. She may not be carrying explosives, but Epiphany could be just as dangerous. But the border guards don't think so, this time.

We also get a new passenger in our carriage. A respectable-looking middle-aged Chinese guy in a dark suit with small round glasses and a briefcase. He wouldn't look out of place sporting a bowler hat, and if he did he'd look exactly like a Chinese Mr Benn. He turns out to be a professor at the University in Beijing going back from a home visit. He speaks good English. His name, he says, is Yang – whether Mr Yang or just Yang I'm not sure. We introduce ourselves and he bows to us all in turn. When we hesitate over whether to bow back or not he offers us his hand to shake.

'Chinese person try always to be perfect gentleman,' Mr Yang explains. 'Confucius say basis for good society.'

The countryside changes as we roll into China. On our right are scrubby yellow-brown dunes as we skirt the top of the Taklimakan Desert, but on our left are astonishing grasshopper-green fields as far as the eye can see. Bordered in the distance by mountains. The fields are soon dotted with Chinese workers in their trademark pointy limpet hats looking like they've just stepped out of a 1950s picture book.

'Look, the peasants are revolting,' I laugh to Ari, who doesn't get it, and I have to explain it to him, by which time it's already way less funny and I'm wishing I hadn't said it with Mr Yang looking on.

Epiphany says: 'You should admire their simplicity, Casey, they've found true happiness in hard work.' She beams and waves out of the window to the field workers, who look bemused and half-wave back before turning again to their labours. 'In fact they probably pity us weighted down with our money and cares and stuff.'

I bet they're actually thinking: 'You patronising rich Westerners. How dare you come here and wave at us'. But I don't want to say this in front of Mr Yang. So instead I go back to gazing out of the window, and am rewarded by a young boy sitting on the rail-side fence who smiles toothily before giving me the finger.

I wonder what our fellow passengers think about it all, but I'm too scared to ask. Mr Yang's said nothing so far and seems to regard us with mild amusement. I'm about to readdress Epiphany when Ari pipes up:

'Mr Yang? Why does China have so many poor people?'

I cringe a bit, but Mr Yang doesn't seem at all perturbed by Ari's question. He straightens up his glasses, places his hands neatly on his lap and looks for all the world as if he is about to address a room full of students. In many senses he is.

'Young man, you ask a very good question. China history very complicated...' And as we roll gently through field after endless field of paddy and peasants, Mr Yang gives us a potted history of modern China, beginning with the Opium Trade Wars between China and Britain in the nineteenth century when Britain began exporting opium to pay for their tea addiction. I have visions of my Victorian ladies sipping their

253

most British of drinks, grown halfway around the world and paid for by drug trafficking. No wonder the British have such a developed sense of irony.

Next, Mr Yang tells us about the fall of the last emperor of the Qing Dynasty and the formation of the Republic of China in 1912, as China began to look towards Western methods and technologies in order to modernise. Ari is rapt with the stories of emperors, warlords and imperial guards, and Mr Yang obliges by playing up those parts.

In the late 1920s Mao Zedong enters mainstream politics, founding the Soviet Republic of China and starting a civil war that will rage for twenty-three years. Mao won the war and declared a People's Republic of China in 1949, under his Chairmanship. With help from the USSR, Mao imposed industrialisation to end China's dependence on agriculture. This Great Leap Forward involved refusing foreign imports of grain; instead, millions were put to work in the fields to feed industrial workers in the cities. Somewhere between 20 and 70 million peasants starved to death in rural areas. That's potentially the entire population of the UK, wiped out in one failed Communist experiment.

After Stalin's death, Mao split with the more liberal Nikita Khrushchev's Soviet Union, leading eventually to the Cultural Revolution of 1966.

'History, religion, culture – all destroyed. China education, economy, all are in pieces,' Mr Yang explains. 'Mao become god, all-powerful. Everything he say written in "Little Red Book" as you call it, "Quotation from Chairman Mao Zedong".'

'You see these speaker?' Mr Yang says to Ari, pointing outside to a pair of incongruous-looking loudhailers strapped to the top of a telegraph pole in the middle of nowhere. 'These are for people everywhere hear Mao teaching. Central People Broadcasting Station,' he announces ominously as if reading from George Orwell's *Nineteen Eighty-Four*. A bit of a far cry from the BBC I'm thinking. Although I suppose the repeated broadcasting of any one point of view is a brainwashing of sorts.

Clearly he is no fan of 'The Little Red Book', and I suspect that, had he been a university professor at the time, he would have been one of the 'liberal bourgeoisie' which the Revolution sought to eliminate for their radical thinking. And he's probably sticking his neck out by telling us all this, even now.

'Millions of my people do not agree with what I tell you here,' he says, as if reading our thoughts. 'They tell you Mao is great man. They tell you he make China great. That he responsible for China being superpower. He is not. China is great *despite* Mao.' Mr Yang has become quite emotional now, his hands continually straightening his glasses, which are slipping down his nose as he emphasises things with a nod or shake of the head.

'And new leader no better. China only country where 1989 revolution fail. They send tank to crush the people in Tiananmen Square, but this never mention now. Wiped from China history. Tanks crush Chinese people's hearts. China now "superpower". Yes, everything *Made in China* now. But still we pursue Cultural Revolution agenda. China try to 're-educate' Tibetan and Uyghur. All to be Han Chinese.' Mr Yang slams his hand down on the table for emphasis and the violence surprises everyone, including himself.

Epiphany looks up sharply at the mention of her beloved Uyghurs. Clearly this is another side to their story that she was totally unaware of. And here she is about to try to convert them into something else as well. God (or Allah) help them.

* * * * * * *

We reach Urumqi around 8 p.m. and say goodbye to Epiphany. I feel just like I used to when I was a child and Sunday School was over for another week – guiltily happy to escape. It's not that I didn't enjoy our little chats. Just that it could be quite challenging. Still, I came here to be challenged, didn't I? And I wish her well in her own journey of discovery. She'll be alright, with God on her shoulder.

Since we have another day before we reach Lanzhou, we opt for an early night. This allows me to catch up with my reading about China's amazing history and to not think about my parental responsibilities. I must admit I'm still a bit nervous about being in sole charge of a child, especially Ari. I never felt at all worried when the others were here, but now it's just the two of us. I find myself grabbing my rucksack with the knife inside and moving it closer. Maternal instincts or self-preservation?

Just as we're settling down to sleep, Ari suddenly pipes up: 'Why did you apologise to Epiphany earlier?'

My mind does a mental somersault as I realise I'd already repressed the earlier conversation about my religious beliefs, and now I've caught myself out.

'Um, just… because it was the right thing to do.'

'But she was wrong. She shouldn't have said those things to you.' He's defending me, I smile to myself. Oddly, this makes me feel even more magnanimous towards Piff.

'She has just as much right to tell me her views on religion as I do to challenge them. She just shouldn't tell me what to think. Nobody should tell anybody what to believe. Ever. You have to figure these things out for yourself.'

Ari thinks about it for a while then nods and turns over to go to sleep.

'G'night Casey,' he says sleepily. 'I'm glad I'm here with you.'

'Me too,' I reply semi-automatically, thinking that this is a turn up for the books.

When I eventually manage to banish the thoughts of my personal Greek tragedy and fall into a fitful sleep, I have weird dreams of millions of women burning their bras in paddy fields while 'Patricia the Stripper' plays out over the loudspeakers, interspersed with quotations from 'The Little Red Book' and episodes of *The Archers*. Niobe and Ari are walking through the fields towards me but I stumble and wake up suddenly with a Red Guard standing over me and a gun pointing in my face.

CHAPTER 18

The train of thought

'Remember, no matter where you go, there you are.'

Confucius,

The Confucian Analects, 475BC-220AD.

I almost fall out of my bunk with fright. Ari is shaking me awake, shouting: 'The wall. The wall!'

I must be still dreaming my surrealist dreams. But no, this hand on my arm pinching me seems real enough.

'Look, Casey. The Chinese Wall.'

'The Great Wall,' Mr Yang corrects softly and I realise that they are both standing at the window of the carriage looking out at one of the greatest wonders of the world. The only man-made object visible from space. Or so they used to tell us in the days before Google Earth.

It seems incredible that we're actually seeing this iconic entity here in the middle of nowhere, even just a small section of it. Mr Yang tells us that the Wall, which was started a few thousand years BC, eventually stretched over 4,000 miles. As we get nearer to Lanzhou the sections of Wall get more and more impressive. We can make out the distinctive double rows of serrated teeth on the ramparts of the thick walkway, snaking its way improbably up and down steep gradients as if clinging to their side. Some segments are so tantalisingly close to the train track that their impressive scale becomes wildly apparent. My guidebook recounts an old legend that anything up to 3 million Chinese peasants died while building the Great Wall and their bodies were just chucked into the foundations and built on, or their bones ground down for mortar. I don't like to ask Mr Yang about that. It makes Pink Floyd's assertion all the more frightening.

* * * * * * *

We approach Lanzhou towards evening. The fact that we've been travelling in China for well over twenty-four hours gives some idea of its size. Lanzhou is approximately in the middle. Mr Yang will be transferring to another train Beijing-bound, but before he leaves he wants to make sure that Ari and myself will be able to find somewhere to stay for the night. Despite my protests he accompanies us to the taxi rank, fending off the alarming number of Chinese men who rush towards us to carry our bags, to secure our custom for their guesthouse / shop / restaurant. He safely deposits us in a registered taxi and tells me he has told the driver to take us to a hotel he knows, which is nearby. I cannot thank him enough but he seems to consider it his duty as a good Chinese 'gentleman', and *that* he certainly is. I realise that we would have been lost without his assistance, adrift in the sea of Chinese faces and characters, unable to read even a simple road sign, and incapable of differentiating between a good deal and a total rip-off. Thanks, Mr Yang.

After the relative quiet of the trains we've been on for the last couple of days, I feel unprepared for the rushing onslaught of China. I know there are 1.3 billion people in China, and that one in five people on the planet is Chinese, but I didn't know what that would be like in reality. It feels like all of them are here, squashed into Lanzhou. The pavements are so full that people spill out on to the streets, while the road is chock-full of cars, trucks, vans, lorries and motorbikes all spewing out choking exhaust fumes to mix with the already polluted air. You can literally see the smog level on the street, reaching up to the second storey of the buildings like a river of toxic air. Through this we can barely make out the mountains that surround us and the muddy Yellow River on which the city sits. Thank God for aircon, even if it's so noisy we can barely hear ourselves think.

The taxi weaves its way through the erratic and noisy traffic, along streets lined with huge grey high-rises and dilapidated tenement blocks. I realise that the picture of China I had in my head when planning this trip was completely tea-plantation green, and the only buildings were delicate ancient pagodas and temples. The reality of the growing economic superpower is way more urbanised. The taxi eventually deposits us at the improbably-named *Peach Blossom Castle Hotel*.

At the Reception I realise, with a bit of a start, that everyone assumes that Ari is my son. After the first few times of trying to explain that he's actually nothing to do with me and that his father left him with me in Kazakhstan while he flew out to Saudi, I give in and just go with it. It brings me the uncomfortable realisation that I should share a room with him. He's as keen on the idea as me (i.e. not at all), but he's not even thirteen years old and I couldn't forgive myself if anything happened. I'm still very new at this parenting lark.

So here we are, sitting on our twin beds. A maid in China and the Boy Wonder.

'What now, Casey?' Ari looks expectantly at me for the next big thing. And I suddenly realise that I haven't got a plan. I haven't thought beyond getting Ari safely to China, without

Danny by our side, or Epiphany's heavenly guidance or trusty Alice. I look around the room for inspiration. Two narrow beds with what were once pandas on the bedspreads; lank, thin silver-grey curtains, a view over the Yellow River which lives up to its name, and the smogged-up cityscape; faded yellowing flock wallpaper with a silver and brown geometric design in the vague shape of mountains. Something Mr Yang said to us is nagging at the back of my brain. Hmmm. There is one place I've always wanted to go. A place that feels like it's at the very ends of the earth. The ultimate adventure destination.

'Let's go to Tibet!' I say with feeling.

Ari grins and nods his agreement, before flipping open his PSP and leaving me to figure out the details on my own.

Later I ask the receptionist how we can get visas for Tibet. After a lot of to-ing and fro-ing between the dozens of smiling Chinese people who appear all to work behind the desk, a young guy appears at our side. He's wearing a red Man Utd shirt with Fu Manchu jet-black hair and a moustache like two slugs hanging off his top lip.

It turns out that you can only get into (the Autonomous Region of) Tibet if you are part of a tour party as you require a special permit as well as a visa, and these are only granted to tours. Fu Man U says that he can organise all of this for us for the day after tomorrow. And just like that, off goes another complete stranger with our passports and money. This is becoming a habit I just can't get used to, and I begin to wonder if Western society is a bit too controlled. Maybe we *should* be more trusting. But with no way of telling whether we're being totally ripped off or not I reserve my final judgement, and hope to see Fu Man U in a couple of days.

* * * * * * *

Two days later, Ari and I have 'done' all the cultural sites of Lanzhou: the Yellow River, White Pagoda Mountain, Zhongshan Bridge, Five Springs Mountain, the night market and the Memorial of the Eighth Route Army Office. More exhausting has been dealing with the ubiquitous postcard and souvenir sellers, and the beggars pulling our sleeves and trying to blackmail us into buying their wares. There's only so many jingling hand massage balls and six-inch-high terracotta warriors one can purchase. By the afternoon of day two we'd taken refuge in our hotel room watching the tidal flow: the sea of smog starts rising as soon as the sun is up, visibly climbing up to face height by about mid-afternoon, totally covering you by evening, and subsiding at night.

In the evening we find an internet shop and talk briefly to Danny who's arrived in Riyadh. He says it's hot and dry (in both senses) and the women are all in the veil. It's the closest to hell he's ever been, Danny comments, but the work is going well. Ari and I both reassure him that everything is fine with us, and there's nothing a mid-life-crisised lesbian and a twelve-year-old boy together can't handle. We make a plan to meet in Nepal's capital, Kathmandu, in a week's time.

Back at Peach Blossom, Fu Man U arrives with newly stamped visas and train tickets for the next day. He very grandly announces that we are going to travel on the newly-built Qinghai-Tibet railway, the world's highest railway track, whose inaugural journey is tomorrow. God only knows how he has secured tickets (at a higher price than originally agreed, of course). I grudgingly pay the extra for this pioneering journey. One for the scrapbooks, I suppose, not that we have any choice.

Ari and I spend our last morning in Lanzhou doing a bit of shopping as we haven't brought any warm clothes for Tibet. In the market I manage to get us both kitted out in winter woollies for around $10 each: Full ski-suits from head to toe, big jumpers, hats, scarves and gloves. We feel stupidly sweaty trying all this on in the 35 degree heat, and the locals clearly think we're laughingly bonkers, but we're prepared for anything now.

When we return to the hotel we get everything packed and take turns to change in the bathroom as has become our habit since sharing a room together. I don't know which of us is more shy of the other. When I come out of the bathroom Ari's sitting on the bed with the passports and visas open in his hand. I make a lunge for them but it's too late, he's already seen it.

'Your name's not Casey,' he accuses me bluntly.

'It's none of your business,' I reply just as curtly.

Ari looks angry and hurt as if I've misled him in some way. As if I've pretended to be someone or something I'm not, which isn't true.

'Look, those are just the names I was baptised with, but nobody uses them. Not since I was a little kid. I use my initials: K C, but everyone assumes it's 'Casey' so... Casey it is. Just like no one calls you Aristotle, just Ari,' I explain with finality and take the passports and visas from him.

Ari looks at me for a few seconds, studying my face. He seems to come to some decision.

'OK,' he says, and smiles. For a second I think he's giving in without a fight, but then he adds, with a cheeky smile: 'As long as you're nice to me, and never tell me off for anything, and let me do whatever I want, then I'll never tell anyone that your real name's Katharine Celeste...' He squeals as I dive on top of him and start tickling him.

'If you... ever say those... names again I'll... tickle you until you die laughing.' I yelp as he tries to fight me off, both of us laughing so hard we nearly fall off the bed. 'I mean it,' I add as Ari gasps for breath.

'I was... hmmph... right,' he shrieks as I tickle him again. 'You are KFC!'

Yeah, and I know what the 'F' stands for, I think, silently berating my adoptive parents once again for their baptismal battiness.

* * * * * * *

Our inaugural train departs in the afternoon amid huge fanfare, with a cutting of ribbons and speeches by Chinese officials. It all seems rather like departing on the maiden voyage of the *QE2*, or perhaps the Orient Express. The train itself is sparkling new and pretty luxurious, a testament to Chinese engineering and manufacturing at its height. It's 'sweet' as Ari puts it. The only sour note is that just when we're boarding we're handed a leaflet by a group of noisy protesters, a mixture of Tibetan and Western faces, who are swiftly ushered away by Chinese guards, and none too gently. The leaflet asserts that this railway (originally conceived by Mao more than forty years ago) is yet another example of China assimilating Tibet into the mainstream, and warns us of the dangers inherent in such a move: 'strengthening China's military and political grip on Tibet, and increasing immigration thereby deliberately diluting its unique culture'. The leaflet asks people to boycott the train. I think about the political prisoners Mr Yang told us about, held in detention centres for daring to protest against China's occupation of Tibet. Now I feel like a scab crossing a picket line. Suddenly I don't feel like a very socially, morally or environmentally responsible tourist as I settle down in my luxury berth with my luxury blankets, about to enjoy a first-class meal in my deluxe restaurant car rolling into an occupied country.

* * * * * * *

I have plenty of time to think about this as we travel through southern China en route for Tibet. Overnight we pass through Xining and Golmud, steadily gaining altitude from 1,500 metres in Lanzhou to 4,500 metres when we wake up in Naqu. There are a lot of station stops where passengers pour off the train to take photos and then pour back on as the guard blows his whistle. Standing in the middle of the vast Qiangtang plain, Naqu railway station offers amazing views of crystal clear lakes reflecting the ice blue and white sky that seems to go on for ever. Surrounding us are what the guide refers to as jokuls, which I take to mean the magnificent jagged mountain peaks that frame our view, which is nothing short of spectacular.

On the vast grassy plain we can see yaks and sheep grazing amongst the scattered tents of the nomadic tribes who pass through here. I am in awe of the majestic mountain scenery and pondering the incongruity of this iron road thundering through places which the Tibetans regard as sacred, and which belong to another time and place. The train brings tourists to gawp at people who are amongst the poorest on earth, and who live in occupied territory while their spiritual leader, the Dalai Lama, is in exile.

I look at my ward, Ari, who's chirpier than ever now that he thinks he holds something on me. He's happily surveying the scenes outside the window with all the innocence bestowed on him by his youth, while listening to music on his iPod. As I'm scrabbling about in my bag for some chew bars to keep us going I realise that he's grabbed the leaflet from the table to read. Still with his earphones in. I wonder that he can concentrate with the tiny cymbals clashing in his ears.

I scooch across to sit beside him and read the leaflet, which describes the apparent attempt of the Chinese to expunge Buddhism from Tibet, destroying 6000 monasteries in the process. About how it's still a crime to possess any image of the Dalai Lama.

'I've heard of the Dalai Lama,' Ari tells me. 'Mum's talked about him, but I always thought he sounded like a super furry animal.'

I laugh. I quite like the Super Furry Animals. Conquering utopia in space chariots. I have to admit that I don't know much about the Dalai Lama except that he's been living in exile in India since the 1960s and won the Nobel Peace Prize in 1989. I tell Ari this much.

'But why doesn't the Dalai Lama fight to get his country back from the Chinese?' Ari asks, perfectly reasonably. After all, he is the country's leader. But he's more of a spiritual leader.

'Sometimes fighting isn't the answer, Ari, even when things are totally unjust. And anyway, there are more ways of fighting than violence.'

'What do you mean?'

'Peaceful protest, like Gandhi. Have you heard of Mahatma Gandhi?'

'Maybe,' Ari says doubtfully.

'Gandhi was a great leader of India who didn't believe in violence as a way of fighting oppression. He protested at the British occupation of India using boycotts, peace marches and eventually a hunger strike. Gandhi used peaceful means because he believed in religious and political tolerance – that people could and should live peacefully side by side whatever their race, colour, religion, caste and beliefs. He believed that no one was better than anyone else, that everyone was equal in the eyes of God. Eventually Gandhi helped achieve independence for India in 1947. He inspired people like Martin Luther King and Nelson Mandela in their peaceful protests for freedom from oppression. We can learn a lot from Gandhi. He once said: "An eye for an eye makes the whole world blind."

Ari thinks for a moment.

'So is that what the Dalai Lama is doing for Tibet? Is he peacefully protesting?' Ari sounds out the words as if they hold little weight in a violent world which recognises only chaos and anarchy as reasonable responses.

'Well, yes, Ari, he is...'

'Then he's not doing a very good job,' Ari interrupts impatiently. Hmmm, I try again, in my best parental tone.

'...and so were those people at the station who gave us this leaflet so that now we know something more about what's happening in Tibet.'

Ari shrugs as if to say 'and what are we going to do about it?' And I wonder for a second time whether we should be boycotting Tibet as a peaceful protest. Or what? Bashing off emails and signing petitions seems ineffectual at the best of times, but sometimes it's the best we can do. Isn't it? How do you explain that to a twelve-year-old who gets his idea of justice from 'Street Fighter'?

* * * * * * *

A few hours later, my doubts about the trip are all but forgotten as we see Lhasa shining in the distance. The ancient Forbidden City of Tibet. I can scarcely believe that we're here. This seems *so* far removed from where we started this journey in South London just over a month ago. And we've seen and experienced so much en route.

As we disembark I immediately feel very foolish about the fact that we're dressed in our ski-suits and woollies. The temperature must be in the low twenties and we're sweating like a couple of blubber whales in Florida. We quickly strip down to T-shirts, squinting in the bright sunlight. Who knew we might get a suntan in Tibet?

Our tour party is herded like cattle over to an ancient-looking minibus which takes us to a seedy-looking guesthouse majestically called 'Grand Unified People's Hotel' but which, in reality, looks more like a Blackpool B&B. The warmth of the welcome almost makes up for the fact that our room contains two of the tiniest wooden beds I've ever seen, like children's beds, and an ensuite which is actually *in the room*: a shower cubicle standing in one corner beside a small sink. It's draughty, poorly-lit and I spy a few cockroaches lurking like omnipresent travelling companions, but this is Tibet! We're in Tibet! And I'd put up with a lot just for that.

Downstairs the lobby is full of chubby Westerners boasting in loud voices about having just *done* Everest base camp. Ari expresses the opinion that he'd quite like to *do* it too, which is a shame as I've signed us up for a more spiritual option: a five-day trek to the remote Rezhen Ashram, starting at 6 a.m. the following morning!

* * * * * * *

At 5 a.m. we're woken by a loud banging on the door reverberating through the paper-thin walls enough to wake most of the occupants of this floor. One up all up. Luckily, it turns out that most of our floor *is* going on the trek. Seven large Germans and a Canadian couple.

After a hearty breakfast of hot porridge and green tea, and eschewing the cold shower (no hot water this morning), we all kit up with an ill-fitting knapsack filled with rented sleeping bags and warm blankets. Oh, and we're all given daft woollen pompom hats bearing the unfortunate acronym of our hotel

(GUPH) presumably as much for advertising as to distinguish us from other tour groups.

First of all we're bussed out to see the Potala Palace, former residence of the Dalai Lama, high up on the roof of the world. We're driven through the dusty streets, bustling with life even at this early hour, past shops decked in incongruous neon lights called 'Krishna Hardware' and 'Buddha's Fancy Clothes'. It reminds us that commercialism (at least China's version of it) has infiltrated even here. Meanwhile soldiers of The People's Army on every street corner 'keeping the peace' remind us of China's other grip of control here.

The palace rises up out of the hilltop it rests on like an overgrown Soviet holiday complex. There are thirteen stories and over a thousand rooms in a fetching mixture of white, brown and yellow. None of the ethereal magic you might expect from the home of the Dalai Lama.

Looking down on Lhasa is equally lacking in magical qualities. *Lhasa* means 'shrine' in Tibetan, and conjures up mind pictures of delicate stupas and pagodas, dreaming spires and mythical Tibetan beauty. But in fact it's more like looking down on Bradford when it was at the height of industrialisation – lots of low 1950s factory-looking buildings huddling together for comfort on the flat grey plain, plonked incongruously in this majestic mountain setting. I guess Paradise is seldom the way you expect it to be.

The other thing that shocks me is the begging. As soon as our bus stops outside the palace we're besieged by raggedy Tibetan children holding out their hands, pointing to their mouths, loudly demanding money or sweets or anything we can give them. The large Germans produce a bag of sweets and are practically knocked over in the rush. A lot of the children follow us round our entire tour, and around each corner there seem to be more of them.

After a cup of hot tea (with salted yak butter, the local delicacy) we're packed back into the bus and driven off across the plain to the edge of nowhere, where a row of tatty huts apparently marks the beginning of our trek. Then we set off into the mountains.

The path we're following is little more than a foot-wide yak track, and the yaks still use it. Several times we have to step to the side to let beasts pass us, laden with goods, their bells tinkling and hot breath stinking. The track is stony and uneven so you have to watch every footstep, especially where it drops away on one side down a sheer mountainside. But the view is breathtakingly spectactular as high above us on all sides snow-capped mountain peaks lay their claim on a piece of piercing blue sky. If God dwelled anywhere on the earth, surely it would be here. We progress slowly as the large Germans struggle along, needing frequent stops. Ari, meanwhile, looks like he's got a manic lamb tied to his head with his pompoms waving madly as he leaps from rock to rock like a seasoned mountain goat.

A couple of hours later we fall into step with some smiling Buddhist monks in their saffron robes, also bound for the monastery. They seem to bound effortlessly from rock to rock, and beam on seeing us. One of them hands us a leaflet while another one gives us a flower, which I tuck in the rim of my beanie. Smiling like a hippy, I trek along feeling like we've finally found some freedom and happiness in the beautiful mountains of Tibet. This feeling is shattered when we stop for a tea break and the monks suddenly turn on the hard sell, trying to foist little religious trinkets and prayer beads on us. I guess I thought there would be a big dividing line between commercialism and spiritual awakening, but apparently here the one is the price of the other.

CHAPTER 19

Seven days in Tibet

'Say not, "I have found the truth," but rather, "I have found a truth".'

Khalil Gibran,
The Prophet, 1923.

When we finally stop for the night all of us are exhausted. We've been trekking for around five hours but it feels more like ten. Our guesthouse is one of several, forming a small village and apparently catering exclusively to the passing trade of tourists and monks. The simple clapboard structures are oddly reminiscent of alpine chalets – painted wooden shutters and pointed verandahs – only sadly without the jacuzzis, or chalet maids. The pleasant tinkling of the bells around the necks of the local yak herd only adds to this displaced imagery.

Our little party is shown into a long unisex dormitory lined with simple wooden bunk beds, and left to shower and change before dinner. Through the window at the end of the room the sun is setting a spectacular salmon pink against the jagged mountains. We go outside to watch its splendid progression. Just as well, since it turns out that the single shower cubicle is located outside in the courtyard and is shared by several guesthouses. So we join the back of a queue of Western travellers

271

all attempting to look cool and zen-like while clutching floral toiletry bags and garish, moth-eaten hotel towels. The water is barely lukewarm and spurts at you from an old hose rigged to the ceiling while you hop about, contorting to wash all over as quickly as possible as the temperature plummets to zero with the setting sun.

After a dinner of yak stew the Germans and Canadians start to play cards. The Germans soundly, and with great pleasure, beat the Canadians at several different versions of Last Card, after which I hear one of the Canadians muttering angrily about karma failing them.

'What's karma?' Ari asks me later as we brush our teeth at the communal tap in the courtyard.

'Well, I think it's basically that Buddhism sees the world as completely interconnected, and that all our actions have consequences on others. So, for example, when we hurt someone, in the end that'll end up hurting us. And conversely when we do good to other people we'll end up benefitting ourselves. Kinda like Jesus saying: "do unto others as you would have them do to you".'

Ari's eyes widen in the dark.

'How long does karma last?' he asks after a pause.

'Grnnnph,' I say thoughtfully, with a mouthful of bristles. 'I dunno, Ari. I dunno.'

* * * * * * *

We settle into our bunks, tucking in all the blankets we can find, and keeping our woolly hats on. I decide to read my monk's leaflet while the candles last; there's no electricity in the mountains after sundown and the darkness is complete up here. The leaflet shows a picture of one of the 'head teachers' at the monastery, all smiley and happy, and looking suspiciously like a Tibetan Elvis, with retro seventies hair and sideburns. It summarises the teachings of the Buddha in three lines:

1. Don't do negative things
2. Do positive things
3. Train the mind to be happy

Simple then. Just, basically, be happy.

As religious doctrines go, *happiness* seems very appealing. In contrast to what I remember from Sunday School teachings of Christianity, which was more about being *good*. Buddhism doesn't fight for dominance amongst the other world religions; doesn't proclaim that there is only one true God; doesn't chide you for wearing clothes made of two different kinds of cloth, or not covering yourself head-to-foot in a veil. Buddhism isn't about blind faith in a saviour, or about a church of rules and dogma, but about happiness in ourselves. Maybe Buddhism is the answer?

I lie on my bunk exhausted both mentally and physically, but somehow feeling more alert and alive than I have done in years. I'd forgotten what it's like to feel bruised, really knocked out from a hard day's play. I also feel really *safe*. I can't quite explain it – like nothing bad could ever happen to me, to us, here. It's a strange feeling and I almost feel ashamed for bringing a weapon here for self-defence. I resolve to abandon my knife at the earliest opportunity.

Ari is lying on his bunk above me, with his arms and legs flung out like a starfish abandoned by the tide. He's probably already fast asleep. It's just me and my Buddhist thoughts. I've never really tried to meditate before, but if ever, now's the time to try. I relax and attempt to let the concepts of love and happiness drift through my mind… but all I can now hear is the 'tst tst tst tst grrrrowowow meeeeeerrrrr' emanating from

Ari's earphones. I thought he was sparko but now I can see his fingers tapping on the side of the bunk in time to the music.

'What on earth are you listening to, Ari?' I poke him in the back from the underside of the bunk.

His head appears over the bunkside, frowning. I motion for him to take off his earphones and repeat my question.

'You wouldn't know them. They're Northern,' he answers imperiously, like I'm a seventy-five-year-old Southern Jessie who's never listened to *Top of the Pops* in her life.

'Try me,' I challenge, hoping to God I will have heard of them, and readying myself to pretend.

'They're called the Arctic Monkeys,' he says with a flourish, as if producing a rabbit from a hat. But I know that rabbit.

'No way. *Whatever People Say I Am, That's What I'm Not*? I *love* that album. My favourite's "I Bet You Look Good on the Dancefloor".' I start to sing the chorus tunelessly.

Ari looks at me incredulously, as if I've just told him I know his innermost secrets. Oh yeah, not such a grandma now, huh? Into the disbelieving pause I pour further proof: 'I went to see them in Sheffield, you know.' For a moment I think Ari is going to actually implode as he mouths 'no way' back at me, his eyebrows crawling higher and higher up his forehead as he tries to process this discombobulating information. Then his eyes widen and he cracks a huge smile.

'No wonder you're such a *mardy bum*!' he says cheekily, disappearing from my view with what looked like a hint of him actually being impressed. Must be the poor light in here. I smile to myself, wondering about the weird serendipity of the situation. Almost like it's karma.

I'm just settling down to try to meditate again when Ari sticks his head over the bunk.

'Do you think Danny's going to come and live with me and Mum?' he asks me out of nowhere.

274

'Um, why do you ask that?' I need to tread carefully here. I don't know what Danny's said to him.

'Because I overheard him talking to you about working near where we live.' He looks at me expectantly.

'Oh right, and that's all?'

'Well, I know that him and Mum are getting on much better now, but I don't think that she'll really want him to live with us,' he says earnestly.

'Yeah, I think you're right, Ari. I think Danny wants to live near you so that he can spend more time with you. Would that... Would you like that?'

Ari pauses in contemplation, then shrugs. 'Yeah. He's all right,' he concludes grudgingly. High praise indeed!

'The thing is,' I say gently, wondering how best to say this, 'I don't think he's going to get back with your mum.' I try to smooth the path.

Ari looks at me as if I'm the dumbest person in the world.

'I know that, K C,' he pronounces the syllables very slowly as if to the hard of understanding, his eyes wide with incredulity at my stupidity: 'She's gay.'

Oh. Right. He knows then. I wasn't sure. I feel myself blushing, because the subject's never come up before between us and I've no idea what he thinks about it. I wonder if he knows about me? Ari watches me reddening, then he starts to smile.

'I *knew* it,' he says triumphantly. He pauses slightly for effect before adding: 'You're gay as well, aren't you.' He says it as if he's just solved an Agatha Christie mystery, or placed the last piece in the jigsaw, or, more likely, knocked someone out on his 'Street Fighter' game.

I smile back at him, glad it's out in the open.

'Yep,' I reply, relieved. 'That I am. I'm here, I'm queer, I'm going to drink up all my beer!' I half-sing to him, grabbing my half-drunk Tsingtao from dinner and downing the contents.

Ari giggles, but hasn't quite finished questioning me.

'How come you haven't got a girlfriend?' he wants to know. Ah me. Not that. I've had enough of everyone here asking why I haven't got a husband, I don't need politically correct questioning too. I shrug, wondering what trite response will shut him up best: It's me? It's them? It's complicated?

I plump for: 'I just haven't found the right one yet.'

Ari smiles a little enigmatically and allows me to get away with that one; even though from his perspective I'm probably well over the hill and better get my skates on if I'm not to be left on the shelf like my 'Spinsters Abroad'.

I go to sleep thinking about happiness and how dependent it seems to be on other people. How we think that having someone else somehow completes us, like we're not able to be complete on our own; and how we think we've found that happiness, over and over, but how it always seems to slip away again.

* * * * * * *

The next two days' trekking are really hard work. A full six to seven hours a day of plodding up and down mountainsides until I'm not sure which is worse – the up or the down. Every step of the 'up' makes my quad muscles burn to melting point, but every step of the 'down' makes my knees feel like they're about to crumble. Plus my neck hurts from always having to look down at my feet to make sure the next foothold is safe and won't catapult me down the mountainside. I barely get to see the breathtaking scenery except when we stop for water or tea or chocolate bars which enterprising kids are selling at the side of the track. 'LAST MARS BARS FOR 10 MILES!' one sign tells us, clearly a young entrepreneur who'll go far, especially when we find an identical sign just around the next corner.

On the afternoon of the third day, when all of us are just about to give ourselves up to sky burials, we finally spy the monastery sitting atop a mountain straight ahead. Its walls are fluttering with hundreds of pastel-coloured triangular prayer flags on strings (and not a red flag of China in sight). Our joy at seeing our final destination is tempered by the realisation that we have to trek up the mountain to reach it. I feel I know what climbing Everest is like now. After two and a half days of trekking in the highest mountains in the world Ari and I sleep like logs, despite being on spartan wooden bunks in a seven by seven foot monk's cell. It's a deeply happy, dreamless, Buddhist sleep.

* * * * * * *

In the morning we're woken before sunrise for group yoga. It makes me feel like a cross between an ascetic hermit and a suburban housewife. Fed with the ubiquitous Tsampa 'porridge' (barley flour mixed with Tibetan salted yak butter tea, and yoghurt) we all sit on the bare wooden floor and await spiritual stretching and transcendental fulfilment. I've no idea what exactly we're meant to be doing, and as my bum goes numb and my teeth start chattering I'm getting more and more perplexed.

I guess we're meant to be meditating, but I've no idea how to do it, and besides, I'd be more likely to fall asleep if I closed my eyes. That is, if it weren't so bloody cold. Beside me, Ari's eyes are starting to droop and he slumps against my shoulder. As I look down at his tousled mess of hair I feel a pang of... something I can't quite name. I gaze down at the boy and think what a strange world this is, what a long journey we've all made to get this far, and how I didn't expect things to turn out this way.

I had been sitting cross-legged on the floor of the Rezhen Ashram since 4 a.m., watching the sun rise over the Tibetan Plateau, while trying to achieve enlightenment. I thought I'd finally got it, but then I lost it, and then I sneezed. Loudly.

I want the ground to open up and swallow me like the failed experiment in enlightenment I really am. Grasshopper has well and truly ripped the rice paper this time. As my sneeze reverberates around the room like an avalanche, others stir from their reverie. But before I can apologise or even acknowledge it, Tibetan Elvis appears at the front of the hall, as if bidden by my sneeze. It's the guy from the leaflets. I'm not sure whether to clap and cheer or swoon. Neither seems quite appropriate, but then what is 'appropriate' in this situation? Elvis in robes grabs the microphone, and for a second I think he's going to burst into 'Crying in the Chapel', but instead he launches into a spirited outline of 'The Buddhist Way'.

Elvis tells us that the Buddhist principle of detachment is one of the keys to greater happiness. Realising and accepting that everything is impermanent, and that our lives are the creation of our minds. Nothing is 'real', so why worry so much about it? Life is precious, but this too shall pass. I feel like my brain is exploding. After the session is finally over and the sun is high in the sky, Ari turns to me.

'Does that mean that I should be happy about the fact that Mum might die of the cancer if it comes back?' He looks anguished, as if he's just found out that Santa Claus is the harbinger of death.

'Oh Ari, I don't think it's saying that at all,' I start, but I'm not sure how to go on. 'I think what they're saying is not that we shouldn't love people or care if they live or die, but that we should accept that everything passes in the end.' Is that it?

'And that's supposed to make us happier?' he asks doubtfully.

'Yeah, well, I'm not really sure that I'm explaining it all that well.' I'm not at all sure that I understand it myself. 'Perhaps it would be better to focus on the impermanence, that nothing is here for ever. So you could take that to mean that the suffering your mum feels now will pass, and the worry that you have about her, that too will pass.'

'No, it won't,' Ari says emphatically. 'I'll always worry about her.' He turns away from me and my Buddhist teaching and stares out of the window at the glorious view. Does it still seem so glorious to him, in the middle of his anxiety?

I wish I could give him better guidance, better reassurance. I hesitatingly place a comforting hand on Ari's shoulder and practise some loving kindness, concentrating on my inner happiness and then Ari's, and then Danny's and Niobe's. He doesn't flinch and even, after a second or two, appears to relax just a little bit. It feels like a prayer, but more immediate somehow.

Over lunch I reflect on the morning's events. I found enlightenment. I lost it. But I found something else as well. Something like a greater connection... with Ari, with myself, with... I don't know... everything.

The funny thing about enlightenment, I think, is that the word was originally used in Europe to denote emancipation of thought from religious doctrine. Whereas before, the church had been so powerful as to have you burned alive if you so much as hinted that you didn't believe every single word was gospel truth. So enlightenment meant freedom of thought, allowance of human reason instead of divine inspiration. In the Buddhist context it means freedom from feelings of need, anger and suffering, amongst other things, in order to achieve true peace. So really, rationality and freedom from thinking are at opposite ends of the scale... are they? My brain hurts. It's either altitude sickness or an overdose of meditation.

After lunch we're conducted in a spiritual exploration of the big Buddhist mantras: 'Ong Namo Guru Dev Namo' – greetings to the creator, the spirit teacher – a mantra used to tune in to your higher self before meditation; 'Sa Ta Na Ma' – all that ever was, creativity, destruction and regeneration – the cycle of life and a catalyst for change; and 'Om, Mani, Padme, Hum' which, according to the 14th Dalai Lama, is a means by which one can transform oneself into a Buddha. If reciting these simple words can transform me into an enlightened one, a Buddha, then I'm all for it. I scribble all these things down in my notebook but somehow, when I read them back later, they don't feel as magical as when Guru Elvis explained them. Exhausted, Ari and I get another early night after more yoga and a light supper. He's evidently not in the mood to talk tonight, and I feel like a rubber band that's been stretched in all directions and then let go to curl in a crinkled heap back where I started, all knotty and spent.

* * * * * * *

The next day we have to leave again. Another two and a half days of punishing trekking along the mountain tracks. Oh I love to go a-wandering, but sometimes a cable car wouldn't go amiss. Even reciting my new Buddhist mantras over and over doesn't really block out the pain. I clutch both ends of the white prayer scarves of friendship we have been presented with by the monks (in exchange for a 'small donation'), and think of flying.

By the time we finally reach the relatively suburban-feeling Lhasa I'm almost on my knees and have to crawl back to the hotel to have a rest before I can face the world again.

Ah the trials of (nearly middle) age. I grab a disco nap and try to soothe my weary body by enlivening my mind with the Buddhist concepts I've learned. Oddly I find that the hardest one is *love*. Tibetan Elvis said that we should train ourselves to believe that nobody in the world is more worthy of love than yourself. *My*self. It's about nurturing that small centre of love, peace, security and happiness inside. It's not just about giving to others (and not counting the cost, as I was taught), but about loving yourself so that you can love others. It sounds more *Marie Claire* than Buddha, but it makes sense. I just seem to find it really hard to do for some reason.

* * * * * * *

After embalming my knees in Tiger Balm, Ari forces me to take one last spin around town to do some last-minute souvenir shopping. He has bounded down the mountains like a young buck, and now seems excited at the prospect of getting back to civilisation. Because I've been concentrating on the pain in my legs while trying to maintain a dignified Buddhist serenity, I don't notice until it's too late that we're being followed by a gaggle of youths. It's not until they've completely surrounded us in a corner of a small market that I realise they're out to rob us. I suddenly feel hands in my pockets, in my rucksack, everywhere. I grab Ari closer to me and start yelling at them to go away. I look around trying to attract the attention of someone else in the market but the women look away and the men hurry on by. I guess this is what you get for being a stupid foreign tourist letting down their guard.

I'm not afraid for myself or my belongings but for Ari. Having said that, I'm not about to give up my rucksack and all my stuff without a fight either. So I grab Ari and shove him behind me, putting my rucksack between me and the lads who must be in their late teens, shaven-headed but not very monkish. I manoeuvre into a corner to protect Ari.

'I've got a knife!' I shout, trying to emulate Crocodile Dundee or someone very brave, which I don't feel right now. I rummage in my rucksack frantically trying to get my fingers on the knife I'm so glad I didn't get rid of yet. The lads are jostling me and trying to wrestle the bag from me. I can feel Ari's bony hands grabbing on to me and can almost feel the fear that's gripped him. That makes me angry. How dare these lads threaten a woman and a twelve-year-old boy? I finally manage to grab hold of the knife handle and produce it with a flourish, still in its sheath and looking a lot smaller than I imagined it would. I have a sudden worry that they will produce a huge khukuri and respond with: 'That's not a knife... *that*'s a knife!' But, to my relief, it seems to have the desired effect. The lads in front of me stop their clamouring and jostling and take a step back. But instead of clearing off, they stand their ground, looking me in the eye with a glimmer of... what? Amusement?

Before I know what's happening the lad in front of me, the ringleader, has grabbed the knife from my hand and run off laughing and shouting, the others following him making rude gestures and loud noises. Ari and I slump to the ground in shock.

'Are you OK?' I ask him, and in reply he leans into my arms and stays there. I hug him tightly until someone finally comes over to check on us.

'These boys,' says a wiry old man with a sigh and a smile. 'They cannot be taught.'

Can't be taught? Yes they can. Bring back corporal punishment, I'm thinking very un-Buddhistly, as we're helped to our feet. Where were these Tibetan Samaritans when we got attacked? I feel like we've been mugged in Santa's Grotto by elves. I can't get my head round it. I feel stupid and embarrassed,

282

especially for not protecting Ari better. I look down at him, still clinging to my arm, the stuffing knocked out of him. I feel my anger rising once more. The heady feeling of safety and happiness I've had since arriving here in Tibet evaporates. I feel totally disillusioned. I guess good and evil exist everywhere, even in places that feel like heaven.

Ari and I head back to the more populated part of town and gravitate towards the crowded backpacker internet café where we feel much safer. After a calming hot chocolate, we confirm our flight to Kathmandu the next day. Our last stop. Our money's all but run out and Danny's new work contract means he has to move on, and Niobe's doing much better after her operation, so... It looks like our adventure's coming to an end. Danny's emailed that he can get us flights back to Blighty in a few days.

I suddenly realise that I really don't want to go home. I don't even want to think about it. It's been such an adventure and I've been having such a good time, even with all the ups and downs. I realise that I've even enjoyed spending time with Ari these last few days. Turns out the kid's all right, after all.

We call Danny and arrange our meeting in Kathmandu tomorrow. He tells us that Niobe's making a great recovery, which is the best news. Ari and I agree not to tell Danny about what just happened. I tell myself it's because we don't want to worry him, but it's also because I don't want him to think that I'm completely incompetent, idiotic and reckless. Danny's a bit evasive on the call and says he has a surprise for us but won't say what. I have a sudden fear that he's going to announce that he's decided to move to Saudi with the contract. Oh Danny, please don't do this again. It's Ari's birthday next week and he's genuinely excited about seeing Danny again. Don't run away. Just when everything seems to be working out for the best in the best of all possible worlds.

CHAPTER 20

Twenty-four hours from Tulse Hill

'You must live in the present, launch yourself on every wave, find your eternity in each moment. Fools stand on their island opportunities and look toward another land. There is no other land; there is no other life but this.'

Henry David Thoreau,
Journal 12, 1859.

'Look, Casey. Everest!' Ari tugs at my arm as everyone in the plane rushes over to the right-hand side to get a look, and I'm frantic that we might suddenly bank and fall out of the sky.

'Which one is it?' I ask, puzzled that the world's tallest mountain isn't sticking out like a sore thumb, way above the neighbouring peaks. Another passenger, nose glued to the window beside me, explains that Everest is only just taller than its neighbours: Lhotse and Nuptse, so it's easy to get confused. In fact *Chomolungma*, 'Mother of the Universe' as the Tibetans call her, or *Sagarmatha*, 'Goddess of the Sky' as she's known in Nepal, doesn't appear taller than the others at all from this angle. I feel kind of cheated. I imagined Everest to be standing alone, in the full majesty of its glory – long, straight sides like a storybook mountain, rising up to an incomparable pinnacle well above everything around it. Instead it's like looking down into the open mouth of a great white shark, rows of serrated teeth jostling for space. Once again I'm disappointed, because I'd preordained what I thought the experience would be like. What was it Guru Elvis said: if we have no expectations, we can never be disappointed.

I sneak a look at Ari who's excitedly surveying the mountain range below, all thoughts of yesterday's incident having apparently evaporated. They say kids bounce back from adversity more quickly, or maybe, after all, he *does* feel pretty safe with me (Crocodile Dunderhead moment notwithstanding).

Being so high above the world, in the fluffy white clouds, always makes me think about God. It must be all the religious picturebooks I had as a child. I start wondering whether I feel any closer to having some answers about the meaning of life now. I feel like I've learned so much on this journey, and yet in some ways I still know nothing. I feel like Socrates but it doesn't make me feel any cleverer. I wonder if there really is an answer at all. Or are we still looking because the answer *isn't* out there? Or because it's personal? It varies from person to person? Is it like the ultimate unknowable, like the existence of God being unprovable? Maybe it isn't a secret, it doesn't actually exist. There is no meaning...? Well, there won't be much meaning for Ari if Danny's decided to cut and run again...

* * * * * * *

By the time I stir from my reverie we're landing in Nepal. Kathmandu's Tribhuvan airport looks like a big shed in a field. Like a very small Luton airport without the shops and cafés. We're standing in line to get our visas stamped when Ari jumps, and yells: 'It's *Mum!* Casey, look, it's my mum!'

I look through the window where he's pointing and see Danny standing with a tall, slim woman wearing a headscarf. They're both waving. So this is Danny's last surprise. What a relief! I'm so pleased for Ari. For all of them. I watch Ari grinning and waving madly at them both. Niobe looks even more gorgeous in person, I can't help thinking, and start blushing furiously, turning my head away so that nobody sees. I have to hold Ari back from running straight through, as we have an agonising ten-minute wait to get to the front of the queue, and a heart-stopping moment when I think they're not going to stamp our passports because I'm not Ari's guardian.

'His mother and father are right over there,' I plead with the guard, but he has to have a languid conversation with his friend, with both of them looking at us and then at Danny and Niobe before stamping the passports and handing them back to us.

I've never seen Ari so happy and animated as we all greet each other in that shed at the top of the world. Niobe is visibly weak, but overjoyed at seeing Ari who looks like he might never let go of her. I take the opportunity to sneak a proper look at her. She has amazing cheekbones set in smooth olive skin, petite features, long eyelashes and the most stunning emerald green eyes I've ever seen in my entire life, like Greek seas on a summer's day, glistening with sunlight and laughter.

'I tried to make her stay at the hotel but she insisted on coming down here to meet you guys,' Danny grins, breaking into my daydream.

'I'm fine. I've done nothing but sleep since the operation.' Niobe grimaces playfully at him. 'And I couldn't wait to see my boy!' She hugs Ari gingerly, protecting her right side. 'Couldn't let you celebrate your thirteenth birthday without me,' she adds with a huge smile.

'It's true, you've been great company,' Danny grins to Niobe mock-sarcastically. 'It's been like a narcoleptics' tea party.'

Niobe digs Dan in the side playfully with a finger and I suddenly catch a glimpse of the chemistry there must have once been between them, which has now settled into what seems like a good friendship.

'And it's nice to meet you too, finally.' She turns to me with those piercing eyes and gives me a full-on beaming smile and a hug too. I'm grinning like an idiot, and full of emotions carried on butterfly wings inside my stomach that I can't quite pin down. I feel carried away in the moment. I'm stupidly happy to see both Danny and Niobe, and for a second I forget that this marks the beginning of the end of our adventure.

Danny steers us through the waiting crowds of hangers-on demanding to take our bags and begging for money to an incongruous-looking big shiny Mercedes, which he has apparently rented for a few days to ferry us around the city. I climb into the front to let Niobe sit with Ari in the back, but regret this almost instantly when Danny swings out into the traffic and it's total mayhem on the roads. There are cars, motorbikes, bicycles, rickshaws, tuk-tuks, pedestrians and holy cows to negotiate in the very narrow maze of streets that wind through the city. Cows are sacred here so you risk eternal damnation by hitting them. Pedestrians aren't sacred, but as many of them are Westerners, you risk eternal lawsuits by hitting them, so Danny goes carefully. Soon he is swearing and using the horn like a native. As we've learned on our journey it seems to be the only way to get through.

Niobe, I notice in the mirror, holds herself uncomfortably

during the journey, which isn't made any better by the obstacle course of potholes and the starting and stopping for crossing cows. So we're all relieved to finally reach the hotel. Danny has booked two twin rooms, as the hotel was almost full, so it looks like I'm sharing with him. But at least it has a bar with plenty of comfy seats and good food so we all spend a fantastic evening just sitting together enjoying being here. Ari is a little overexcited and overtired after all the trekking, so he reluctantly goes to bed around 8 p.m., but Danny, Niobe and I sit up talking and drinking for another hour or so.

I'm also overexcited and overtired, which makes me gabble on about anything and everything. I tell them about our experiences at the Buddhist monastery and about my thoughts on enlightenment and the meaning of life, glad to have an adult audience to bounce ideas off. And Nib, as Danny calls her, is a great conversationalist, on all topics it seems. I can see where Ari gets his enquiring mind from.

'You're very earnest, aren't you?' Nib is smiling at me, and I can't tell if it's slightly mocking. Danny is looking at me funny now, also smiling.

'Yeah, her middle name's Earnest,' he chips in with a knowing grin (and I suddenly wonder if Ari's told him about discovering my real name).

'Like Ernesto Che Guevara?' I say hopefully.

'No, like Ernest in a handbag.' Danny grins.

'A *handbag?!*' Nib and I chorus, collapsing in fits of laughter until she clutches her side in pain. She has a beautiful laugh, I notice.

I'd rather hoped that my name on this trip might be 'fun', but Fun Che Guevara doesn't quite have the same ring. It just sounds like a noodle dish.

We're still giggling like children when we notice that Nib looks about to collapse, so reluctantly the three of us retire on a high; exhausted but exhilarated. I really don't want any of this to end.

* * * * * * *

In the morning Ari's up bright and early, still overexcited by the presence of his mother. He wakes us all up for breakfast and then wants to drag his mum out sightseeing, but she's understandably tired from the flight and still recovering from the operation, so she wisely decides to rest up for the morning. I'm exhausted from the trek and my knees are still sore so I'm more than happy to stay with Niobe, while Danny takes a slightly unwilling Ari out for a morning's sightseeing, and to 'reconnect'.

So Nib and I settle back into the comfy chairs downstairs and order coffee. She wants to know all about the trip, how Ari's been, and more about my thoughts on the meaning of life, despite her teasing me about being so earnest. I tell her that Ari's been fine, *good* really, although he's been very worried about her. Nib confides in me that she feels guilty about the cancer because it worries him so, and because there's no one for him to talk to. She says he won't talk to the school counsellor, so she's really happy he's been talking to me.

'I've been no great shakes,' I tell her. 'In fact I don't really know how to talk to kids,' I admit.

'I think that's why he likes you so much, you don't talk down to him.' Likes me? Likes me, does he? I guess that's possible. I don't know what to say.

'Well, anyway, he's got Danny too now,' I blurt. 'Is he...?'

'Moving back to the north with his job, yes,' Nib smiles. 'We'll see how that goes, but I'm glad he's spending more time with Ari, he needs a good male role model.'

'Shame it's not just a male model he needs,' I say before I can stop myself, then blush. 'Sorry, I didn't mean...'

Nib laughs that wonderful laugh.

'No, it's OK, I know what you mean.'

Nib is so easy to talk to that I find myself asking her about the cancer, despite my intentions not to pry. But she tells me quite candidly about her shock and horror when she discovered the second lump (three years after the first one), how she struggled with how and what to tell Ari, about the radiotherapy she'll be having for the next six weeks, about overcoming her fear of what might happen by doing counselling and practising positive thought; and about the real fight she had with the medical staff to let her come away like this now. In return I end up expounding all my theories of the great search for the meaning of life, and the existence or otherwise of a God or higher power. Somehow I find myself telling her my innermost fears about humanity and religion – that I believe in the power of rational thought and logical questioning as a guiding principle in life, but yet I also find it hard to dismiss a spiritual dimension.

'But the thing I find hardest,' I tell her, 'is believing in the words of *divinely inspired* gurus, prophets or vicars. I just think that if we accept that all men are equal then we have to accept that all of them are just winging it the same as the rest of us. So we shouldn't just accept someone else's word for anything unless we can verify it to be true for ourselves.'

'Then you're denying the superior wisdom of any teachers,' Nib the teacher challenges, with a smile; and she has such a beautiful smile that it makes *me* smile.

'No, well...' I laugh. 'I think what I would say is that we *can* learn from others but that we shouldn't just take someone else's word as gospel truth without some level of critical thought. You see, the problem with externalising the source of all wisdom for me, is the negation of personal responsibility. And we all have to take personal responsibility for our lives, don't we?'

'You *are* earnest, aren't you!' Nib laughs and pats me on the knee. 'Shall we order some cakes?'

'Yes. Sorry.' I'm flustered by her hand on my knee. 'Am I boring you?'

'Not at all. In fact it's refreshing to find someone who actually thinks about these things. I thought it was just me. I don't often come across people I can talk to about stuff like this. We're quite similar, you and I, I think.'

Nib orders some cakes and more coffee, and as she turns back from talking to the waiter I'm suddenly hyper-aware that I'm staring at her, which just makes me feel like a nervous teenager. I want desperately to be cool, to dazzle her with my sparkling repartee and make her like me, but all I can think about is how beautiful she is and how the sunlight seems to be sitting in her emerald eyes, making them seem like glittering pools of knowledge and power and love and... I realise she's looking at me expectantly, wanting to carry on the conversation. *Say something clever* I beg myself.

'So, er, do you... Um, do you, believe in anything?' I manage to get out.

'Well, I'm not sure I would call it "belief". I guess I'm more of a rationalist than a Platonist.'

I nod sagely, so glad she's not laughing at me, thinking that 'Platonic' is the last thing on my mind right now; and then, as if the effort of being this serious and holding all my feelings inside is just too much for me, I burst out laughing. She looks at me quizzically.

I blush furiously.

'I'm sorry, it's a dumb in-joke from my Classics class. Whenever someone says *Platonist* all I hear is *Platypus!*'

There's a silent pause. Why did I say that? Why am I such a klutz at conversation? We were doing well, we were talking about sensible, intelligent stuff and then I have to go and say *Platypus*. I glance up at Nib, not wanting to see the disappointment in her eyes, but she's leaning towards me conspiratorially and says, totally deadpan: 'What do you get if you put a cat in a room with a duck?... A duck-filled-fatty-puss.'

The coffee and cakes arrive, interrupting our laughter. I haven't enjoyed myself like this for such a long time it feels almost alien. I just haven't felt this alive in years. Maybe it's the culmination of this adventure of a lifetime. Maybe it's the coffee and sugar rush. But I don't think it's just that. I look up at Nib and have to remind myself that this is Danny's ex-wife I'm talking to here, and Ari's mother... but that's no reason why she can't also be my... friend.

'So what's so rational about not being a Platypus then?' I grin.

Nib explains that, to her, Platonism is like believing in divine revelation rather than believing that we can understand everything through logic and rational reasoning. Now I pride myself on being a rational thinker but for me, I guess, in *my* life, even if I have issues with a guiding divinity, I do still believe in *some* sort of universal spirit (like a father God, mother nature, Gaia, or a creative power... light... energy... love). This, for me, doesn't take away any of my own personal responsibility for my life, love, well-being and happiness, but does allow me to think of myself as a created being still with infinite possibility (not predetermined), and I tell her this.

How for me it's about 'spirituality' more than 'religion'. How what I really yearn for is a considered, personally relevant, reasonable, loving, working faith. Faith *can* make you a better, more caring, more outwardly-focused person. 'Religion' can be bad, but so can any organised group of people with an axe to grind and a belief that *they're* right and everyone else is wrong; like terrorist cells. I think back to my feelings of abandonment and loneliness when the people I held closest, my parents and the church, turned their back on me for being gay. And yet here I am, after all these years, still clinging to the vestiges of my faith; because it's something bigger and stronger than me.

'So you *do* believe in something beyond rational thought,' Nib frowns slightly.

'Yes, I do, but I also think that's a rational thing to do. I believe that things will work out for the best, and that somewhere out there, there is a benign "force" looking out for me.'

'Isn't this just what you want to believe?' she asks, without sarcasm.

'Yes, maybe. But I've thought about it, a lot, and this is what I believe,' I say decisively, surprising even myself that I've finally been able to articulate my beliefs.

Nib sits back in her seat and thinks for a minute before saying, rather unexpectedly: 'I envy you that belief.' I'm taken aback.

'Do you really envy me, or pity me?' I grin at her ruefully.

She laughs. 'Both, probably, but mainly envy…' she frowns and stops talking.

'What?' I coax.

'Well, you seem to have this real urge to belong – to some place, some viewpoint, some… something. But,' she scratches her head absent-mindedly. 'I don't know, you seem like you're just fighting it, really hard.'

* * * * * * *

Time seems to fly while we talk and I realise that I'm guiltily annoyed when Danny and Ari turn up to have lunch with us. Ari is full of the sights and sounds of Kathmandu. He insists that we both have to come out in the afternoon and Danny agrees to drive us all to see some of the Buddhist stupas, Hindu temples and downtown Thamel – the famed backpacker district. So that's what we do.

Kathmandu appears to be a peaceful world melting pot where anything goes. Buddhist and Hindu religions rub shoulders very happily, while the King's Palace sits alongside the hippy tourist district. It's hard to believe that we're currently in the middle of a Nepalese Civil War between the Maoist rebels and the government, which has been 'raging' since 1996.

It's rainy season in Nepal and the deluge starts mid-afternoon as we're on our way to the outskirts of Kathmandu to see the sprawling Pashupatinath Hindu Temple. The clouds have been hanging around all morning just gathering strength for their assault and when it comes it's violent. Even with the windscreen wipers on full pelt Danny struggles to see in front of the car, and the streets quickly become more like riverbeds. At least the pedestrians take cover, leaving the road free for us and the holy cows who don't seem to mind the rain in the least.

We're not allowed inside Pashupatinath Temple itself, as we're not Hindu, but our guide takes us to watch the cremation of bodies on the banks of the holy Bagmati river. An endless parade of bodies are stripped, washed, painted, wrapped in white cloth, covered in wood and straw and then set on fire on platforms sticking out into the dark waters. It's quite a shocking scene and I can't help thinking it's not really the normal sort of fare for tourists, especially with a kid. But our guide assures us it's all perfectly normal. After all, the people are dead – they don't mind. It's the most holy temple of Shiva in all Nepal, and a most auspicious send-off. Because the Bagmati runs into the holy Ganges, Hindus believe that anyone cremated here will be released from the otherwise eternal cycle of rebirth – 'a lucky escape' our guide tells us.

I can't help noticing however that just downstream of the cremations, groups of men are sifting through the debris and retrieving everything from jewellery to gold teeth – well, they say you can't take it with you. I guess a 'lucky' cremation is lucky for everyone round here. Ari is totally unfazed by all of this, basking in the protection of his mother's presence, and our guide even takes a photo of the four of us standing there high above the smoking pyres, surrounded by large white cows, monkeys and umbrellas. I feel slightly like a spare wheel in this unconventional family picture, but none of the others seems to think anything of it and Danny and Nib both put their arms round me while I, in turn, hold Ari in front of us. I feel surrounded by an odd feeling of serenity, joy and love in these most unlikely surroundings.

* * * * * * *

I wake up the next morning realising that it's Day Forty of our travels. I wonder if that's significant? Forty days in the wilderness and all that. Nearly six weeks since we left dear old London town. I think about all the things that have happened to us on our adventure. The people we've met and the things we've seen. What a trip!

We have four days in Kathmandu before we fly back home on Saturday, and we spend our time exploring the city in our luxury Mercedes, with short forays on foot to spare Nib from getting too tired, and to spare us all from the rain and the begging.

Kathmandu is a truly magical place, even in the rainy season. Everywhere we're greeted with a cheery 'Namaste!' with prayer-hands and a little bow of the head. And the architecture of the historical buildings is stunning: the enormous round Boudhanath stupa with its shining white golden-topped dome and stylised all-seeing eyes like a cartoon villain; the Monkey Temple with its swollen columns and giant-hatted Buddha teeming with holy monkeys; the precariously-balanced and rather Islamic-looking single finger of Bhimsen Tower, like a straightened-Pisa; the giant rotating prayer drums; the omnipresent colourful fluttering prayer flags; and the statues of more gods and goddesses than you can shake a stick at: Vishnu, Ganesh, Shiva, Laxmi, Kumari, Devi, Kali, Padmapani, Tara, Yama, Gita, Bhakti, Hanuman, Brahma, Buddha.

Nib still needs lots of rest, and the rains sometimes get the better of us, so we also spend plenty of time in the hotel just chilling and talking. About all sorts of things: life, the universe and everything. The evenings we spend in the local restaurants and rooftop bars with spectacular views of the surrounding mountains (when the clouds part). It's absolutely enchanting, and these are the most enjoyable and peaceful few days of my life.

* * * * * * *

'I suppose it comes down to whether or not you believe that we have a soul,' Nib is saying to me over pre-dinner cocktails on Thursday night vis-à-vis the existence of God being one of life's 'Big Questions'.

The three of us are waiting for Danny who's making a few work calls before dinner. We're sitting on the rooftop terrace, and the setting sun is glinting on Nib's face and lighting up her green irises so that I can see that they're not a uniform colour but pools of varying shades, like a mountaintop lake reflecting the clouds as they skeeter by above. I'm trying to process what she's saying but all my brain is telling me is how amazing she is. I try to tear my gaze away before Ari notices.

'B...but surely you, you do, don't you?' I stutter. I'm suddenly taken aback that she might not. I hadn't considered that anyone could not believe such a fundamental truism.

'There's no proof for anything beyond our physical selves.'

'Yes there is,' pipes up Ari, looking like a mini new age hippy in his multi-coloured coarse wool shirt from a fairtrade shop in Thamel. 'Mrs MacDougall told us the soul weighs twenty-one grams.'

'Mrs MacDougall is his extremely evangelical RE teacher,' Nib explains, raising her eyebrows at her handsome son in his embroidered finery. She herself is looking resplendent in a dark green brocaded trouser suit from the same place. It matches her eyes as the darkness of the evening settles around us.

'They still have religious ed. in schools? I'm shocked!' I say in mock horror, trying to regain my composure.

Nib pats me on the arm pretending to comfort me and winks, turning my heart to jelly.

'It's OK,' she says. 'I tell him to listen to his iPod during lessons.'

'You do *not!*' Ari cries, then realises that we're joking. 'Anyway, it's true. She said that they measured dogs when they died and they didn't lose any weight but humans lost 21 grams.'

'Thus proving that we should definitely let sleeping dogs lie, eh?' I quip.

'Especially when the dog's had its day,' Nib adds, grinning wickedly.

'What are you talking about?' Ari asks, thinking perhaps we're making fun of him. 'You two are drunk!' He goes back to playing on his PSP.

'Not yet,' Nib says cheekily, turning back to me. 'Anyway, I think that the most interesting thing is that humans have a need to believe in the soul as incorporeal, not physical. That's what makes us different from dogs. But we can't *know* whether it exists or not, can we?' She looks me directly in the eye, making me shift my gaze elsewhere so I can think properly.

'But you may as well ask: how do you know love exists? We just *know* these things,' I argue, a bit embarrassed at the example my brain chose, but Nib doesn't seem to notice.

'We *want* to believe in them. Maybe "love" is nothing more than a series of chemical reactions in the brain. Maybe the soul is nothing more than that. Maybe even the notions of God, heaven, hell and all the rest of it are nothing more than that.'

I'm silent for a second. I've never thought of it like that before. So reductionist.

'You make it sound like it's a bit of a crutch believing in any of this,' I say, perhaps a bit more defensively than I mean to.

Nib looks at me and thinks for a second. 'Well, maybe I do think that about some people. Not you. I think you've made a choice about what you believe, because you *want* to believe, you *need* to believe that there is something more to life than just the physical reality.'

'Something beyond the *nasty, brutish and short* thing?'

'Mmmm. Hobbes.' She nods at me, smiling.

Another stupid memory from my university days is triggered and I break into a wide smile. 'You know, not that I want you to think that I'm a complete idiot or anything, but I once wrote in a student essay that the philosopher Hobbes's first name was Russell. I guess it was just my brain playing word association.'

Nib howls with laughter and has to clutch her side, making both of us wince.

'At least you didn't say it was Calvin,' she giggles.

'Well, I don't know which is worse really – a cartoon tiger or a kettle?' I burst into more laughter.

'I think there could be something deep in that,' Nib counters, mock-serious, 'but I think I'll need a bit of time to figure out what.'

'Take all the time you need. I'm not going anywhere,' I say, before my brain engages with the words.

Nib pauses almost imperceptibly in her laughter, while my heart does a little leap and I have to look away. After what seems like an age of her smiling at me, she says: 'I think what you're looking for is something that satisfies and motivates you both emotionally and spiritually. Something that justifies and explains your... *passion* for life.'

'*Passion*?' I look back at her, trying to control my beating heart and ignore the fact that Ari is still within earshot. I catch a glimpse of myself in a silver tray as a waiter walks past: a men's white shirt tucked into shapeless jeans, my too-long hair pushed up under my beanie. Not your average picture of a passionate woman. Nib's regarding me with a faraway look in her eyes, like she's slightly sad about something. Like she's thinking about something she might have had once and lost.

'Yes, I think *passion* is the very word,' she says thoughtfully, looking me directly in the eye. Then she finishes her drink and collects Ari into her arms gently. 'Now, young man. Is it time for dinner yet?'

* * * * * * *

It's Ari's thirteenth birthday tomorrow and Nib, Danny and I have hatched a surprise for him, besides his mum being here I mean, and after dinner all four of us gather in Nib and Ari's room. Ari looks slightly apprehensive, especially after witnessing Nib and my conversations earlier. He must think we're about to lecture him on something.

'You know, thirteen is a very special age,' Danny says to Ari.

'Is it?' he answers, his eyes widening.

'Yes,' says his mum. 'In Judaism it's the age at which a boy comes of age – the Bar Mitzvah.'

'But we're not Jewish,' Ari says, confused.

'No, but the principle still applies. It's the age at which you're reckoned to know for yourself the difference between right and wrong.'

'And in Australia, thirteen is the age at which young Aboriginal boys go walkabout in the desert for six months and fend for themselves as a rite of passage to adulthood,' Danny adds. Ari pales.

'And you know that your birthday, 14th July, is Bastille Day in France?' I ask him. He shakes his head. 'It's the anniversary of the storming of the Bastille; a turning point in the French Revolution, which led to the "Declaration of the Rights of Man"... I thought it was an interesting point,' I add to Nib and Danny, who both laugh.

Ari is looking decidedly worried, like we're about to circumcise him or send him off into the mountains to climb Everest to prove his manhood or something.

'So, tomorrow...' Niobe starts, with a big smile. 'You get to choose whatever you want to do for the day.'

Ari practically laughs with relief.

'Anything?' he asks excitedly.

'Yes, anything. But we all have to do it together,' she adds, and for a moment Ari's brow darkens as if he might have been wanting to spend his birthday just with his mum. But it passes almost immediately, because maybe spending it with his dad as well is something good. And me? Well, I come as part of the package right now. Ari says he'll need to think about it and goes off with Danny to catch one more stunning view of the city at night before bed.

'Now then, Casey,' Nib turns to me, 'I think it's time I gave you a haircut.'

'What? No! I mean, that's very kind and all but, really, it's not necessary.' I hastily tuck some stray strands of hair up under my beanie.

'Hmmm, that's what Ari said, but then it's his birthday so I let him off, but you…' She looks at me almost tenderly and gently lifts the beanie off my head. 'You have no excuse for not letting me practise my hairdressing skills, do you?'

I gulp, feeling naked without my protective beanie. But somehow Nib makes it feel OK. And somehow I manage not to jump as she softly strokes my hair and begins to cut and shape my unkempt locks, although every touch feels like electricity.

* * * * * * *

In the morning Ari comes downstairs clutching the guidebook I lent him, grinning all over his face.

'What happened to your hair?' he asks me baldly, doing a double-take.

'Your mum,' I tell him, trying not to blush too furiously.

'Oh. Looks nice,' he says casually. And Danny nods his agreement, only he also smiles at me for a very long time afterwards too.

Ari won't tell us where he's decided to go but says he'll direct Danny in the car. After opening birthday cards and having breakfast we set off on our last big adventure, with Ari up front commanding the unfeasible Mercedes through the crowded streets. Our first stop is the Tibetan Refugee Camp. The refugees, many of whom have been here for the majority

301

of their lives, make carpets and other crafts to sell to support themselves. Nib buys a lovely rug with an intricately woven dragon pattern while Ari gets a black and white *Om* T-shirt.

Back to Kathmandu for lunch, and then while Ari drags Danny off to try to find our afternoon's attraction, Nib and I do a spot of shopping for Ari's birthday presents. I buy Ari a big notebook made of locally handmade paper with a woven cover in the pattern of a sacred mandala with a mountain in the middle, to remind him of the journey. I buy myself one too as a keepsake and in lieu of the new hat I would have bought, only I'm quite liking my new haircut and it feels more 'me' now; like I'm finally out in the open somehow. Not hiding. Nib is getting tired I can tell, but she doesn't want to spoil Ari's big day. I'm trying to get her to have another coffee and sit awhile at the café when Ari and Danny hurry up excitedly.

'OK, come on!' Ari says, grabbing at his mother's arm.

'OK, OK, hold your horses,' she says, getting unsteadily to her feet. I take her other arm to steady her, hoping it's not a long walk.

'Where are we going?' I ask Danny, but he puts his finger to his lips and points at Ari who's grinning like a Cheshire cat. Whatever it is, he's absolutely over the moon about it, and it's clearly meant to be a secret. I've never seen him looking so radiant. For the first time since I met him he has actually transformed into that saintly image of childlike innocence I had before I met him at Trowell Services. That seems *so* long ago. Back then I couldn't imagine ever getting on with the brat, let alone liking him.

We stop outside an unprepossessing building with a sign displaying a body mapped over with strange lines and points. The sign says 'AYURVEDIC AND TANTRIC HEALING CENTER'. Nib and I look at each other and then at the boys, unsure what we're meant to do next.

'It's for you, Mum,' Ari bursts out, dragging her inside. 'It's a healing centre. For your cancer,' he adds by way of explanation.

'Oh,' Nib says. I look at Danny, trying to figure out why he has allowed Ari to get involved in this thing, which is either pure juju or, at best, a worthless and exploitative laying on of hands. But Danny gives me a look that says 'just go with it', and so we do.

'He insisted,' Danny whispers to me as Ari leads Nib up to the desk and helps the man to find the appointment he has just made a few minutes ago. Nib shoots us a look that is somewhere between 'help me!' and 'why not, what harm can it do?' as she is led into the treatment room and Ari is ushered out.

'I know it might not work,' Ari says earnestly as we sit there in silence. 'But I thought we should try it, as we're here, and your guidebook said that Nepal is the best place for this kind of healing. It's a holy centre or sacred or something. And the man said that cancer can be caused by deep emotional trauma and that this can release it... Or something like that.' Oh boy, my guidebook has a lot to answer for. I steal a glance at Danny but his face gives nothing away. Still, they say travel's meant to broaden the mind, and if I'm willing to believe in a creative force in the universe, why not a healing force? And why not this? Besides, it's more than touching that Ari has chosen this for his birthday treat.

* * * * * * *

In the evening we take Ari for a birthday meal out – our last supper, if you will. Ari keeps asking his mum if she's feeling any better after her treatment earlier, and she keeps reassuring him that she thinks she does while trying not to give him false hope. It's the final evening of our big adventure; the last time we'll all be together like this, away from normal life back home. *Home?* It doesn't even seem the right word any more.

Ari finally goes to bed full of the day's adventures and filled to the very brim with tiredness. Danny, Nib and I stay up talking for a little while longer, eking out the last dregs of it; none of us seemingly wanting it to be over. But I guess it finally is. As we all reluctantly head off to bed Nib takes me aside momentarily.

'Thank you. For everything. This has been an amazing trip,' she says, and gives me a quick kiss beside my mouth. Barely touching me, the place where her lips alight seems to burn like a beacon in the night.

I blush and mumble something about it being amazing for me too, and nice to meet her and, oh God it's so embarrassing that I'm almost glad to get inside my room and close the door. Thankfully Danny's in the bathroom so can't read what's written large across my face over the burning kissmark branded on my cheek. My mind is turned upside down. I don't know what to think. My mind casts back to our earlier conversations and the way she touched my hair when she cut it. I want to believe in something. I want to believe in *love*. Of course I do, but past experience has instilled a caution in me. Do I find it harder to believe in love than I do to believe in God?

I feign sleep when Danny comes back in, and lie awake for a long time with all these thoughts flying around my brain. I finally fall into the familar nightmare. I'm back on the beach in Greece again. Sara is laughing at me standing alone on the beach, thinking she's drowned. I'm up to my waist in the dark waters unable to go on or go back. She leaves me a note in our hotel room telling me she's leaving me, telling me I'm a fool, telling me to get over myself and my fear of the sea, as if it were that easy. Then she's gone and I'm underwater, drowning, choking in seaweed. I wake in the middle of the night sweating and confused, not knowing where I am until I hear Danny's reassuring snores in the blackness and it brings me back to dry land, my bed, Kathmandu. I fall back into a fitful sleep to dream of Nib walking out of the sea like Ursula Andress and taking my hand and walking with me along the golden beach. When I wake I know that more than ever before, I don't want any of this to end.

EPILOGUE

The end and a new beginning

'Happiness therefore seems to be complete and self-sufficient, and is the end of what has come to pass.'
Aristotle, *Nichomachean Ethics*, c340 BC.

Somewhere over India, at 35,000 feet, and with Ari, Danny and Niobe sleeping deeply beside me, I can finally let my thoughts run free and try to make sense of everything. The whole trip has been eye-opening, but Kathmandu has certainly been the highlight and what's keeping me awake right now. I'm just gazing dreamily at the clouds, trying to cement these memories into my mind, when I notice that Danny's eyes are open and he's looking at me with a strange expression in his eyes.

'What?' I ask, immediately blushing for no reason.

'Nothing. Just wondering what you're gonna do when you get home, that's all.'

'What, after I unpack and have an Indian takeaway you mean?'

'No, I mean, you're not going back to live with your parents in Scarborough, are you?' He asks it as if I'm contemplating becoming a nun. He pulls himself up straight in his chair, squaring his shoulders and then pulling a ludicrous face at me, which makes me laugh. This is followed fleetingly by a frown. But not fleetingly enough for the new Casey – the one who now notices these things about people.

'What's up, Danny?' I ask with genuine affection. For a second his features look alarmingly like they might crumple, but they compose themselves quickly.

'Casey,' he begins emphatically. Worryingly. 'I guess I want to thank you for letting me come on this trip with you. I, er...' He looks pained, as if it's costing him emotional pennies to say this. 'I was a bit... lost, I guess, I... I just want you to know that I wouldn't have wanted to do this trip with anyone else but you. When we got back in touch you made me feel... grounded, solid, for the first time in a long time. It was high time for me to grow up and you helped me to do that. You...' The pain seems to become an agony. 'You kinda rescued me,' he blurts out, reddening almost imperceptibly beneath his tan. He catches my eye and we share a nanosecond's acknowledgement before both bursting out laughing like the kids we once were. Still are. For ever. But it touches me still.

'What about you, Casey?' he's asking now, like I have to reciprocate with the same sort of life-changing admission. I sigh.

'Ah, me. What about me indeed.' I smile at him. 'I don't know, Danny. I think I need a change too.'

'You know Ari's very fond of you,' he says. 'And so is Nib.' He raises an eyebrow suggestively.

'Ah shutup.' I punch him on the arm to hide my embarrassment.

'OK, OK, but it would be nice for all of us if you were around. I mean it. It's been great doing this trip with you. I've had a lot of fun, and I've enjoyed spending time with you.'

'Daniel O'Connor, are you chatting me up *again?*' I laugh, and duck out of the way as he lunges for my arm. He grabs me and gives me a huge bear hug.

'You wouldn't go out with me if I was the last man on the planet, Casey Jones, but you're my best mate and I don't want to lose that.' He holds me tight for a few moments longer and then lets me go.

I'm so moved by his little speech that I have to quickly wipe away a little tear from my eye as I straighten myself up in my seat. I hope he doesn't notice, but I suppose I shouldn't care if he does. Oh Danny, my first love and my best friend, this is what 'family' and belonging is all about, I think, as I flick sugar packets at him to cover my emotion.

* * * * * * *

On landing at Heathrow twelve hours later, Danny, Ari, Nib and I drag ourselves through the airport in a semi-zombie state and transfer on to our short flight to Manchester. It's all a very long way from Shangri-La. All of life's little ordinarinesses seem foreign and strange: being able to drink water from a tap, being able to flush toilet paper down a sit-down toilet, and the guarantee of a hot power shower at the end of the day. Ah, perhaps true bliss *is* to be found in the simple things.

* * * * * * *

I can't sleep on this flight either. Jetlag, and a certain creeping anxiety and excitement about the future all conspire to keep me awake. Nib's last words to me in Kathmandu are also ringing in my ears: 'Believe in yourself, Casey.' After all my talk of belief in things this has knocked me for six: 'I think that you're someone to believe in.'

308

In the end I give up on sleep and get out my notebook and begin to write out some of my thoughts and *learnings* for Ari before I start to forget. As I sit with pen poised, thinking about why this is important, to make the world a more understandable place, a less scary place for Ari, I realise that trying to actually *make* the world a better place for Ari to grow up into is something worthwhile.

I write at the top of the first page a quote from my Ernest, Ernesto (Che) Guevara, about letting the world change you before you can change the world.

Then underneath I write:

There is no guidebook to life. We all have to figure out our own way, but we can learn from our parents, teachers, friends and other wise people around us and those who have gone before. These are just some of the things I've learned so far on my journey, in the hope that it might help you on yours.

I've learned that life doesn't always turn out the way you expect it or necessarily want it to. I've learned that you cannot know all the answers, and that the more answers you find, the more questions you'll want to ask. In life I have been disappointed, thrown, shaken, and stirred. I have loved and been loved and live to love again. I have experienced the joys of passion and possibility, of laughing in the face of danger, of feeling the fear and doing it anyway. I've also known deep, deep boredom and unhappiness with my lot. I've learned that some days are better than others, and that the grass always looks greener on the other side but that this is usually a trick of the light. I've learned that learning is a goal in itself, a reward in itself and a profound frustration. And I've learned that this is all normal.

I've learned that life really is what you make it. No one will bring your life to you. Don't fall into the trap of believing that you're a passenger in your life; be the driver. I've learned that there's no such thing as a perfect world, because people are imperfect, because we always have a choice (free will). We can choose whether to do right or wrong. Use your freedom of choice wisely, because it affects the kind of world that you build around you. Remember that the Buddha said: 'Our life is the creation of our mind'.' In other words, nothing just *is* except that we make it so. It's like the glass half-full thing – if we think life is a bowl of roses then it by and large will be. The power of positive thought should not be underestimated. So think positive thoughts, Ari!

One of the most important things I've learned is that all those little 'crutches' that help people get through life – religion, marriage, children, career – they're not necessarily bad things; you just have to make them work for you and not the other way around. I think I was a bit scared of falling into bear traps, and I thought myself strong for avoiding them, but really I was just running away from things I didn't understand. But you make your own rules, so make sure they're *good* and *right* and *true* for you, and stick to them. Live your own life and be proud of who you are.

Here are some 'rules' I'm going to try to live by, that I've gathered from some good teachers and wise people, and some that I even thought of myself:

- *Be shrewd, but as far as possible love and trust others. We need a sense of belonging.*
- *Be open to life and all its possibilities, but be careful – not everything is good for you.*

- *Try always to see life from the other person's perspective as well as your own.*
- *Try to do only what you believe in your heart to be good and right and true.*
- *Figure out what the meaning of life is for you, and choose your destiny well, but remember that it's never too late, so don't ever despair.*
- *Don't waste time worrying about things. If something needs changing change it, if it can be changed. If it can't, change yourself or your attitude to it.*
- *Form your own views by reading, discussing and experience, but always be prepared to change your mind.*
- *Be open to difference and don't be scared by what is not like you. Remember, it takes different strokes to move the world.*
- *Practise what you love, every day.*
- *Follow your dreams for they are what keeps you alive.*

Then I dig around inside my bag and find the two scraps of paper I'd been using as bookmarks in the guidebook, and I write out the quote from *A Return to Love*, by Marianne Williamson; used by Nelson Mandela during his inaugural speech as, miraculously, President of South Africa, 1994, after his long imprisonment. It talks about the fear that we all have, that we misconstrue as being a fear of our own inadequacy, when, in fact, Williamson asserts, what we're really afraid of is our own power. She asks why we constantly put ourselves down and play small when that doesn't serve anyone? The world needs us to use our talents and to shine, and this, in turn, encourages others to do the same, so that the world ends up a much better place.

And lastly I copy out the well-worn words of my favourite poem, by Max Ehrmann: 'Desiderata'. I've carried this around with me throughout our travels. It's got me through some tough times in my life when I've lost my way and can't see a place for myself in the world – most particularly after she-who-must-not... After Sara.

I especially like how Ehrmann talks about walking quietly through the noisy world and finding our peace in silence. About trying to see the best in the people you meet. Listening properly and speaking truthfully. Not letting life's trials make you bitter, or blind you to the good stuff.

But my favourite bit is where the poem speaks about us all being children of the universe, with an intrinsic right to be here; each allotted our place, just like the stars in the sky. How the world is a beautiful place despite all the shit that happens. So we should try to be happy!

I sit back and look at what I've written, smiling. As an afterthought, underneath the quotes, I write:

Always be prepared, Ari. And always carry dental floss. I got a piece of meat stuck in my teeth on that Chinese train that irritated me for days – I'm sure I've started an abscess now.

And above all, this one thing: Don't read this stuff and expect it to tell you all there is to know about the meaning of life. Or even to understand it all right now. You have to go out and find things for yourself. Oh, and sometimes you don't have to wait for life to change you before you can change the world, by the way. I think Che Guevara got that wrong.'

I pause, pen in hand. There's something not quite right about ending it there. There's something missing. Something about not necessarily needing to travel the world to find answers (although it's fun). Something about the truth being inside, and not having to look too far for love and belonging. I smile to myself. I know how to put it in a way Ari will understand:

As the inimitable Arctic Monkeys once sang: Dorothy was right.

* * * * * * *

Back home at the vicarage, I'm halfway through my traveller's tales over dinner with my parents when my mobile rings. Dad frowns at me as I make a lunge for it.

'Hello?' I say hopefully, thinking it might be Danny arranging a meet up, or Ari calling for life advice, or...

'Hi. How're you doing?' It's Nib! 'I thought I'd call and see how you're standing up to the interrogations.' She laughs that beautiful laugh and I can feel myself blushing.

'Is it Danny?' my mum asks, seeing me blush.

'No, it's Niobe, Mum, she needs to talk to me about something *urgent* to do with Danny and Ari,' I say hastily withdrawing from the room to the fading cries of my mother telling me not to be too long as my dinner'll get cold.

Nib laughs again. 'So, how is it?' she asks me.

'Actually, it's OK,' I say. Thinking that it's really more than OK, it's really quite nice to be home again with Mum and Dad and Dixon. For now at least. And, maybe, it's finally time to talk.

'That's good,' Nib says.

There's a slight pause.

'In fact I do have something very urgent to ask you,' she continues, slightly hesitantly.

'Oh yes?'

'Yes, I need to know when you're coming over to see us. We miss you. And I want to talk to you about something Ari's got into his head.'

'What?'

'Well, he's insisting that we do something to help the Tibetan refugees, and I thought that with your charity background that would be something more up your street. And there are quite a few good charities in the Derby area that are always looking for good staff with experience, especially ones who've worked in The Big Smoke. And a friend of mine has a room to rent in Matlock, just down the road...'

I smile. 'Are you trying to organise my life for me?' I ask teasingly.

'No. Well... yes. Somebody has to! You said that you didn't really know what you were going to do next, so I thought I'd suggest something which means that Danny and Ari and I get to see a bit more of you now we've all found you...' She says this hurriedly and then fades out as if suddenly wondering if she's gone too far.

'Let me think about it,' I say slowly. 'I'll have to consult my people, of course, and then there's the small matter of leaving the home comforts of the vicarage behind...'

'Oh well, of course if it's all too much...' she replies play-mockingly.

'I'll be there first thing in the morning!' I tell her, jokingly. In fact I haven't actually unpacked yet and it would be nice to just up and off first thing and embark on a whole new adventure. But there are some things I need to sort out here first.

* * * * * * *

I remember my mother singing to me to soothe me to sleep when I was little, 'It's a Small World After All'. When I hit my rebellious years and she was still trying to soothe me with the same song I would think, yes, Mum, Dad, your world is very small, but there's a great big world out there for me, and I can't wait to get out there.

Now I finally get it. I see that the world actually is pretty small, in the sense that people the world over are just people, friendship is friendship, love is love, and everyone just does the best they can.

Disclaimer

Historical accounts are fallible. So am I. Any historical or factual inaccuracies are my responsibility, but may also be a matter of opinion.

Acknowledgements

Writing and publishing a debut novel is very much like embarking on a long journey for which one is largely unprepared. I wouldn't have made it to the end of this particularly long adventure without the many people who inspired and supported me along the way.

My writing vehicle would probably never have got out of the starting grid if it weren't for a number of inspiring teachers early on in my life, particularly Mrs Lindsey-Jane Griffin, Dr Richard Wilkinson and Mrs Ruth Macdonald who helped me move from stabilisers to a big girl writing (and thinking) bike. Professor Paul Webley also pushed me (literally at times) in the right direction.

Some early map-reading guidance was provided by The West Cork Ladies Creative Collective (Iseult & Leeanne, Helen & Eithne, Toma & Carmel, Sarah & Dee) who braved the first drafts; while later compass bearings were provided by the Brighton Friends' Centre Creative Writing Course Alumni Group (notably Rebecca, Roger and Philip) who were endlessly patient and encouraging with the final drafts.

My wonderful wife, Lada, has become a very capable chief mechanic, team leader and race engineer, making sure everything runs smoothly in the background and pretty much single-handedly keeping all the wheels on. While my parents, Mary and Keith, have always provided the breakdown cover

I needed on rainy days, and cheered me on proudly from the sidelines.

When I'd nearly run out of steam, The RedDoor Press team (Clare, Heather, Anna and Lizzie) appeared at the finish, and their belief in me and my vision for this book, and their invaluable support through the whole publishing process, carried me over the line. After a dozen years of trying to get published, their independent and innovative approach was a godsend. Thanks also to Emily for the fabulous ice cream cover design, and to Jen at Fuzzy Flamingo for the funky fonts – my hot wheels and decals.

Lastly, all travelling companions are a welcome bonus on life's journey, and in this regard I must above all thank the Birds and the Bees!

About the author

Photograph courtesy of GFW Clothing

Cat Walker was born and raised in the sunny seaside town of Scarborough in North Yorkshire. She is a grown up eternal student, with many and various jobs under her belt, and a passion for travel, which has seen her wandering the globe in search of the truth. *The Scoop* is her debut novel. Cat currently lives in Brighton with her wife and baby son. Cat Walker is not having a mid-life crisis!

@CatWalkerAuthor
catwalkerauthor.com

Find out more about RedDoor
Press and sign up to our
newsletter to hear about our
latest releases, author events,
exciting **competitions**
and more at

reddoorpress.co.uk

YOU CAN ALSO FOLLOW US:

 @RedDoorBooks

 Facebook.com/RedDoorPress

 @RedDoorBooks